TO THE STAFF OF
THE JABBERWOCKY:

THANK YOU FOR HELPING
MY LAUNCH MY NEW NOVEL
I HOPE YOU ENJOY IT
(AND SELL A LOT!)

DAVID MATHIS
'09'

A Memory of Kassendahl

DAVID MATHIAS

authorHOUSE®

AuthorHouse™
1663 Liberty Drive
Bloomington, IN 47403
www.authorhouse.com
Phone: 1-800-839-8640

First published by AuthorHouse 8/31/2009

ISBN: 978-1-4490-0667-9 (e)
ISBN: 978-1-4490-0665-5 (sc)
ISBN: 978-1-4490-0666-2 (hc)

Printed in the United States of America
Bloomington, Indiana

This book is printed on acid-free paper.

DEDICATION

To Amber, my partner, my inspiration and my example.

DAVID MATHIAS

ACKNOWLEDGEMENTS

I'd like to acknowledge the ones before me - my grandfather, Mathew, father, Raymond and Uncle William, who taught me how to drive a tractor, put up shocks, load hay, thresh oats, keep bee's and all the other early ways of farming, before these ways were forgotten. These were the men who instilled a sense of spirit in me that left me curious about how much I could accomplish and how far I could go. My father taught me honesty, integrity and gave me a set of values that I've carried with me my entire life.

I'd also like to thank my editor, Ruth Records for her patience, advice and good spirit, and Diane Barton for her work on the book cover.

1

The afternoon sun shone brightly as a herd of dairy cattle moved about in a small pasture, sparse from over-grazing. On the other side of an old fence in an area more shaded, the grass was greener, taller but just out of reach. A single cow reached its head below the lower of two rusty barbed wires that made the division between the farmer's fields. It stretched and leaned hard to get to the taller grass now just within reach of its tongue. Soon it was joined by other cows and the tall, green grass could be reached by pushing against the rusting barbed wire. The barbed wire screeched as it was pulled through the rusty fence staples. One by one, the staples were pulled free from the rotting post. Within minutes the low and rusting thread of wire snapped and gave way to the movement of the herd. The cows moved over the remaining wire and a very thin, weathered and rotting post yielded to the force. All at once the herd of almost twenty-five cows was grazing in the neighbor's field.

Matt Miller and his son John were donned in beekeeping attire as they saw to the hives in the small orchard near their house. Matt's wife Katherine hung laundry on the line not far away. Their hired hand, a middle-aged man, was near an open shed greasing up the hay loader and tractor. Dust billowed as an old truck came down their long driveway and pulled into the yard. They all looked up from their tasks as their neighbor, Harlan, stopped his truck and stepped out.

He tipped his broad-brimmed straw hat back and wiped his brow with his hand. "Hello, Miller's…your cows busted through the east fenceline." he said with a smile. Then he cocked his head to the side and spat as far as he could into the dry dirt.

Matt Miller waved an arm at him as if to tell him to hold on. After another minute, Matt and John put the last of the frames back into place, set the cover back on the hive and walked toward their neighbor. As they moved away from the hive and toward Harlan, they each removed their screened hats and long gloves. Matt wiped the sweat from his brow with his long denim sleeve.

"Well, I'm sorry about that, Harlan. I planned on splitting the north forty and moving them just as soon as we were done haying that field." Matt Miller said.

"Not a problem, Mattie. The boys and I rounded them up and patched the fence good enough for now, but I don't think it'll keep them cows out for long, wire's pretty rusty." After a pause, he continued. "How's the corn?"

"Pretty near knee-high. Got it in early thanks to a good Spring – and yours?" Matt smiled as he brushed a few bees away.

"Same here – it'll be a bumper crop if we don't get a dry spell. Well, I best be getting back."

"Have a glass of lemonade?" Katherine asked. Harlan smiled.

"Some other time, Katherine, thanks the same." Harlan tipped his hat to her, Matt and John, got into his truck and drove away.

"John, you best take a load of hay out to the pasture. After tonight, we'll have to keep them in the barnyard until you and Steeg can get a new fence strung."

"Yes, sir." John replied.

Morning sun glistened over the gentle hills of the east field of Matt Miller's farm and illuminated the tips of every stalk of wheat as they slowly danced in the gentle breeze. To most it would seem calm, but summer mornings were warm and welcoming to the birds, insects and every other living thing. If you studied the earth closely enough, within arm's reach you could witness an abundant bustling of life.

It was June 13,1944, and U.S. Troops had just landed at Normandy a week earlier. The world was at war - a world far from this field. It wasn't a war that Matt Miller had started or knew much about, but he had a son over there and this made it his war as well. Matt Miller's other son was here at home on the farm where he could see him every day - work with him, and teach him the things he would need to know in order to achieve something of meaning and value in this world. As much as he needed his son's help, he placed greater value on being able to watch his son become a man and take on a character of his own.

Two men were now preparing an early start on what remained of the two-strand fence work. Previous days of work were productive and this day would be the last that they could devote before haying began. When completed, the cattle would be able to graze in a field farther east and near the edge of the woods and swamp where it was too shady and low for crops, but rich for grass. The McCormick tractor had been filled with gas the night before. It was good practice to prepare the tractor before it was put away in the shed each night. The cedar posts, sledge hammer and metal tool box were on the farm cart glistening with dew that was quickly drying from the morning heat. A small cart that held a large spool of barbed wire was still hitched behind the tractor. The screen door swung open and slammed shut behind the two men clothed in denim jeans, sleeveless t-shirts, plaid cotton shirts with sleeves rolled up and straw hats.

Steeg was the hired hand, a Swedish immigrant who had moved down from the forest country of northern Wisconsin. He was tall blonde-haired man with a solemn expression, high cheek bones and a long blonde moustache. He was a part of this farm for as long as John could remember. As a child growing up, John had always called him Mr. Onsgaard, but now that John had made that measured growth into manhood, he was at ease calling him Steeg as the other men in town did. John earned this status to be an equal and Steeg granted it to him. And the name "Steeg" seemed to fit this man like the brim of his well-worn hat. It was still early in the morning and already the brims of their hats were wet with the first sweat of the day.

Matt's son John was a strong, and good-looking young man with blonde hair and brown eyes that gave him a look of innocence. He had just turned eighteen on the first day of June, and, having registered for the draft, expected to be called at any time. Throughout the days, he would sometimes strain to hear if Ma were calling from the house or ringing the dinner bell at a time other than the ceremonial noon. He was waiting for his call to duty.

This was Wisconsin, the dairy state, a land settled mostly by German Catholic Immigrants. Many people still spoke German, especially the older ones. Sometimes German was spoken in front of the children when the adults didn't want the young ones to know what they were talking about. The people found it funny though, that the children all picked up the language, and by the time most of them were twelve they could speak their native tongue nearly as well as their fathers, mothers and grandparents.

Out on the fenceline, Steeg was digging a hole as John unloaded cedar posts from a two-wheeled trailer. John carried a half dozen posts over his left shoulder. He laid a post every twelve feet - stepping out four long steps as a measure. After dropping the last post, he turned and started walking back to

Steeg. John broke the long silence. "So, Steeg, what would you be doing if you weren't doing this?"

"I suppose I'd finish getting the hay loader ready." came his reply.

"No, I mean what would you be doing if you weren't working here on the farm?"

After a long pause Steeg answered. "Suppose I'd be up north logging…I don't know."

Moments later, sensing that John was looking for conversation, Steeg continued, "What about you?"

John was quick to answer. "I'd be traveling the world, looking for treasure. Maybe I'd be an anthropologist or archeologist. I like all of that old stuff and the hunt that goes with it. I'd like to go to college someday, but Ma and Pa don't have the kind of money to help me out and I don't have much saved. I was thinking that after I come back from the war I could work for a year or two and then go to college. Not much adventure here on the farm - unless you want to consider that time awhile back when the bull broke his stanchion and ran around the yard. I never saw Pa move so fast." A few more minutes passed and then John continued, "Maybe I'd search for the Holy Grail." He let out a little laugh. Then his expression changed as if he were thinking 'why not'? "I want to ride on the Orient Express, I want to walk on the Great Wall of China, and I want to climb the Eiffel tower. I want suitcases loaded with stickers, labels and tags from countries that I've visited all over the world!"

"Well, I suppose…suitcases with labels…" Steeg said quietly keeping his laughter to himself.

"Seriously, Steeg, there is a big world out there. I hope to see some of it when I go off to the war".

Steeg's expression was suddenly terse. "You might see more than you bargain for. Besides, you have everything in the world right here. You have the farm, the land, the Kassendahl and all its beauty." His words, which almost seemed to be scolding at first, turned warm and sensitive.

John had a puzzled look on his face. "The Kassendahl?" he asked.

"Yes, Kassendahl, I saw you by the stream one time with a young lady. Kassendahl…kissing place, you know, a special place that you never forget." Steeg said with a smile.

John knew that Steeg was right about the kissing place and it was a place he would never forget. A little embarrassed that his rendezvous received such exposure, John hurried to get the subject back on track.

"I love this farm, but I don't want to spend my whole life here wondering what's out there. Hopefully, in a month I'll be in the war fighting side by side with Bill. Who knows, if I'm over there when the war ends…maybe I'll stay awhile, see Europe, travel around Italy, France…maybe England."

Steeg laid the posthole digger off to the side as John dropped a post into the new hole. The cedar posts were sharpened at one end and, after starting a hole with the post-hole digger as deep as they could reach, a sledgehammer was used to drive the pointed end of the post down square and true. The two men took great pride in making sure the fence was in a straight line so that any man from now and on down through the years could stand at the end of the field, look down the fence line and see how straight and true a job these men had done. And a strong fence gave all of them a confidence that their cows would not be wandering off into the swamp. Steeg felt concerned for John who obviously wanted to talk more about the world on the other side of these fences. He wanted to continue the conversation with John, but he wasn't sure that he could or even should try to explain the devastation of war, the disorder, disruption and ending of people's lives or the destruction of families and homes. To Steeg there was no greater sin than to destroy a family through the taking of a life.

They were hurrying now, to get the last posts set before the noon dinner bell would ring. The sun was straight up in the sky and the mid-morning snack of hard-boiled eggs and salted pork sandwiches made with homemade white bread was long behind them. John held the last post as Steeg grabbed the sledgehammer. His first swing hit straight and true, but the post was not vertical. As John said, "hold up," he reached over the top of the post to straighten it just as the second blow came. In an instant that neither man would ever forget, the force of a grown man swinging a five-pound sledge had hit the top of his right hand.

John screamed out in pain pulling his hand to his chest and covering it with his left-hand, he doubled over and fell to the ground in unbearable, piercing pain. "GOD...Steeg...Oh, my God..."

When John finally opened his eyes, blurred with tears, he could not see Steeg. As he regained some calmness from the pain, he saw Steeg running away, but not toward the farm for help, he was running toward the swamp. Confused and disoriented, John's senses quickly came to him as he took his flannel shirt from the fence post where he had put it earlier that morning. Wrapping it tightly around his bleeding hand, John was compelled with a sense of survival. He wondered where Steeg had gone as he put his focus on his feet and stumbled toward the tractor. One more yell, "Steeg". John started the tractor with left hand, right hand still held tightly to his chest and clinched in a fist, his shirt soaking with blood. The old McCormick tractor got him to the house, but emphasized to him every bump in the farm lane. John reached the house. Ma had a sense that there was trouble - a premonition – as she rushed from the house wiping her hands on her apron and running down the porch steps toward her son.

John shut off the tractor and feeling light-headed, let Ma help him down from the tractor. She took the blood-soaked shirt from his hand to wrap her clean apron around it instead. He looked away as she did this, not wanting to see what he felt. She was somewhat relieved to see that he still had all of his fingers. She caressed his back and shoulder as she led him to the house. John's straw hat fell to the porch and he could feel the wave of cool air ripple through his hair, cooling his hot and sweaty head. He was faint and felt nauseated. Through the narrow slits of his eyelids, he saw the apron quickly turning red from the burst veins in his hand.

"What happened, John?" she asked.

"Had my hand over the top of the post...sledgehammer... must've slipped..." John replied as he winced in pain.

Matt Miller came from the barn and hurried into the kitchen. Seeing the situation, he proceeded to wash his hands in the kitchen sink without a word. He then rushed over to John as Katie picked up the earpiece and cranked the wooden wall phone to make a call. She was able to reach Doc Smith at his office in nearby Calvary Station. She was relieved to hear his voice and thankful that he was tending to routine office visits at this moment and not out seeing patients in their homes.

"Doc, Katie Miller here. There's been an accident."

There was a long pause as Katherine's face creased with concern and mild panic, her hands trembling as she held the earpiece. "His hand...it was hit with a sledgehammer." She paused, took a breath, wiped her brow and eyes with a towel and continued, "Pretty bad - no, I can't tell. We have it wrapped to stop the bleeding, but it's soaking through". There was another pause as she listened intently. "Yes, yes. Okay...goodbye".

Katherine turned to her husband Matt. "Get some ice from the freezer," she ordered before realizing that he had already taken the ice tray from the freezer and was crushing the cubes in a towel. She took the towel full of crushed ice and wrapped it around John's hand.

"John, Doc Smith will be here in about twenty minutes. Can you be strong until he gets here?" she asked.

John just winced in pain and nodded. "Let's get him to the parlor...grab some towels, Mattie".

Matt and Katie walked John to the couch in the parlor and helped him rest back. Matt laid towels on the floor near John and tucked more towels near his side. A long quick trail of blood ran down John's arm and dripped to the floor.

"Best keep your arm raised a bit, John." Matt said. Putting a pillow behind John's head, Matt wiped the sweat from his son's forehead with his handkerchief before it reached his eyes.

"Where's Steeg?" Matt asked quietly. There was no response except for a look of confusion in John's teary eyes.

Katherine went to the kitchen, took a fresh white apron from the top drawer and put it on, tying it in the front. She then put both hands on the kitchen table, gripping the edge tightly. She lowered her head, closed her eyes and took in a deep breath. There had been accidents on the farm before, but none like this and not to her baby. In a few seconds she was prepared again to deal with the responsibilities of being a farm wife.

It was more than a half-hour before Doc Smith arrived. He was greeted by Matt Miller holding the screen door open.

"He's in the parlor. Near as we can tell, he had his hand over the top of a fence post and the farmhand must have hit it with the sledge." Mister Miller said.

Doc Smith nodded at Katie as he hurried into the parlor. He set his black bag down and opened it, taking out a light and stethoscope. He lifted John's eyelids one at a time, and shined the light into each. He placed his stethoscope into his ears and placed the cold end onto John's chest. The coolness of the instrument caused John to open his eyes slightly, but he was in too much pain to talk. He knew now that the doctor had arrived and he could leave everything in his hands. Doc Smith carefully removed the towel from John's hand. Katherine was right there to take the bloody, wet towel from the doctor. Most of the bleeding had stopped although more blood began to trickle out as Doc Smith felt the swollen hand. John grimaced in pain as the Doctor pressed into the flesh of his hand to determine if bones had been broken. After a minute, the conclusion was clear.

"John has compound fractures on all four of his fingers and there may likely be several breaks on his carpals and metacarpals as well. There are twenty-seven bones in the human hand, it's likely that there are many more breaks than we'll even be able to see with an x-ray. There is so much swelling right now that it's hard to tell just how bad the damage is. The thumb was probably spared as it was off to the side of the post when the hammer hit". Doc Smith informed Matt and Katherine Miller.

"Oh, my God." was all that Katherine could say as she drew her hand up to her mouth. Matt put his arm around Katherine's shoulder.

"How long will he be in pain?" Matt asked.

"Oh, it'll be very intense for the first few days. I'd say in a week it'll just throb and the pain will be more dull and aching." Doc Smith said. "Keep it elevated so the blood isn't rushing to the hand." Ma wiped her eyes with her apron and struggled to hide her worry from John. Doc Smith said, "Once the swelling has come down a bit I can set the fingers in a cast so that they heal straight, but for now just keep him comfortable as best you can. I don't even want to put in stitches until that swelling comes down. I'll dress the wound and then come back tomorrow. From there we can determine when he'll be in shape to come in for an x-ray."

Ma brought John ice throughout the afternoon and clean linen from the old bed sheet she had torn up to wrap around the wound. He kept it elevated to keep the pain down as much as possible. Doc Smith gave John a shot of morphine before he left and gave Ma a bottle of pills for him to take as needed for the pain. The injection took effect and John slept for a very long time. He was only half-awake when Ma was changing the blood-drenched dressing in the middle of the night. Matt cut down the legs of a small wooden table and set it beside the couch so that it stood at the right height to elevate John's arm. He taped an old quilt across the table top to make it comfortable.

In the weeks that followed, it was determined that John would never be able to pull a trigger. The combined skills required to hold a gun steadily, sight in a target and pull the trigger could not be done with accuracy and consistency. For medical reasons, he was now excused from all branches of the military. The recruiters advised John that he could check back if he felt his condition would change, but the look on their faces told him that they didn't expect this to happen. Much to his disappointment, John would never be able to wear a uniform in the service of his country.

John's feelings were mixed. All he had wanted was to enlist in the Army just as his brother Bill had. He had imagined how the townspeople would talk about Matt and Katherine's sons. The brothers who fought in the war together and how there would be stories of their heroic journeys. But John also thought of those who didn't come back. Michael Koenigs and his brother Pat were both killed in action - both gone. Bumps Walber was shot on the German front, had his right leg amputated, spent weeks in an Army hospital and then died from an infection. These were classmates - these were people John knew, had played with as a boy - living breathing people no more. Now he had to re-think his future. He loved the farm and their home, but didn't want to think in terms of his life following so closely that of his father's. The world was changing and he knew the era of the family farm would someday be gone. He felt that the war was one way for him to get a start somewhere away from these fields and this little town.

In that split second, John's plans for his life were changed forever. There was neither a contingency plan nor a reason for the healthy and confident young man to think he should ever need one. The first thing to do now was to heal and determine the limitations he would now have. His life and his future, as always, were in God's hands.

Steeg never returned to the farmhouse. He left all of his belongings. Matt and Katherine figured that he was so scared (or so sorry) for what had happened that he felt he needed to leave the farm without an explanation or even a note. Word around town at the tavern in the days and weeks that followed implied that Steeg was seen thumbing rides toward the north. He was probably headed back up to Phelps near the Michigan border where his family had settled after the move here from Sweden. The northern part of Wisconsin reminded many of the immigrants of their homeland. As enough families congregated from old country to the new, life became more comfortable for them. Now a son would return and would have to start his life over again. This did not need to be.

2

John spent the weeks following the accident, slowly learning to contribute to the farm chores in any way that he could. He grasped for any opportunity to show his father that he could triumph over this or any other obstacle that confronted him. He was handicapped, and the family had lost their farmhand as well. John did not want his parents to suffer for his accident. Cousins from the other end of town came to help with the fieldwork, but seldom came early enough or stayed late enough for milking the cows. After some time, he found that he could drive a tractor again. The pace was slow and he could maneuver the tractor with his left hand and to some extent hold the steering wheel with his injured right hand. When he'd hit a small rock or furrow it would send pain shooting through his hand and up his arm, but he learned to live with the pain rather than live with the feeling of being useless on the farm. From time to time, he'd accidentally bang his hand and the frailness of his situation would come back to him. All in all, John felt satisfaction knowing that he was being of help, and it took his mind off of his condition.

John drove the Chevrolet to town early one morning with Ma to get groceries at Diederich's store, in preparation for the July 4th weekend. Ma would be baking pies for the church bake sale that would be held at the town picnic.

Leo Diederich always wore a short-sleeved white T-shirt and overalls, except if it was to Church on Sunday - which he seldom attended. John remembered seeing Mr. Diederich in Church as a child and catching himself staring at this man who came to church with Mrs. Diederich, but looked so different from the neck down. He never had a bad word to say about anyone, after all, everyone in town was a customer. Had Mr. Diederich chosen any other path in life John could not imagine him being anyone but the kind man at the grocery store. Leo had a peculiar twitch and every once in awhile mid-sentence would strain the muscles in his neck as if exaggerating the vowel "E", but with mouth closed. He carried about him the wisdom of a man who had seen it all, but the humility of a man smart enough to only mind his own business and to make an occasional comment about the weather and the war effort. He had his own philosophy, but was cognizant of who was listening and kept his words simple. Mr. Diederich extended credit to everyone in town who needed it, and with a war going on, many did. If someone couldn't pay their bill, it didn't seem to matter, and if it did matter, it surely wasn't discussed with anyone else in the store. A few people in town were known to park outside and wait for others to go in ahead of them just to take advantage of his grace and demeanor, knowing Leo wouldn't bring up the topic of past dues in front of others.

As John held the door open for his mother he looked over at the steel rings that were set into the concrete for tethering horses and remembered how he'd play with them as a child.

"Afternoon, John,…Katherine." Leo said respectfully.

"Hello, Mr. Diederich." John replied.

"Hello, Leo." Ma said gently.

Emil Wegner was in the store, a man who seldom spoke. It was more likely that you'd get an uncomfortable stare from the big, burly man who carried the odor of the barn with him wherever he went. His eyes were a light grey and the whites of his eyes always appeared yellow and bloodshot. Children who came into the store when he was there would keep their distance and try not to look his way, although they could still feel his stare.

"Heard about your little misfortune, John. That's got to be one heck of a hurt."

"Oh yeah, I think I've had enough pain to last me a good long time."

"Well let's hope so," Leo said with a broad smile. He had a way of bringing a smile out of everyone.

Ma continued to pick baking supplies off of the shelves and smiled as she listened in on the two men. She had to squeeze between the boxes of bananas that were in the center of the store and Emil Wegner. She inconspicuously held her breath for a few brief seconds as she made her way clear of him and over to the shelves where the bags of sugar were kept.

"Tommy Kraus left this morning for training." Leo said.

"That so?" John replied having already heard this, but leaving open-ended responses made for better conversation.

"Won't be long before he's over there…what's the word on you there? Don't suppose there's much they could find for you to do."

"Can't shoot a gun…can't hold a flag…I suppose I'd make a good target, but it looks like this won't be a war for me."

Leo let out a little chuckle and Emil Wegner just stared.

Then John stated simply, "4F".

"Just as well, John, Matt and Katherine need you on the farm. One son off to war will have to be enough from the Miller family." Leo responded.

Ma's expression went to sadness as she thought about William, John's older brother who was stationed in Europe in the middle of it all.

Ma had placed everything from her list onto the counter and Leo started writing the name of each item on his green order pad. When he had finished, he punched the prices of each item on his adding machine and it spewed a long white ribbon with the total.

Ma paid up her account plus what was being purchased this day. She wasn't one to let these things go too long and feel obliged. If anything else had to wait, it had to wait. Keeping up and being able to hold her head high meant more than having the things in life that she wished for. No one knew how long this war would last. She learned from the hard life that everyone in those times had, that you must learn to want what you already have. John loaded the groceries into the back seat, right-hand cupped underneath, still wrapped heavily in bandages that now didn't need to be changed quite as often.

Katherine asked John to drive her to do a few other errands this morning. This included stopping at Mrs. Koenen's house to pick up some rhubarb for her pies. Katherine and Gladys spoke for quite awhile as John sat on the fender of the dusty old Chevrolet. Mrs. Koenen's Irish setter came up to John and sniffed at his left hand. Her dog came from a litter that the Millers' setter had had on the farm many years earlier. John pet the dog and it followed him over to sit in the shade, against the white picket fence. They waited for the ladies to finish getting caught up on talk about their gardens, the farm work, and only a small amount of gossip. As the two ladies finished up, they walked toward the car. Mrs. Koenen asked how John's hand was and although it still hurt very much, John responded that he was fine and getting better every day.

As they pulled up the long farm lane John could see a large unfamiliar truck backed up to the barn. Ma didn't seem to pay attention, which made the situation stranger to John. John pulled around the yard and brought the car to a stop. Standing up from the door of the car, his right arm elevated over the top of the open door, he squinted in the bright sun to see who was at the barn. "Zigglebauer's Cattle Company, Mount Calvary,

Wisc." was painted on the door. The hand-painted words were fading and the door had a distinct spray of dried manure that the rain could not wash away. Pauly, as everybody around called him, was standing at the truck, foot poised on running board, and picking away at the dried manure spattered and dried onto the truck door. This was just another of his little diversions while negotiating price on a herd of cattle that he knew the owner intended to part with.

Pauly Zigglebauer had Matt Miller at a disadvantage. He knew there wasn't much demand for dairy cattle while the war was going on. Most farmers in this area had all that they could handle just to milk the herds that they had. John closed in slowly, respectful of his father's business, to see if he could find out was happening. Finally an excuse came to mind and John called over to Pa in a voice loud enough to assure him that he was far enough away not to be eavesdropping on their conversation.

"Pa, Ma needs you in the kitchen right away." Matt Miller lifted his head to see John.

"It'll only take a minute, Pa, but she says she needs you this minute."

Pa looked back and forth between Pauly and his son and finally, as if being shaken from a daydream said, "Sure, ya, I'll be right there." Then he turned to Zigglebauer. "Pauly, I'll be right back. Seems that Katie needs me for a minute."

"Hurry back, Mattie, or I just might take off with these here cattle of yours and forget to pay."

Matt went up to the house. John had gone quickly back to the car, grabbed a bag of groceries with some awkwardness and double-stepped up the porch. Ma pushed the screen door open as John approached and he came into the kitchen setting the groceries down on to the kitchen table. In an almost combined move, John swung around from setting the groceries down to confronting his father face to face. His whole life had been with respect and a distinct set of protocol with family members. Today was different.

"Pa, what are you doing? I mean what is…why is Zigglebauer here? What's going on? What's he doing with our cattle on his truck?

"John, your mother and I are getting too old for this. We love this land, we love farming as my father did before me and his father before him, but it's getting to be too much. It's time now. You brother is off at war. The only reason they took him is because you and Steeg were both here to help Ma and me with the farm. Your sisters are both married and moved away and only come around with their husbands and the grandchildren when it's threshing time or sometimes to help with loading hay into the barn. They have lives of their own. When Bill comes back from the war he'll probably want to get a job at one of the factories and raise a family of his own. I don't want him coming home from doing his country's service and feeling that he has an obligation to this farm."

"But what about me?" John asked with some trepidation, realizing that he stood there with his right hand bandaged halfway up his forearm.

"You love this farm too, John, I know this. You love to farm as we do, but you were meant to be more than a farmer."

Matt wasn't comfortable with this conversation and, thank God, conversations like this had been few over the years. His eyes darted back and forth slowly from Ma's eyes to the groceries, to John's eyes and sometimes to the floor, but only for a split second. He felt there should be no guilt in what he was doing, but he did feel a little ashamed for not telling John before Pauly Zigglebauer had come this day.

"I struck a deal with the Weber's to rent the land and they'll be allowed to use the hay barn as they see fit. Roger Weber will finish off the harvest this fall and we'll be paid back for the price of the seed and what's fair for planting and cultivating. Roger Weber is as honest a man you'll ever find. He's been a neighbor for years and his father before him. I trust he'll treat the land as if it was his own." Pa was speaking more at ease now that more details were being shared. "John, I see the books you're reading. I hear you talk with your friends after church about traveling, spending time up north. A young man with your mind should be thinking about college...I'm only sorry that your mother and I don't make the kind of money it takes to help you out..."

"Okay, Pa, okay, it makes sense and you're right. You're right. But for crying out loud don't let that Pauly Zigglebauer put you over a barrel - put *us* over a barrel!"

"No one's going to put us over a barrel, John."

John walked with his father back to the cattle truck where Pauly was again lazily picking away more of the dried manure from the door of the truck.

"Oh, ya, Matt, glad you came back, so...let's settle up here. Thirty a head going to do it?" Pauly spewed his words with a mix of spit and tobacco juice. You never wanted to be too close when this man launched his words.

Now it was John's turn to be a part of these dealings. "Okay, let's settle up, Pauly. But first, let's cut the bullshit. If we don't get top dollar for this herd, then there's no deal, plain and simple and you can just unload them and put them back in the barn."

"Oh, wait a minute, you must be John." Pauly began, trying to regain some territorial ground.

"Yeah, that's me. We'll take forty-five bucks a head and not a penny less." Pa looked at John with a mix of surprise and pride. Pauly's eyes darted over to Matt as if to plead his case on higher ground.

"Don't look at me, Pauly. You heard the man." Matt would have been happy with thirty, but was enjoying this moment.

Pauly stammered, looked back and forth between the two Miller men, looked back at the manure-spattered door of his truck as if to remember whom he was by looking at his name on the door and finally spewed out, "Sure, ya, okay then – that's okay by me. They're a fine bunch of animals and you got a deal. Might be a little bit more than I wanted to pay, but that's okay." He added, "I'll be okay with this one." as if these two men now standing very tall really cared. The Miller men knew quite well that Zigglebauer would make out very well for himself as he sold them off.

That evening, two very tired men came to the house, washed up and had a meal laid out for them that they typically wouldn't see unless it was Sunday or if extended family were over. It was Ma's way of saying thanks, her way of showing her pride, her respect and probably most of all, her relief.

"No more milking." she said. "No more getting up before sunrise and getting to bed late at night." she continued.

John held a large, full glass of milk into the air to make a toast and realizing the contents of his glass said, "Let's have a toast and be happy anyway."

Ma and Pa both laughed. Their old and weathered faces much happier than John had seen in a long time. It was a laugh that was loud and from the heart, ending in sighs and mixed emotions. The day had been filled with more emotion than they were used to. Most days were very scheduled and uneventful and they liked it this way. Now the routine would be different - very different! The Miller's had farmed this land for generations. In the sense of how things were all around them, it was a legacy. The change would be hard, but welcomed! Pa would still plan on getting up early, as would Ma. They kept some chickens and Pa still had the two draft horses. He had not made them a part of the deal, thinking about the times he and Katherine would hitch up the old buggy and take it down to the creek for picnics.

John sat out on the front porch and thought about everything that had happened that day. A lot of events and sentiment squeezed into one afternoon and now the cool evening would let him spread his thoughts apart.

Matt Miller came out of the house and stood near the porch swing where John was sitting. John broke the silence.

"Think I'll look for a job up north."

"Where abouts?" his father asked.

"Eagle River or Phelps, I think."

"Good fishing up there. Something you've never had time for before today." Matt said.

"Well, we'll see." John said. And again the two were silent, taking in the starry night.

3

In the days that followed, John took on a quiet and thoughtful demeanor, much different from the man he had proven himself to be when he stood firm with selling off the herd. He and Pa had cleaned out the barn for the last time other than the stalls and equipment needed for the draft horses, Strawberry and Mr. Duke. In the evening John would sort through his things - books to take, and things to leave. A list was made and maps were studied. Steeg had come from a part of Wisconsin near Eagle River, close to the border of Upper Michigan. It was far, but not too far so John would be able to return home for a visit once in awhile. He had never been too far from home. There was an occasional trip to Staceyville, Iowa to visit relatives. These were the relatives who ventured far from the family for no distinct purpose, but that they were set on starting a creamery. There were a couple of trips with friends to the Mississippi to fish. There were fish a lot closer, but not as big when one added the thrill of driving across the state, making eventful stops along the way, and taking in the beauty of the great river. John loved the Mississippi, but was curious about the north - curious about the land that Steeg had talked about so many times.

One Friday night at the supper table over the fish and potatoes that Ma had fried up, John announced his decision. "Ma, Pa, I'm going to leave tomorrow for Eagle River." He was careful not to use the word "move" for he had never "moved" anywhere before and, being the youngest, had some reservation over leaving his parents alone, aging and still having responsibilities of lawn, garden, and beekeeping.

"Tommy Horsch can come over to mow the lawn. I spoke with his brother Mark about it and all you have to do is call. Tommy can use our mower and he'd be glad to lend a hand with some of the yard work. He likes to mow lawn and does a good job of it." John's words suddenly became a little disjointed as he realized he had strayed from what he intended to talk about.

Softly his father spoke, "Okay, then. That sounds good. I think you'll find work that you can do up there, even with one hand." Weaving in a little humor and making him feel at ease was the Millers' way of condoning and granting their support. John recognized this trait and saw it in himself from time to time. When he would recognize that his speech would respectfully mimic his father's, it would make him feel proud. As a boy, seen around town on his bike, people would ask, 'Whose boy are you?' He would reply, 'Matt Miller's son.' The replies were always the same, 'He's a good man, your dad', 'good man', 'good man - and a good card player…honest'.

"I'll pack up some sandwiches for you to take. What time?" Ma asked as if to get into the conversation and acknowledge her harmony, as well.

"Well, I was thinking that noon would be best. I'm going to hitch a ride up 'cause I really don't need to take a car. Hitchin's easy and plenty of people stop. You meet some real good people that way."

Katherine gave Matt a look and he knew just what it meant, so he responded, "Oh, I don't know, John, why don't you take the pickup at least? We don't have a need for it anymore since we don't have to haul grain to the mill and back."

John didn't expect to be offered the truck. The thought hadn't even crossed his mind. John was soft, but excited in his reply, "If you're sure it's okay, that'd be great. Now that you think about it, it's faster and it'll make it easier for me to come back for visits." John was always careful to be assuring in his choice of words and tone.

Katherine and Matt Miller looked at each other. The last of their children was getting ready to leave. There was more emotion again and someone had to think quickly to change the subject and mood. John chimed out a little loudly, "So, I see we got a letter from Bill."

"That was the other day and you already read it." Ma said in a remindful tone.

"Oh yeah, I know. I'm just glad he's doing fine and he's safe and all."

"For now." Ma replied and then repeated in a gentle tone, "For now."

The three finished their meal in near silence only being cracked by the occasional comment on how good the fish tasted and the usual topic at a farmer's table, the weather.

John woke early the next morning, but not as early as Ma and Pa. They had coffee on and Ma was already cooking up a big breakfast of ham, eggs, sausage, toast and the last of the milk that came from their farm. They all were thoughtful of what this meant, buying milk at Diederich's store. It would be milk that had come from a dairy and came in a bottle. No cream to be skimmed from the top and the flavor would definitely need some getting used to. But they still had their chickens and this meant fresh eggs. John brought his suitcase and canvas bag down the stairs all neatly packed the night and days before.

With the truck he could bring a little more and use this opportunity to pack a peach crate with some of his favorite books. He ran back up the stairs for his books with great leaps. Ma and Pa looked at each other as they heard him run up the stairs. How long would it be before anyone ran up the stairs like that? Grandchildren ran up and down the stairs when they came to visit but their's were little steps, these were the long leaping steps of their young son - this young man who had been such a part of their lives and was with them through all of their changes.

John ate everything on his plate and in these times of tightening their belts, commented on having both sausage and ham even though he knew this was an occasion. After a few trips between the bathroom and his bedroom to make sure nothing was forgotten, John made his final walk through the kitchen where Ma had now finished wrapping up a large lunch sack for him, and Pa sat quietly, thoughtful and expressionless. Men in this family never hugged, certainly never kissed, and almost never shook hands, unless in some gesture of gaming. John didn't want to break with the custom and so only offered his left hand to shake even though he wanted desperately to know what it was like to hug his father. Children got hugs, but as they grew older the distance grew further. John knew he was loved by his father and didn't need to make the situation awkward by startling his father with behavioral changes. They shook hands and even looked into each other's eyes, but for only a second. There was the understanding that if you let someone look too long into your eyes they would see your soul or be able to read your emotions, maybe both.

Ma was different. Her family hugged and gave little smooching kisses on the cheek. Today's peck on the cheek was a little longer. In fact, she took seconds as tears formed in her eyes. "Oh John...we love you, Son. Please, be careful and make sure to write."

John nodded as he hugged his mother and whispered toward her ear, "I love you too, Ma, both of you." This is as close as he would ever get to tell his father that he loved him - 'I love you' through an interpreter. She hugged him for a long time and John looked over her shoulder at his father and rolled his eyes. Matt smiled and held back a laugh.

John drove down the farm lane as Ma and Pa watched from the sitting room window. When he left, they were in the kitchen, but he knew they would be looking and probably getting very sad and so he beeped the truck horn long and with sudden bursts to let them remember the occasion in a less-somber mood.

John drove through all of the towns he had known his whole life. He stopped in Chilton to say goodbye to Linda Nicolet, a girl who had *somewhat* broken his heart. She was different from all of the other girls. So special that she was easier to forgive. He pulled up to her house, but no one was home. 'Just as well', John thought, 'I'd probably choke on my words'.

He and Linda had once "skinny dipped" at Giltner's Pond together. It was a pond surrounded by woods and was not open to the public. All alone, they had discovered the beauty of their own bodies without crossing beyond a very warm hug in the cool water. She was the same girl that Steeg had seen John with at the Kassendahl.

John wished he could let everyone know that he was leaving, that he was getting out of this little town and wouldn't be here when all of his old friends were standing around on Saturday nights wondering what to do.

John saw a couple of people he knew walking on the sidewalk, but only beeped the horn and waved, yelling out the window, "Going up north!" Now John settled back in the seat, his right-hand still only slightly bandaged, cupping the top of the steering wheel which kept it elevated and relieved some of the throbbing. His left arm was perched on the open window, a full tank that he had topped off from the bright orange gas barrel by the corncrib, and nothing else to think about except putting some miles behind him.

4

Nearly six hours later, John pulled into Eagle River. He had
been driving all day and had only stopped once to stretch
and check his map. He thought this might be a good time to ask
around about jobs. The pickup truck was carefully parked a few
spaces down from the Hunter and Fisherman's Bar. John walked
past the bakery, its windows offering a sparse display of a few
loaves of bread and two pies. The store between the bakery and
the tavern had been closed and yellowed newspapers covered the
windows and glass door. Across the street there was a grocery
store and an undertaker's parlor with a casket displayed in the
storefront. It was combined with a tailor shop. A few other
stores lined the main street and people were walking about
doing their business in town. John took it all in and then walked
into the bar. This time of afternoon, there were only two men
seated at the bar, smoking cigarettes. They had shot glasses and
half-empty glasses of beer resting within reach. They craned
their necks to see who broke the silence and cast a shadow in
the doorway. Both men squinted to keep the unwanted sunlight
from their eyes and neither man spoke. John gave a slight smile
and nodded at the two men. Then he made eye contact with the
bartender who had been reading his newspaper at the other end
of the bar. He was a short man with black hair combed over to
conceal his baldness and a heavy growth of whiskers.

The bartender folded his paper, set it down and got up from his stool to come over to the end of the bar closest to the entrance where John stood now, standing tall to stretch his back after the long ride and holding the bar rail with both hands. "What'll it be?" the bartender asked.

"Have any cold beer?" John asked.

The bartender gave John a blank stare as if to suggest that the question was not worthy of response.

"What'll it be?" the bartender repeated.

"Any kind." John replied.

"Shorty?" asked the bartender.

"Long-neck." Replied John with a little more confidence. The bartender turned, stooped over and opened the glass-door of the refrigerator giving a welcomed gust of cool air to the patrons. He opened the bottle on the well-worn brass bottle opener mounted on the mullion of the refrigerated cabinet, the bottle cap dropping into the long tin receptacle labeled "Hamm's, From the Land of Sky Blue Waters." There was a picture of an Indian woman in a canoe. John laid a quarter on the bar and held out his good hand to receive the beer. The bartender took a coaster with his left hand, flipped it skillfully in front of his customer and placed the bottle firmly on the coaster which caused a little foam to escape from the bottle top. The bartender quickly snatched up the quarter and turned to his cash register. This was a repetitive dance that left no room for thinking, making this an ideal business for the man who wanted to conceal his demons. Short glasses of draft beer throughout the day to be sociable with his clients, day in, day out and he could maintain a steady hand to pour beer and enough of his wit to make proper change. He submitted occasional additions to the conversations with only enough personality to keep what few customers he had, coming back.

John took a long drink from the bottle and looked around studying the walls. Very little of the varnished pine wall was exposed between the mounted trophy fish, deer heads, moose and other local animals that gave their lives to adorn the walls of the Hunter and Fisherman's Bar. The stuffed snow geese suspended with fish line from the ceiling had turned a light shade of brown from the years of smoke that drifted up from the countless men who stood beneath and told each other exaggerated stories of their latest escapades in the great north woods. These days there were fewer men, however. The war had taken most of the bar owner's business away. What men remained almost never brought their girlfriends or wives to the bar to have a few drinks and some laughs as they had years ago. These were lean times for the bar. If it weren't for the older men in the area who felt the slow steady sting of age and needed a place to forget, there would be no business at all.

John struck up his nerve and after carefully choosing his words asked, "Any jobs in these parts? Been thinking I'd like to try my hand at logging".

The two old men at the bar only had to crane their necks a more comfortable ninety degrees to address the young man who stood to their left. The man closest to John studied him up and down noticing the wrapped right hand, and after enough time had passed for his thoughts to come, he replied, "Sure you can spare one?"

The two old men burst out in laughter and even the bartender had to look above the paper he had returned to, to give a half-grin while shaking his head.

Having sensed their pride in discovering the funniest remark of the day, the second man said, "Sure don't look like you'd be too damn good with an axe! What'd you do? Chop the other one off?" The two men continued in their hearty laugh occasionally coughing and choking up years of deposits from their lungs.

John grinned politely and played along, nodding his head to acknowledge that they had in fact made a very funny observation. Finally, as the laughter died off a bit and it was obvious that another clever remark would be a long way off, John made another effort to ask since he was sure these two old men had forgotten the question by this time.

"Logging any good up here?" John asked. It was one of those questions that he knew sounded kind of stupid just as he was asking it. This second attempt drew no openings for the men and their faces quickly turned somber.

"Logging?" the man on the right spoke up looking at his beer glass. "Logging ain't for shit unless you want to work for one of the biggest crooks in Vilas County. Most camps is closed or near-closed, torn down or burned up." He continued.

"Why's that?" John quickly asked now that he was starting to get a serious response.

The old man conjured up the nerve to let out all of his pent-up feelings, enough to draw his focus from his near-empty glass of beer to look John directly in the eye. Speaking more loudly now and shaking his head from side to side the old man responded, "'Cause that old bastard Anderson went and forced the decent men out of the business. He struck up so many deals with the devil that a good honest man can't make shit from logging no more. Cheated…robbed…took from everybody till there was no more to take." The old man's voice trailed off and his limp head turned again to his glass as if to say he had said it all.

Feeling the awkwardness and sore nerves that he had struck, John let the next couple of minutes go by in silence with only an occasional murmur heard from the man on the left. The muttering was not recognizable but probably nothing worth hearing. John continued to drink his cold Huber beer in long deep gulps as if to hurry this little hell along.

Finally John spoke up again, "Nice, weather up here. I bet the fishing's good." Now with a few brief words, he brought the old men out of their deep depression to a moderately less depressed state.

"Can't complain." The man on the left said.

"Pulling some nice Walleye's out of Big Twin." The man on the right chimed in.

"That so?" John remarked. The man on the left said, "ya, ya, ya…nice sized fish. Good eatin' size."

"I'll have to get out there." John responded.

Now it was the man on the right's turn to contribute his attempt at humor, "You could drag that stump of a hand you got there in the water, shake it around a little…and you might bring up a good sized Musky!" Now both men laughed loudly again. The bartender didn't look up from his paper this time. But this was enough of a diversion for John to swig down the last of his beer, grin and give the men a casual left-handed salute as he stepped backward toward the door.

"Thanks, I'll have to remember that one. See ya."

John shrugged it off. Better luck next time he thought to himself. John got into the truck, started it up and drove north out of town on Military Road headed for Phelps. A few miles out of town a large buck deer pranced across the road in front of John. He slammed on the brakes and gasped at the size of this animal. It's large new horns still covered in velvet, the buck made it across the road in only a few leaps, its large white tail stood straight up and waved like a flag as he disappeared into the thick brush. Now, close behind came the doe. Smaller, and just as beautiful, it pranced behind its mate. John kept the truck motionless for another half-minute as if to wait for another surprise before the brakes were released. The gas pedal was slowly pushed by its driver and the pickup truck again started down the road.

John saw the sign: "Phelps three miles". Then up ahead spotted a large, shiny dark blue sedan with clean white-walled tires pulled over to the side of the road. An old man was walking around and pounding his fist on the hood of the car. John slowed up and pulled alongside.

"Got a problem?" John shouted above the sound of his engine.

"No I just stopped to pick flowers! Of course I got a problem! Damn thing just stopped!" the old man said in disgust.

John held up his left palm to the man and nodded his head in motion to signal that it was all right and he was pulling ahead to stop. John pulled up in front of the car and shut off the truck. The old man was still walking around the car, this time with a cane that he pulled from the car through an open window. Now he could smack the wheels, tires and any other part he wanted as if it would work a miracle.

John asked "Mind if I take a look?"

"Naw, go ahead." the old man agreed.

John got into the man's car. It smelled of cigars, but it was a beautiful newer car and otherwise very clean. John turned the key and the engine turned, but did not start. John got out of the car quickly and popped open the hood. John knew a lot about cars, tractors, trucks, anything with an engine. He spun the wing nut loose that held the huge air cleaner on top of the carburetor. Looking down into the carburetor, John could see that it was dry, without any trace of gasoline. Now, setting the air cleaner down on the road in front of the car making sure to set it in a clean spot, John went around to the gas cap and removed it. John made a little tapping sound with the gas cap against the stem of the gas tank and listened as he held his ear close by, the sound echoed, the tank was empty.

"No gas." John told the man, as he stood upright.

"That so?" the old man questioned.

John offered, "I can give you a lift into town to get some gas if you'd like."

"And leave my new car here for someone to steal or vandalize?" the old man stiffly responded.

"Well, I guess I could run to town and bring back some gasoline. Enough to get you back to town anyway." The old man just nodded looking around.

"I'll do that then." John concluded. "You wait here and I'll be right back." he said.

"Now where in the hell do you think I'm going to go?" the old man mumbled under his breath.

Kind of a grouchy guy John thought to himself as he closed the hood of the car and headed for the pickup. John drove into Phelps and as he slowed down for the city speed limit, noticed a sign reading 'Rooms for Rent.' An elderly lady was hanging bed sheets on a clothesline. She wore a blue and white gingham dress with a white apron tied around her waist. She reached to the top of the high line stretched to allow room for the sheets to hang in the warm breeze without touching the ground. For a moment he remembered his mother and how he would hand her clothes pins when he was a small boy, too young for farm work. He would run around between the sheets hanging on the clothes line and play hide and seek with his mother.

John pulled his eyes back to the road and spotted the only service station in town. He purchased thirty cents worth of gas in a red can borrowed from the station owner who kept it for just such occasions, then he quickly returned to the stranded man. The old man looked somewhat surprised, but happy as John stopped the truck, got out and produced a red gasoline can from the bed of the truck. The old man just stood still. Only his head followed John's every move as he poured gasoline into the tank and then a little that was saved was poured into the carburetor to prime the engine. John got in and after a few tries, the car started right up. John revved the engine a bit to make sure it was going to stay running and then got out of the car, replaced the air cleaner and slammed the hood shut.

"That'll be thirty cents for the gas, sir." John said. The old man still looked a bit unbelieving.

"I'll do you one better than that." the old man said as he extended a business card to John held between the two fingertips.

"You stop by Camp Nine tomorrow, and I'll give you your thirty cents or something better." John looked the man over and then took the card in his fingers, the old man still holding on. Then their eyes made contact. The old man said "That okay by you?"

John replied, "Okay by me." The old man released the card. John then stood aside as the old man opened the car door and got in. His head could barely be seen above the huge dashboard as he reached up to shift the car into gear and drive away. John watched as the old man drove away and the big bright blue car got smaller in the distance. He was standing there now with a card in his hand. He looked down and read:

C.A. Anderson Lumber Company, Incorporated
C.A. Anderson
Proprietor
Phelps, Wisconsin

John stared at the card with indecision. Was this a stroke of luck or just some strange chance encounter that should be ignored? After all, it was only thirty cents. He wouldn't have to show up tomorrow, but he did say he would. What was there to lose? This was the man that not more than a half-hour ago the old men were cursing about at the bar. John placed the card up under the sun visor, looked over his shoulder to make sure the road behind him was clear, and turned the truck around heading again to Phelps.

Back in town John noted an interesting site, a shabbily-dressed man sitting on a bench in front of a bar. The man had his left arm extended over the back of the bench and several small birds were sitting on his arm eating seed that he was taking from a crumpled paper bag and placing on to his sleeve. His eyes appeared closed as if caught in a dream and he wore a broad, nearly toothless smile. At his feet there was a wooden box with a handle and a wire mesh door. Nearby another man stood. This man wore a full, well-trimmed beard and was better dressed.

The seated man opened his eyes just wide enough to notice John watching him. He held up the index finger of his right hand to signal John's attention and said, "Now here's the trick." He stood up and slowly moved his left arm in a wide circle while the birds clung tightly and a few small finches fluttered loose. John's expression showed amazement and the old man yelled out, "Pine sap!" The other man laughed as did John.

"Great show!" John yelled out to the man.

John drove along slowly. He noticed old men fishing off of the pier, their coffee cans with bait and newspapers nearby. There was a dry goods store, a hardware store and a funeral home along one block and a movie theatre, bar and two closed up storefronts on the other side of the street. Cabins lined the south shore of Big Twin Lake and the sunlight glistened on the waters as he stood there for a moment appreciating the beauty. He pulled up to the series of cabins that had the 'Room for Rent' sign out in front. He knocked at the door and the lady he had seen earlier appeared, recognizable by her dress and hair. She had a pleasant smile and John found himself staring into her dark eyes.

"How much for a room?" John asked.

"Day, week or month?" the lady replied.

"Depends, I guess." John said. This drew no response and so John continued, "A week to start with, I guess, and we'll see where it goes from there."

"I have one room right now. The cottages I rent to the tourists. Come end of season I shut everything down. Takes too much to heat everything and the pipes freeze up. So if you want the room it'll be five dollars in advance and five dollars a week. If you move on, just give me a week's notice so I can put the sign back up. No women in your room and no liquor on the premises and I'll expect you to keep your room neat." The lady said.

"Not a problem with that," John assured his new landlady. She produced a guest log from a table just inside the doorway and handed it to John. John reached in his pocket and produced a five-dollar bill and handed it to the lady.

"You have a job?" She asked as she handed him a pencil. John wrote his name and date and handed it back.

"No…but I'm looking."

She raised an eyebrow.

"If you know of anyone hiring around here…"John continued.

She spun the book around to read it and said, "Thank you, John Miller, I'll write you a receipt." She went back in through the screen door and placed the guest log back on the table, then opened the kitchen drawer retrieving the receipt book.

John stood outside and looked at the lake. The two old fishermen were calling it a day, one of them holding up a long stringer of fish – Bass and Walleye, the other closing up his tackle box.

The lady returned with the receipt. "Here you go," she said. "They might be looking for men at the lumber company. Not too many young men around with the war and all."

"I didn't get your name, Madam." John asked.

"Alice Stephan." the lady replied. "You can call me Alice. I've lived here my whole life. This was my father's place."

"Well, pleased to meet you Alice. You won't have any trouble out of me, I can assure you." And after a deep breath he continued, "I guess I'll go downtown and find a store to get some groceries."

"That would be John Phelps' grocery store – only grocery store in town." Alice replied. "You can park your truck over there under that maple tree. Enjoy your stay and good luck with your job search, Mr. Miller…I'm sure you'll do fine. There's always work for a man with spirit." she said.

"John will do." He offered.

She smiled and he smiled back as he turned and walked back to the truck.

5

As the sun set over the west shore of Big Twin Lake, John sat on the wooden lawn chair with its blistered white paint deep in thought. The last couple of days had brought him more change than he had seen in his eighteen years in this life. He knew there was so much to learn, so much to see and so many things to do. In a way, John felt some guilt that people he knew, friends from school, were on the other side of the world fighting a war so that he and everyone back home could have this precious freedom and that he could sit here watching the glimmering waters. He heard voices in the background. Some of the other renters had made a small fire in the circular piling of stones that lay in the center of the yard. A screen door closed and footsteps approached. John did not move but sat motionless, tired and watching the last sunlight of the day sink into the big lake.

A voice seemed to come out of nowhere "Finding your way around alright?" John turned and saw Alice walking over from the house.

"Oh, yes – thanks for asking. It's very peaceful up here." After a minute, John continued, " My dad used to come up to this area when he was younger, told me a lot of stories of hunting and fishing here. One time he got between a mother bear and her cub - said he 'just got the heck out of there'," John said. He smiled when he thought about his dad as a young man running from a bear.

"Oh? How wonderful that you can be in an area where your father spent time. It'll give you so much to talk about when you see him next," she said.

"Yeah, I guess so," John responded thoughtfully.

"Well, I have some chores to do so you have a good night, John."

"Thank you, Alice, same to you."

She glanced at John's bandaged hand and had a sympathetic expression, but said nothing. They exchanged smiles and she headed back to the house. John slept well that night, too tired to ponder the fact that he was in a different bed, different room, and different land.

The next morning John was awakened to the sound of screen doors slamming and voices of the Chicago men who had come up here to rent cabins so that they could fish, and that meant four o'clock in the morning. John now lay in the wooden bunk, eyes open and trying to convince himself that his first day living in the north should start early just like any other day had been on the farm. He was a little stiff from the worn mattress and the fact that he now had to sleep in a more dedicated position so as not to lay on his healing hand. He held it up and stared at if for a moment. Then started peeling off the remaining bandage exposing the warm, moist hand to the fresh air. Scabs had formed and he could move his fingers a little bit. His forearm bore colors of yellow, blue, black and red. He thought this might be a good day to discard the bandage and start letting the wounds get some fresh air. Pa had always told him that this is the best thing for healing a wound. He stared at his bare right hand and tried stretching out and bending his mangled fingers. It was painful, not excruciating, but enough to make him realize that finding work up here that he could do might be a little more challenging than he had thought.

Buttoning his shirt and tying shoelaces was still a chore with one good hand but each day he found it a little easier. After getting dressed and cleaned up at the sink in his room, John pulled a new pair of leather work gloves from his canvas pack. Ma had given them to him last Christmas and since his old pair was still good enough for work on the farm, he had saved this pair for later. John felt this to be the appropriate time to tear the gloves from the staple and cardboard band that bound them. Slowly he pulled the right glove over his right hand, ever so slowly tugging at this side and then the other. Maybe a quarter of an inch each time, John maneuvered the glove over his hand, guiding the fingers into their places. After minutes of struggle the glove was on. Now John could pull the left glove on pulling the cuff of the glove with his teeth. John flexed his hands in the gloves, the left hand could make a fist, the right hand could barely move. It was stiff and sore and still gave John a lot of pain.

It was still early as John stepped outside. He looked down the road and noticed a café. It was a small wood-framed building connected to what looked like a converted railroad car with a sign mounted to the roof which read "The Spot Lunch." Below that, a separate but attached sign read "Dinners – Lunches" and "Enjoy Pepsi-Cola – hits the spot." The lights were on and it appeared that they were open and serving breakfast. John walked down the road, arms folded on his chest since he couldn't put his gloved hands into his pants pockets. He saw a car coming toward him. It was a large beige colored 1937 Auburn Boattail Speedster, a beautiful car, and so out of place here in the north woods. As it passed, John turned his head to see the gleaming Boattail cruise by.

As he got closer to the diner he could make out the cook, waitress and a few people sitting at the counter having their coffee cups re-filled. The waitress had dark brown hair worn in a ponytail and looked like she could have been an actress. She sure is pretty, John whispered to himself. John stepped inside and the bell above the door jingled. Both the cook and the waitress looked up to see who had come in - this time a stranger. "Morning," John said.

"Morning, sit anywhere." the girl replied. The cook went back to pouring pancake batter on the grill.

John took a stool at the counter and looked up to read the chalkboard menu that hung above the back wall.

"Coffee?" the girl asked.

"Sure." replied John without so much as a thought. He hadn't been a big coffee drinker but thought, 'If I'm going to work up here like a man, I've got to drink up here like a man – might as well get used to coffee.'

"Take cream?" the girl asked.

"Yes, please...and sugar too." John responded. The girl smiled, finished pouring the coffee and went to set it back on the burner. She picked up her order pad and looked up at John. He noticed her waiting and they gave each other a quick smile. John's mind raced as he tried to think of something to say.

"Nice weather up here... but a little chilly." he said, implying that he wasn't from the area.

"Oh yes, it's been real nice. It's always a little brisk in the morning, but it'll warm up nicely in a couple hours. Before you know it, it'll be fall. Where are you from?" the girl asked.

"Oh, I don't think you've probably ever heard of the town, but it's basically around the east shore of Lake Winnebago." Everyone knew where Lake Winnebago was since it was the largest lake in Wisconsin.

"Try me." the girl said smiling.

"Mount Calvary." John responded looking into her dark eyes for some sign of recognition.

She squinted her eyes in thought and then popped them wide open. "Nope, can't say that I have, but you never know, I might just get there someday." This comment made John realize that she had probably spent her whole life up here just as he had spent his whole life down there.

John ordered pancakes, bacon and a glass of juice. The waitress called the order back to the cook and then continued with busy work behind the counter. Every once in a while the cook would look up and notice the little show she was putting on for their new customer at the counter and would shake his head.

"Here you go." she handed John his breakfast.

"Looks good." John said and he commenced to set his napkin, cover the pancakes with syrup, pick up his fork and dig in. The cook rolled his eyes.

About halfway through the stack John asked, "So, what's your name, if you don't mind my asking?"

The girl smiled and replied, "Abigail…Abigail Spence."

"Abigail … Abigail…" John repeated softly to himself. Where he had come from all of the girls carried names like Kathy, Mary, Christine, and the like. The name Abigail was new to him.

"My name is John, John Miller". Abigail reached out a hand to shake.

"Pleased to meet you." she said with a broad smile that showed her beautiful white teeth.

"And very pleased to meet you, Abigail," John replied.

"You can call me Abby." she said.

John set down his fork and extended his left hand which seemed a little awkward and a bit embarrassing. "Injured my right hand awhile back." he said.

She produced a sad face. "I was wondering why the gloves… nothing serious I hope."

"I'll be fine. Everything heals in time." John said.

Abby went back to wait on other customers. As John was eating, he felt as if someone were watching him. He turned at the waist enough to look out the window. The man he had seen with the bird man was standing outside with his hands resting on the sill, looking in. The cook came from behind the grill carrying a cup of coffee and a paper bag. He set both down on the end of the counter and opened the window. "Morning, Eddy," the cook said.

"Morning." the old man replied as he stared at the bag and the coffee. The cook handed over the bag and the coffee. Eddy strained his neck a bit to get a look at the waitress, grabbed the bag and coffee and in an instant was gone. John thought the event was a little strange.

After John finished his meal, Abby came over with the pot of coffee. He really didn't want any more, but thought it would give her an excuse to keep coming back and give him an excuse to continue to receive her attention.

"Top it off?" she asked.

"You bet...good coffee." he replied. "There was a rather curious fellow here just now." John said as he nodded toward the window.

"Oh, I think that fellow goes by the name of Eddy...at least that's what I've heard Harvey call him...Eddy. I think he's kind of new to the area...I've seen him around town a couple of times with Dido." Abby said.

"Dido?" John questioned.

"Yeah, a shabby old man who feeds the birds." Abby said.

"Oh yeah...I've seen him...pine sap." John exclaimed.

Abby laughed. "Yes sir, that would be the man." she said with another broad smile.

"So what do you do up here when you're not working?" John asked.

This got the attention of Harvey, the cook, who looked up and gave a stare, then shook his head as he went back to what he was doing. He should have been used to innocent flirtations, but he had had other waitresses run off with customers before and not come back. Abby noticed the look from her boss and kept her voice low.

"Sometimes there's live music at the dance hall in Conover. It's really pretty and they have real pretty lights. On a hot summer night it can be a lot of fun. Other than that, everyone just hunts and fishes and works".

"Have you ever seen an Auburn Boattail Speedster?" John asked.

She gave a curious look. "Can't say that I have."

"It's one of the most beautiful cars ever made. The back end comes to a point like a boat."

"And…" she asked curiously.

"Well, I just saw one this morning – on my way here…it seemed kind of out of place for Northern Wisconsin."

"Really?" she asked with sincere interest.

"I couldn't believe it. You must have some rich people living up here."

"I've heard of a few. But just to let you in on a little secret, John… (She leaned forward to whisper) I have to work for a living so I'm not traveling in those circles these days!"

John laughed. "Speaking of work, is there much going on around here at the lumber camps or mills?" John had no intention of working in a splinter factory as they were referred to - his intent was to give the question greater room for response.

"Lumber camps are all over the place, but not enough men and too many trees." She replied. "I would have thought if you were interested in millwork you might have tried the paper mills down there in the Fox Valley where you passed through on your way up here."

"Oh, I'm not so much interested in paper mills or millwork in general. I'd rather be working out in the sunshine."

"Well then, you might try Anderson Lumber. Most people don't care for the man, but he's got the jobs," she said. Abby noticed that there were customers waiting for her. John noticed also and gave her a nod. John continued to eat breakfast and in a few minutes, was finished. Abby stopped by with an arm full of plates and set John's bill in front of him, giving him another smile.

John could see that Abby was getting busier as more men came in for breakfast. He looked at the bill, took a couple of dollars from his wallet and left them on the counter. As he was leaving he said, "Maybe see you around some time?'

"Don't be a stranger… John." Abby said.

Hearing her speak his name gave John a warm feeling. He had met a beautiful girl, the sun was rising, and he wondered what else the day had in store for him.

John saw a small sign about fifty feet away pointing the way to the C. A. Anderson Lumber Company. John went back to the cabins, got into his truck and started off for the lumber camp. About three miles south of town he could make out a sign for Camp Nine. It was a small sign and would have been very easy to miss had it not been for the sparse trees, piles of smoldering brush piles and stacks of logs piled all around. The drive in was muddy and had very deep ruts. More than a couple of times the pickup truck bottomed out with a thud that sent John bouncing up and hitting his head. John slowed the truck and, as he pulled around the log piles to the area where the office and bunkhouses stood, he couldn't help but think about having to crawl under the truck and inspect for any damage.

A small sign over the door of a wooden building read: "C. A. Anderson Lumber Company, Limited" and below that, "Camp Nine". John pulled up and shut off the truck. He could see men starting to amble around the camp, men making trips from the bunkhouse to the privy and back. These were some of the dirtiest, filthiest men he had ever seen. Not one of them could walk ten feet without hacking up something that they would launch as far as they could and not a smile among the whole bunch. Smoke billowed from the bunkhouses as men carried in chopped wood to stoke pot-bellied stoves.

There was no sign of the big blue car and John knew he had shown up way too early. Some of the men would give a glance at him as they went about their morning business. Suddenly John saw one large man shove another man back and forth near one of the garbage barrels until the large man finally clutched the other with both hands and yelled something within inches of the other man's face. He then gave a shove and the man fell backwards, stumbling over some chopped wood and finally landing in the mud. The winner of this scrap stood there for another few seconds to make sure the defeated man stayed there and that this score had been settled. The man then ambled back into the bunkhouse slamming the door behind him. John quickly got out of his truck and with some hesitation, walked over to the man and offered his hand to help him up. The man was so much smaller than the man who had pushed him, it was clearly an unfair match.

"Let me give you a hand." John offered softly.

The man laid there for a moment on his back, butt and elbows. He was evaluating what had just happened to him, and the stranger who offered his hand. He finally reached out to accept the help offered to him. The man had black hair and dark skin, at first making John think he might be an Indian, but the man spoke, "gracias…gracias sënor…sir…thank you".

"You're a long way from home."

The man responded, "Everyone here is a long way from home." His accent was heavy and John was a impressed that the man spoke English so well.

John helped the man to his feet and introduced himself, "Name's John Miller, what's yours?"

"Manuel." The man replied, "Manuel Ochoa, Camp Nine Cook."

"You're the cook? Well, I guess you've got work to do. Probably some pretty hungry men waiting for you to do your work."

"Si...yes, I need to hurry." Manuel thanked John again and with several nodding bows turned and ran to another building that also had a small sign that simply read "canteen." Below the word were letters crudely painted in parenthesis: "cantina".

John looked around at the various buildings, some barely standing, pieces of machinery, cans of kerosene and gasoline, and trucks parked at one end of the camp. There was a building labeled "maintenance" and there were partially dismantled chainsaws strewn all about, some mechanical parts stuck into the mud as if planted and perhaps expected to grow. John checked his pocket watch, the one given to him by his father on his fifteenth birthday. It was seven a.m. and John stood around thinking it might have been a good idea to set a time for meeting with this old man. Just then one of the bunkhouse doors flung open and out stepped the large man who had been fighting with Manuel. He let out a tremendous belch followed by other bodily noises as if forced. He stood there and then noticed John. Grinning to find that he had had an audience for his performance, he started walking over toward John.

"What the hell you looking at?" the man asked.

"Not a thing." John said in a matter of fact tone.

"Not a thing, huh?" the man replied. John didn't say a word.

"So, what the hell are you doing here, boy?" the man asked.

"Come to talk with Mr. Anderson. I have an appointment to see him." John stated.

"You looking for work here, boy?" the man asked.

"Maybe...not sure, guess that would be up to the boss." John responded.

"Come to work all fixed up and brand new leather gloves, huh?" The man now seemed to be challenging.

John looked the fat man in the eye and didn't say a word. They stood and stared at each other in silence for a moment and then the man let out another belch and John could make out the smell of the man's disgusting breath in the cool morning air. Just then a car pulled into the yard, a familiar bright blue car that brought a little bit of relief to John.

"Well there you go, boy. Old Charles Alexander Anderson here to your beckoned call." The fat man chortled, turned and walked away.

The car pulled up next to John's truck and the old man shut off the engine. He gathered up some papers and stuffed them into a leather case. After what seemed like several long minutes the man finally emerged from his car and stepped onto the boardwalk that spanned the front of the building. He walked up to John.

John said, "Morning Sir".

The old man stared at John for a second as if to recognize him. "What're you doing here?" the old man asked.

"You told me to stop by today, sir. I'm the guy who got your car running yesterday out there on Military Road. You were out of gas, remember?" John asked.

"Oh, hell, yes, I remember. I'm just having some fun with you." the old man said.

John was relieved. The old man fumbled with his key in the lock of the door, finally spinning the key all around and pushing the office door open.

"Come in then," the old man invited. The two men stepped into the office. Although this was just a field office, it was kept impeccably clean and organized. The old man set his leather brief case on top of his desk, took off his coat, hung it onto a coat tree near the door, and invited John to have a seat. John sat down in one of the two chairs positioned across the large desk.

The old man walked over to the kerosene heater and turned up the heat. He walked around the desk and sat down. He took his case from the pile of papers on his desk and fumbled through a few envelopes before setting them down.

"Do you know why you're here?" the old man asked.

"Well sir, as I recall you said you'd either pay me the thirty cents I spent to put gasoline into your car or you'd have something better." John spoke with confidence. "Is that how you recall it, sir?" John asked looking straight into the man's eyes.

"Yes, yes, of course I remember and I'll get right to the point. You strike me as an honest young man. Where are you from, son?" the man now spoke with warmth in his voice.

"A small town near Fond du Lac, east shore of Lake Winnebago, a town called Mount Calvary." John answered.

"I know it well, son. Elmer Magnon still have a tavern over there in Petersburg?" the man asked.

John seemed surprised at the question and stammered, "Yes, yes sir, in fact he's a good friend of my father."

"What's your father's name?" asked the man.

"Matt... Mathew Miller, sir." John responded.

"Nope, no I can't say that I know him. Might have heard the name...not sure... but there's a lot of a good people from that part of the state." After a moment of nodding the man continued, "You a farmer or just fond of pickup trucks?"

"Born and raised on the farm, sir." John answered.

"Well, truth is, I need some help up here in the camp. Lost a lot of good men to the war effort including my right-hand man, my office clerk, don't know when or if he'll be coming back. Of all that's left not one could count to a hundred if their lives depended on it, mostly immigrants and old men. Got one fat foreman running this camp and I wouldn't trust him to keep anything straight as far as keeping records. I need someone who's sharp, good with numbers and can be trusted. You that man?" the man asked.

"Yes sir, in fact I'm very good with numbers. I kept track of all of the milk production records, breeding records, anything that needed to be kept track of on the farm sir," John spoke with pride.

"What's your name again, young man?" the man asked.

"John Miller, sir." John responded.

"Well John, if you want a job as records clerk for the C. A. Anderson Lumber Company, I'm offering it. I'll start you off at twenty-five dollars a week and you can fill up your tank as you need since you'll need your truck to get from camp to camp. Things work out, after awhile I could go thirty a week." The man offered.

"Well sir, my answer is, yes." John replied. Mr. Anderson extended his right hand to shake on the deal and was met with John's left hand.

Charles Anderson reached into his pocket and pulled out a handful of change. He poked and moved the coins around until he produced a quarter and a nickel. He picked them up and handed the coins to John. He gave a nod as if to convey that they were settled up for the debt of the previous day.

"You trusted me for thirty cents, John. It's good to be able to trust people, just be careful about the people you put your trust in." John took the coins with his left hand and gave an understanding nod back to the man.

"What's with your right hand? Now that I think of it, it was bandaged up yesterday." Anderson said.

"Nothing much sir, just learning to write left-handed, shouldn't be a problem sir."

"Let's get to it then, John. I'll show you around, and then we'll come back here, and then I'll show you what's all involved with keeping the records."

The two men walked out to the yard as the workers were coming out of the canteen from breakfast. Not too much more than a couple dozen men at this camp not including the cook,

Manuel, John thought to himself, quick to survey the workforce. Then out came the fat man who again stopped in his tracks to look at John and Mr. Anderson.

"We have a new records clerk joining us this day, Nelson" Anderson called over to the fat man. The fat man, Nelson replied, "That's good, sir, pleased to hear it. This clerk got a name?"

"John Miller, Mr. Nelson, pleased to make your acquaintance." John spoke up in behalf of Anderson.

"Well, Miller, I'm the camp foreman...the wood boss. I'm sure you and I are going to get along just fine." Nelson said with a laugh. A slight look of concern came over John's face. Nelson finished the introduction with another loud belch and scratched his fat gut. Nelson extended his hand to shake and John extended his left hand.

"Wrong hand, Miller." Nelson grabbed for John's right hand and Mr. Anderson quickly brushed Nelson's arm aside. Nelson laughed.

"Got to have a firm handshake, right boy?"

"Knock it off!" Anderson told him and continued to mumble under his breath, something that sounded like 'Idiot'.

"Don't listen to his B.S., I'm the boss here and that's all you have to remember, John."

Then the old man turned toward Nelson. "Nelson, it's almost half-past seven the men should be out in the swamp cutting by now. Damn it, man." Anderson turned toward John. "This is just what I'm talking about. No ambition here, no drive. I want this changed. I want this camp to run the way it used to. I want all the camps to run the way they used to before this war." Anderson said.

Anderson climbed into the passenger side of John's truck. "Come on, I'll show you around the camps. You're probably wondering why I'd have a shiftless fat ass wood boss like Nelson in my company. Well, I might as well tell you...you'd hear the story from someone eventually. You see Nelson's father was a long-time employee here. A few years back a hydraulic line snapped on a skidder and a load of logs rolled off crushing the old man's legs. I thought he was going to die…but he pulled through. I visited that poor bastard every evening in the hospital. Spent my own money to make sure he got the best care he could get. Then he shows his gratitude by finding a lawyer to go after me saying that the condition of the equipment had been reported as a potential safety violation. You know… all that crap. Well, to make a long story short we reached a settlement giving the old man a decent retirement and his son a management position in the company. I've long since regretted that second part of the deal. His old man passed on a year ago, but I haven't had anyone come forward to take his place."

The two men drove from camp to camp looking over the terrain, Anderson talking about trees and how the war was bringing in orders to be filled. Throughout the day John's new boss showed him the books that he kept, records of production, maps of land that the company owned or leased, lease agreements with the state and private landowners and the listing of employees. Anderson introduced John to the secretary and bookkeeper and they explained how the payroll was kept. John scanned down the list of employees. In the listing for employees of Camp Four he saw the name, Onsgaard. Perhaps a relative, perhaps his friend, in either case John felt curious and a bit excited to see this name.

"I have a son back in Minneapolis. He's finishing up college next year and my hope is that he comes out here to take my place. I have business interests back in the cities that I need to tend to and my plan is to be back there in a year. That's enough for today John. You get yourself acquainted with the men. Treat them well and they'll treat you well. Treat them too well and they'll walk all over you…it's a balancing act, but I think you've got the brains and integrity it takes to make this work. Prove me right." Anderson said.

"Yes sir, Mr. Anderson. I'll see you in the morning." John said.

"No you won't. I have some business at the mill to tend to. You're on your own." Anderson said as he grabbed his leather case from his desk and headed toward the door. He turned and tossed the keys to John.

"Here, you'll need these. That'll be your desk over there. Any office supplies you need, you let the girls know, or else you just pick up in town and charge them to my account. I'll see you day after tomorrow. So long, John, and welcome to the lumber business." Anderson said with a distinguished smile.

John spent the rest of the day getting familiar with the business, the camp and what was expected of him. The ladies in the office gave John their version of how things should be done and what they thought would be expected of John. They also threw in a little gossip and a few good stories.

"The big thing to look out for is accidents…remember that, John Miller" one of the old ladies told him while the other nodded silently with eyebrows raised. "There's plenty of accidents around the equipment." she continued.

"Lot's of accidents" the other chimed in.

That evening John thought he'd stop by the Spot Lunch Café to see if Abby was still working. He thought that, with the good fortune of finding work, he just might have the good fortune of getting a date. John stepped into the café and hesitated. An older woman was behind the counter and although he wanted to turn around and leave, he couldn't think of an excuse that would allow him to do so without a little embarrassment. And so he sat at the counter and ordered a sandwich and glass of milk for his supper.

"Abby working tomorrow?" John asked

The waitress gave a smile as she cocked her head to look him over. "So you're the one." she said with a grin.

"The one what…?

"The one she was talking about all afternoon."

"Oh? Well, I hope it was me." John replied with a curious look.

"Name John?" she asked.

"Yes…John Miller."

"Yep…you're the one." she said with a wink and grin. "She starts at five AM."

"Oh…thanks. Do you mind if I just take my sandwich to go?" John didn't wait for an answer before gulping down the entire glass of milk.

The waitress laughed and took a small paper bag for his sandwich from under the counter.

6

John was glad to find work so quickly and that the need for manpower was as great as he had heard. John knew it was the war, some luck and probably some Divine Intervention. The only down side John could see so far was a fat crew foreman who seemed to single him out for no apparent reason. Perhaps it was because John was not like the others. John was articulate and clean, two qualities that were rare in this group. Whatever it was, John was not going to let this man get under his skin and thought best to keep his distance as much as possible, if nothing else to stay clear of the man's foul smell and disgusting habits.

John took to his tasks well. His farm experience gave him the skills he needed to work well with numbers, analyze work, schedule work and study work methods, always keeping his mind open to better ways to optimize the crew's efforts. John was quick to sort out the more productive workers, to watch and learn from them. The men liked John and were glad to share what they knew with him.

In the weeks that followed, the weather grew cooler, especially at night. It was now late September, and between the cooler temperatures and some sincere conversation from time to time, the men were producing more than the months prior to John's arrival. John made daily trips to each of the camps to check the counts of logs harvested. He made maps for himself - at first to keep from getting lost, but later to keep track of where the hardwoods, softwoods, and the older stands of pine could be found. He learned quickly to distinguish the various hardwoods and softwoods: maple, elm, basswood, cottonwood, poplar, aspen, larch and birch. In these days the crews were mostly cutting softwood, red, white and jack pines. Occasionally spruce and hemlock were taken. John assessed this industry quickly and concluded that there was a lot of waste and if he studied long enough, there would be ways to increase the yield. Choice trees were cut and often crushed other growth as they fell. The tops were left where they lay and it would kill any undergrowth. Unfortunately, dry branches were good kindling for forest fires and the men had to stop work a couple of times each summer to put out fires that had gotten out of control. In the vast forest that spanned a half million acres a single fire could result in devastation. John would mention these concerns to Mr. Anderson when they were both in the office at the end of the day. Anderson smoked his pipe and would nod occasionally making an understanding remark.

Charles Anderson asked John to do an audit of production at Camp Four. John would need to dedicate a full day including travel time for the task. Camp Four was a group of men who worked with little to no supervision and stayed in an old bunkhouse. Having been one of the older camps, they had more comforts than the newer camps. Men had their own bunks and more room for privacy. Nelson had informed the crew the day before that the new records clerk was coming and would be verifying some information. John had suggested arriving at noon so that the men could all be gathered for lunch and he would not be cutting into their production time. John also wanted to use this time to bring the men some iced lemonade and had purchased several gallons of it from Abby at the Spot Lunch café. John had been taking evening meals there with some regularity over the weeks and was beginning to learn more about this girl.

Arriving at Camp Four, John set out the lemonade on a makeshift table of logs and a few scrap boards. John invited the men to help themselves and then take a seat so that he could address them all at one time. The men began to congregate as John got his clipboard from the pickup truck. Still curious about the name 'Onsgaard' that he had seen on the employee listing, John looked over the men as they came out from the logging trail to the clearing. John saw Steeg Onsgaard and thinking he would make a surprise of it, kept moving around with his back turned to Steeg. Turning around with the brim of his cap pulled down and holding the clipboard to partially covered his face, he yelled to the men to form a straight line and call their names as they came up to him so that he could take count of the men.

John kept his head down as he moved toward a familiar man sitting near a bull dozer. John announced his name "Onsgaard", lowered the clipboard, looked up at Steeg and asked, "I think we already know each other."

Steeg's jaw dropped and his mind raced for words that wouldn't come. John broke the silence with a soft voice, "Why'd you leave the farm, Steeg?"

Steeg could only come up with two words, "I'm sorry." He stammered a bit and quietly said, "I guess I was scared."

John extended his left hand to shake and said, "We missed you Steeg, you shouldn't have left us, but Ma and Pa understand."

Steeg nodded, looked around and then realized how strange this situation really was and asked, "So what are you doing here?"

"Heard so much about these great north woods from you that I thought I'd come up here and see for myself. Pa sold off the herd and started renting out the land, time for both of them to take life a little easier. Got a job with this outfit the very first day up here and that's about it. Well, I best get to work here."

After finishing taking names John told the men to take a break and go ahead and have lunch as he would explain the procedure they would use for the audit. John poured two glasses of cold lemonade for he and Steeg and the two men walked off to sit down by a tree and catch up on how their lives had changed over the last few months. John headed back for the office at Camp Nine a little happier this day to have found an old friend and make sure all was forgiven.

That evening John drove over to the Spot Lunch Café to return the glass gallon jars. As he pulled into the parking lot he noticed Eddy by the window again and thought it seemed a little strange. Returning the jars was a good excuse to see Abby again. It was seven o'clock and she was just getting off of work. John came into the café with jars in hand and set them on the counter. She greeted him with a smile and came over to the counter as John was sitting down.

"Don't get too comfortable, that is unless you're too tired to take a girl out to watch the sunset over the lake," she said with a smirk.

"A great idea to finish off a great day. Say, your boss seems like he's in a pretty good mood today." John said.

"Well, I have to tell you a secret…Harvey's been getting money in the mail…cash…about once a month someone sends him a fifty dollar bill! Fifty dollars, John - some months it seems like that's just what the café needs to pull us through. I think whoever it is, they're a real angel." Abby said with confidence.

"Wow, a fifty dollar bill with no explanation, no notes… nothing?" John asked.

"No return address, no nothing, just a crisp fifty dollar bill" Abby replied.

"I wish whoever it was had my address." John said. Then John proceeded to tell her about the small world they lived in and finding his old friend Steeg over at Camp Four.

She paused as she was taking off her apron and said, "Really? John that's great news, I'm happy for you." She gave him a little hug and untied her apron, quickly hung it up, wrote out the time on her time card and called out to the cook, "Good night, Harvey, see you in the morning."

By the time Harvey looked up from cleaning the grill, Abby was already heading for the door with her arm wrapped around John's. John glanced back and noticed Harvey placing a plate of food and a cup of coffee on the step of the café. Eddy walked over, grabbed the food and took it away.

The two sat on a large flat rock overlooking Big Twin Lake and talked as the sun was setting.

"So, you really haven't told me too much about your life… that is, I'd like to know a lot more about you." John said.

"Not much to tell. I'm an orphan. I was raised by my aunt Helen over in Three Lakes. My mother died when I was a baby and I never knew my father." Abby told John with a hint of sadness in her voice.

"Sorry to hear that." John said.

"Don't be, I'm fine with it. I just wonder what it would have been like to have a mother and father like the other children in school. I would have liked to have brothers and sisters, but that's life I guess. I have other people in my life now that my aunt passed away…you know, friends, people that seem like family to me" Abby said. The air began to get a bit chilly and John offered Abby his wool jacket. He helped to put it over her shoulders and she leaned over to him as he put his arm around her and they both held this moment in silence. John turned his head toward Abby and she turned her head up to him and they kissed. They continued to embrace and kiss, as the sun set over the lake and it was getting dark. The two walked over to John's truck.

"Would you like to go to the Vilas County Fair, John?" Abby asked.

"Well…"

"I don't mean to be forward…I really don't. It's just that the fair starts this weekend and you probably wouldn't have any way of knowing that and…"

"Yes…I'd love to, Abby."

"Okay then." Abby leaned up to John and gave him a little kiss on the cheek. "Good night, John."

"Good night, Abby."

The next morning John's alarm clock went off and in the shock of awakening, he accidentally hit it, sending it across the room where it continued to ring loudly. He sprang to his feet and stumbled across the floor to shut off the alarm, shivering in the early morning cold. He shut off the clock and jumped back into bed to savor the warmth of the blankets and quilts piled high. Eyes opened, John thought for a moment about missing work or at the very least showing up a little late today. He wanted to live the previous night over again and again, but in a few minutes time gave in to the fact that it was a new day, a work day, and he needed to report for work. He had a man transferring to Camp Nine and he didn't want to be late.

There was thick dew over John's truck and with the sun coming up, steam began to rise from the hood and the top. John kicked up dew from the thick grass as he headed to the truck, shivering a bit from the cool morning air. He turned the key and his faithful truck started. John let it warm up as he wiped condensation from the inside of the windshield with the sleeve of his jacket. He had left his window open a bit from the drive home the night before. John arrived at Camp Nine and parked in front of the canteen. He swung open the door to find breakfast in full process. Manuel was dishing out huge bowls of oatmeal that the men took over to their tables where they poured heaping spoons of brown sugar, raisins, and nuts. Hot coffee flowed into cups everywhere and there were many men still in line. John walked briskly around behind the counter and grabbed an extra apron. He asked Manuel for another big spoon, "La cuchara grande" he shouted over the noise of the men. Manuel handed John a spoon and he proceeded to dish out bowls of the steaming oatmeal for the men. Manuel smiled briefly and continued to tend to the boiling water he had going for the next batch. Manuel handed John a cast iron frying pan and instructed him to fry up more bacon.

"This is your frying pan." Manuel said with a smile.

John said, "Thanks, no one has ever given me a frying pan before." But the attempt at humor was lost in the language. John found his way around the kitchen and proceeded to fry up thick slabs of bacon. John enjoyed helping and seeing the men eat a hearty meal. There was a sense of camaraderie that he hadn't seen before.

Nelson walked in and the noise quieted down a bit. Men who were looking around talking and laughing were now looking down at their plates and bowls. Nelson walked up to the counter.

"Spic – get me a bowl of oatmeal and some toast…and hurry it up."

John grabbed Manuel's arm as he reached for a bowl. John looked at Nelson, he could feel his heart beating faster and adrenaline rushing.

"What's the problem?" Nelson asked.

"This man's not a *spic*." John said.

"Okay then, tell your stinking Mexican amigo to get me my breakfast."

John began to feel a little more in control like the day he took charge of the cattle sale. "The only thing stinking in this canteen is on the other side of this counter." John said.

There was now a silence in the room.

"You ready to get the crap beat out of you?" Nelson barked. Before John could answer, a voice came from across the room.

"Lay a hand on that young man, and you'll have to answer to all of us – starting with me." It was Steeg. He stood up and all eyes were on him. Nelson looked around nervously.

"Think I'm afraid of a bunch of old farts like you? Besides, I was just having some fun with the boy." Nelson said with a nervous smile. "Now that you got everyone's attention maybe you could ask Sënor Cook here to dish me up a bowl of oatmeal… please!" Nelson craned his neck around to see if his sarcastic tone of voice met with everyone's approval.

John let go of Manuel's arm and gave him a nod. One of the men yelled, 'fat ass.' Nelson looked around quickly, but all of the men were now laughing. This was the first time any of the men showed the disrespect they were feeling and now he had had his share of embarrassment for the morning.

Nelson yelled, "That's enough out of all of you."

Things quieted back down and the men started talking among themselves again. There were a few nods toward John as the men commented on the way he handled himself. John felt relief, continued frying bacon and tried to ignore the occasional stare that he knew was coming from Nelson.

These days were unseasonably hot. Earlier in the week, while running errands for the company, John saw a poster in town announcing the Vilas County Fair. John was thinking about the fair this morning and looking forward to spending time with Abby.

Later that morning, John went to the office and suggested to Mr. Anderson that if he could get a few gallons of lemonade from town, it would refresh the men and help increase production.

"Good idea, John. That's something Nelson never would have figured out and you know why?"

"No sir."

"Because it's just plain common sense and the man doesn't have any."

"That might be, sir. Well, I best get going. It'll take them awhile to make up a few gallons of lemonade."

"Well go on, John – get down to that café in town – get a move on."

"Yes sir." John grinned as he drove to the Spot Lunch Café.

As John walked in, he saw Abby sweeping the floor. She looked up, saw John and called out in surprise, "Hello, John." She put down the broom and moved quickly to him.

"Hi Abby - good to see you. Do you think Harvey could make up about five gallons of lemonade?"

Abby turned and yelled to Harvey. "Harvey, five gallons of lemonade, if you please."

Harvey put down his paper and gave her a wink.

She turned to John. "Tomorrow's the fair."

"I know. It's all I can think about."

Abby helped John load up the lemonade into his truck. The two smiled and Abby brushed her hand over John's as she said, "Goodbye, see you tomorrow."

John grinned and winked as he climbed into his truck. He leaned out the open window and watched as she walked back toward the café. She turned her head to get one more look and John tipped his hat to her. She gave a little wave of her hand.

The next morning John picked up Abby at her small house on Scattering Rice lake. She was wearing a blue checkered dress and she had a light blue sweater wrapped around her shoulders. John got out of his truck and came around to open the door for her. They arrived at the fair and were excited to see the large tents. There were smells of food cooking, popcorn, cotton candy and occasionally cigar smoke from a few of the older men who sat on wooden folding chairs as they watched people. John bought cotton candy and the couple shared it.

They strolled around looking at people and trying a few of the games. John knocked down the milk bottles with a strong pitch. The disfigurement of his fingers actually helped his grip on the ball and he was both surprised and proud. Abby picked a simple necklace as John's prize. John had a bit of a hard time helping her put it on and he noticed a few people looking at his disfigured hand. Eventually Abby reached back and hooked the clasp. They walked down to the river and sat on the grassy bank. There were children running around close by and John could feel their stares as he leaned over and kissed Abby.

After talking for a long time, the couple sat quietly. John laid back and Abby laid with her head on his stomach. They watched the clouds and then the silence was broken by the sound of John's stomach growling. Abby began laughing.

"John Miller…I think someone's hungry."

"Who? Not me." But then his stomach growled again followed by more laughter, now from both of them.

"Let's get something to eat." Abby suggested.

"Okay, you talked me into it."

"I think your stomach had something to say about it too!" she said as she stood up.

"I know a really nice restaurant here in Eagle River and it's not too far away. Can we go there, John? Please?"

"Absolutely." John stood up and reached his hands into his pockets. When Abby was turned away to leave, John took the money out of his pocket and fanned the bills enough to see that he only had two dollars and a little change left.

John and Abby walked to the Copper Kettle restaurant on the main street. Abby led the way, pulling John by his arm. John slowed up as they got to the entrance. There was a copy of the menu taped up in the window and John was quickly studying the prices. He followed Abby inside and over to a booth where they sat across from each other. An older waitress came up to them.

"Afternoon…can I get you something to drink?"

"Just water for me." John said.

"I'll have a coke, please." Abby said.

"I'll be right back with your drinks. Today's special is meatloaf. It comes with mashed potatoes, gravy and a vegetable for two and a quarter."

"Oh, that sounds really good doesn't it, John? Mmmmmmm."

"Hmmm…I don't know, Abby."

"Oh you absolutely have to have the meatloaf special, John. You're still a growing man and you need to quiet down that growling animal in your stomach."

John gave a little laugh. Abby leaned forward and then John felt her hand tapping his knee under the table. He looked over at Abby and she was nodding her head. He gave a curious look and she tapped his knee again. John reached under the table and felt her hand. She slipped something into his hand. He took it and looked over as he moved his hand within view. It was a five-dollar bill.

"I can't take this."

"You most certainly can, John." She whispered.

"Well, I'll pay you back." he said.

"You already have…by being my friend."

"Abby…you are amazing."

"John, you're the one who's amazing and you don't even realize it."

"Abby, you're making me blush, but I'm still paying you back…as soon as I get my next paycheck, I promise."

Just then the waitress came back. "Ready to order?"

"I'll have the meatloaf special." John said. The waitress wrote it down.

"And you, Miss?"

"I'm not very hungry…thanks."

The waitress rolled her eyes and walked away with their order.

"Now why did you do that, Abby?"

"Probably because I think I love you, John…at least, that is, I think so. So you see, I don't need to eat."

"What?"

"I'm not saying it again, John. But if you insist, I will have some of your mashed potatoes."

The couple shared the meal and had enough money for a slice of pie. They spent the afternoon walking around the fair. They stopped at a booth where a photographer took their pictures together and a photo of each. They gave the man the last two dollars they had and Abby's address so that he could send the photos to her after the pictures were developed.

That night there was a small fireworks display, but for the couple it was magnified by the reflections on the water and the feeling that was growing in their hearts.

7

Over the next few weeks, the romance between John and Abby grew. They were young and they knew the world held many experiences for them as individuals, but somehow they felt that they were meant to be together.

John drove Abby to a cabin just south of town that had been abandoned. The windows were boarded up and it looked as if it needed some repairs. There was an old barn behind the house that had seen better days. It had old gray cedar boards and the north side of the barn had a thick growth of gray moss and lichen. John and Abby walked hand in hand to a spot behind the barn that overlooked the meadow. The tall grass appeared as shimmering waves of russet and auburn as it swayed softly in the breeze.

"I love this old place. Found it a few weeks ago when I was driving out to one of the job sites. Turns out it belongs to Mr. Anderson. I saw it on the plat sheets." John moved his hand over the tops of the tall grasses. "It reminds me of a place back home, the Kassendahl." John said as he looked out over the field. Abby didn't respond and he knew immediately that he had spoken a word that left her in query. He smiled at her.

"It's a Norwegian word…it means 'kissing place'. John was almost blushing just to say the words to her. Abby grinned and her face was glowing. She put her hand up to shield her eyes from the sun as she glanced out over the meadow.

"Then that's what we'll call it, Kassendahl." she said.

"Can we name a place that isn't ours…that we don't own?" John asked, not expecting a response, but if there were an explanation he would expect it to be a rational one.

She simply said, "We just did."

John looked at her and smiled as she continued to look over the field. He felt a surge of ardor as his heart beat forcefully. He had never had a feeling like this in his life, it could only be called love. Her gaze came to John's smile. She took her hand from her forehead and she gave a little laugh.

"We don't have to own something or some place to make it special to us. This place, Kassendahl, this time in our lives can be ours forever. We'll just keep it in our hearts." she said as she put her hand on her heart. Then she continued, "Do you feel something, John? It's like…"

"You don't need to explain." he said. "Yes, yes, I do feel it."

She took his hand and softly placed it over her heart. "My God, John, I've never felt this way before…not with anyone… ever…" Her words drifted off as the smile left her face. John felt her warm skin and her heart was pounding just as heavily as his. He took his hand away so that he could wrap his arms around her. Then he kissed her passionately. She gave back to him in every way.

They spent the rest of the day together enjoying the sounds of the wind and the warmth of the sun. They watched eagles, deer, rabbits and squirrels and laughed as they named every one of them, each name sillier than the last. But when the laughter subsided, they shared their dreams and spoke of the future as if they would never be apart.

8

It was now early November and Alice was closing up the cottages. The tourist season was well over and John had recently found a room in town to rent.

"Well, John Miller, it's been a pleasure. I hope you'll consider moving back in the spring. The cottages are just too hard to heat in the winter months." Alice said.

"The pleasure has been all mine, Alice. I might be back in the spring, you never know."

The two shook hands and smiled. As John walked away, he turned to take in one last look and saw Alice smiling at him, she gave a friendly wave and for a moment, he felt as if she were a relative saying goodbye.

John drove to his new place, a room above Jester's bar downtown. There weren't a lot of places to choose from in a small town such as this. The building resembled a big box with asphalt siding that everyone referred to as Polish brick. There was a back entrance and a long straight stairway leading up to the rooms that lined the long narrow hallway. John was lucky to get an open room at the very front of the building and this afforded him a window looking out over Big Twin Lake. Other boarders, especially those on the South side were not as lucky since Jester's tall two-story building was built only a few feet away from the movie theatre next door. Very little light got in and the view was of the brick and mortar next door with the occasional bird's nest or spider's web. John was often too tired at the end of the long day to do much more than just kick off his boots, lie on the bed and gaze at the sunset over Big Twin. The lake would soon be completely frozen. The fishing shanties would not go out for another month to make sure the ice was thick enough, but there were always those who were a little too anxious and always the stories of someone going through to a watery grave. Some of the men who did break through the ice and survived to tell about it would often foolishly return figuring that lightning could not strike twice in the same place.

In these last few months, John became quite skillful at his work. He focused on efficiency and left no stone unturned from how to keep the saws sharper to maximizing the hours of daylight by diverting other chores for evening hours. He remembered his father talking about 'division of labor' – having men specialize on a particular job instead of multiple tasks. He assigned a few of the older men strictly to keeping the logging trails clear for the equipment. John, being diligent and always wanting to please his boss, kept clear and concise records, learned enough of the various languages of the immigrant workers to speak socially and always looked for competence as well as small and affordable ways of rewarding the crews. Nelson saw how the men dedicated themselves to John and he felt that John and all the other men in the camp lacked respect for him. Any attempts that Nelson made to be nice to the men were noticed as insincere but the men, "jacks" as they were called, played along for fear that this man would make their lives a living hell.

One evening, John was locking up the office. He was working late, putting things in order before the Thanksgiving weekend which he hoped to spend back at the farm. He noticed a light on at the maintenance shed. He went over to see if "Doc" Fitzgerald was in. Thomas Fitzgerald, the camp "dentist" filed and set teeth on the chainsaws and the broad crosscut saws in the evening after the jack's dropped them off at the end of a long and abusive day. He was a shorter man who always wore a brimless welding cap. He had curly red hair that jutted out the sides of his cap. For all the time that John was employed by the company, he had never seen Doc without his cap.

"Hey, Doc, how are things?" John asked, speaking loudly over the sound of the grinder and trying not to startle the man so intensely working. Doc looked up from his work peering over the top of his round safety glasses with side shields that bore a film of gray metal dust.

"John! How are you doing?"

"Can't complain, Doc, and it wouldn't do much good if I did...pretty cold this morning." John replied.

"Colder than Cheyenne in January." Doc replied. Doc had used this expression often. He had been to Wyoming once when he was young and was stuck in Cheyenne during one of the coldest days of the year.

"These guys toss their chainsaws here at the end of the day like it's their dirty laundry. Then it's my job to spiff them up and make them work like new by morning. Sometimes I feel like an elf!" Doc gave out a laugh. "And it's a thankless job 'cuz they just come back the same way next day." Doc shut off the grinder and gave a deep sigh. He reached up to his forehead and rubbed hard as if his many years of hard-earned wrinkles would wipe away. Then to John's surprise, Doc removed his welding cap to reveal a very bald and shiny scalp. John caught himself starring for a brief minute.

"The older jack's seem to be okay on the saws. They work at a steady pace and keep the chains well oiled. But some of these younger guys keep on running them dry and wrecking the teeth." Doc grumbled. Then Doc realized that he was speaking with a young man. "Sorry, John, I sure didn't mean any offense by that." Doc spoke softly, apologetically, looking directly into John's eyes.

"No offense taken." John replied. "Here's what we'll do…if it's all right with you, we'll paint a number on each of the saws and assign them to the men. Then we'll instruct the men on how to maintain them better. It could be a language issue too so we'll demonstrate clearly so we can make sure they understand."

"That's a good idea, John, let's do that…good idea." Then to change the subject and lighten things up, Doc announced, "Got a fresh pot of coffee, John - just made it – it's a bit strong and bitter, but it'll wake you up before it kills you."

"How could I turn down an offer like that?" John replied with a grin.

Doc got up and grabbed a white porcelain coffee cup from the shelf near the pot and blew out some dust. After inspecting it under a nearby work lamp and not satisfied with the cleanliness, reached into a wooden drawer and took out a clean shop rag. He wiped clean the inside and rim of the cup in a circular motion, blew away any remaining dust and then upon final inspection grunted, "There, well…maybe there's a little dirt there, but it shouldn't kill you and if it does, I'll speak well of you at your funeral." Doc laughed again, set the cup down and proceeded to pour from the dull and dented aluminum coffee pot. Doc filled his own cup as well, much less concerned over what might have floated in as he worked. John now took his coffee black like all the other men and had developed quite a fondness for it.

Doc brought over both cups and sat down on a chair across from John.

"You'd think business would be down a bit with the war and all. Darned if we aren't busier than ever, but with half the men. They might not be building houses, but they're building a lot of training camps. I read, too, that Uncle Sam's building wood framed airplanes, P-40's I believe. Navy, too, for that matter, building PT boats – all wood," Doc went on to say. John nodded respectfully as Doc spoke. He was by far one of the brightest men in the employment of the company and always reading anything he could get his hands on.

John replied, "Paper mills have been buying up a lot of hemlock for liner board - a lot of demand for cardboard cartons, too."

"Got to ship all them supplies in something." Doc remarked.

The two men nodded and sipped their coffee.

Doc then got a little distant, staring into his coffee cup.

"What's the matter Doc?" John asked.

"Got a son fighting the war over in Germany. His name's Michael Donovan Fitzgerald." Doc said with pride. "I sure do miss him. He's in the same outfit as another kid from Eagle River. That kids folks got a letter the other week. Turns out that they've both been seeing quite a bit of action. Small skirmishes mostly, he added. At the end of one fight, he said my son dragged a wounded kraut back across the lines so that his comrades would find him." Doc said with dignity in his voice.

"Probably saved the man's life." John responded.

"No doubt." Doc answered.

"He did the right thing…the Christian thing to do considering the circumstances." John said. Doc had a proud look on his face.

"Has Michael written to you or Mrs. Fitzgerald?" John asked. Doc became quiet and distant. Then finally Doc broke the silence.

"Maggie died years ago. Michael was at school, came home to find that his mother had hung herself. Doctor said she must have been depressed for some time. I didn't see it and when I did, I didn't know what to do about it. To be honest with you I almost thought maybe she was seeing another man. I don't know for sure what made me think that…I guess it was just a feeling. Strange how one day can change the course of your entire life. Michael became very withdrawn. I think somehow he always blamed me. We were never quite the same even though I'm all he has left." Doc said sadly. "I didn't even know he had joined the army until a week after he was gone. Just sent a postcard…that's all." Doc said.

John felt bad for having stirred up such memories. He tried to think of a way to change the subject. Glancing around the shop he noticed a violin case setting atop the workbench. "What's that Doc? A violin? My father plays…"

"Does he now? And how about you?" Doc asked.

"He taught me some. He was just starting to teach me about a year ago. I was picking it up pretty well. Now with this (lifting his crippled right hand) I don't know, but I did bring my violin up north here. I have it in my room just waiting for the day when I might be able to play it again."

Doc went over to the bench and carefully took the violin from the case.

"John, men have overcome much greater obstacles than the ones you face." Doc sat back down and rested the violin on his lap while he tightened up the bow. John sat quietly as Doc plucked the strings and turned the pegs to tune the instrument. Then he softly played a somber and sweet song. It was simple and it was beautiful. John hadn't heard the violin played this way since his father played when John was recovering from the accident. Since his arrival here, his exposure to music had been limited to the radio in his truck and at the bars and café. This was nice, this was pleasant, and this was a good evening. Doc handed the violin over to John. John gave a little grin and propped it under his chin. After a bit of apprehension John began to play. Doc pulled a harmonica from his bib overalls and began to play along. The two men smiled at each other and laughed at a few sour notes. John was playing a country song called "Li'l Liza Jane".

9

John had enjoyed Thanksgiving with his parents at the farm a few weeks earlier and now it was almost Christmas. It seemed to be ideal weather for harvesting timber. In the Summer, men had to tolerate insufferable heat. Now the logs were easier to move along the frozen ground. Even the horses seemed to be more cooperative these days as they pulled large sleds of logs from the forests.

John put a kettle on the stove for a cup of tea and began to pack his suitcase for the trip back home for Christmas. He had a couple of small gifts that still needed to be wrapped, but he knew he'd have some time before the family exchange of gifts on Christmas Eve. He put them in his suitcase and placed some shirts and pants over the top of them. The tea kettle whistled and John went to the stove and poured the hot water into his cup. He was looking forward to seeing his parents and maybe to seeing a few friends and relatives. Even though he had just visited his parents a month earlier at Thanksgiving, he enjoyed his time with them and was looking forward to another Christmas at the farm. It seemed strange to be away, to be involved in such different work, and to meet and get to know new people. John liked his new life very much. He thought about asking Abby to come home to the farm with him, but thought perhaps his mother would be upset that he was getting so involved with a young lady in so short a time. John felt a little somber and as he wound down for bed, realized that he had not had his tea. He went to bed that night thinking about the events of the day.

John awoke the next morning to a cold room and wrapping himself in a blanket, sprang across the room to turn up the gas heater. He could see his breath and that was enough to signal to him that this was a good morning to pull his clothes into bed and get dressed item by item under the covers. John peered out the window to see that they were having a blizzard. The sky was gray and snow had drifted across the street outside. John began to have doubts as to whether he would be able to leave Phelps and make the trip home. After awhile the room became warmer and now dressed, John could put on the socks he had hung by the heater.

John walked down the wide covered stairway that ran between the buildings to the street below. The truck was covered with snow and drifts were all around the vehicle. Shoveling the truck out would do no good if the street wouldn't be plowed and in storms like this it wasn't uncommon to have the road drift over within a half hour of plowing. John thought as long as he was out in the cold he would walk to the Spot Lunch and have breakfast. Harvey lived about fifty feet from the café and so John knew there would be a pretty good chance that the restaurant would be open. John trudged through the knee-deep snow to the café. Upon arriving at the café, he had to grab the nearby shovel and clear the stoop in order to get the door open.

"Morning, Harvey." John called.

"You gotta be nuts to be out in a storm like this…I guess that'd be both of us, huh?" Harvey replied.

John sat at the counter and Harvey poured him a cup of coffee. The café was warm and empty. Harvey dug around under the counter and produced a newspaper.

"Here you go, its yesterday's paper, best I can do. Won't get a paper today, probably won't even get the mail."

"That's okay, thanks." John sorted through the newspaper and arranged it on the counter so that he could warm his left hand in his pocket and his right hand on the steaming cup of coffee.

John heard the bell of the café door and turned to see Alice come in and close the door quickly behind her. He had not seen her since moving into his room at Jesters. All of her winter wrappings had a coating of snow and she quickly grabbed a nearby broom to sweep away the snow that she had brought in on her boots.

"Well, good morning, John, nice to see you," she said her words producing steam through the scarf. "Going home for the holidays?" she asked.

"If I can get out through this snow. I guess I trusted Mother Nature too much." John replied.

"Come over to the house, you can use my phone to call long distance to your mom and dad." Alice offered.

"Thanks, Alice, that would be great. I'll leave you some money for the call." John said.

"Oh, don't worry about it, it's Christmas time."

The door opened again and in came Abby. She was wearing a thick wool coat with a crocheted scarf around her face and stocking cap pulled down tight over her ears and forehead. She sat beside him at the counter and pulled her scarf below her chin.

"So what are your plans for Christmas, John? Think you'll get out of here later today?" she asked.

"Looks pretty doubtful. I'll call home long distance later. I suppose I could consider this an opportunity to see what Christmas in Phelps is like." John replied.

"I'm not doing anything later." Abby spoke so only John could hear as she reached down to pull off a boot and winked.

"Well, we could spend Christmas Eve together if you'd like. It could be pretty nice, I suppose." John's manner was a little awkward but inside he was feeling warm and excited.

Abby pulled the other boot loose. "I'll make dinner. It'll be very nice and besides I got you a Christmas gift." she said.

"You shouldn't have...but yes, I'd love to come over." John said.

"I live on Scattering Rice Lake, last cabin at the end of the south road." Abby told John. John knew quite well where Abby lived, but she didn't want Harvey or Alice to think that he had been over to her house in a way that wasn't proper. John figured this out from her expression and simply smiled.

John spent the rest of the day checking in on some of the elderly people in town to make sure they had heat and weren't out trying to shovel out of this mess. He went over to Alice's to use the phone to call home. Ma seemed a little down, but happy to hear John's voice. She comforted John and made him feel okay that he wasn't going to be there.

"We didn't have much planned for this Christmas anyhow, not with the war and all. Don't worry, we'll see you when we see you and that's just the way it'll be this year" she said.

Pa took the phone for a while and mostly talked about his new car. It was a brand new Ford, it was the first time ever that he had purchased anything so bright and shiny blue. John seemed amazed that his father was capable of overcoming his phobia about being noticed in town, surely everyone would talk and point at Matt Miller in his shiny blue car. Pa asked about lumbering in this weather and seemed very curious, but then realized that this was a long distance call and must be costing a fortune and so he cut the conversation short.

John arrived at the cabin where Abby lived at three o'clock and knocked at the door. Abby had been cleaning up and opened the door. John came in and looked around. The cottage was small and in many ways old-fashioned. The walls and ceiling were knotty pine, stained a honey-brown color. There was a large field stone fireplace that dominated the room. The walls were filled with mounted fish, antlers and photos of men holding oars lined with dozens of huge fish.

Abby noticed John looking around. "No, they're not my doing. They came with the place. They belong to the owner and he didn't have any other place to keep them. I've gotten rather used to them. I've even given some of them names."

"I think the place looks great." John replied. There was a small Christmas tree in the corner. It was lit with colored bulbs but nothing else.

"We can finish decorating the tree together. I thought I'd bake some cookies as soon as the bread is done." she said.

"That sounds like fun." John said. Then he walked to the windows facing west. Children were playing out on the frozen ice and the sounds of laughter seemed especially pleasant. Snowflakes drifted from the sky in chaos as some of the children tried catching them on their tongues. The sun came and went from behind the clouds, shifting shadows that resulted in a dreamlike display. It was a joy for John to sense their happiness from the warmth of Abby's cottage.

"I can't wait to give you your present." Abby said with excitement.

John gave her a suspicious look as he could hear whimpering noises and scratching coming from behind a door. Abby noticed that John heard the noise and smiled.

"Can I give it to you now? Oh, please?" she pleaded. John smiled.

"Sure." Abby carefully opened her bedroom door and there sat a brown puppy suddenly amazed by her stocking feet.

"You got me a dog?" John asked with a surprised voice.

"What do you think? Isn't she beautiful?" Abby asked. John stood quietly.

"She's beautiful – Irish Setter?" he asked.

"Yes, I remember you telling me about an Irish Setter that you had on the farm. And then by chance, I heard someone at the café talking about a litter of Setters…do you like her?"

John stooped down and the pup took its glance from Abby's socks and pranced to John. John picked her up and she dove for his face, licking and sniffing. John laughed.

"She sure is frisky. What's her name?" John asked.

"She doesn't have a name. I think she wants you to name her." Abby said. She was now smiling and more excited that John seemed to be accepting the gift.

"I don't have a place to keep her…not yet anyway."

"She can stay here until you have a place where you can keep her." Abby offered.

John continued to stroke and scratch the pup.

"Rusty!" John said.

Abby raised her eyebrows and repeated, "Rusty? That's a great name…it fits her well." Abby continued.

After Rusty was tired from her play, she fell asleep on a rug by the gas heater. Abby and John played checkers, drank hot cider and talked. The wind had died down earlier, but the snow hadn't stopped falling, the sun finally gave up and the sky was now a pale gray and at this moment, with the children all gone to their homes, there was a silence all around.

Abby suggested that John make a fire to take the chill off and he quickly rose to the occasion. They prepared a meal together, enjoyed their simple dinner and now sat on the floor in front of the blazing fire. They talked about life, friends, family, the war and what the future might have in store.

Finally, from nowhere Abby broke the mood and springing to her feet exclaimed, "I almost forgot, I have a bottle of wine. It wouldn't be Christmas without a toast." She returned from the kitchen with a bottle, corkscrew and two kitchen glasses. Handing it to John she said, "Here - a job for a man! I don't have any wine glasses so I guess these will have to do."

John opened the bottle and poured wine into the glasses. "Here's to a wonderful Christmas." he said.

"Here's to Christmas together." Abby replied. They sipped from their glasses. Abby set her glass down, looked deep into John's eyes and then with a simple gesture, pointed to her lips. John leaned in and the couple kissed long and gently. Abby reached over and pulled a blanket from the couch. John eased her back to the rug and moving over her, put his hand behind her neck and pulled her face to his. He kissed her slowly, passionately and with a feeling he had never felt before. The couple, tired from the gentle events of the day, lay in each others arms, Abby's head resting on John's chest. He thought she was sleeping as he held his lips to her hair and whispered, "I believe that if I held you in my heart, all the dreams of this ambitious mind would be realized."

She whispered in reply, "Believe."

John said goodbye to Rusty. He promised he would come over often to play with her and work hard to find a new home for her. John and Abby kissed goodbye to a day they never wanted to end.

In the weeks that followed, John continued to brave the cold days and enjoy the warm. Throughout his workdays, he saw bear, deer, pheasants, fox, wolves and a wide variety of wildlife surviving the winter world. The days when he could see Abby made things even better. He wanted to be careful with her. He wanted to be close enough to let her know how he felt, but distant enough not to smother her nor for him to become too close.

10

Since John had come to the lumber company, he had kept his dealings with Nelson to the minimum. Occasionally he would run into him and the outcome could never be predicted. There were times that Nelson was mean and irritable and times that he seemed friendly, but that was usually after he had been drinking. On one such occasion after work when the men were playing cards, Nelson mentioned to John that they had negotiated a special hunting permit to be able to take deer any time of the year. John suspected that this was just a lie and that by telling him, Nelson was somehow convincing himself that it was the truth. John accepted that he was still young, just off the farm literally and that he could be naïve at times. He also accepted that there were people that could never be trusted, people that thought they were getting away with something by lying to themselves to make themselves feel better about who they were. He accepted that those people would in turn, lie to others and he knew that Nelson was a man who lacked both character and integrity. As long as he carried weight in this company, John knew that continuing to keep his distance from Nelson would be the best thing to do.

When deer were hunted to supplement the food supply at the camp, it was Manuel's chore to hang the deer carcasses to let the blood drain and to butcher and preserve the meat. Venison stew was a common meal and the men liked how Manuel seasoned it to disguise the gamey taste.

It was getting to be a long winter, but luckily there were only a few days with blizzard conditions in which the men couldn't work. On one such occasion, with drifts of snow well over the road, there were still some who could make it to town to drink and gamble away a week's wages at Jester's Bar.

One Saturday evening in late February, John decided to patronize the establishment of his winter landlord and have a couple of beers. The bar was fairly crowded considering the hard times. The war was being fought on both fronts. The British were conducting heavy raids on German cities while the Americans had just landed on Iwo Jima. The United States had just begun a rationing of coffee and those who could afford it were buying war bonds. John made his way to the bar and ordered a beer. He glanced over his shoulder to see the old man with the wooden box that he had seen his first day in town. The wire mesh door was open and the man was holding a pet porcupine on his lap feeding him peanuts. John took his beer and walked over to the man.

"That's quite the critter." John said.

"His name's Mister Eggbert, and he does not care to be called a critter." the man said.

"And you must be Dido.' John said.

"A fine reputation always precedes the best of us." Dido said. Mister Eggbert continued to carefully peel the shell off of the peanut he had been working on and as the two nuts were out of the shell, Dido held up his finger. "And what is our arrangement Mister Eggbert?" The animal paused as if he understood every word.

"That's right, one for you and one for me." Dido said as he divided the peanuts between them. He smashed one with his beer glass, wiped it off the edge of the table into his other hand and popped it into his mouth without regard for dirt or porcupine saliva.

"Don't have quite the bite I used to." he said with his near toothless grin. His companion Eddy laughed and took a drink.

John smiled and said, "I'd pet him, but he seems a little prickly."

"That's alright…Mister Eggbert just likes his nose rubbed… go on…it's okay." Dido said.

John carefully rubbed Mister Eggbert's nose and the porcupine stood on his hind legs stretching his nose into the air apparently loving the attention.

Introductions were made and John offered to buy the two men a beer, but they declined. Two men at the bar were shaking dice for money.

"Three sixes." Dido whispered.

'Three sixes…beat that!' One man at the bar shouted to the other.

"Four five's." Dido whispered again.

'Take that! Four fives!' The other man shouted.

John looked at Eddy and asked, "What's he doing? How's he doing that?"

Eddy simply smiled and shrugged.

The first man at the bar yelled over to Dido as he was shaking the cup, "I need you, Dido my friend…what's it going to be?"

Dido was silent. The man slammed the cup down and yelled again, "Come on Dido…I know you know." Dido was silent.

"Oh forget you!" the man yelled in frustration but before he lifted the cup Dido whispered to Eddy, "Another six."

"Four sixes…beats four five's!" the man yelled.

John looked at Eddy again and spoke softly, "Is he cheating?"

"Oh heaven's no, son" Eddy replied. "It's just a little gift of his."

"Haven't I seen you at the Spot Lunch?" John said.

"I've been known to frequent the café on occasion, yes." Eddy said. With that, John stood and smiled.

"Well, nice to meet the both of you." John said. The two men smiled and nodded in return. Then someone put a nickel in the juke box.

"Benny Goodman, Woody Herman and Sammy Kaye." Dido whispered to Mr. Eggbert but just loud enough for John to hear. And then as John was walking away the song "Jersey Bounce" by Benny Goodman came on. John shook his head in disbelief smiling. He sat at the bar making occasional conversation with the local men. He finished his beer and headed upstairs to his room to turn in for the evening.

Later that night there came a knock at John's door. Jester had come to John's door with Eddy. Eddy had too much to drink and had stayed long after everyone else had left including his friend Dido. Jester was concerned that he would drop over drunk in a snow drift somewhere and freeze to death in his sleep. Nobody knew where the man lived or even if he had a home. Eddy stood there as Jester suggested that maybe he could stay the night on John's floor since kicking him out would be cruel by any man's standards. Jester's real name was Chester Alvin, the son of Jukka Alvin, an immigrant from Finland. (The name Jester came into being from the slurred speech of one of his customers) He was a tall man with no hair on top but a long beard and chest hair that stuck out from his open collar. Jester told John he would knock two dollars off of his rent if he would agree to let Eddy stay the night and John said that wouldn't be necessary. The floor was warmed from the heat of the bar room below. Jester came back and tossed in a few thick wool blankets that he had pulled from a hall closet, blankets that had been left by previous tenants over the years.

"Okay this one time, Jester, but I have work in the morning and he's got to get up when I get up." John said.

"Don't worry, John. I'd give him a ride if I could, but I got sick kids at home and the wife called asking for some help. And I'd take him to my place with me, but the Misses would never go for it. I come in early to clean up the bar and if he's still here, I'll bring him downstairs." Jester said.

Eddy smelled of beer and after grabbing the blankets, dropped to the floor and quickly fell asleep. John lay awake thinking about the oddity of it all, but concluded that it was just one night. Eddy would make noises from time to time and mumbled in his sleep. He spoke louder at times and it sounded as if he were calling to children. He sobbed and moaned until he drifted back to sleep.

The next morning John woke Eddy and told him he'd have to leave.

"I'll buy you breakfast at the Spot Lunch." John said to entice him to move faster.

"Can't eat...not now." the old man said.

John gave the man a puzzled look. "Well...sorry, but you can't stay here, I have to go to work...I can give you a ride though." John said.

The elderly man got up and with trembling hands, wiped his neatly-trimmed beard. John poured Eddy a cup of coffee.

"You talk in your sleep." John said.

"What did I say if I might ask?" the old man asked.

"Something about your children...you married?" John asked.

"She passed on after giving birth to my little angels...twins." Eddy spoke quietly.

"Sorry for asking sir – I didn't mean to bring up any bad memories," John said. "Where are your children, what happened to them...do you ever see them?" John asked.

"I see my little girl every chance I can get, she's beautiful and seems happy. My son fought in the war and they just brought him back." Eddy now looked distant and John thought that perhaps his son had been killed.

"Can you stay with your daughter today?" John asked.

"I'm afraid that's not possible," Eddy said. The response and Eddy's tone of voice left John puzzled and the room became silent. John kept about his business getting ready for work and was folding the blankets when he noticed that Eddy was reading a telegram.

"Something important?" John asked. Eddy crumbled up the telegram and stuffed it in his pocket without saying a word. Telegrams were usually bad news. He then looked directly into John's eyes and said, "Thank you young man, I hope I haven't been a trouble to you."

"You're welcome. And I hope everything works out with your children." John shrugged it off and left the room for a minute to put the blankets back in the hall closet where he knew Jester kept them.

John yelled to Eddy from the hallway, "We could use some extra help at the camp if you're interested in a job." But there was no response.

Then John heard his violin being played with great skill. When he returned, Eddy quickly put it down.

"Was that you?" John asked. Eddy softly wiped his hand across the top of the violin and didn't say a word.

"I must go, and I thank you again for your generosity and warm spirit." Eddy said with a sincere tone in his voice. With that Eddy opened the door and left quickly.

John noticed a piece of paper Eddy had left on his table. It simply read, "Hebrews 13:1-2". John was intrigued by this man, but couldn't think about it now. It was time for work and yet he had to know what Eddy had meant and took his Bible from his nightstand and looked up Hebrews 13:1-2.

"Christians, keep on loving one another. Don't neglect to welcome guests. This is how some without knowing it had angels as guests."

John closed his violin case and left for work thinking about the old man.

11

The next evening, Eddy stood among the trees and watched as the Spot Lunch café was being closed. He stood there in silence for a long time. Finally Abby came out and he watched her walk toward her car. He approached slowly and she turned, suddenly startled by his advance.

"Abby" he said softly. If you could give an old man a ride, there's something I'd like to show you."

She was frightened and confused. This was the somewhat disheveled old man that she had seen around for the last few months, for the most part, a stranger. She figured him for the type that you know only by name and know nothing about except what you hear. But she hadn't seen this character in weeks and he looked different. She barely recognized this clean-shaven and well-dressed man. Could he be mean, harmful? She hesitated nervously and against all sense of reason said, "Get in." Abby kept focused on the road despite the nervousness she felt from this man staring at her. She was wondering what had possessed her to give this man a ride.

Eddy noticed her nervousness and said, "Girl, don't be afraid, I would never hurt you. I would never hurt anyone, but especially not you." His tone sounded so sincere, but something kept telling her that this was unusual and she remained cautious. She thought it best to show that she had the upper hand.

"So, you said you wanted to show me something…what is it?" Abby said with regained confidence.

"Pull over here under the streetlight." he said. Abby reasoned that if this man had any harmful intentions he surely wouldn't want to carry them out in the light and with people still on the street.

Eddy produced the telegram from his pocket and smoothed the wrinkles from it on the dashboard of her car. He handed it to Abby. "Read it." he said calmly.

Recipient: Edward David Baker

Mr. Baker – we regret to inform you that your son, Sergeant Anthony Thomas Baker was injured in the line of duty – 2nd January, 1945 – stop – sent to Copley Hospital, 507 Dempster Street, Chicago, Illinois – stop – Condition improving – The United States Armed Forces thank you and our prayers are with you and family for an expedient recovery - stop

Abby folded the telegram and handed it back to the man. "I'm sorry to hear…but what does this have to do with me?" she asked.

After a pause, he wiped a tear from each eye and said, "I'm Edward Baker…Anthony is my son and your twin brother… Abby, you're my daughter."

Abby was stunned. "You're my father…you're my father?"

Eddy looked away. "Please don't be alarmed, Abby, I'm not quite what you think I am." he said.

"You're my father…how can you prove this…how do I know this isn't some trick? she asked.

"You and Anthony were born September 18th of 1923 in Eagle River…you weighed in at eight pounds, two ounces. Your mother's name was Barbara, you were raised by your Uncle Ted and Aunt Helen in Three Lakes. Your Aunt Helen who passed away a few years ago. Helen was your mother's sister and their last name before marriage was Spence.

She stared at the man in disbelief. "Your mother and I lived in Chicago and would come here to spend summers at our house on the lake. I had a successful and well-managed business that allowed me to take summer months here. It was here that you and your brother were born. Your mother took ill and passed away within a few days of your birth...and here...here's a copy of your birth certificate and the one for Anthony." Mr. Baker produced two folded certificates from his jacket pocket.

Abby took the birth certificates and unfolded them. She studied one and then the other. "My mother passed on?" Abby asked, now beginning to believe.

"I didn't know how to deal with her death. She meant the world to me and I never expected such an ending to the miracle of your births. Helen stepped in quickly to help. I returned to Chicago to my business, but returned in two months with a nurse to take Anthony. I just couldn't take you from Helen – it would have broken her heart. Anthony's nurse's name was Ester, and she took care of him most of the time seeing to his feedings and naps and such. I needed to continue with my business. I stopped coming up here when you were just starting to walk. Your aunt and I thought it best if I stayed out of the picture. She and Ted could not conceive and we agreed that it would be best this way. We were never sure if we were doing the right thing, but as time went by it seemed that there was no turning back. I sent money every month and wrote often to inquire about you, but after a couple of years your Uncle Ted became rather resentful and didn't want to take the chance that I would come and take you back. He took you and Helen and moved around...enough times that it was almost impossible to find a trace. When Anthony went off to the European front last summer, I came back up here looking for you…it was difficult to find you since there were no records to speak of but finally I did. But then, not knowing how to deal with the situation once I found you, I kept my distance. I knew that this moment would eventually come and I am so sorry that this is such a shock. Whenever I came to the Spot Lunch it was to see you."

"So, let me get this straight…I have a brother, Anthony and he's in a hospital in Chicago." Abby stated.

"Yes, Abby…yes." he said.

"I don't have enough money saved to make a trip to Chicago, and I don't know as if my car will make the trip." Abby said, now thinking more clearly and accepting her new reality.

"Abby…I may have looked a little shabby at times and I'm often seen in the company of the local man they call Dido. That's a bit of a story as well, and there's more to it all than meets the eye. His name is Daniel D. O'Day…he was an inventor, a man with several patents and inventions to his name. He had always been an old business acquaintance and family friend. Some years back, like many people, he fell on hard times. But anyway, there is a purpose for all of this, and I hope you'll understand. Although I've grown tired of the hypocrisy and air of the wealthy, I have never lost control of my business back in Chicago. Money is not a concern and if you'll park your car at the lake house, we'll take my car to the train station. We'll have a chance to talk more about that on our journey. I'll call my staff and tell them to expect us. They'll pick us up at Union Station and take us to the hospital straight away. Now if you don't mind giving me a ride home we can leave in the morning. But I do have one stop to make, I need to drop off a package in town…"

"You're my father…you're really my father…and I have a brother…I have family." Abby stated again.

"Yes dear, and I'm so sorry for the shock. In time, as we get to know each other and catch up on the last nineteen years, you might even come to feel a little something for me…maybe forgive me for not being in your life…maybe. I hope that's possible."

And in that moment Abby took her father's hand and grasped it tightly. "Oh…I'm so happy and I'm so sad…but mostly happy." she said. Then she put the car in gear and drove her father home. When she pulled up to the lake house she was amazed. She had heard of places like this along the lake but had only seen one or two on occasion. It was a huge log home with a gate house secluded among acres of tall pine trees. A snow covered stone wall extended back into the pines. As they approached the large wrought iron gates, suspended on the two large fieldstone columns at each side of the entrance, they slowly swung open. Abby took his hand again and gave it a little kiss.

Then he pulled her hand up to his lips and gave her hand a kiss. "Good night Abby, sleep well." he said.

"Good night…father'.

"The train leaves at ten-fifteen so if you'll stop by at 9:00 AM, I'll be ready.

That night Abby packed a suitcase, the only one she had. It was an older suitcase she had gotten from her aunt. It was a little frayed and one of the metal corners was missing. Abby didn't have many clothes, but she did have a blue checkered dress that she folded carefully. Although it was a bit old, it was the nicest dress she owned. She chose the skirt and blouse she would wear on the trip and set them across a kitchen chair. When she was done she wrote a note to John explaining that she would be gone for awhile. She put the note in an envelope and wrote his name on it. That night she barely slept. She found herself asking if this was all real. If it wasn't true what kind of cruel prank could this be? No…it wasn't a prank…he knew too much…the lake house.

This was real and she was about to leave on a trip that would continue to change her life.

She woke early and sprang out of bed. She washed up at the sink, brushed her teeth and hair and put on a little make-up. She ran out to her car and started it so that it would be warm when she carried Rusty out. She tossed her hairbrush and a few small items into the suitcase and looked around the rooms of her cabin. Rusty was still sleepy as Abby put her in a box she had stuffed with an old blanket. She carried the puppy out to her car and then ran back to lock her door. She stopped for a second as she looked at her cabin, taking it in for what might be a long time.

She drove into the yard of her father's lake home. Now in the morning light she was even more impressed with the circular driveway, the dormers, windows, the large oak door and wrought iron details all around. It had a stately charm about it that was unique for its Northwood's setting. She left the car running and went to the front door, passing various small granite statues, each cloaked in a veil of fresh snow. As she passed the garage she looked in, holding her hands to the sides of her face she saw the boat-shaped back end of his car, the 1937 Auburn that John had asked her about when they first met. Her breath quickly clouded the glass. Suddenly, Edward opened the door.

"Good Morning, Abby." he said brightly.

"Good Morning."

"I do hope you slept well…I didn't. I kept thinking of how cruel it was for me to spring all of this on you so late in the evening. I would have waited for a better way to tell you, but having received the telegram about your brother, I didn't think there was any other choice."

"Well…now that you mention it, I had a hard time drifting off. As far as everything else, I still need some time to accept all of this." she said.

"Oh, I was afraid of that. With all of the time and thought I gave to the whole thing…well, and then to find out about

Anthony…that changed everything. I did call home early this morning and the report I got was that he is stable. I believe he's going to pull through quite well. He has that tough Baker spirit. Come to think of it I imagine you have a bit of that self-sureness as well. Am I right?"

"I guess I am a bit confident…but isn't that a learned trait?"

"Sometimes, but I like to think there's a lot to what kind of blood courses through your veins. Well, enough on that for now. We can re-visit that subject on the long train ride ahead of us. We have so much catching up to do."

Edward reached for his suitcases, but Abby quickly picked them up. They were leather with bright brass corners, buckles, escutcheons and a brass plate on each of the cases with her father's monogram. Edward grabbed his briefcase.

"Thank you, Abby." He locked the door and got into the car as Abby put the suitcases in the back seat.

They started off down the road and Edward gave one last look at his lake house.

Then glancing over at Abby, he remarked, "You have the same eyes."

"I beg your pardon?"

"You and Anthony…you'll see."

"We need to make one very quick stop…it'll just take a few minutes. I have to let Harvey know what's going on and leave my dog with him."

"Of course, Abby."

That afternoon John and Steeg were grinning from ear to ear as they drove up to the Spot Lunch to buy some sodas after work. John was hoping to invite Abby to go see "Meet Me In St. Louis" with him at the theatre. Steeg dropped himself onto a rustic cedar chair that sat behind the front door, exhausted from a hard days work.

John was excited and walked into the café. "Harvey, is Abby here?" he asked.

Harvey came from behind the counter and in a quiet voice said, "She's not here, stopped in this morning and said that she was leaving and didn't know when she'd be back." John's smile stopped. "Oh…okay. If she comes around, just let her know I said hello…okay? And let her know…never mind. Thanks Harvey."

"Well, wait a minute, John…she left a letter for you." Harvey pulled a box from behind the counter. "And this dog." he continued.

"Rusty." John said softly.

Harvey took the folded envelope from his back pocket and handed it to John.

Dear John,

I'm headed to Chicago. I don't know how to explain this and so I'm not going to try in this letter. Something wonderful has happened and I'm not sure at this time when I'll be back. I don't know where to begin. I've let Harvey know to hire someone to help him and that I'm sorry for the way I'm leaving…short notice and all. I have so much to tell you. My life has changed so much in this little bit of time. I will miss you and think about you often. I hope you will think of me from time to time as well. I hope to see you soon. I know Rusty will be happy with you.

With Love and Fondness,
Abby

John, disappointed, left the café and stood there for a moment looking around. "Where's the soda?" Steeg asked.

"I think we're ready for a beer." John replied.

In the next couple of weeks there was no word from Abby. John read the letter several times. It left so much to be explained and seemed so mysterious. "With Love and Fondness." John thought about these words and then put the letter back in the envelope and put it in the bottom of his dresser drawer. John wondered if she had found somebody else, perhaps an old boyfriend. After all, that would explain a lot. John let himself feel hurt for the first week, but then put his focus on work.

12

The train arrived at Union Station. Abby was enjoying looking at the different people so different in their dress from what she was accustomed in the north. She spotted a distinguished looking man wearing a tweed jacket. He had a beautiful well-groomed moustache and gentle eyes. Abby and her father gathered their things. She noticed her father looking at her from time to time and just smiling. She smiled back, but could feel the anxiety of all of the sudden changes and reassured herself that it would take time. Abby followed her father as they stepped down from the train. She noticed the man in the tweed jacket again and he approached them. He smiled broadly and extended his hand to take her father's suitcase.

"Mister Baker, so good to see you sir."

"Thank you, Stephen, good to see you as well…I can carry my case, but please let me introduce my daughter, Abigail…I mean, Abby."

"Hello, Miss Baker, so nice to finally make your acquaintance after all these years. Please let me take your suitcase."

"Abby, this is Stephen." her father said.

"So pleased to meet you, Stephen…may I call you that? Stephen that is."

The man laughed pleasantly. "But of course, Miss Abby, of course." he said.

"Stephen is a gentleman's gentleman." her father said. The look on Abby's face was a bit at a loss. "The family assistant… butler." he continued.

"Oh my, I see." Abby smiled with a bit of embarrassment.

"And may I take you suitcase, Miss Abby?" Stephen repeated.

"Yes…yes of course, thank you." she said.

Edward shifted his suitcase to his left hand and put his right arm around Abby.

"Come, Abby…let me introduce you to Chicago."

"What is the latest news on Anthony?" Edward asked Stephen with concern.

"Oh, he's doing very well sir. The hospital is very grateful for your generous gift and Doctor Maguire asked me to assure you that Anthony is getting the best of care."

"Excellent, Stephen, we'll go there tomorrow after lunch… give Abby some time to get used to things and a little more time for Anthony to rest. Please take some of his books over to him this afternoon."

"Already done sir…but I'd be glad to take some more if you'd like." Stephen replied.

"No, no need, Stephen…I'll call him when we get home and let him know that I'm back…that we're back." Edward began to wonder just how he would break the news of Anthony's sister to him.

Edward and Abby followed Stephen out to the street. Abby continued to look at all the people, sailors, soldiers, women in beautiful dresses and men in suits. She couldn't remember ever seeing so many people. Abby found herself staring up at the buildings. To her it was breathtaking. They approached a large black car and the driver wearing a black uniform and cap, quickly jumped out and moved briskly to open the rear door.

"Good afternoon, sir." he spoke as he bowed slightly.

"Hello, Freddie…nice to see you." Edward said. "This is my daughter, Abby." he said proudly. Freddie nodded his head respectfully.

"Perhaps you'll drive her to some of the shops tomorrow morning…after we've had time to rest." Edward suggested.

"Of course, sir, it would be my pleasure." Freddie gave Abby a friendly smile. He would enjoy having a pretty girl to drive around his city instead of the usual elderly men. Stephen loaded the suitcases into the trunk as Abby and her father got into the car. Abby breathed in the smell of the car and looked around at the luxurious interior. There were little tables that folded down and even a bar. Stephen got into the front seat with Freddie and instructed him to take them home.

Abby continued to look around as the car drove on, looking down every intersecting street, at all of the signs and again so many people.

"Abby, perhaps I could have my secretary, Joan, take you shopping tomorrow…she has very good taste and I'm sure the two of you would have a very good time of it." Abby immediately thought of money.

"Oh…I really didn't bring much money with me." she whispered not wanting to be overheard by the gentlemen in the front seat. Edward gave her a puzzled look, but before speaking, remembered that any awkwardness of the situation, any misunderstanding, any discomfort was all somehow his responsibility for not having pursued her years earlier. He pressed a button and a glass window went up between them and the staff.

"Abby, dear Abby…think of it this way, I owe you about eighteen years worth of birthday gifts and Christmas gifts…not to mention all of the spoiling that I have been deprived of giving you. My secretary will give you spending money and she'll sign for all of your purchases. I know this will all take some getting used to, but trust me, your life will be forever changed…as will mine and Anthony's. There are things that you'll learn over time." he said.

"Such as...?" she asked.

"Well, for example, that with wealth comes responsibility. I worked very hard to build this business...oh, of course, there was something there to begin with. Your grandfather started the business, but it was all very modest until I took over at the helm." he said.

"Just what kind of business is this?" Abby asked.

"Medical equipment...all sorts and naturally in very high demand with the war and all, but that's exactly what I mean. We will not profit at the expense of American lives and that is why we make certain to donate equipment and supplies generously whenever and wherever we can. We establish quota's and profit levels that are required to sustain and grow the business and provide for the well-being of our valued employees, but beyond that, in this time of need, we give whatever we can." he explained.

Abby felt proud and knew that growing to love a man of such generosity would not be as difficult as she might have thought earlier.

They arrived at a very tall building on Ontario Street. Abby strained her neck trying to see the top. Stephen opened the door for her and she stepped out immediately noticing how different the air was from that to which she was accustomed. Edward walked around behind the car and offered her his arm. Freddie took the luggage from the trunk and Stephen signaled for the doorman. Abby looked around. She had never been waited on in her life and it brought a smile to her face. The doorman walked briskly to greet Mr. Baker.

"Good Day, Mister Baker."

"Hello, Stanley, this is my daughter, Abby. She'll be staying with us for some time. I'm sure you'll make her feel welcomed."

"Certainly sir, pleased to meet you, Miss Baker."

It took Abby a second to remember her new name.

The elevator door opened and Abby was amazed by the beautiful inlaid wood. Her father put his arm around Abby to guide her onto the elevator. Stephen moved the suitcases onto the elevator and pressed the button for the 18th floor. Abby was taken aback by the movement of the elevator, but quickly regained her poise. When the elevator opened, Stephen held the door open until Edward and Abby were off.

"This way, Abby." Edward said as he moved down the hallway taking keys from his pocket. There were only two doors, one across from the other. Edward put his key into the lock of the door to the left and opened it.

"After you, Abby." he said as he held the door open for her.

Abby walked in and was astonished to see the beautiful apartment. It was elegantly furnished and through the open curtains she could see the city skyline.

"Oh, my…God."

"Do you approve?" he asked her with a smile.

"Oh my, yes…I've never been in such a beautiful apartment. It's wonderful."

"And there's a room made up just for you. Right this way." He opened the door to a stunning bedroom at the southwest corner of the apartment. Abby walked in and tears formed in her eyes.

"My secretary, Joan, helped to pick out the furnishings. You'll meet her tomorrow."

"Oh, my God, it's so beautiful."

"Stephen, please set Abby's suitcase on the bed so she can get unpacked and settled in."

"Yes sir."

"Stephen generally makes our meals, but I thought we'd go out tonight to have a little celebration of our reunion, Abby. It's a bit early for dinner and a bit late for much of anything else, so if you don't mind, I'd like to call the office. If you get hungry, just let Stephen know and he can fix you something. Stephen, would you please make reservations with Morton's for dinner?"

"Usual table?"

"No, something out in the open. I have a daughter to show off!"

Yes, sir, will there be anything else?"

"Father…I'm afraid I'm wearing about the best dress I own. I don't think I could go to a fancy restaurant in this." Abby said with some embarrassment.

"Nonsense, you look fine. But if it'd make you feel more comfortable, perhaps I could get Joan to bring something over for you."

"I'd hate to have her bother."

"Don't worry about it. I'll have her swing by Marshall Field's and pick something out for you to wear this evening. Now, I'll give her a call and you can get settled in. Again, if there's anything else you need, just let Stephen know."

With that, Edward left Abby and went back into the living room.

"My room is just down the hall if you need anything." Stephen said to Abby.

"Thank you, Stephen." Abby closed the door and spun around quickly, as if she was afraid that it would all disappear. She leaned back against the door and looked around the room. It was larger than her whole cabin back home. She opened the closet doors and dresser drawers. She couldn't imagine that someone would own enough clothes and shoes to fill so much space. She opened another door expecting to find another closet, but instead found her own bathroom. He father had even gone to the trouble of having a basket of toiletries setting on the small table in the corner. She began to unpack, and her clothes looked small as they only took up half of one drawer. She had only packed one extra pair of shoes and it looked lonely sitting in the closet and so Abby took off the shoes she was wearing and set them along side.

Abby threw herself onto the bed and stared at the ceiling. She couldn't believe that it had only been twenty-four hours since she met her father. Her whole life had literally changed in a day and would never be the same. She felt breathless from the excitement (or perhaps it was the altitude) she had never been in such a tall building in all her life, but now she was going to live in one. She also felt the separation anxiety from having left her cabin so quickly and without the opportunity to say goodbye to John in a more appropriate way and to assure him that she would only be gone a few months. She wanted to tell him so much and to share with him everything in her life. There was nothing more exciting than this.

Abby noticed a writing desk in her room and examined it more closely opening the hinged top to reveal paper, envelopes and an assortment of writing gadgets. Abby pulled out the chair, sat down and ran her hands over the beautiful wood. Then she took pen and paper and wrote the following:

> *Dear John,*
>
> *I meant to tell you all of this when I return but I think I'll be here in Chicago for some time – maybe a few months. I'm so sorry that I didn't have an opportunity to tell you in person, I'm sure as you read this letter, you'll understand. I'm not sure where to start but do you remember me telling you that I'm an orphan? Well, I'm not. I just found out the other night that I have a father, Edward Baker and that I also have a twin brother, Anthony. I was raised by my aunt and uncle and I'll tell you more about that when I see you again – I hope soon. I miss you so much.*

Anthony was wounded in the war and that's part of the reason my father came looking for me. We are going to see him today and I'm so excited. I'm actually going to meet my brother for the first time, I can't believe it. I wish you were here. It's hard to explain but I always felt that I had a brother ever since I was little.

I can't tell you how wonderful I feel, like I finally belong somewhere. There's so much more to tell you John but I think we're going to be leaving soon for the hospital and I haven't much time. I hope you will write to me soon.

John, I love you. I love you so much. I hope to be back in your arms again soon at Kassendahl.

Love with all my heart,
Abby

Abby should have been exhausted from the long train, but she was excited and after only a few minutes got up to explore the apartment. She quietly went out into the hallway in her stocking feet and into the living room. It was all so elegant. In a small room off of the living room she could hear her father on the phone.

"Yes, Joan, that sounds wonderful, just put it all on the account and while you're at it why don't you pick out something nice for yourself as well…alright then…and please try to be here by six-thirty so that Abby has enough time to get herself ready. Thank you…Bye now."

Edward looked up as he was hanging up the phone to see Abby walking around the living room. She came over to the den where her father was starting to go through the mail.

"Have I thanked you?" she asked.

"I'm sure you have. Joan will be over, no later than six-thirty with a couple of dresses for you to choose from for dinner. This will work out nicely – we'll be able to go visit Tony early in the morning."

"I can't wait…I'm so excited." Abby said.

"Well, if you don't mind, Abby, I'm going to get a bit of rest."

Abby gave her father a kiss on the cheek.

"Well, I'll try to get some rest, as well, but I don't think I'll be able to sleep." she said.

Abby went to her room and did manage to sleep a bit, but was awakened by a knock at her door.

"Miss Abby."

"Yes."

"Stephen here – Mr. Baker's secretary is here with some packages for you."

"I'll be right there."

Abby quickly brushed her hair in the mirror and then went to the living room. Joan was a young lady, perhaps in her early thirties with wavy blonde hair and bright blue eyes. She was neatly dressed and was just taking off her coat when Abby came in. She quickly made her way across the room with her arms extended.

"Why, you must be Abby. My you are beautiful and I can see the family resemblance…it's remarkable. I'm Joan." She wrapped her arms around Abby and gave her a warm hug. Abby gave a little hug back as she was still trying to get used to all of it.

"Hello, Joan."

"I'll lay all of the dresses out and you can pick which one you want to wear this evening and then I'll just put the others in your closet. I guessed at your shoe size and picked up a few pair for you to choose from as well. Now…I wasn't sure if you had a coat or not and so I picked out a fur wrap that I thought would go nicely with any of the dresses. Oh, and I picked up a nice warm bathrobe and slippers – that was your father's idea."

"Oh my…" Abby picked up a light blue dress and held it up to her. "It's heavenly."

"It'll look great on you. I'll just put these others in your closet. Now your father tells me that tomorrow after you've met Tony, you and I are going shopping. So if you want to return any of these or if anything doesn't fit, I'll just take care of it."

Joan and Abby picked up the clothes and shoes and took them to Abby's bedroom. Joan stayed to help Abby put up her hair and get ready.

That evening, Abby and her father went to dinner and Abby had her first glass of champagne. She had never been to such a nice restaurant and had never seen so many beautifully dressed people. But tonight she was beginning to feel more comfortable about her surroundings.

13

Abby woke up and took a minute to remember where she was. She ran her hand across the soft sheets and looked over at the curtains. She slipped out of bed, put on her new bathrobe and slid her feet into her new slippers. She walked to the window pulling open the curtains to see snow blowing past. She braced herself and she looked down to the street below. The sidewalks were already filled with people and cars, buses and trucks filled the streets. The sun was coming up over Lake Michigan and there was smoke and steam rising from the rooftops all around.

Abby went to the kitchen where she found Stephen making breakfast.

"Good morning, Miss Abby. How did you sleep?"

"Good morning, Stephen. To be honest, I've slept better. I think it's going to take me a day or two to get used to all of the changes. I'm also so excited about meeting my brother."

"Well, you can always rest this afternoon before you go shopping."

Abby could see her father enter the dining room adjacent to the kitchen. He was dressed in a fine brown suit and had the morning paper in his hand. Abby walked into the dining room.

"Good Morning, Father."

"Good Morning, Abby. I imagine you tossed and turned a bit. Was it the dinner or the excitement?"

"A bit of both – that was the biggest and most tender steak I've ever had. Come to think of it, I can't remember the last time I had a steak."

"I'm glad you enjoyed it."

Stephen brought a tray with coffee and glasses of juice and set them down in front of the two place settings at opposite ends of the table.

"Freddie will be picking us up in an hour. Stephen, I'd like you to come to the hospital with us and consult with Doctor Maguire to see what we need to make Tony's room more conducive to his needs. Just as soon as they'll let us have him we'll be bringing him home to recover. Then I'd like you to see if Doctor Maguire can recommend a nurse that we can hire for as long as it takes."

"Yes sir."

"You can do that?" Abby asked. Why, of course dear." Edward looked a little shocked.

Stephen brought a tray with bowls of cereal and set one in front of each of them.

"Oh Father, I've written a letter to my friend back home. Can we mail it today?"

"Of course, just give it to Stephen and he'll see to it."

"I'd be glad to, Miss Abby." Stephen said.

They arrived at the hospital and Stephen walked in ahead of Abby and her father. He approached the desk and informed the attendant that Mr. Baker was here to see his son, Anthony. Just as Abby and her father approached the desk, another woman within hearing range came over briskly and greeted them with a bright smile.

"Good Morning, Mr. Baker, I'm Miss Ford. If you'll come this way I'll escort you to your son's room." Then she turned back to the attendant and said, "Call Doctor Maguire right away and let him know that I'm taking Mr. Baker to see his son."

She turned to Abby and extended her hand. "I'm so sorry, I'm Miss Ford, and you are?"

"Abigail...Baker." she said while giving her father a look that almost seemed to ask for an endorsement. He smiled to her and gave a wink. She could tell he approved and was happy.

Abby continued, "I'm Anthony's sister."

"Of course you are, dear, I can see the resemblance. He'll be so happy to see you. He's really doing quite well this morning."

By then they reached the door to his room. Miss Ford went in ahead of them.

"Good Morning, Sergeant Baker. You have some very special guests to see you."

Mr. Baker made his way to the side of the bed as Abby stayed back a few feet. She looked around at the equipment. Anthony had a leg in traction and a bandage wrapped around his forehead. His right arm was in a cast and just the fingers were exposed.

"Tony."

"Father." This one word was all Mr. Baker needed to hear to bring a tear to his eyes.

"Son...I've brought someone to meet you, someone who is uniquely a part of your life. Anthony, this is your sister Abby."

Abby stepped up to the bed now and found herself captivated by his face. She studied him closely especially his eyes.

"Abby." was all he said and now his eyes were watering.

Abby had told herself that morning that no matter what, she wouldn't cry, but there was no preparing her for this and the tears came quickly.

"Anthony." She carefully reached down and put her hand on his left hand. He gripped her hand and began to move his mouth, but no words came and he cried. Abby put her right hand on his head and drew herself near. She whispered, "It's alright Anthony. No one is going to separate us again, and a tear ran down her cheek. Edward looked away and his hand fumbled in his pocket, but Stephen quickly produced a neatly folded handkerchief and Edward quickly took it. Mr. Baker wiped his eyes and Miss Ford brought him a glass of water. "No, thank you – it's alright." he said to her. He turned back to his children and placed a hand on each of them.

"My children…sometimes we don't know why we make the judgments that we do…why we do the things that seem right at the time. We're humans and we believe that the story we're writing in our heads will have the happy ending we want everyone near us to have. I'm sorry that I didn't keep you together, but when it all started, it seemed like the right thing to do although a voice inside me made me feel uneasy for so many years. Then you go on telling yourself that someday it'll be for the best. When that voice inside finally screams loud enough you can't help but listen and realize that maybe it's too late. Then you start to regret and it's the regret that forces you to do what you should have done years earlier. You realize that it seems impossible to correct the past and you can only pray that the ones you've hurt will forgive you."

Abby began to openly cry. Stephen made eye contact with Miss Ford and they left the room quietly.

"I'm sorry, my children. That's all I can say."

Abby pulled away and looked directly at her father. "No… no…no don't be sorry, we're here now – together."

She turned completely to her father and gave him a strong and firm hug. With some resistance he reached his arms around her and hugged her back. A big smile came across her face as she turned back to Anthony.

"We have a lot of catching up to do." She laughed. Anthony wiped his eyes with his good hand.

"You have my laugh…it's a good laugh." he said with a broad smile.

"There you go, Anthony. We have lot's of new memories to make." Abby said as she now gave him a warm hug.

14

N elson was having a cup of coffee in the office. He sat at the south wall looking out into the yard. He chewed on the stub of an old cigar and rubbed his thick whiskers. The ladies in the office would give each other a glance or a smirk when they would notice Nelson scratching himself or making some obscene noise.

The mailman arrived and the office ladies were thankful for the distraction even though it was a brief visit.

'Good morning, ladies!' he said as he gave a bundled stack of letters to one of the office ladies. The ladies simply nodded and smiled to him. 'Nice weather today.' He tipped his hat and left before either could answer.

As one lady shuffled through the stack of letters she found one addressed to John. She noticed the hand-writing and return address and assumed that it was from a woman.

"Letter here addressed to John." she said to the other.

Nelson became agitated. He had been enjoying this peaceful moment before the start of his work day even though his mere presence infringed on the peacefulness of the early morning that the ladies had been enjoying. He was now thinking about John Miller and how his life had been so much easier before this kid came to the camp. He put his coffee cup down with a slam that startled the ladies.

"I'm going out to the camps." he said abruptly.

"Well, if you're going to see John would you give him this letter, please?" The lady said as she held it up. Nelson snatched the letter out of her hand and shoved it in his jacket pocket. He went out of the door and it slammed behind him.

The lady looked over at the other and said, "I have a feeling I shouldn't have given him that letter." The other lady shrugged.

Nelson drove down the road, pulled over and stopped. He cranked open his window. He took matches from his pocket and lit up the cigar he had hanging in his mouth. Then as he put the matches back in his pocket his hand touched the letter that had been given to him. He took out the letter, looked at it and saw John Miller's name. That was about all he needed to see right now. He crumbled the letter and threw it out the window. He closed the window, put the truck in gear and drove off into town to buy a pint of whiskey.

15

It was early in April of 1945 and the war continued without John. It had been three longs months since Abby left. He had thought about her every day and prayed that she was safe.

He had received a letter from his brother Bill and after reading of some of their near escapes and the deaths of some of Bill's friends, thought that perhaps he was meant to be here in Wisconsin. John began to think that this was his destiny and that with faith and prayer, he would ride along this course of his life and see where it would take him.

Although there was still a thin layer of ice on the lakes, the men had already taken to working in their shirts, without coats. Production was steadily increasing as conditions became more pleasant. Anderson had commended John on sticking to it through the winter and keeping production at a good pace despite the tough conditions. Anderson also shared with John some news that he had received. The state would lease an additional two thousand acres to the C. A. Anderson Company starting on May first. John was pleased that Mr. Anderson would share this news with him.

"What kind of trees can we expect to be harvesting there?" John asked.

"Mostly maple, some hemlock. We'll take a drive out and look things over...but I don't think we can take the contract."

Anderson replied and then continued with some trepidation, "The problem is that we don't have enough men." John and Anderson sat and looked around in thoughtful silence until John finally announced,

"I just might have an answer to that, sir."

"What's that?" asked Anderson.

"There are Prisoner of War Camps in the state. Close to three hundred of them. There's one down by Chilton on the county fairgrounds. They're holding Germans until the war is over."

Anderson stared at John and asked, "What good does that do us, John?"

"Well, sir, they're loaning these men out to canning companies and other concerns to offset the cost of keeping them. The canning companies are paying them nineteen dollars a week. We can match that and make it worthwhile bringing a busload of them up here. Only thing is that we'd have to put a guard on duty. From what I hear, at one camp they have three men guarding over twelve hundred prisoners. I don't think Uncle Sam feels too threatened by these men." John spoke with enthusiasm.

"Well, you might have something there, John, except there'd be a heck of a lot of Germans up here and we have enough of a language barrier as it is." Anderson said.

"Well sir, I might have that covered too. I speak some German, enough to get by and give instructions. My parents spoke German on the farm all the time. Steeg Onsgaard from Camp Four speaks some German too. We could drive down to Calumet County, meet with the authorities and send one of our men along back with them by bus. There's plenty of bunkroom available and, if need be, we could set up tents for the summer months." John said.

"Let me think about this… no, wait a minute, let's do it." Anderson remarked.

John drove over to the camp where Steeg had been working under Nelson's supervision that day. John had with him, a written note from Mr. Anderson excusing Steeg from work for the next week. The note read:

"Let John take Steeg from the camp for the next week or so. They're going to round up some P.O.W.'s and Steeg speaks some German. Any problem with this – come see me. Signed: C. A."

John pulled into the clearing where Nelson was sitting under the shade of a tall pine. He saw John pull into the camp, got up and walked over to John's truck. John handed the note to Nelson from the open window. Nelson became enraged and swore at John for taking one of his men. Spit flew from his mouth as he cursed John. John tipped his hat and replied with a courteous: "Thank you for your contribution to the cause," and in a few minutes drove off with Steeg.

The two men set out on Sunday morning on the seven-hour drive. John left Rusty at the camp where Manuel would look after her as if she were his own. Anderson gave John some cash as expense money and Manuel packed up a big basket of sandwiches - good sandwiches, not the kind he would fix for Nelson.

With this being done, John and Steeg drove the long and bumpy road out of the county, heading south. They arrived in Chilton at around seven o'clock and found a room for the night. Monday morning the two men drove over to the County Fairgrounds and found the office. The fences around the fairgrounds were not very secure and when John had asked the innkeeper about the prisoner of war camp the night before, he knew nothing about it. It wasn't kept secret, but at the same time it was not advertised, either. The German prisoners were treated well and since the majority of people living in Wisconsin had been of German ancestry, there were often cases of prisoners being loaned out to different businesses with no more than a signature.

Daniel Justinger was the chief in charge of the camp and appeared to be more than happy to loan out a couple dozen prisoners. After all, there would be fewer mouths to feed and the camp could make a little profit from the deal.

"How many do you want, Mr. Miller?" Justinger asked. "Take the whole lot if you want." he continued.

"We'd be very happy with a busload sir, about thirty men in all." John said.

"I'll need some time to select the men and have them pack up what gear they've got. Some of them might be loaned out right now for night shift at the cannery and won't be back until tomorrow. Best if you'd stay the night. We'll get you out of here with them first thing tomorrow." Justinger said.

"Fair enough." John replied and the two men set off for a day of rest and relaxation.

John and Steeg drove to the farmstead and both Ma and Pa were happy to see both of them. It was a little awkward at first for Steeg, having left as he did, but Matt and Katherine made him feel at home again. They had even boxed up his things to take back with him. The old place looked great and it did John's heart good to see how well the Weber family had been keeping up the place. They had even put a fresh coat of paint on the barn and sheds. John and Steeg drove the ten miles back to Chilton in the late-afternoon. John wanted to look up some old friends, one in particular and Steeg just wanted to walk around town. He hadn't been in a town this size for some time and just wanted to feel the sidewalk beneath his feet. John dropped Steeg off at the south end of town, the two of them agreeing that they would meet for a late supper at the bowling lanes.

Steeg was walking along admiring how different the houses looked from those that were built up north. Clapboard siding and clean white picket fences appeared to be typical in this area. Suddenly one house caught Steeg's attention. There was a woman on her knees crying in the front yard and a blanket draped over her porch. Steeg's immediate thought was that perhaps the woman had just lost a loved one in the war. He approached her as she knelt weeping in her front yard. He was cautious not to startle her until she finally sensed him near and, gaining her composure, looked up at him.

"Sorry, Ma'am, I didn't mean to scare you. Just wanted to know if there was anything I could do." Steeg asked with all sincerity. The woman got up, went over to the porch and pulled the blanket down. Painted on the side of the porch were the words: "slut" and "whore". Who would do such a thing? Steeg thought to himself.

"My husband was killed in the war, I have nothing. Why is this happening to me?" the woman asked, not expecting an answer.

Steeg said, "There, Ma'am, if you've got some paint and thinner I can clean that off for you."

"That would be so kind of you, so kind." the woman said. Steeg introduced himself as she put the blanket back over the porch. The two of them went to the shed in back and found a small amount of paint in a can. There was a dried film of paint on the surface, but under the film was enough paint to take care of the situation. Steeg found some sandpaper and gasoline in the shed as well, and went about thinning the paint, then sanding and painting over the words that someone had painted to wound this woman's heart.

The woman's name was Jane Grace. She brought out a cold soda for Steeg as he worked on the porch. A couple of times while he worked, women would walk by and stare. One lady came out of her house across the street. Steeg could sense that she was staring for the longest time. Slowly, Steeg turned his head to make eye contact with the woman. She shook her head from side to side, turned and went back inside of her house. Yes, it is a shame Steeg thought to himself.

Jane came out and sat on the porch steps to keep Steeg company. She asked him many questions about where he was from and the type of work he was accustomed to doing. Finally she asked, "And what brings you to this fine town?" with a hint of sarcasm.

Steeg said, "We come here to pick up some of the Germans from the camp to bring back up north to work." He still spoke with a heavy accent.

"Oh, is that so?" Jane replied. "How many prisoners?" she asked, seeming very curious.

"Maybe thirty." Steeg replied. At this last comment she seemed a little distracted and as if she needed to do something. Steeg finished up painting the porch and put the materials back in the shed.

"You can clean up in the kitchen sink if you'd like, Mr. Steeg." she said.

"Please ma'am, call me Steeg." he said.

"Well, Steeg it is then." She replied and gave him a flirtatious wink. It had been a long time since Steeg had had a woman wink at him and he felt his heart beating with excitement. Steeg cleaned up and Jane handed him a clean, fresh towel. He was not accustomed to such cleanliness, at least not since he had left the Miller's farm.

Jane said, "Thank you so much," and stood on her tiptoes to give Steeg a kiss on the cheek. "Thank you so much…Steeg," she said softly.

Steeg gave a smile and a nod and headed for the door.

Steeg walked back to the motel at a brisk pace. He had Jane on his mind and suddenly he had lost interest in looking at the neighborhood. It was late afternoon now, close to the time when Steeg would meet John for supper at the bowling alley. He saw the pickup truck at the motel and went to the room the two men shared. John was asleep on one of the beds, tired from his afternoon.

Steeg woke him up and said, "John, John, I think I've got something to do this evening. If it's all right with you I'll want to pass on supper."

"Gee, Steeg, I've never seen you like this before. Is everything okay?" John asked.

"Oh yes sir, yes, John." Steeg replied. "I met a woman this afternoon, a widow lady and I want to go back to see her." Steeg said.

"Well, that's great." John said as he slapped Steeg on the back. "Why don't you take the truck? I won't need it. I may stop to see an old friend, but he lives close by and I can walk." John suggested.

"Good, thank you, that's a real good idea, John." Steeg said.

That evening Steeg drove to Jane's house, pulled up and shut off the truck. He sat there in silence looking at the flowers he had picked for her. A few snatched from a couple of different yards so that no one would notice or if they did, they wouldn't care. After awhile he mustered up enough courage to proceed. He walked along her sidewalk and up the porch steps. He stood at the screen door in silence trying to think of words, kind and gentle words. He needed to think of the kind of words that a woman would want to hear and yet not be offended since she was a widow and all.

As he stood there he suddenly heard sounds from inside. The door was open and he could hear sounds through the screen door. They were sounds of a woman moaning and he thought she might be crying again, maybe over the loss of her husband. Steeg opened the screen door quietly and stepped inside. He thought that he might bring her a pleasant surprise with the flowers. Steeg walked a few steps in and suddenly saw a drab-brown shirt hung over a dining room chair. He stopped dead in his tracks as he saw the familiar initials on the back of the shirt: " P.O.W." Now he heard sounds of a man moaning as well. Steeg dropped the flowers to the floor and backed up to the screen door. He quickly left the house and walked quietly to the truck trying hard to control his emotions. Anger, hurt, and a pain Steeg had not known before, the feeling of having been deceived. Steeg started the truck and drove to the bowling lanes where he knew John would be, tears forming in his eyes.

Steeg came into the bar after gaining his composure and saw John sitting there.

"How was your evening? Hey, why are you back so soon?" John asked.

Steeg just said, "Oh, she had other plans." John ordered up a beer for Steeg as he took a seat next to him. There were quite a few people at the bowling lanes for a weekday night. Steeg looked around and saw a table of customers that disturbed him. Over in the corner there were four German prisoners, their P.O.W. jackets on in full view of everyone. With them there were two guards in uniform with their guns leaning against the wall, all of them drinking together from a pitcher of beer.

Before taking the beer that had just been placed before him, Steeg turned and walked over to the men at the table. "These are prisoners! They have killed your brothers, your fathers and neighbors. Take them to the prison where they belong." Steeg shouted. The guards, suddenly solemn, leaned forward and sat upright. The prisoners too, had known that this man was alarmed at the fraternization that was taking place.

One of the guards finally spoke, "We didn't mean any harm, these men are safe. They're no threat." He began, but words trailed off as he realized that the man was right, they needed to do their jobs although they would rather do it in a bar.

"Take these prisoners back to the prison or I will take them there for you and see that you're reprimanded. You are being derelict in your duties and a disgrace to your community and country." Steeg commanded.

No more needed to be said. The men got up, the guards gathered the rifles that they had left against the wall.

John sat looking at Steeg and after what seemed like minutes, spoke, "I'm proud of you, Steeg, proud to be your friend." John knew that something had happened earlier this evening to provoke such a reaction, but this was one of those things best left alone. John and Steeg drove back to the motel, Steeg just looking out the window.

16

John saw the men and Steeg off at the bus station. Steeg couldn't help but look over the thirty-two men given to his custody and wonder if any of them had been the man in the arms of the sad woman he had spent his afternoon with. The night before, after the two men arrived back at the hotel, Steeg told John of his sad experience. After the bus had left with Steeg and the prisoners on board, John asked Justinger if he knew of this woman.

Justinger said, "Yeah, unfortunately all of the men here know about her. Her husband is stationed over in Guadalcanal."

John asked, "You mean to tell me she's not a widow?"

"No, Miller, but I'd guess that some day... if and when Mr. Grace comes back, he might just wish that she was."

No more was said about the incident and it occurred to John how much he was learning about people. Thinking about the incident made him sad and reflective. John drove his truck to the gas station, ordered the attendant, "filler up", paid his bill and began the drive back to the north. He thought that if he speeded up a bit he could follow the bus and in spirit, keep Steeg company on his long trip back.

For a few extra dollars, the bus driver drove the men directly to the lumber company. Anderson came out of his office as the bus drove in. He was excited that John and Steeg had produced what John had promised, a group of men to harvest timber from the newly leased land. Nelson came out of the office shortly behind Anderson and scuttled over to the bus to inspect the new crew and display to the boss that he would take things over from here.

"What a bunch of good for nuthin's" Nelson barked.

"Oh shut up, Nelson. They look just fine to me. If there's any that are good for nothing then you make something out of them." Anderson snapped back.

Nelson looked at the ground, then grabbed the clipboard with the crew register out of Steeg's hands. "It's about time you got back from your little vacation." Nelson said to Steeg.

Steeg simply smiled beneath the long mustache that hung far over his lip.

"Good job, John." Anderson said as he patted John on the back.

"Thank you, sir." John said with his usual modesty.

"Now we can boost output, can't we?" Anderson continued.

Nelson put Steeg in charge of the Germans and the plan was to keep the entire group together only for the first week to make certain that the men learned the basic instructions and could cross-train each other. By the end of the first week they found that the Germans had not only learned the equipment and processes, but had assembled their own production methods to maximize efficiency. They were organized, hard-working and they never complained. There was very little supervision needed. Northern Wisconsin any time of year was better than being at the Russian front and the prisoners were grateful to be gainfully employed and in surroundings that reminded them of their home. When John made his rounds he took the opportunity to practice his German with the men, usually one-on-one. John gave particular attention to a man named Helmut

Gerhard. Helmut was young, about John's age and seemed to understand John's German.

Wie sind Sie und sind wie die Arbeit?

"How are you and how is the work?" John asked.

Gut, sehr gut vielen Dank. Die Arbeit ist fein und die Luft ist gut zu atmen.

"The work is good. Thank you and the air is good to breathe." Helmut responded with a grin.

Wir haben viel Arbeit und der wir sind dankbar für ihre Bemühungen.

"We have a lot of work and we thank you for your efforts." John said smiling as he patted Helmut on the back.

Ja, vielen Dank aber nur, bis der Krieg über ist.

"Yes, thank you but only until the war is over." Helmut said with a broad smile.

Sehr gut. Vielleicht können Sie der Koch einiges Rezepts lehren?

"Very good. Maybe you can teach the cook some recipes?" John asked.

Das wäre gut. Vielen Dank vielen Dank.

"That would be good. Thank you, thank you." Helmut said as he returned his attention to his work.

John felt good about how his German was coming back to him. It felt good to make a positive contribution to the company. The days were bringing more hours of sunlight and production was increasing.

One wet morning Nelson was getting a crew together to start cutting on a new section. There was a heavy fog and mist. The men were cold and several were grouped under canvas tarps to keep the rain off.

One old man who was simply called Guzikowski yelled above the noise to Nelson, "Don't make sense to work in this."

Nelson gave the man a hard stare. He yelled at the men and pushed a few around. The jacks had been working hard and a few were mending injuries. There were always injuries, sometimes serious. Climbing and walking on slick bark was hazardous and the little production they would get on these days hardly made up for the lost production from men nursing sprains and cuts. Nelson continued to yell at the men to get on the truck and many did so grudgingly.

Guzikowski spoke up again, "Trying to work on a day like this…someone may not come home."

Nelson yelled, "Shut your yap and get on the truck. Maybe that someone will be you!"

Nelson was trying in his own way, to increase his production, compete with John. He also seemed to enjoy pushing men past their limits. The cold, icy rain continued through the day. Sometimes the sun would break through the dark clouds but only long enough for the men to see where they had been slipping and struggling through the mud and ice. Nelson sat in his truck while the men worked, most of the time wadding hard boiled eggs into his mouth and eating sandwiches his wife had prepared for him the night before.

At the end of the day Nelson went around to the men and instructed them to pack up and head to the truck.

'Pack up..' one of the men started to yell to the others.

Nelson grabbed the man by the arm "Shut your mouth. I give the orders around here." The man looked at Nelson in disbelief and grabbed his saw.

Nelson went from group to group and herded the men toward the truck. This was a little unusual as his regular routine was to sit in his truck and blow the horn. Nelson peered around as the men got onto the truck. He got into the cab and started the engine. One of the men reached around the canvas tarp that covered the back of the truck and slapped his hand on the driver's side window. Nelson rolled the window down a few inches.

"Guzikowski's not here sir," the man said.

"Who's that?" Nelson asked although he knew all of the men's names.

"The old Pollock...the one who spoke back to you this morning."

"Don't worry about it, he got on one of the other trucks." Nelson replied. The jack thought this a bit curious, but knew better than to disagree with the wood boss.

The man who took notice of the missing man spoke up above the sound of the truck and the rain, "Boss says don't worry about it."

One of the men yelled back, "What the hell does that mean? I just saw him over in that grove 'bout half-hour ago."

"Boss say's don't worry about it!" The man yelled back over the noise of the truck.

Nelson drove the men back to the camp. The bunk house at Camp Nine was cold and empty, Guzikowski wasn't there. He was still in the grove among the logs that had been cut. The old man was cold and shivering and against his better judgment, started walking toward where he thought the lane was, leaving his saw and grabbing only a canvas tarp that he had used earlier in the day to cover the gasoline can, tool box and other things he had hauled out to the cutting. The wind picked up and sprayed a hard icy rain from the leaves into his face. He stumbled over some branches and fell. He spun around as he got up and now as it was getting dark, he realized he had lost his direction. He began walking, stumbling over rocks and branches that he couldn't see. He called out, but knew it was hopeless against the sound of the wind. He listened, but heard nothing. He thought that if he could find his chainsaw he could use the fuel to start a fire, but realized now that he had no idea of where his gear was. He pulled his coat over his head and crumpled to the ground at the base of a large pine tree. He sobbed as he realized his situation was hopeless. The best he could do would be to try to make it through the night without freezing. His leather boots were wet, his socks were wet. He covered himself with the wet canvas tarp and prayed.

17

John drove into the yard of Camp Nine. He had a satchel of paperwork with him as he headed toward the office. It was cold and wet but the rain had stopped. One of the men hurried from the canteen toward John.

"John, something's happened." he said.

"What is it?" John responded.

"Guzikowski ain't in the camp. Nelson said he took him back to camp yesterday while we was cutting at the new section, but when we got back here no one seen him. We checked all over. We was going to ask Nelson to use a truck and go looking for him but…" The man trailed off.

John responded quickly. "Grab a half dozen guys and meet me back here at the truck.

"Sure thing, John." The man said and hurried off. John went to the office and tossed his satchel on to his desk. He grabbed a box from a shelf and digging through it, pulled out a cigar box. He hurried back to the truck and the men were already waiting for him. John opened the box and handed out whistles to the men.

"Who saw him last?" John asked the men.

"I did." Responded one of the men. He was a man they just called Jensen, a big and strong man from Norway who spoke in broken English. "We work 'bout fifty yard part near a…a grove on the other side of a little hill. Not much lane cut so we hike in pretty far. That is where Nelson told me and Guz to cut. Come afternoon, Nelson come over by me, say the Polack was already back so don't worry." Jensen spoke as if he had a hard lump in his throat. The men knew how serious this was.

"We start at that spot and spread out in each direction. We blow the whistle one short blast every five minutes so we don't get too far apart." John demonstrated. "If you spot him, you whistle three long blasts." John demonstrated again. "When we hear those three whistles, everyone heads back to the truck." John directed. Everyone nodded. "Everyone clear on this?" John asked, now looking for a firm response. The men spoke up in agreement.

"What's all the whistling about?" Nelson asked as he stepped out of the canteen. John looked over and then told the men to get in the back of the truck. "Where the hell you think you're going with my men?" Nelson barked at John. John didn't respond. He got into his truck, started the engine and began driving. "I asked you a question you son-of-a-bitch." Nelson yelled as he hurried toward the truck pulling his suspenders up. John drove off.

All of the men went with Jensen to the spot near the grove where they had been cutting and spread out from there as planned. John stayed with Jensen. They looked for a trail, broken branches, footprints, anything that the forest would tell them. An hour later, Jensen saw a brown canvas tarp with two boots extending from it.

Jensen yelled, "John, John!" Then he remembered the whistle, fumbled for it in his pocket and blew three long blasts. John came running. Jensen stood frozen in his tracks. There was no movement from beneath the tarp.

Jensen wrapped the stiff canvas around the man and lifted him on to his shoulder. The two men walked out of the woods in silence.

John and the men recovered Guzikowski's body and drove him to the hospital where the coroner met them. John called Mr. Anderson and explained what had happened by all accounts from the men.

"John, I'm putting you in charge." Anderson spoke firmly.

"In charge of the cutting operation?" John asked.

"No, John, in charge of the whole thing. I'm going to be spending more time tending to my business back in the cities. Maybe with you in charge we won't have accidents like this. Tell the office ladies to pay for the funeral, send flowers to the family if he's got one. I'll draft up an agreement with regards to your title, responsibilities, wages, and so on. I'll tell Nelson myself. He's not going to be too thrilled about it, but that's the least of my concerns." There was a brief silence. "Any questions?"

"No sir,...thank you." John said.

18

It was the middle of May and Abby's father was having the apartment prepared for Anthony's move home. He had been hospitalized for just over four months and Abby visited him as often as it was possible for her. Stephen had a hospital bed moved in and modifications were made to accommodate his wheelchair. Nurses were being interviewed and Mister Baker consulted with Stephen to make sure they were hiring not only the one who would be best for Anthony, but would be suitable in the household as well, since they didn't know how long the process of healing would be.

Abby had gone shopping and now had more clothes at one time than she had had over the course of her life. Anthony told her all about growing up in the city, the private school he attended and the summers at camp. He told her that he had always felt that something was missing and she knew exactly what he meant. Anthony's friends would come to visit and in the evenings they would play board games and laugh a lot. She enjoyed the company of Anthony's friends, but at times she felt a little out of place. She wondered if they would even talk to her if she was the Abby from the Spot Lunch Café. She wondered if they knew what it was like to work hard for what you wanted, like John. She wondered if they would accept her if she was with John and how they would treat him. Her father would talk with her often and she shared some of her concerns with him. He assured her that there was no way of knowing what went on inside peoples' minds, but that one thing was for sure, you could never place one hundred percent of your faith in people and that if you ever did, that's when you'd be hurt. Abby was realizing that her father had a wisdom that she had never known before. She had not seen this wisdom in her uncle Ted who had raised her, and she certainly did not see it in Harvey at the café. It made her want to know more. She wanted to read the books in her father's library. She wanted to go on to further her education and find her place in this world. For the first time in her life she was a part of something and it made her want more.

Abby wondered why she had not heard from John and it left her sad at times. She was worried that perhaps John had found someone else, but she still wanted their relationship to exist in some way and she felt that perhaps they would be able to pick up again where they left off when she would return home. But home was beginning to feel like a moving target. Where was her home now, she wondered? She knew one thing for sure, she didn't want John to know about her father's wealth. She didn't know how he would accept it. Perhaps, because he came from such a humble life, he would resent her because of her father's money. Maybe he would grow to only love her because of her father's wealth. She didn't want either scenario, and so she would do her best to keep it from him until she knew what his reaction would be. She wrote John a letter:

> **Dear John,**
>   *I miss you terribly. I love you so much and want to be with you. I wish that you would write so that I know you are well. I worry about you in your dangerous job and would give anything if you would come to Chicago to be with me.*

**Please, John, it's been months, please write to me
and let me know that you still love me.**

Abby read the letter several times. She thought that maybe
it sounded too desperate. After all, it had been some time
now since she had written to him and he had not responded.
Maybe he didn't love her as much as she had thought. After
several minutes of procrastination, she tore the letter into
little pieces and tossed them into her wastebasket. She
took out her paper and pen and wrote a new letter, one that
was more about her new family and not one that could be
interpreted as forlorn:

> **Dear John,**
>   **Anthony and I have been spending a lot of
> time together. It's hard to explain the feeling, but
> I'll try. It's as if a part of me has been found a
> part that has been missing all these years. I can
> hear it in his laughter and I see it in his eyes.**
>   **I don't know why you haven't written to me. I
> wonder if you've found someone else. If that's the
> case I can understand, but I hope we'll always
> remain friends.**
>   **Love Abby.**

Days later, John received the letter and it hurt him. Who
was Anthony and why would Abby think that John would
want to write to her if she was with another man. He didn't
even know where she was before receiving this letter – how
could he have written? John could not remember a time in
his life when he felt so low. He brushed the papers aside on
his desk, and folded his fingers into each other as he bowed
his head and prayed, Lord, I don't know why all of this is
happening, but it must be happening for a reason. Do you

have a bigger plan that I can't see from my perspective? I'll try to understand…I'll try to be strong, but I need your help to do that, Lord.

19

The Chicago sunlight was streaming into Abby's room. It was now the first day of June and she was beginning to feel very comfortable with the city, and she knew that having a family was now a big part of it. She had been shopping with Joan several times in the past week and sometimes they would get together for coffee at one of the many small cafés. Abby would think of John from time to time and her heart ached. She wondered why he hadn't written back. She wondered if he had met someone else. She wrote another letter one evening and then crumbled it up and threw it away. If he had feelings for her, he would write.

Abby sat near her bedroom window, enjoying a cup of tea and reading a new novel entitled, "The Fountainhead". It was given to her by her father one evening when he came home from work. She imagined herself as Gail and John as Roark as she became immersed in the book. She would look out of the window from time to time as clouds would move past the sun. She liked the way shadows were cast over buildings while others were brightly lit and only blocks away. Maybe someday John would move to Chicago to be with her. He would become an architect or a successful businessman who came home to her every night. They would have dinner and there would be children, lots of children who loved their father and pleaded for his attention so they could tell him of something wonderful that they had seen or experienced that day. He would pick them all up and give them lots of hugs and kisses. He would read to them as she would sit nearby and watch lovingly. He would promise to take them to the Field Museum or on some other adventure and then, when they were all tired from the excitement, she would help him carry the little ones to their beds, tuck them in and kiss them goodnight.

It seemed like a fairytale dream, but with her father's wealth and position, he could help make that dream come true. This dream and many more.

Abby heard some noise and voices coming from the living room and quickly placed her photo of John into the book as a marker. She set the book down, picked up her tea cup and jumped up from her chair to rush out of the room, only stopping for a second to glance in the mirror. She hurried into the living room just as her father was taking off his black overcoat and handing it to Stephen.

"Just in time, Abby. He's here." Mr. Baker announced.

"Oh, this is wonderful, I'm sure he's excited. Where is he?"

"He and the nurse should be coming up the elevator right about now. Freddie is helping with the wheelchair and I came up ahead to make sure we didn't have any obstacles lying around."

"May I go out into the hallway and greet them?" Abby asked eagerly.

"Absolutely, dear."

Abby rushed out into the hallway and stood at the elevator. She looked up to see the arrow move past the numbers until it finally stopped on their floor. The elevator door opened and Anthony glanced up at Abby, giving her a big smile.

"Hello, brother-dearest! My, I've always wanted to say that." Abby was beaming with excitement. She leaned down to give her brother a hug and he responded with open arms.

"Hello, Sis! I've always wanted to say that, too! Hey, if I'm not mistaken, that smells like Stephen's famous meatloaf cooking. My God, I've missed his cooking."

"Close, Tony, it's steak. Big, juicy, thick steaks. Stephen showed them to me when he came back from the market today. And we're having baked potatoes with lots of stuffing and vegetables…and German chocolate cake for dessert. He said it's your favorite." Tony smiled and a concerned look came over Abby's face. "Is it still your favorite dessert? I mean…being a German recipe and all?"

Tony laughed out loud and then, realizing the absurdity of what she said, Abby began to laugh as well. "Sis, this is Liz, she's going to be my nurse for the next few months, or however long it takes me to start walking again."

Elizabeth Knoll was a tall, dark-haired woman with deep brown eyes. She was new at nursing and had just started working with Copley Hospital a few weeks earlier. She was young and strong, having a specialization in physical therapy and training in massage. Edward did not disclose the full scope of Anthony's physical problems, sparing her the agony and him the embarrassment. Elizabeth would be available twenty-four hours a day to help Anthony with everything he needed in order to make a full recovery and to eventually join his father in the family's business.

"Pleased to meet you, Liz. I'm Abby. Thank you so much for looking after my brother."

"I'm pleased to meet you as well, Abby. Would you get the door please?" Elizabeth asked, but then the door opened and Stephen held it so that the nurse could push the wooden wheelchair into the apartment. Abby walked behind. The wheelchair was manufactured by Edwards company, Baker Medical Corporation, and custom-made for Anthony's height and comfort. The seat, backrest and leg supports were all thickly padded and covered in a soft brown leather. Edward Baker hoped he would never have to produce equipment that his own children would need, but since one of his children did, it would be the best.

"This will take some getting used to." Anthony said.

"You'll do fine, Tony. Father's had a few rooms fixed up for you, even special bathroom fixtures and accessories to make it easy for you until you can walk again."

Anthony seemed to force a smile. The doctors had told him that there was a chance he may never walk again, but he wouldn't burden his new sister with this bit of news.

Stephen took Elizabeth's coat and spoke with her about her accommodations and the family schedule for meals and time together as Abby took the handles of the wheelchair and moved Anthony into the living room.

"Is this alright? I thought you'd like to be near the window since we're getting some nice sunlight this afternoon."

"This is fine, Abby. Please, don't make a fuss. I think I'd just like to relax a bit before supper. Maybe you can tell me some more about your life growing up in northern Wisconsin."

"I'd be happy to. I'm going to go get a picture of my boyfriend, John. I'll be right back." Abby rushed out of the room and then returned in a minute with her book. "I'm reading a great book. Father brought it home for me."

Just then, Edward entered the room having just changed into more casual clothes and a silk smoking jacket.

"Thank you again, father." Abby called to him and he raised his eyebrows. "The book!" she added.

"Oh, you're welcome. Please let me know what it's about when you're finished, but just don't tell me the ending." he said with a smile. Edward walked over to his son and sat in a large, comfortable chair. His nurse appeared to feel a bit uncomfortable.

"Elizabeth, please, please come in and make yourself at home. After all, you're going to be here for an indeterminate amount of time and your comfort is very important to us. I know that Stephen showed you around the other day, but if there's more you'd like to see of the apartment, please, do not hesitate to let us know. I'm sure in a day or two you'll become acclimated to our schedule and I trust you will find your accommodations comfortable." Edward spoke with a calming voice, one that seemed very natural for him. He had learned long ago not to put on pretenses, whether in negotiating business or talking with loved ones.

"Thank you, Mister Baker. My studio apartment is lovely and I really appreciate every kindness shown to me. Stephen has been very helpful, indeed. I do want to tell you that the fitness room you built for Anthony will surely help speed his recovery. It truly is wonderful and I can't wait to put him to work!" She looked at Anthony with a warm smile as she said this and Abby took notice.

Stephen entered the room. "Fifteen minutes before dinner is served." Edward gave Stephen a nod that he had come to understand. "May I get anyone a drink?" he added, and then nodded back at Mister Baker.

"I'll have a cold beer, Stephen!" Anthony called out.

"I stocked your favorite brand just yesterday, Anthony." Stephen said proudly.

"Miss Elizabeth? May I get you a beverage before dinner?" Stephen asked with a smile.

"Oh, um...no thank you, Stephen. I'm fine."

"Miss Abby?" Stephen asked.

"Nothing for me, Stephen. I'll just have Marion pour some more hot water into my tea cup." Abby said as she reached for the cup she had set on the coffee table.

Stephen quickly dashed to where Abby was sitting and took the tea cup from her.

"I have it, Miss Abby. Please...enjoy this moment with your family." Stephen said in a pleasant voice.

Edward Baker leaned forward in his chair, looking into Elizabeth's eyes.

"And please tell me, what regimen do you have planned for Anthony's recovery?" he asked.

She leaned forward and placed her hand on Anthony's knee. "Tomorrow morning we'll start with a good breakfast and then two solid hours of exercise, weights, stretches and then an hour to relax...massage, and then another hour of work before lunch." Abby noticed the way Elizabeth looked at Anthony as she said the words, 'relax...massage' and it made her wonder for brief seconds if she was planning something.

Abby excused herself to freshen up a bit before dinner and as she left the room, she glanced back to notice Elizabeth smiling at Anthony. It was more than a smile, it seemed flirtatious. Abby told herself that she shouldn't read too much into such a gesture and that the right thing to do would be to let it go, but not too far.

20

John was working hard every day and seeing to his duties with skill and dedication. Anderson drove out to Camp Nine where John was taking count of logs.

"Good Morning, John. The new crew is producing well. Maybe when the war ends some of these guys will stay on." Anderson said.

"There's always the possibility." John said with his usual optimism.

"Where are you staying these days?" Anderson asked.

"Well sir, still above Jester's Bar. I intended to move back to Alice's a month ago, but she's not opening the cottages now until mid-summer. She's off visiting her sister in Arizona. I miss the view of the lake in the morning." John said.

Anderson looked off at the horizon as he spoke, "I've got a cabin…an old camp actually. It's about two miles south of town as the crow flies. It's been abandoned for about three or four years now. If you're interested I'll sell it to you along with forty acres. I sold it on land contract to a Finnish guy. He tried farming the land after we logged it off back in the thirties, but he couldn't make a go of it - got into some trouble moon-shining - and to make a long story short, I got it back after he moved on. There's an old barn with it."

John knew immediately that his employer was talking about the place that he and Abby had named Kassendahl. He became excited about the opportunity, but was hesitant. He didn't feel that he could afford the place and it would feel different without Abby. He thought about the prospect of her returning someday to find that he owned the Kassendahl.

"I don't know sir…I don't have a lot saved at the moment. I've been sending money back home to my folks. It sure would be a great place for Rusty."

"Rusty?" the old man asked.

"My dog. I built a dog house for her behind Doc's shop."

"John, you can have it for $1,500. I'll draft up a contract if you're interested. I'll even throw in some milled stock to help you get the place in shape. My son, Charlie, stayed out there a couple of summers back…complained about the roof leaking… never did a thing to fix it though. Got that lazy streak from his mother's side I'd say."

By now John's mind was racing. He'd love to have a place of his own, but this place more than anyplace on earth. He became a bit anxious.

"Would you mind if I drive out to take a look at it over my lunch break?"

"John, this pile of logs isn't going anywhere, let's take a drive over there right now!" Anderson said.

John and his boss drove over to the cabin. The drive in was covered with tall grass and halfway in John had to get out and move a tree branch that had fallen. Unlike most of the single-story log cabins he had seen at other camps, this one had a tall steep roof. Mr. Anderson produced a key from his pocket and unlocked the front door. It took a bit of effort as the lock was rusty and the door needed a good push to get it open. There was a large open room that had served as bunking quarters at one time and a steep stairs that led to a loft that had been used as a bedroom when Mr. Anderson's son had stayed there. There was a broken window in the kitchen and the remains of a dead raccoon under the stairs. Near the large stone fireplace there was a hole in the floor from the rain that had leaked around the chimney and settled in a low spot. The windows had curtains that were dirty, and the cobwebs that clung to them held many a fly that had been caught trying to escape through the window.

"Needs a little work wouldn't you say, John?"

"I could have this place looking like new in a couple of weeks." John said with confidence.

The two men walked outside and John took in the view of the rolling meadow and the wild flowers. "Kassendahl" John whispered under his breath.

"What's that, John?" Anderson asked.

"Nothing, sir."

"There's the small barn, over there's another shed and a sauna." Anderson said. "There's indoor plumbing…my son could never live in a place without all of the convenience's of a modern home. The well and septic system are good, as far as I know…oh, and if you're interested, you can have that sailboat parked in the shed. That was Charlie's, but I'm not going to deal with it."

"I think you've got a deal sir. I can give you $750 tomorrow and, if it's okay with you, the balance in payments." John offered.

"Well, John, I had planned on giving you a raise. You've taken to this business like I've never seen anyone do. That's why I put you in charge. You've got production way up and you're dedicated, I can see that. Not like that lard-ass, Nelson." Anderson looked out over the tree line. "The raise I was going to give you will offset the payments…you agree to stay on for another year at the same pay and that'll take care of the balance. That way you can still send some money home to the folks, you got yourself a house and land, and I got you on board for another year. Sound like a deal?"

John couldn't contain his joy at this proposition. "Yes sir, you've got a deal." John extended his right hand. Anderson took it softly and then gently gripped it and the two men shook. Mr. Anderson handed John the key.

That evening after work John went to the general store and picked up a broom, some lye, bleach, pail, detergent and other cleaning utensils.

He turned down the next aisle to see Alice Stephen paying for a few groceries at the checkout.

"Well hello, John." she said.

"Oh hello, Alice. I thought you were out in Arizona."

"I just got back two days ago." she said.

"I'm glad to run into you. I hope you're not offended, but I won't be in need a room this summer. I just bought a house!" John said.

"Well, that is wonderful news, John…say, will you be needing some furniture and curtains? she asked.

"Oh, I suppose I will…but, I'm a little short on money at the moment. I had just enough for the down payment and I don't get paid for another week." John said.

"Oh, John." Alice laughed. "I have so many old chairs, tables and all of those things that I've amassed over the years. You'd be doing me a favor to help me get rid of some of it. Stop by when you can with your truck and we'll go through the rafters out in the shed. You can help yourself to what's ever up there". She said.

"Wow, that's great. I don't know how to repay you." John said.

"You'd be doing me a favor so don't think twice about it." She said. She took her change, picked up her groceries and gave him a smile as she backed up toward the door. "You just stop by when you can. Make it around supper and we can share a meal and some pie - like old times."

John's next stop was Jesters Bar to inform his landlord that he would be moving out. The bar was empty except for Dido and his friend Mr. Eggbert. They sat in the corner as Dido carefully petted his friend. John glanced over at the old man.

"Dido seems mighty happy today...so does Mr. Eggbert." John said.

"You'd be happy, too, if someone left you a coat and it had a hundred dollar bill in the pocket."

"Is that right?" John stated.

"Dido sometimes stays in a room behind the church rectory... said there was a package on his doorstep with his name on it and that's it...lucky bastard."

"Not a shabby coat either from the looks of it." John said. "I'd like to give you notice that I'll be moving out...I bought a house, a cabin just south of town."

"Well congratulations, John. We'll miss having you around town. Hey wait a minute." He walked through the doorway with the small sign above that read, 'private', and soon returned from the back with a bottle wrapped in a newspaper. "Here you go, John...a little something to celebrate with." He spoke in almost a whisper and nodded toward Dido. It was obvious that he didn't want it getting around that he might have a generous streak. Something like that could put you out of business.

John nodded that he understood, but neither of them needed to be overly concerned as Dido was engaged in deep conversation with his friend Mr. Eggbert. John kept his voice low, "Thanks, Chester...that's really nice of you. If you're in the neighborhood sometime, stop in and we'll have a beer. It's just a couple miles south of town," John headed toward the door concealing the bottle under his arm.

"I'll do that, John...you take care now." Jester said as he went back to his paper.

Over the next couple of weeks John worked on his new home. His first chore was to take a shovel and remove the raccoon remains from under the stairs. Then he set about patching any spots under the eaves where animals could get in. He had glass cut at the hardware store and bought glazing putty to fix the kitchen window. He cut copper flashing and took a pail of tar to fix the chimney leak, and he took Mr. Anderson up on his offer of milled lumber to repair the floor. Alice provided a table and set of chairs, a large rug, and a set of dishes and silverware. She showed up one Saturday with curtains which she measured and hemmed up to fit his windows. They enjoyed a cup of tea in his backyard sitting on furniture that he himself had made with soft cedar and made smooth with a drawknife and sandpaper. He gave the chairs and small table a coat of green paint to keep them from graying in the weather. The back yard was nothing more than a small area of lawn which he mowed with an old rotary mower. He was proud of his work and enjoyed having Alice as his first guest, but had hoped in his heart that his first guest would have been Abby. From time to time he would think about her and miss her. He wondered why he hadn't heard from her. He still held on to the dream that one day she would come back, knock on his door and he would welcome her to their new home. But he kept reminding himself that this was a dream. Maybe she would never return.

John pulled the sailboat from the shed and braced it up with timbers. He took a pail of water and some bleach and set about cleaning it. John didn't know anything about sailboats. This was a vessel used strictly for pleasure and all he had known were boats used for fishing. But nonetheless, John methodically set about raising the mast and setting up the sail which had been stored in a canvas bag hanging from the shed rafters to keep mice from it. He was a bit surprised when a gust of wind came up and jarred the craft from its timbers. John immediately lowered the sail and put it away for the day.

He asked around town and found an older man who sailed. John sheepishly admitted that he knew nothing of the sport and asked him if a little information could be shared. The man was eager to share what he could which included maneuvering a boat with the wind as well as tacking into the wind. All of this made sense to John and he was now eager to try it all out.

21

William Miller lay in a cold, wet and muddy foxhole. He had been there for three days with the frozen corpse of a Nazi not more than four feet away. The shelling had been going on day and night with only a few hours of silence at a time. William kept low. He knew where the enemy was, but he didn't know where the men from his troop were other than the ones he had seen get hit. He had finished the last of his rations but his thoughts weren't of food. From his position he could not tell where the enemy was and so he couldn't discern whether it was safe to leave.

In the first two days he could faintly make out the sound of voices in the distance, but with the sound of the wind as it blew through the trees, and the bombing and gunfire he could hear, it was difficult to distinguish whether the voices were those of Americans or those who would gun him down. Giving away his position would mean either being rescued or immediately killed.

William tried to keep awake but would give in to a few hours of sleep late at night. He thought about escaping but then saw a camp of Germans a few hundred feet away sitting around a fire. There were several and they appeared to be heavily armed.

The next morning when there was enough light, he took some folded paper from his backpack and dug deep into the pockets finally finding a pencil, wrote the following:

Dear John,

I've been in this foxhole for three days with very little food. A few feet away there's the corpse of a nazi I killed with my bayonet. He was scared and cried for his mother as he lay dying. I put his helmet over his open eyes. I think most of the guys from my outfit are dead. I'm not sure where I am except that there's a farm on the other side of a hill about three hundred yards away. I could hear cows until about a day ago. I imagine they've been killed and eaten. I try not to think about food but visualize myself going over there and strangling one of those chickens I hear in the morning. I remember how Ma would collect eggs every morning. We always had fresh eggs didn't we? I could hear the enemy walk around near this hole I'm in but they never spotted me. The hole's partly covered by the stump of a large tree that got shot down. The nights are cold, very cold and I have all that I can do to keep from freezing to death. I took the coat from this guy but it doesn't help much. I think I've got frostbite on all of my toes – I can't feel them at all. When I hear footsteps and voices nearby, I crawl up as far under the stump as I can to conceal the mist of my breath. But the weather was warm earlier this morning and this guy's starting to stink. I've thought about making a run for it but not sure where to run to. I keep listening – trying to hear the voices and make out what they're saying. Hoping I'll hear English one of these times and I'll be able to get the hell out of this hole. I hope you don't enlist John. I hope to hell you don't enlist. A letter from Ma got to me a few months ago and she said you moved up north. Stay there. You never listened to me too much when we were kids. You were the stubborn one. But listen to me now John – war really is hell. I think about this German I killed. I didn't have a choice. If I would have let him go he would have brought the others to me and I wouldn't be writing this letter. I think, who was this guy? For all we know he might have been a distant cousin. He was a man just like you or me. He probably had a family. Maybe a wife and kids and now he's dead and starting to rot. I don't know if I'll get out of this mess but if I do it'll be a miracle – nothing less. I don't have a way out – not this time. I'll keep this letter on me and so if you're reading this I'm probably dead. I love you brother.

William

William folded the letter and placed it on a dry spot nearby. He thought about his brother, his parents and the farm. He would give anything to be home with them or at the very least, to be able to see their faces one more time. Then William took a fresh sheet of paper and wrote another letter.

Dear Ma and Pa,

Not much going on over here. The countryside is beautiful – just like Wisconsin. I probably put on ten pounds. I had eggs this morning Ma and it made me think of you. Then my bunkmate and I had a whole chicken to eat. I heard cows the other morning and it made me a little homesick but I'll be home before you know it. I wonder where our relatives are and I hope they're surviving the war. Maybe when this mess is all over I'll have some time on my hands and I'll be able to look some of them up. I find myself with a lot of time to think about things and mostly I think about how nice it is on our farm. I remember what it's like to watch the wheat gently blowing in the morning sun – golden. There's a farm not too far from where I'm writing this. I wish I could just put down my gun and go over and help with the chores. Wouldn't that be a surprise to them? I hope you're both doing well. I hope John's working hard up north – I'm sure he his. He's a good kid – I mean "man". Gee, I can't believe my little brother is making his way in the world. After I'm home maybe I'll go up north and get him out in a boat for some fishing. I'll bet there's some big ones up there. I wonder how Strawberry and Mr. Duke are doing. They sure are hard working horses. I imagine there'll be a lot of work for me to catch up on when I'm home, even if we're not going to farm anymore. I don't think the war will go on much longer – things seem to be pretty quiet where I am. I got your letters a few months ago. Thanks for writing but if you don't get a chance to write for awhile don't worry about it. I'll probably be home before you know it. I love you both very much and I'm looking forward to Ma's cooking and listening to my Pa's violin.

William

He carefully searched through his pack and found two envelopes, this is all he would need. He folded each letter and put them in separate envelopes. Then folded them again and put them into his top shirt pocket under his coat. He prayed the Lord's Prayer and Psalm Twenty-three, then made the sign of the cross and pulled himself out of the foxhole. He ran up the hill and toward the farm.

22

Early one Saturday morning in July, John stepped out into his yard. He looked at the sky and took note of the wind. Enough to move a boat. John hitched the boat trailer to his truck, put the sail, an oar, life jacket and other gear into the back of the truck and headed for Big Twin Lake. John took the boat to a landing that was quiet and secluded. The last thing he wanted was to make a mistake that would result in him ramming a few fishermen or capsizing the boat only feet from shore. John set the boat in the water and tied it to the wooden dock. He drove his truck and trailer down the lane a bit to leave the landing open. He strapped on the life jacket, took the oar and moved the boat out about fifty feet from the pier. John carefully hooked the sail to the line and raised it up. The wind immediately filled the sail and to John's surprise and pleasure he was sailing. John sailed the large lake for nearly two hours. He sailed with the wind, skillfully tacked into the wind and was beginning to feel rather confident. John enjoyed moving quietly with the wind. It was exhilarating to him and he couldn't wait to tell his parents of his new hobby.

John brought the boat about to the east end of the lake. There was a bar there and John thought it'd be a good place to rest for awhile. As he came near the shore he saw a few people fishing from the pier and a fellow about his age standing on the pier smoking a cigarette and drinking a beer. John dropped the sail a bit early and then used his oar to get the boat closer to the pier. He felt the young man staring at him and he felt a bit embarrassed at his inexperience.

"Good wind?" The young man asked.

"Yes, I'd say so, actually...um, my first time sailing." John responded with a little embarrassment.

"That right?" The young man asked. John nodded. "Nice boat...where'd you get it?

"Well, it was actually given to me by my boss." John answered.

"I'm glad old Charles Anderson is generous to somebody." The young man said.

"How did you know...?"

"My father...that's my boat, or at least it was." The young man said.

"You're Charles junior?" John asked.

"Charlie will do. Yeah, that'd be me. Just here for the Fourth of July weekend...but thought I'd stay a bit longer. You must be the farmer my old man was telling me about. So you move from the farm to the boondocks of northern Wisconsin...big move."

John ignored the comment and extended his hand for a shake. "I'm John Miller...I guess you'll be wanting your boat back?"

Charlie Anderson ignored John's gesture and took a long drink from his beer. Finishing it off, he tossed the empty bottle into the lake and took a long drag from his cigarette. "Naw, that's okay, Miller. You keep it, the old dog can buy me a new one. Besides it looked like you really got a blast out of it...wish I could get excited about the little crap in life. " Young Anderson responded.

"Your father told me that you were finishing up college out east." John said.

Young Anderson gave a blank expression and then took a long, final drag from his cigarette and flicked it to the water. Then after a long silence he noticed John's disfigured right hand.

"What the hell happened to you?" he asked.

"Had an accident on the farm last year, it hasn't healed just right...but I get by. Had to learn how to write all over again and ..."

"I didn't ask for your life story, Miller...Christ."

John's expression changed. He looked away and then started tying off the boat. Young Anderson laughed.

"What's the matter, Miller? Hurt your feelings? I figured you'd be a lot tougher...what, with working with my old man and all."

"Tough enough." John responded.

"Come on, Miller." Anderson pointed across the road. "There's a bar...least you can do is buy me a beer for taking my boat."

John nodded. "Fair enough." he said.

The two young men went into the Holiday Bar. The walls were filled with mounted trophy fish, deer heads, antlers, a black bear and a very large moose head. There was a glass case with a large muskie positioned as if it were ready to swallow a muskrat swimming just above its mouth. There was no one in the bar.

Anderson yelled, "Where the hell's the bartender...come on, I need a beer!"

An older lady came out from the back tying an apron around her waist. She gave Anderson a cold look.

"What can I get for you?" She asked.

"Two shots brandy, two beers...tall ones...and cold." He commanded.

John gave her an apologetic look and she set up the glasses.

"Bring the dice cup." Anderson instructed as he lit up a cigarette with his silver lighter. He threw a money clip on the bar and it held several large bills. "Shake for this round." he said as he shook the dice cup and slammed it down on the bar. He lifted off the cup and swept away two of the dice, leaving three fives. He shook the other two dice and slammed the cup down. "Five fives! Beat that Miller." Anderson said proudly.

John swept up the dice and put them in the cup. John gave a few shakes and poured out four sixes and a two. John gave Anderson a sly look, took the two, loaded it into the cup, gave two shakes and slammed the cup down. Anderson put his hand over John's hand, holding the cup down.

"Make it interesting?" Anderson asked.

"Like how?" John asked.

"Throw a ten spot on." Anderson said.

Ten dollars was a lot of money to John, but he felt compelled to keep up with the rich kid's game.

"Just a ten spot?" John asked.

"A twenty then." Anderson said. John nodded and Anderson lifted his hand from John's.

John lifted the cup to reveal another six.

"Damn!" Anderson shouted. John smiled. Anderson took a twenty from his money clip and tossed it toward John.

"Lucky bastard." he said.

The two men tossed back their shots of brandy and chased them with their beers.

"Maybe pool's more your game" John said. Anderson gave a slight smile.

"Don't tell me you had a pool table out in the barn, farmer."

"Naw...but the chickens like an occasional game of poker."

Young Anderson laughed and racked up the balls.

The two young men continued to spend the afternoon drinking, shooting pool and occasionally betting. They were both feeling the effects of the alcohol.

"Time to go...but I'm not sure if I can sail." John said.

"Come on, let's make a sailor out of you. Where did you put in?" Anderson asked.

"Wally's Bait Shop at the Southwest end. Listen…I know when I've had enough, I'm not going to sail in this condition." John said.

"Alright, listen up, I'll sail us both back there and then you give me a ride back here to get my car." Anderson said. "A final voyage with my old boat…but pay attention, I'll teach you a few things about sailing."

"Let's go." John said. He picked up a pile of bills from the bar, folded them and put them in his pocket.

The two men got into the sailboat. John strapped on the life jacket. "Only have one jacket…but there's a cushion." John said.

"I don't need one." Anderson said.

John untied the boat and Anderson raised the main sail. It was early evening and the wind picked up. The waves were choppy and John began to sober up quickly. The boat was tossed and Anderson kept up with the wind, tacking back and forth across the long lake. When they were getting near shore John spotted a jagged rock ahead.

"Watch that rock!" John yelled to Charlie.

"Don't worry…big baby." Anderson laughed loudly, but in a split-second, grazed the side of the rock and fell from the boat. John leapt to the back of the boat and grabbed the rudder. He loosened the rope and dropped the mainsail, then grabbed the seat cushion and dove from the boat into the cold water. He came up and gasped for air looking around. Anderson was about twenty feet away. John swam to him. Anderson was flailing his arms and gasping for air. John grabbed Charlie's jacket and raised him up, pushing the cushion to his chest. Anderson clung to the cushion. The two men looked at each other with an understanding and John swam to the boat that bobbed up and down over the waves. He reached the boat and raised the sail while holding the rudder with his leg making the boat turn sharply to port side. The boat quickly moved around in a large circle and John managed to bring it close enough to reach Charlie with the oar. Charlie grabbed the oar and John managed to tip the man into the boat. Overwhelmed by the booze and the freezing water, Charlie lay in the bow of the boat gasping.

"Stay down!" John yelled. He turned the sail and rudder and brought the boat into shore, jumping out into the shallow water. Charlie got out of the boat and staggered toward the shore still holding the seat cushion to his chest with his left arm. The two men got the boat loaded onto the trailer and strapped down. When the they finally got into the truck they sat for a moment shaking off the cold. Charlie had an angry look on his face.

"You didn't save my life Miller...I'm an excellent swimmer... just caught off-guard. You didn't save my life". Charlie's words seemed disturbing to John.

Finally Charlie let out a laugh, "Man! That water's cold! Let's get the hell out of here."

John was eager to relieve the tension, "Yeah...darn cold.

Charlie looked out the window and said, "Thanks."

John drove Charlie over to the Holiday Bar to get his car. "I suppose I'll see you around, Miller, take care of that boat." Charlie said.

"So long." John said.

John drove back to his cabin thinking about how strange this fellow had been, what his mother would call "spoiled rotten". But it also seemed that Charlie had his good-natured side.

23

Ablue car pulled into the yard of Alice's cottages. An older man in simple clothes and a broad-brimmed hat got out and looked around. He walked over to the door with the small sign that read 'office' and knocked at her door.

Alice came to the door and pulled the curtain aside. Then she let the curtain fall back and opened the door.

"Can I help you?"

"I'm looking for my son." the man said.

She looked the man in the face closely. "Mr. Miller?" she asked.

"Yes, you must be Alice. John told me all about you. You see, I have his address, but I just need to get some directions." Matt Miller said.

"Please, come in." she replied. "Can I get you a cup of tea, Mr. Miller?"

"Please, call me Matt. And, yes…a cup of tea would be very nice. Thank you."

"Have a seat. I have some apple pie. I made it yesterday from dried apples I picked in September. Would you like a slice?"

"That would be nice." he told his hostess.

Matt Miller walked around the room. It felt good to stretch his legs after the long drive. He looked at the photos on the wall, the framed embroidery, the picture of Jesus and the crucifix hanging above the doorway. He glanced out the window and watched men ice-fishing out on the lake.

Alice glanced out the door at the blue car. "You didn't bring Mrs. Miller with you?"

"No, she's not feeling well these days."

"You seem very quiet Mr. Miller...I mean Matt. I can sense that something's not quite right...tell me."

Matt Miller took two folded envelopes from his coat pocket.

24

When John arrived home from his day of sailing, he was surprised to see a blue car in his yard. As he got closer to the house he saw his father sitting on the front porch.

"Pa…I'm sure happy to see you."

"Hello, John."

"You wouldn't believe the day I've had." John noticed the somber look on his father's face. He suddenly felt a knot in his stomach.

"Pa? What are you doing here?"

"William was killed in the war."

John slumped back against the porch rail and slid down to the floor. "Oh no, Pa." John began to cry quietly.

"His body is being flown back. We'll bury him on that little hill where your grandparents are buried. We tried to call up here but couldn't get through." Matt Miller produced a letter from his pocket, still sealed, and gave it go John. John simply held the envelope, not knowing what to do.

His father continued, "I don't understand. He wrote to us and it sounded as if he would be home soon. It sounded as if the war was passing him by. I don't understand why this had to be our William…I don't understand."

John didn't know how to respond to his father. He was beginning to realize that he knew nothing about the war. It changed everyone who lived through it and everyone who didn't. It was as if in that very moment, the *glory* of war was gone. John opened the front door and the two men stepped inside.

25

Anthony rang the small bell on his nightstand furiously. He had been ringing it off and on for several minutes without a response. In anger he finally threw the bell at the door, just as Elizabeth was coming in. The noise jolted her and she entered the room cautiously.

"Anthony, I'm so sorry, what is it?" she pleaded.

"Damn! I had an accident, I'm sorry." he said, now calming.

"No, no, Anthony, that's why I'm here – to help. I'm just sorry I couldn't get here in time. Here, let me help with that." She pulled back his sheets as he looked away, out the window, obviously feeling embarrassed by the situation.

"It's alright, Anthony, I'll get a warm washcloth and towels, I'll be right back." With that, she left the room in a hurry with the wet sheets bundled in her arms. He continued to look out the window and a tear formed in his eye. Just then, Abby came down the hall and began to open his door.

"Don't come in here!" He shouted. She quickly shut the door and turned just as Elizabeth was coming down the hall with a bucket of warm water and towels.

"Don't go in there, Abby!" Elizabeth warned in a whispering tone.

"Okay, okay, I'm sorry – I didn't know." Abby returned to her room feeling a bit uncomfortable. Elizabeth hurried in to Anthony.

He could feel the warm washcloth over his private area, but as her hands moved over his legs he felt nothing. To lessen their awkward emotions she placed a dry towel over his midsection.

Anthony now watched her. "The bedpan was out of reach. I guess we shouldn't let that happen again."

She looked up at Anthony and smiled as she continued to wipe his legs. "Don't worry, first night home and all…we'll get it figured out." She assured him and he gave a weak smile. "We might as well get you dressed. Would you like to wear the brown slacks?" She pointed to a pair of pants she had picked out the night before and hung on his closet door.

"Yes, that'll be fine." His answer was instinctive. She knelt down to get his legs into the slacks. "Damn it, Elizabeth! When will the feeling come back to my legs?" He asked emotionally.

"Give it time, Anthony, the shrapnel tore things up near your spine. You were lucky to survive."

"Lucky, huh?" He looked out the window to the gray wetness that streaked the buildings in his view.

"Doctor Maguire wants to do the surgery, but we need to wait until the threat of doing more damage is behind us. Perhaps in another month. And in the meantime, you'll be surprised at how much your body will heal on its own." She looked up at him and then continued, "I promise, Anthony." He looked down at her with a solemn expression.

"After breakfast, we'll start working on it." he said with surety in his voice.

Sometime later, Elizabeth wheeled Anthony to the dining room. Abby took a few seconds before she could make eye contact.

"I'm sorry, sister, we were off to a bit of a rough start this morning."

"That's alright, Anthony, I...I didn't know." she said apologetically.

He smiled at her as Stephen came to the table and set a neatly-cut grapefruit in front of him.

"Thank you, Stephen." he said looking up. "Where's Father this morning?" He asked.

"Freddie has already taken him to the office. They were out of here by seven." Stephen replied.

"And what plans do you have for today, Abby?" Anthony asked.

"Nothing for this morning, but Freddie is picking me up later to go have lunch with Dad." She said with some excitement. "My life here...things here are so different." she added.

"And what would you be doing if you were still in Wisconsin?" Anthony asked.

"Well, right about now I'd be serving breakfast to my customers as the Spot Lunch. John would probably be sitting at the counter and smiling at me and I'd be topping off his coffee..." She smiled. At that moment, Stephen poured more coffee into her cup.

"That's it?" Anthony asked and then realized he might have insulted her in some small way, but before he could diminish the effect of his words, she spoke up.

"Oh, I know it doesn't seem like much of a life to you, but it's the only life I've known. Until father came along, my customers were like my family. And John..." She became quiet.

"Have you heard from John?" Anthony asked. Abby had told Anthony about John shortly after she met her brother.

Abby looked away and then back again as if she was ready to say something but she stopped. She didn't know what to say. She felt an aching in her heart and thinking of John this morning only made it hurt more.

Elizabeth joined Abby and Anthony at the table and placed her napkin on her lap.

Stephen returned from the kitchen with plates of eggs, bacon and toast for the brother and sister. Elizabeth was hoping to join in the conversation, but could sense that whatever words the two were having, must have been completed.

"Get plenty to eat, Anthony, we need to continue your stretches and training." She finally said with a smile. Anthony simply smiled at Elizabeth.

Abby crumbled her napkin and set it on her plate. "Excuse me, please." she said as she got up and left.

"What's the matter, Anthony?"

"Don't worry, she'll be alright. She's just missing someone. I told her once that she should find someone new, someone here in Chicago. I'll never mention that idea again! She must really be crazy about the guy." Anthony said.

26

It was late November and logs were now being pulled from the forest by teams of horses and large sleds. Tractors, even with chains proved futile in the unseasonably deep snow and if one got stuck it could waste a better part of the day to get it out. Living conditions in the bunkhouses was pretty bleak. The men who slept in the bunks below were too cold through the night, the men who slept in the bunks above, too hot. Keeping clean for the men was often too much of a challenge. The summer months meant grabbing a bar of soap, a towel and heading for the closest lake. The more concerned men would boil up water and sponge-bathe on a regular basis. The less concerned would just go without. Lice were a constant problem and when the men would do laundry, the surface of the water would be covered with the thick scum of floating lice. Communicating good hygiene habits to the men in different languages was a challenge but, John would try. Without seeing results, John could not tell if the men didn't understand or didn't care and so he resolved that there were just some of both.

John stopped in at the canteen and found Manuel staring off into space. "Manuel…hey, Manuel wake up." John called to him.

Manuel looked startled and then smiled. "Hello John." he said.

"Is there something wrong, Amigo?" John asked.

"You know…it is strange sometimes. You get a feeling that you can not explain…as if something is going to happen…you don't know what, but it is bad." Manuel spoke.

"Yes, I think I know that feeling. What do you think it is?" John asked.

"I do not know, but it gives me a chill, and so I was praying." Manuel said.

"Well, like most feelings it will probably go away." John said. With that, John filled his canteen with coffee and set off to work.

Arvin and James Krueger of the Krueger Lumber Company came to Anderson's office later that day. The father and son team owned and managed one of the larger lumber businesses in northern Wisconsin. A man in his early sixties with dark eyes and well-kept white hair, Arvin was born into the lumber business started by his grandfather. His son James never really knew hard times, but he knew hard work. His father had brought him up through the company starting out as a child bringing water to the jacks. There wasn't a timbered section of any northern county that Arvin's family did not know about. Prior to this visit, Krueger had been logging primarily in nearby Florence County. Now his crews had been working very close to property lines that bordered those of C. A. Anderson. Mr. Anderson produced a box of cigars. His son Charlie reached for one and Charles senior snapped the lid closed. "Guests first!" he said. Arvin and James each took a cigar from the box and then Mr. Anderson offered the box to Charlie.

The four men sat and smoked cigars, each one bragging to the other about how they were profiting from this unfortunate war. There was plenty of business for all of them. Mr. Anderson opened an oak cabinet and brought out a cut-glass decanter. He held his cigar in his teeth and pulled four glasses from the cabinet. Turning each over, he poured scotch from the decanter, filling each of the glasses half full. The men now drank to their success and glasses were re-filled more than once. Charlie and James made light conversation about college.

"You back up here for good?" James asked.

"Hell, no…probably for a year, learn the business, make some money and move back to Minneapolis." Young Anderson replied.

The older Anderson called to John who was working in his office in the back of the building, "John, come out here. I'd like you to meet a couple of scoundrels." The four men laughed loudly. John came out from the back office and introductions were made. By this time John was using his right hand more regularly and found that if he cautioned people as to his condition, he could shake hands right-handed.

"We're having a little something to take away the chill." Charlie said, and then poured a little scotch into a glass and gave it to John with a light-hearted wink. John looked over at Mr. Anderson and his face conveyed that he was looking for permission. Mr. Anderson gave a nod and John took a sip of the scotch.

Then as if to show John how the rich live, Charlie made an announcement. "Gentlemen, I just had one hell of an idea, let's see just how good a crew of scrubs you've got there at the Krueger Company and have ourselves a little contest."

"What you have in mind, Charlie?" The older Krueger asked.

"Let's say we see how much our men can harvest in a week, equal number of men and similar stands of timber." Charlie said.

Krueger said," You've piqued my interest Charlie." Then he turned to the elder Anderson. "What do you say Charles?"

"Well…I don't know. You rush men along and it usually results in waste and accidents." The older Anderson said.

Then James chimed in, "Only if there's betting involved…got to have a bet to make it worth the effort." Charlie and their guests were all in agreement and so finally Mr. Anderson acquiesced.

"John, grab some paper and a pen and write the terms of the contest." Charlie ordered.

"And what do you propose a suitable prize for the men whose crew produces the most logs cut at the end of seven days?" Mr. Krueger asked.

"Five thousand dollars seem fair to you?" Charlie asked. He gave a glance over to John to see reaction. John was a little shocked at how these men could throw their money around like this, but did nothing more than raise an eyebrow. His father would have had to break his back for a couple of years to earn that kind of money and these men treated it as pocket change.

"That's a lot of money…but it'll certainly make it worth the effort." Mr. Krueger said.

"Five thousand it is." Charlie answered for all of them.

John drafted up the conditions and wager and the two fathers signed. Then John signed as witness. The contest would start on Sunday at noon and end the following Sunday at noon. The sounding of the church bell in town would mark the end of the contest. John excused himself to return to his work and let the two competing families continue their conversations in private.

After Krueger left, Charlie called John back to their office. "John, I need you to drive out and get Nelson back here. I don't want to waste a minute preparing for this challenge. Today is Thursday. I want to find a good stand of timber with clear trails going in. I want the best men selected. I want all saws sharp and replacements ready so no one is left standing idle. I'll give you and Nelson both a little bonus for incentive when we win. In turn, Nelson can ride those men hard, promise them a few days off with pay, whatever it takes we're going to win this contest."

Charlie was now dishing out orders as if he already owned his father's company. His father let him assume some weight and was in a way, glad that his son was showing an interest. Even if it was the sport of competition, how was this any different from the way the world really ran?

John spoke up, "I can make sure we have the most efficient means of pulling the logs out, well-fed and fresh teams of horses, greased skids on the sleds if we have to, accurate measuring and regular counts to keep on track. I'll set up benchmarks so that we know we're on target, but sir, with all due respect, I don't need a bonus or incentive to do this. It's my job and I'd be happy with a little time off like the rest of the men."

Charlie said, "Nonsense John. A hundred bucks for you if we win…if we don't, well…"

John drove out to the camp where Nelson was and informed Nelson that C. A. wanted to see him right away. Nelson moved at a snail's pace just to piss John off, but after John left in his truck, Nelson hurried as quickly as he could.

Nelson pulled into the yard at Camp Nine. He hurried out of his truck stumbling and almost falling to the ground. He ran up the three steps to the porch of the office, entered and walked briskly up to Mr. Anderson's desk panting heavily.

"Yes, Mr. Anderson, Miller said you wanted to see me, sir." The fat man managed to get his words out before needing to gulp more air.

"No, I wanted to see you!" The young Anderson spoke. "Have a seat Nelson. We've got a challenge ahead of us and you're not going to foul it up." The young man said. Charlie Anderson went into the details of the contest.

Both companies had seven days to harvest as much timber they could. Measures would have to be set in place to make sure all men were kept honest. John was sent to Krueger's camp to make sure they started at noon and not a minute too soon. A brief inspection was carried out of the lumberman's camp to make sure that there had not been any stockpiling in advance. Krueger sent a man to Anderson's camp to make sure of the same. John held a pocket watch in his right hand and a shotgun pointed to the sky in his left hand. John shot one blast from the shotgun to mark the start and the men commenced cutting. The shot echoed and could be heard at Anderson's camp where Krueger's man too, shot into the air to signal the start of the great race. John headed toward his truck putting the shotgun into its case. He waved to James Krueger and wished him luck. Krueger acknowledged and replied in same.

In the days that followed the jacks felled trees as if they had as much at stake as Mr. Anderson. They took to their own betting and many men bet more than they had. The two lumber barons' had employed the aid of a local bookkeeper and accountant to keep track of the logs that were being brought into a clearing near the edge of town. Logs were measured for length and girth, carefully recorded and the results locked up in a safe every night. The jacks worked from sunup to sunset. The German prisoners were working just as hard as the other men, giving their best effort. Breaks were scarce, but John made sure the men were well rested, well fed and well motivated. Nelson on the other hand just wanted the men to work, work as if there wasn't a spare minute, then work some more. John found himself laboring harder to un-do the pressure that Nelson did each time he opened his mouth.

By the following Sunday each company had cut and stacked hundreds of trees of all species and sizes. Word spread quickly in the Northwoods and throughout the week people came from all of the neighboring counties to look at the field where the two companies had brought their timber. Bets were made and men scratched their chins trying to evaluate which man might be ahead. It was too close to tell. Now on this morning of the contest all men were working at full speed. The weather was warm for a winter's day and a thick, dense fog hung in the air.

The jacks worked in their wool shirts, buttons loosened to expose the whites of their long johns underneath. The pressure was on and no one put it there more than Nelson. He was not about to let anyone beat him and rob him of his prize. Anderson had offered Nelson fifty dollars if they won and a week off without pay, but plenty of humiliation in the town if they lost.

All hands were being used. Manuel the camp cook was recruited into driving a team of horses and sled. It was eleven o'clock and the sled that Manuel was in charge of was still being loaded. John closed in to look.

"Load anymore on this one and the team will never be able to pull it." John yelled to Nelson.

"They damn well better pull it." Nelson growled back. The men were strapping the chains over the top of the load and getting ready to send this load off.

"Overloading it is no assurance of getting it to the churchyard." John said.

"I'll show you my insurance." Nelson barked. He wrapped a chain around one more log and hooked it to the back of the sled.

"There's my insurance. That and the fact that he's going to take a shortcut across the lake." Nelson said with urgent pride.

"Manuel, don't listen to him. The ice is still too thin and this load is too heavy." John advised. Manuel looked at John and with silent concern, nodded in agreement.

Nelson came storming over and grabbed John by his collar. "You might be the new boss, Miller, but you ain't running *this* show. Young Anderson put me in charge of this contest." Nelson snapped. Nelson yelled to Manuel, "Boy, you better go across that lake as I say and you better do it now!" Nelson slapped the butt of the horse nearest him and yelled, "Go on. Go on. Go!"

The team of horses jerked hard against their harness and the sled began to move. Nelson continued to hit the horse with a large stick he had picked up from the ground and continued to yell as he struggled to run alongside. Manuel shook the reigns as the horses picked up momentum. Now the slack of the chain from the extra log that Nelson had added began to lessen and the last load of trees from the C. A. Anderson Company was on its way to the churchyard.

Nelson jumped into his truck and took off for town. The men were never told to stop, but could see that they had done their jobs right up to the end and started to rest. John too got into his truck and headed for town with a few of the men in back. The Anderson's and Krueger's were already there, each of them strutting around the log piles and assessing the results. Krueger's last load had arrived and the men began to unload and stack the logs and count. The rules clearly called out that logs still left on a sled were not to be included. Mr. Anderson began to look a little concerned and checked his pocket watch.

Nelson arrived at the yard and hesitated to get out of his truck. It was now eleven-thirty and even at full pace they would need twenty of those minutes to unload and stack the logs. John arrived at the yard and carried his clipboard with him as he approached the auditors. John checked and double-checked the numbers. It was hard to believe, but with the last load coming they would actually pull ahead and win. It was eleven forty-five and Nelson was pacing back and forth. He smoked a short cigar and swore under his breath about what he was going to do to *that Mexican*. John was worried and thought it best to drive back down deerskin road to locate the last load. Anderson was beginning to shake his head in doubt and occasionally sent angry stares over to Nelson who did his best to avoid them.

John drove fast but carefully in the dense fog expecting at any time to see the team of horses coming north toward him. There was no team in sight and John came closer and closer to the Lake Road. They probably got stuck or ended up spilling the load with all of that weight, John thought to himself. He turned right on Lake Road and now was sure that something had gone wrong. He saw plenty of hoof prints on the road, but he knew they could have been from any previous load. He pulled up within viewing distance of the clearing at the north end of the lake and could see no tracks coming from the ice. John turned the truck around and looked at his watch. Five minutes to twelve, they had lost the contest. John drove around the lake to the south end where they loaded the last load. John got out of his truck and walked over to the men still resting.

"Well, did we win?" one of the men asked.

"Afraid it doesn't look that way. Did Manuel come back out this way?" John asked.

"No sir." Another man replied. John now began running out on to the ice following the tracks left by the team of horses and their burden. The snow made a sloshing sound beneath each step and he kicked up wet slush with his knee-high boots. John could finally make out the log and taut chain that Nelson had hooked to the sled. 'Probably got stuck.' John thought, John hoped. He slowed his pace and steadied his breath so that he could hear the sound of the horses – no sound. John stopped in his tracks as he realized the inevitable, the unthinkable. They had gone through the ice. The water was clear and now John could make out something floating several feet below the surface of this shallow lake, the body of Manuel trapped in the reins of the harness. John stood there frozen as the hair from the mains of the horses moved slowly around in the current of the clear water. Just then he heard the church bells. John got down on one knee in the wet snow and bowed his head in prayer.

27

A large crowd was assembled as Abby joined her father at a ribbon-cutting ceremony at the Copley Hospital. She was proud to stand beside her father and hospital dignitaries as they took turns giving brief speeches about the hospital expansion they were dedicating this morning. They told the people, including several reporters, of how they would now be better able to serve the community as their heroic sons returned from the war, many in need of ongoing medical treatment. Abby was introduced to many men and women who all flattered her as the beautiful daughter of such a generous man, a pillar of the community. She could not begin to remember all of their names and could only associate them by the furs they were wearing. At one point she had to excuse herself to find a place where she could gather her thoughts and take a moment to cope with the culture shock.

After the speeches and formalities were concluded, Abby sat with her father at a large table where cake and coffee were being served. A man in his mid-twenties dressed in a brown suit approached Abby and leaned over the table. He extended his hand.

"Miss Baker, my name is Robert Edgerton." he said with a smile. Abby put her fork down and extended her hand which he gently took and held. "I work for your father and wanted to take this opportunity to meet you." He continued to hold her hand; something she wasn't used to. It wasn't an entirely bad feeling, just something new and she was becoming accustomed to many new things.

She smiled, nodding her head slightly and then finally just said, "Hello."

"Your father has told me quite a bit about you."

"Oh, did he?" She responded, not knowing what else she could or should say.

"Oh, nothing too personal, just that you're new to Chicago and spent your entire life in the Northwoods of Wisconsin." He spoke with a broad and bright smile and his brown eyes made Abby feel very comfortable and at ease. He had brown hair that was very neatly combed and a clean-shaven face. When he smiled, Abby noticed the slight dimples and laugh lines that formed on his face. She didn't say a word as she smiled and studied his features. "That must have been an entirely different world for you." he said after several seconds of unusual silence.

She finally reacted. "Yes, yes, it is a different world. It's very beautiful up there and I'm beginning to miss it." She said these words as if she meant it entirely, but somewhere deep down inside, for now, she really wasn't missing the north as much as she was missing John.

She had been watching people since the moment she set foot on the train weeks ago. At first the people looked like anybody she had ever seen in her life. They wore coats and boots, hats and scarves. Every time the train stopped, people would leave and more people would get on. Each time the people changed, their clothes changed, their voices and expressions changed, the things they talked about changed. Conversations about the cold weather and lumbering gave away to conversations about the cold weather and farming. Eventually the people looked completely different and their conversations were about banking, finance and industry. The men smoked cigars and talked about the economy, labor unions and how their stocks were performing. The women talked about parties and shopping, their help and how they were waiting for the war to be over so that they could take a vacation again.

Now, Abby was watching the man in front of her as he tried to carry on a conversation. She knew she wasn't making it easy for him, but she didn't know what to say. Had he been a customer at the Spot Lunch, she might have asked him about the ice fishing or deer hunting. If she was behind the comfort of her counter she could imagine all sorts of things she could talk about with him. And if they needed time to think of something else to think about, she could simply give him a wink and go wait on another customer. Finally, she came back to the world.

"And what is it that you do for my father's company?" she asked proudly.

He took a breath, relieved that she was responding to his presence.

"I'm Vice President of Marketing." he said proudly. Abby was a bit uncomfortable as she wasn't sure what marketing was all about. She just smiled, nodding her head as she often did. It wasn't to acknowledge that she understood so much as it was to let him know that she was listening and he could continue. "My department launches new products, creates advertising strategies, public relations..." He looked into her eyes hoping she would continue to give him that slight nod as she had been doing.

"Of course." She said simply and then noticed a bead of sweat forming on his brow.

"Would you mind if I call you?" he asked.

Abby was suddenly and completely disconnected from the conversation and responded before thinking about the effect of her response as she plainly responded. "What for?"

The young man would have been wounded mortally if this were combat, but it was a ceremony. He was a part of it because he worked for the company that had made a sizeable contribution that resulted in making this event possible. Robert was a confident young man and he had a position of authority and influence. He was taken back by her reaction. The first thought that ran through his mind was that this woman would be a challenge and so worth the effort it would take to get to know her.

"Perhaps I would call to ask you to participate in some upcoming public relation events, reading to patients at the children's hospital, appearances at social events that put the company in a good light, things like that." There was a pause, and then he continued, "Or perhaps you might like to have someone show you the town." He looked so secure as he spoke, so sure of his words and intentions.

She felt warm suddenly and her first instinct was to remove her hat and let her hair down so that the heat would escape her, but she didn't want to draw attention to herself. John was always on her mind, but she was intrigued by this man. She realized that she would need time to sum up the feelings that were pulling her in two different directions. For some reason now, she wanted him to leave.

"Yes, I'd love to. You can get my number from father's assistant, Joan." She couldn't believe what she had just said. She felt like some woman out of a movie, someone completely different from Abby Spence. She felt smug and in control although she knew she wasn't. And so why not continue with the impression. "Now, if you'll excuse me." she said. She picked up her coffee cup and delicately brought it to her lips. She had now moved ahead in this little game.

The smile was gone from Robert's face. "Yes, of course... thank you so much, Miss Baker. I'll give you a call then." he said as he studied her eyes.

Robert stood up and nodded politely at Abby and then smiled again. She gave a hint of a smile and suddenly he was gone. She discretely picked up her napkin and waved it in front of her face to cool herself.

28

The men of the camp took Manuel's death hard. Although the exchange of dialogue was limited because of their language barrier, the men spoke in other ways and their message was always understood. They knew Manuel to be a good-hearted man who would hurt no one. In a way that seemed a little selfish the men would miss his cooking, but more than that, they would miss his familiar smile. No one took it harder than Steeg. In his own soft-spoken ways, Steeg had formed a bond with Manuel. Steeg would miss his little Mexican friend and, together with John, would make sure that a letter was sent to his family back in Mexico City.

Mr. Anderson took the death of Manuel in a different way - with guilt. Anderson kept to himself in the days following the accident. When he would see John he would hesitate to make eye contact and tried to avoid talking about what had happened. Charlie on the other hand, seemed more upset about losing the contest, the money and his right to brag.

The funeral ceremony took place at Saint Mary's Church of Phelps, a small white clapboard Catholic Church where Manuel attended when he could. The service was officiated by Father Roots, a stoic man of German descent whose sermons were typically of fire and brimstone. John, Steeg and four other men served as pallbearers. The service was simple and the casket seemed light, but the hearts of every man in attendance were heavy with grief. Each man knew it could just as easily have been him who took the fateful orders that day. John had driven Mr. Anderson to the service in Mr. Anderson's car and the two men sat in the back of the church. Conspicuously absent was Nelson, the man who ordered Manuel to make that foolish journey across the thin ice of the lake on that early winter day. Manuel was buried later that morning in the church cemetery. Mr. Anderson had taken care of the arrangements including a modest headstone that read, "Manuel Ochoa – Mexico". After the ceremony John drove Anderson back to his home.

"Thank you for paying for the funeral and headstone C. A." John said.

"Well, you have to do these things when you lose a man. It's your obligation. Did you get word off to his family in Mexico?" Mr. Anderson asked.

"Yes, sir, they will try to make the journey up here in the summer to have a small ceremony of their own." John replied.

"Well, they'll have a pleasant surprise when they get here." Anderson said. John asked why.

"I own most of the land in Section 17 including that lake where we lost him. There was no name for the lake but there is now – Manuel Lake." Anderson said with some pride in what he'd done.

John pulled over and stopped the car extending his hand to shake. "That's a very fine and decent gesture C.A., I'm sure his family will appreciate it."

"The contest, the bet…it was all a stupid idea - one that I accepted against my better judgment…I feel responsible." Mr. Anderson said softly. Anderson shook John's hand as he had many times in the past, this time with a little more feeling.

"I'm going to take a few weeks of vacation, John. My daughters, wife and I will be taking a trip to Europe. Then I'll be attending to a few business interests back in Minneapolis when

I return before the holidays. I was going to leave Charlie here to run things but the truth is, he doesn't know much about the operation…and sad to say, doesn't care to know much! You'll be in charge of the operation and I'll call long-distance when I can to check on things. Fair 'nuff'? Anderson asked.

John looked Anderson straight in the eye and responded, "Yes sir, you'll have nothing to be concerned about here."

"I'm sure of that John. Charlie and I will ride to the train station in Eagle River tomorrow morning. Train leaves at eight a.m. I've made a list of things that need to be looked after and you know where all the books are. I know you'll do a good job, John." Anderson said with a slight smile. The first he smiled since the death.

"I'll set about looking for a new cook." John said.

"I've already taken care of that. Arvin Krueger has a woman coming over in a day or two. Name's Hanna…from Hurley, big woman with a good temper. Krueger gave her your name. She'll give a call to the office when she gets into town. She'll need a ride out to the camp. Have the office ladies get all of her personnel information and get her on the payroll." Anderson said.

"Yes sir." John responded.

"Well, John, take good care of things." Anderson said. With that, Mr. Anderson went to his car, giving a simple wave of his hand as he drove away.

A few days after the funeral John was working in his office when one of the office ladies called in.

"John, our new cook's at the train station, says you're to pick her up. Where's she going to be staying? You can't very well have her bunking with the men now can you?"

"Good point,…but I wish you would have said something the other day." John said lightheartedly. "We'll get her a room at Alice's until we get around to partitioning off a room from the west end of the big bunkhouse." John suggested.

The day was unseasonably warm and John enjoyed his drive to Eagle River. He immediately saw Hanna sitting on the bench outside the station. John sounded the horn and waved. Hanna stood up. She stood tall and broad. She was a large woman wearing a man's hat with ear flaps tied up, red wool coat and trousers. She had a large trunk and a suitcase. If she hadn't been the only person sitting at the station John might have had a hard time telling it was her. She gave a nod, picked up her suitcase with one hand and grabbed the handle of her trunk with another. John got out of the truck and walked toward her to give a hand.

"Hello, you must be Hanna…nice to meet you." he said, extending his hand to shake.

She set the trunk down and extended her hand to shake his. "Nice to meet you." she said.

"Let me get that trunk for you." John offered.

"Awfully heavy…brought some of my own pots and pans… don't like cooking with strange pans. I got it." she said. She grabbed the handle of the trunk and dragged it effortlessly to the pickup truck. John opened the tailgate and she slung it onto the bed of the truck in one motion. She tossed her suitcase alongside and climbed into the cab of the truck. The drive back to the camp seemed long, Hanna had little to say and John was getting tired of trying to carry the conversation alone.

John and Hanna arrived at the camp. John took Hanna to the kitchen and introduced her to the two helpers. She gave a nod and went about inspecting the kitchen. The helpers already had a large pot of beans on to boil for supper and were doing their best to bake bread.

'Would you like me to give you a ride to Alice's to get settled in? John asked. Then realizing that he hadn't explained very well, he continued, "It's a group of cottages near town. We took the liberty of getting you a room there until we could get things set up properly for you here."

"Men coming in for supper soon?" she asked.

"Well, actually the men will be here in about an hour." John replied.

"Then, no time to waste, we got a meal to cook." Hanna said.

John went to the office to do some work and Hanna set about instructing the help how she wanted things set. There was no disagreement from these two. She meant business. An hour later Hanna gave the order to ring the dinner bell and the men started coming in.

One of the men saw Hanna and gave out a yell. He went right up to her and said, "Look boys…a woman, we got us a woman cook!" Hanna nodded and gave a little smile. As the man turned around Hanna hit him hard across the back of the head with a cast iron frying pan. The man dropped to the floor. Every man in the canteen stopped what they were doing and stared.

"Anyone else care to make a comment like that?" Hanna asked. There wasn't a sound made.

"I thought so! Eat up boys!" Hanna shouted. The men continued to grab their plates and get in line, stepping over the man lying on the floor.

In the following weeks the men made many adjustments. They had dealt with death in the camp before. Steeg took Manuel's death harder than the others. Steeg was upset and felt like he was ready to break. He knew that Nelson was responsible for Manuel's death. Maybe not directly, but had Nelson not pushed so hard and forced his friend to take the load across the lake this would not have happened. Each day that passed made Steeg angrier inside until he could no longer take it.

29

On Saturday morning, Robert Edgerton stood at his bathroom mirror brushing on a splash of cologne. He was impeccably dressed in a new black pin-striped suit, white pressed shirt with French cuffs and a blue silk tie with streaks of a silver design threaded all through. Earlier, he had polished his black wing-tip shoes so brightly that he could almost see his determined face in the reflection as he buffed every inch.

Robert shared his apartment with another man of roughly the same age, Harry Sieger, an old classmate from college. Harry worked as a patent attorney for a well-established firm in Chicago. Although he was still considered young when compared to his aged associates in the firm, he was beginning to see more and more of the larger cases that came through. Harry didn't take himself quite as seriously as Robert. He had a few extra pounds which he considered a sign of success and wore his black hair combed forward and to the side to conceal his receding hairline. Harry seemed to smoke incessantly although the smoke often stung his eyes. It was the one bad habit he allowed himself to have in the otherwise meticulous apartment. Harry sat on the brown mohair couch reading the Tribune as Robert primped in the mirror.

"So, tell me more about your date!" Harry yelled loud enough to be heard.

"Well, it's not a *date* per se, it's more of a rendezvous. Meeting her for coffee and then a cab ride around the city to show her the sites."

"Sounds like a date to me." Harry mumbled as he turned the pages looking for business opportunities. "Is she a beauty?" Harry shouted back.

"Incredible! And if the old senses are still working like they were back in college days, as pure as the driven snow of the Northwoods!" Robert said proudly.

"A virgin? Robert, you are a devil! Do you suspect the young lady knows that she doesn't stand a chance with you?" Harry joked.

Robert paused for a second, then tilted his head to the left and slicked his hand back across his hair one last time. Satisfied, he came walking into the living room.

"Oh, I'm taking my time with this one. *'Love them and leave them'* is not a part of this plan…not this time. This one is special – very special."

This comment invoked a loud laugh from Harry.

"Do you have any idea how often I've heard you say that?" Then Harry pretended to take a small notebook from his shirt pocket and acted as if he were paging through it. "Let me see here…hmmm…no, no….no…hmmm…looks to me like you've used that line about ten thousand times, my friend."

Robert picked up a section of the newspaper that was scattered on the coffee table, rolled it up and struck a pose as if he were ready to strike his victim. Harry raised his arms as if to defend himself from the apparent attack and then Robert placed the paper back onto the table. He shook his finger at Harry as if to scold him. Harry laughed and then picked up the rolled paper that Robert had just set down, unrolled it and began to comb through the columns looking for something of interest.

"Well, you may be close in your calculation my dear, Harry. However, this one is special in one way that none of the others have ever been…or ever will be." Robert used his words to entice the obvious curiosity from Harry.

Harry looked up from the paper with an inquisitive expression, waiting for more. "Alright, I'm hooked, what is so incredibly special about this girl?" he asked.

"Her old man owns Baker Medical!" Robert spoke as if the victory was already his.

"Jesus, Robert, you son of a gun!" Harry sat, shaking his head in amazement.

"Now you see what I mean by *special*." Robert spoke with surety. Then he sat in the mohair chair next to the couch, and began to put on his black wing-tips.

"So are you going to win her with love or with sex?" Harry asked inquisitively.

Robert raised one eyebrow as he smiled at his friend. "Maybe a little of both." He finally said.

"You lucky bastard!" Harry shook his head in disbelief.

At ten o'clock, Robert was sitting at a table near the large window in the café Atwood on Washington street. He appeared calm as he read the newspaper with indifference. He peered over the top of his paper from time to time, looking for Abby. Eventually a long, black limousine pulled up to the curb. A neatly-dressed chauffer hurried out from behind the wheel and moved around the back of the car to the rear passenger's side door.

Abby was still getting accustomed to being driven and made a conscious effort not to open her own door, something that took great restraint on her part. Freddie opened her door and took her hand. She wore a light blue dress beneath her black wool coat. Her head was covered in a large soft wool hat that matched her coat.

"Please, be careful of the snow, Miss Abby." Freddie cautioned her as he helped her out of the car and safely onto the icy sidewalk.

"Thank you, Freddie." she replied.

"Shall I walk you to the door?" Freddie asked. Abby gave him a smile.

"No thank you, Freddie, I can manage from here." she said.

"It's pretty icy, Miss Abby, I'd feel better if I escorted you in." Freddie was not accustomed to driving a young lady around the city and the thought occurred to him that if anything happened to her, he would be responsible. He thought that it would be a good idea to get a look at the gentleman who was going to be taking her out for the day.

"Alright then." she said as she stood on the sidewalk.

Café Atwood was situated next to the Palmer House, a very famous Chicago hotel located in the heart of the business and theatre district. Freddie closed the door and gave a folded dollar to the doorman from the hotel who approached. The doorman of the hotel was familiar with Freddie as he would often come to pick up clients of Baker Medical and drive them to the company headquarters for meetings. He would make sure that the car was not ticketed while parked for a few minutes at the curb.

Freddie walked with Abby and darted ahead to open the door of the café for her.

"Are you sure you wouldn't rather have me drive you around this morning, Miss?"

"That's a nice thought, Freddie, but I believe Mister Edgerton has made arrangements. And besides, Anthony might want to get out of the apartment today for some fresh air."

"Yes, Miss Abby, but if you need me to come pick you up, you just call Stephen, okay?"

"Yes, Freddie, I will do that, thank you."

Freddie stayed by the door just long enough to get a good look at the man who had just set down his newspaper and stood.

"Miss Baker, so nice to see you again." Robert reached for her hand which she eventually produced. He gently held her hand for a few seconds. He smiled at her and she smiled kindly in return.

"Hello, Robert...you may call me Abby." she said. He had been wondering how long it was going to take for him to win that privilege.

"Thank you, Abby." The couple sat at the table.

"Perhaps you'd care for a cup of coffee, a dessert?" he offered.

"No, nothing for me, thanks...maybe a glass of water."

Robert signaled to the waiter and motioned to his glass of water. The waiter nodded and in a moment, produced a glass of ice water, placing it on a cloth napkin in front of Abby.

"Well then, are you ready for a tour of the city?" He asked her. It seemed like a strange thing to ask since this is why she was meeting him and so he quickly continued, "I thought we'd start off with the Shed Aquarium, they have an incredible variety of exhibits of sea life from around the world."

"Does it cost much?" Abby quickly caught herself, uncomfortable by what she had just asked. Richard gave her a curious look and a slight laugh until he saw her obvious embarrassment.

"Oh, don't worry, today is on me. And besides, your father's company makes quite generous donations to all of the museums annually." he quickly added. Abby was eager to change the subject.

"And then?" she asked.

"We'll have lunch at a very nice hotel downtown and off to the Field Museum. From there, we'll just cab around the city a bit so that I can show you a few of the larger landmarks." He was beginning to feel more at ease as Abby took a sip of her water.

"I'd like to be back by three if that's possible." Abby said.

"Oh...absolutely. I have a cab waiting, so anytime you're ready." His expression was friendly and his words polite. Suddenly, Abby felt a little less tense.

"Alright then, let's go." she said.

The couple toured the aquarium and Abby was absolutely enthralled with everything that she saw. Robert's gait was a little more brisk than Abby's as he had been to the aquarium dozens of times since he was a child. Eventually he was able to realize that Abby had never been to such an exhibit before and he slowed his pace to meet hers. He took a deep breath and made a concerted effort to relax and let her absorb everything she was seeing for the first time. It was not an easy task for him as his whole existence was based upon packing as much into every minute of his day as he could. He was an ambitious man, but today he could slow his stride if that meant getting what he wanted.

Later that afternoon at the Field Museum, Abby paused to look at her watch.

"Oh, my goodness, Robert, it's almost four o'clock. I'm sorry." she said.

"You have nothing to be sorry for, Abby. This is your day. But if you'd like to leave, it's not a problem." His words were comforting to Abby.

"If you don't mind. I have a few things I'd like to do at home before evening." she said apologetically.

"Not at all, Abby. That's the nice thing about the museum, it'll be here for us another day." He put his arm around hers and with his right hand, pointed to a hallway.

"If we go down this hallway, it'll lead us to the main lobby. We can grab our coats and have you back within the hour. Traffic should be light around this time."

Abby considered for a moment about the fact that she had not thought about John all day. The notion made her feel a twinge of guilt and her mind's survival method for dealing with guilt was to tell herself that John probably wasn't thinking of her either.

That evening in his apartment, Robert lounged on the sofa reading "The Moon Is Down" by John Steinbeck. Robert found it difficult to focus as his thoughts would turn to Abby with the turn of every page. He heard a key in the lock and knew that his roommate was home.

"Robert! Let me set my things down and then tell me all about your day." Harry said with a devilish smile. Robert acted annoyed, but was anxious to tell Harry about his time with the boss's daughter. In a couple of minutes, Harry came into the room, having replaced his coat and jacket with a button-up sweater. He sat on the soft, pillowed brown chair and leaned forward putting his elbows on his knees.

"And...?" was all he asked.

"She's incredible, Harry. She has the most beautiful eyes..."

"What color?"

"Brown, I think...maybe hazel. And a smile that could melt any man's heart."

"Did she melt yours, Robert?" Harry asked with a raised eyebrow.

"The only thing that melts my heart is what I can put in the bank – you ought to know that!"

"So, you want to go out and meet up with a few girls at the bar tonight?" Harry asked.

"You bet, just let me get through to the end of this chapter." Robert replied. "It just might be that the only good thing about this war is that there are just so many beautiful women left behind." Harry let out a laugh and Robert smiled.

30

It was late in the evening and Nelson had just eaten at the canteen. Although he had a wife back home on the other side of Big Twin Lake, he liked getting a free meal any time that he could. When Manuel was cook, Nelson used to go behind the counter and help himself to an extra plate most nights to take home to his wife. Hanna wouldn't let Nelson behind the counter and had slapped the top of his hand hard more than once with the large enamel serving spoon. She'd give him a scowl and bare her teeth. This night she was in a better mood and figured since the food was for Nelson's wife that she'd put a plate together for the woman herself.

Nelson carried the covered plate with him and walked across the yard that separated the canteen from the office where his truck was parked. A dark figure came out from behind Nelson's truck and before he could notice, Nelson was struck hard with a steel pipe. A man wearing a scarf around his face to conceal his identity had knocked Nelson down and he hit the ground hard, his plate of food fell from his hand and hit against the side of the truck spewing potatoes, gravy and vegetables against the truck door. The masked man struck him a few more times with the steel pipe and then tossed it aside. He then knelt over the struggling man hitting him hard with his fists. Everything was a blur to Nelson as he tried to keep his eyes open, holding his head up slightly and for a moment grasped the left fist of his assailant. He held it long enough to see a ring and then the right fist struck and his head flew back hitting the ground. The attack continued until Nelson was motionless.

Some time later one of the jacks came out of the canteen and something caught his attention. He ran over to Nelson and knelt down at his side. Nelson's face was swollen, bruised and bloody. The worker ran back to the canteen shouting for help. More men came running out. One man held his ear down close to Nelsons face to listen for any signs of life.

"He's breathing, he's alive!" The man shouted. Hanna came out from the kitchen to see what was going on wiping her hands on her apron. The men wrestled to get the limp and fat man onto the back of his truck. Finding his keys on the ground, two of the men rode in the cab of the truck and two more sat on the back. One man held Nelson's head on his lap so that they didn't end up doing any more damage to the man on the way to the doctor's office in town. As much as the men despised Nelson, he was still a human being and basic human emotions told them that they had to help him. They didn't want another death in the camp even if it was the man who made their lives a daily hell.

The men pulled up to the doctor's office sounding the horn. A light was on and the doctor came downstairs from his apartment above his office to see who was in need of help. It was not uncommon to treat logging accidents, but this was the evening and this emergency came at the doctor's time to rest.

"What have we got here?" the doctor asked excitedly.

"Man's been beaten." one of the men said.

"I can't treat him here. He's got broken bones. Follow me, we have to take him to the hospital in Eagle River." The doctor said.

Nelson would be at the hospital for the next ten days. The swelling in his face had not been reduced by much and there were stitches and two very blackened eyes. There was a large cut on his forehead as well as cuts on his lip and one by his eye that took seven stitches. His left arm was broken from one of the first blows and his right arm was sprained when he tried to break his fall. Nelson's wife Agnes came to see him daily and helped to feed him. She was a small woman, very simple in her dress and appearance. She wore wire-rimmed glasses and a head scarf. She almost never wore make-up, her husband didn't approve. Once when they were dating, when she thought she had done a wonderful job of putting on some lipstick and blush, he told her she looked like a whore. She couldn't remember anymore what it felt like to feel pretty.

Now she could only remember what it felt like to be the wife of Robert Nelson and it wasn't often a feeling she was proud to have. She had her troubles with this man and she had learned to ignore his awful habits, his laughing with a mouth full of food, and the way he snored as he would fall asleep in his chair in the evenings. Sometimes just the way he walked across the room was enough to make her cringe, but he was her husband. She had made a commitment and the arrangement called for "better or worse". She felt sorry for him, for being the way he had become and now she felt sorry for his pain. When she looked in the mirror she saw a woman who was plain and her smile wasn't convincing, even to herself. There weren't many men to choose from in the north. She was sorry that she was desperate and afraid of being left alone, but more often she was sorry that she married him. She had to remember way back to when he was a younger man, when he displayed more manners, more respect and more love. They never had children, something that Agnes often felt sad about. Agnes never got her driver's license and it caused such an inconvenience for her. She had to walk everywhere or ask neighbors for rides so that she could earn a little extra income. She had wanted to learn how to drive, but Nelson told her long ago that she didn't need to.

During her visits to him in the hospital, he would barely say a word. Agnes made the effort of bringing him simple books and magazines to read knowing he would probably only look at the pictures and read an occasional caption if something had caught his interest. Nelson hadn't finished high school. There were many men in this area who were not able to complete high school. They had to help support a family by working on the family farm, in factories or in the forest. Men of determination could still find a way to better themselves despite the lack of a formal education. For Nelson, reading was a challenge and even simple math was something the office ladies were for. He loathed those who succeeded where he failed and books were only a reminder of his frustration. Agnes only kept a few books in the house and would often only read when he was at work or asleep.

It would be two more weeks before the swelling around his eyes would go down enough for him to return to work. Word went around the camp that Nelson had returned. The men passed around a card that most men had all signed welcoming him back. A few names were conspicuously missing. John took up a collection to help the couple out and this effort barely raised ten dollars. John asked Mr. Anderson for permission to take a few dollars from the petty cash box so that the donation wouldn't seem like some kind of cruel joke.

It was now a few days before Christmas and John asked Hanna if she would take some food to the Nelson's with one of the company trucks. Hanna prepared a box of food, beans, venison, a few loaves of bread that she had baked and some cookies. She drove to the Nelson home and knocked at the door.

Agnes pulled the curtain back to see who was there and seeing that it was a woman, felt safe enough to open the door. "Yes?" she asked.

Hanna spoke with a voice unnaturally deep and husky for a woman. "My name's Hanna, Mrs. Nelson…I come from the Anderson Lumber Company…brought you some food to help out until…" She struggled with her words. "Trying to help out any way that we can." she said.

"Oh my, that's wonderful. I'm so glad…my name's Agnes, please come in, come in. This is so nice of you." she said.

Hanna brought the box in and set it on the kitchen table and looked around. The kitchen was sparse, only a few quart jars of canned food setting on the counter. She glanced into the refrigerator as Agnes put the venison away and saw that there wasn't much there. Hanna surmised that this was the home of people in need, but questioned where the paycheck went that Nelson brought home each week.

"I can bring more…Agnes." Hanna said.

Agnes took the edge of her apron and wiped away a few tears. "I don't know how to thank you…this is wonderful, just wonderful." the woman said.

Then Hanna did something that she was not used to doing and hadn't done in a very long time. She awkwardly put her arms out to embrace Agnes. Agnes wrapped her arms around Hanna and began sobbing. Hanna wrapped her arms around Agnes.

"That's alright dear…you go ahead and cry." Hanna said as she slowly and gently tilted her head over the top of Agnes's head. She smelled Agnes's hair and closed her eyes.

Mr. Anderson had been traveling in Europe and had just returned for the holidays. John had not spoken with his employer since before the beating. This day he called long-distance to Mr. Anderson at his home in Minneapolis. He told his boss about the beating and that they had no clues as to who was responsible. Anderson was distraught the report. He had two men in the past year and now his wood boss was out for over three weeks. Anderson expressed his faith in John and that he was confident that they would get through all of this. Life at the camp would go on.

John had set about re-configuring the work teams. Each team would have a fair mix of older men, German prisoners and younger men, mostly boys. John gave direction to the crews, putting together their assignments the night before. John also instituted a reward system that was based upon the number of accident-free work days. He was careful to make sure that the men were well-rested and this helped to keep the men more alert. The crews worked with very little supervision and John was cautious to downplay the fact that production had actually gone up in the past few weeks that Nelson had been out. Nelson would soon be returning to the camp.

John spent the Christmas holiday with his parents on the farm. Matt and Katherine were happy to see their son although it seemed like a somber occasion. John thought about how wonderful the Christmas before had been, when he spent the day with Abby. There hadn't been a word from Bill in some time and they could see that something was troubling John. John told them about the death of Manuel and the beating of the wood boss. Katherine expressed her concern over John's safety in such a dangerous occupation. That night, Matt and Katherine talked in bed about John. It seemed like he was carrying the weight of the world on his shoulders while the rich men who owned such companies made outlandish bets that endangered men's lives. What kind of world was this?

31

Anthony browsed through a magazine in a small hospital room as he passed the time waiting for his x-rays to be processed. It was a small waiting room near Doctor Maguire's office with walls that were a light yellow above and a pale green below. The radiator made the room very warm and the window was only open a few inches as it had been painted a few too many times and couldn't be opened any further. As depressing as the room might have seemed to others awaiting the results of a x-ray exam, Anthony didn't mind, he was home from the war and anything was better than where he had been a year earlier. Elizabeth came into the room.

"I brought you a glass of apple juice, Anthony. It was that, or coffee and I know how that's been keeping you awake lately." she said as she sat down next to him.

"Thanks, Liz." Anthony smiled at Elizabeth as he reached for the glass.

"Oh, and I didn't know if you were hungry and so I brought you a sandwich. It's chicken salad with lettuce. If you're not hungry, I'll give it to Freddie." she said.

"Oh, no, you don't, I'm starving! Thanks, Liz." He quickly took the sandwich from her. "And besides, Freddie keeps a stockpile of snacks under his car seat!"

"Still waiting huh? It shouldn't be too much longer. I'll go see if I can hurry them along." she said as she stood up.

"Oh, no, Liz, stay here with me. There's no hurry. Sit down, relax, stay with me." he said.

She sat back in the mission-styled chair next to Anthony. She moved the chair a few inches from his wheelchair, making sure to leave enough room for Anthony to maneuver easily. She opened her purse and took out a compact, opened it and checked her makeup.

"Why do you do that?" Anthony asked with a smile.

"What do you mean? A girl's got to look her best, doesn't she?"

"You always look great, Liz." he said without looking up from his sandwich as if he were a little shy about saying it.

"Why, thank you, Anthony. That's quite a compliment coming from a…" She stopped mid-sentence.

"From a what?" There was a pause as she closed her mouth and smiled. "Go on, Liz, from a what?" he repeated.

"From such a handsome man as yourself. There, I said it. I wasn't going to, I'll have you know. I have been trying to keep a sense of decorum in our relationship."

Anthony enjoyed hearing this. He was looking at her now and she was blushing, bewildered as to what could be said next. He was technically her employer and didn't want to jeopardize her profession. Should there ever be a dispute between them, it would certainly hurt her reputation with the hospital if there were mention of any incident that was less than professional. He continued to smile and she shifted in her seat.

"Oh, stop that now, Anthony. Change the subject." She spoke as if scolding a child.

"No, I don't think I'm letting you off the hook so easily." he said with a boyish grin.

Doctor Maguire stepped into the room, a clipboard tucked under his elbow.

"Thank God." she whispered in a low tone.

"Well, Anthony, you've made my job a little easier today." the doctor said.

"Why's that?" Anthony asked.

"From what I can tell, I think there's a good amount of healing that has taken place. That crack that we saw a few weeks ago, the one at the corner of the vertebrae, it appears to have fused and so we don't have to worry about that breaking loose and doing damage to the nerves."

"What about my legs?" Anthony asked, his expression now solemn.

"I'd say your chances are much better than what I was suspecting weeks ago. You seem to be getting your strength back slowly and that's good. Your leg muscles have atrophied from not being able to use them, however, there is still nerve damage and we have no way of knowing if the nerves will heal. The spine is very complex."

"And so what do I do in the meantime?" Anthony asked.

"It appears that whatever you and your nurse here have been doing is helping your progress. You seem robust and in good spirits – I say we give it a few more weeks. A good daily routine of exercise and healthy eating is going to continue to be of benefit."

"Well then, that's it?" Anthony asked. The doctor placed his hand on Anthony's shoulder.

"I'm being straight with you, Anthony. Give it time. You made sergeant at an early age. That was no easy task, I'm sure. If I'm not mistaken, you probably did that by applying yourself physically and mentally to the challenges that were placed before you. This is no different."

"Thanks, Doc. Well, Liz, I suppose we can go." Anthony said with a hint of sadness.

"It's good news, Anthony…it is. We'll keep working hard. You'll heal, I just know that you will…you'll walk again." Elizabeth said with a sympathetic smile.

"That's the spirit, Miss Knoll." Doctor Maguire said as he moved toward the door. He opened the door and held it. Elizabeth pushed Anthony's wheelchair out into the hallway as Doctor Maguire smiled and said goodbye. The doctor didn't mind Elizabeth giving Anthony encouragement and telling him that he would walk again, but the doctor wasn't ready to make that same claim.

In the early evening, Edward Baker returned to the apartment as Stephen and Marion were putting the final touches on dinner. There was a small Christmas tree in the corner of the living room and a few presents beneath it. Because of the war, Christmas had been humble this year, even for the wealthy. The table was neatly set as always. Abby, Anthony and Elizabeth played a board game in the living room while they waited.

"Good evening, everyone." Mister Baker greeted them.

"Home rather late this evening, father." Anthony said from across the room.

"I've been working on a deal for some time now, an offer that has turned into a very handsome proposition for all involved." he announced.

"Give us the details." Anthony pleaded.

"Now, now, I don't want you to get involved with the business until you've had a good long time to rest and recuperate from your ordeal. I'll say this, however, it will add several new products to our line of hospital equipment. I purchased the patents some time ago from an old business acquaintance up north for twenty-five thousand. It was a very fair deal. This will give us a definite opportunity to provide a much broader line of medical equipment to hospitals nationwide."

"That's great news, father. Any opportunity for export?" Anthony asked.

"Many opportunities...our manufacturing capabilities allow us to manufacture with higher quality and precision at greater speeds. The new line is already being introduced to our plant in Springfield. We'll take a trip to inspect the start-up once we've given the engineers an opportunity to work out the bugs. As far as export, the market is definitely global, but logistically it's a daunting task to undertake."

Stephen poured Mister Baker a glass of white wine and presented it to his employer. Mister Baker smelled the bouquet for a few seconds and then took a healthy sip.

"It will certainly be a blessing to everyone when this war is over." he said as he looked across the room to his children and Elizabeth.

"And, Elizabeth, what does Doctor Maguire have to say about Anthony's condition?" he asked.

"Good news...yes, he seemed very positive and stated that Anthony is making good progress." She replied with a positive tone. Anthony was pondering her words. Her interpretation was certainly much brighter than what his take was. However, it would be better to let his father think the best.

"Well, that is good news. Keep up the good work, Elizabeth." He then turned to Abby.

"My dear, Abby, what did you do this day?" he asked.

"Robert called and we spoke for a few minutes. He thought that perhaps I could be more involved with the company... with regards to public relations and such. Of course, he said he would have to discuss it with you." She seemed to blush. "And of course, I told him I'd have to discuss it with you, as well." she said.

"Why, that's a wonderful idea. It has always been my first dream to have my children together again someday and my second dream to have the two of you involved with the family business...excellent." He crossed the room and Abby greeted him with a hug. "And have you discussed any details...what you would be doing?" Mister Baker asked.

"Well, if it's alright with you, I would do some charity work with the hospitals. Robert would get some photos and arrange several interviews with the Tribune." she said proudly.

"Good, good." he said as he listened intently.

"I'm glad you approve. It would give me something to do... something good and positive, and since I haven't heard from..." Her words drifted off.

"John?" Edward asked.

"Yes, I suppose he's just very busy with work and all. It's just that I expected to hear from him...and it's Christmas and all." She found herself making excuses for John, defending him and maybe more for her own peace of mind than anything.

"You listen to me, Abby. I'm sure this man loves you – what young man wouldn't? He's probably in the thick of things and just hasn't been able to write. Those men work very hard, very long hours, at the end of the day all they want to see is their pillow. I'm sure when the time is right for both of you, you'll be together again." Her father said with assurance.

"Do you really think so, father?" she asked as a tear slid down her cheek.

"I'm sure of it. In the meantime, I think you're absolutely right to stay active, keep busy, do what you can for the hospitals – not out of a need for publicity for the company, but because it is the right thing to do for the soldiers returning from war, for your community and for yourself." He gave her a wink and drank the rest of the wine from his glass. "Would anyone else care to join me in a glass of wine? We have so much to be grateful for." he said with a warm smile.

Stephen heard the request and entered the room with a tray of glasses, already filled, and offered them to Elizabeth and the twins. Each took a glass and posed, ready for a toast. Edward looked around with concern.

"Stephen, Marion, where are your glasses? Join us." He directed them. Stephen rushed to pour two more glasses and then he and Marion entered the living room with cordial smiles.

"And now, everyone, I'd like to make a toast for this day. To my son, Anthony, and the good news of his therapy, to Elizabeth for her part in his recovery, to Abby for her exiting news and the charitable work she is about to partake in, and to Stephen and Marion for keeping this household together...*we are all so blessed*. May God continue to bless all of us and look after us."

With that, they all raised their glasses in unison and then drank to their father's toast.

32

The men were all instructed to be at Camp Nine on the morning of Nelson's return in late January. It was unseasonably warm this day. Some men stood and others sat around the yard talking among themselves, the Germans in a group of their own. Nelson went to have breakfast in the canteen. He received nothing but a cold look from Hanna. He softly asked for oatmeal and then grabbed a cup to pour coffee for himself. Hanna scooped up a large spoonful of oatmeal and when Nelson wasn't looking she opened her mouth over the ladle to let a stream of saliva trail out...but then couldn't bring herself to do it and dumped the oatmeal into the bowl. She put a piece of dry cold toast on top of the oatmeal and set it on the counter. She felt no pity for this man and now having gotten to know Agnes, wished that she had had the chance to take a few swings at this man herself. Nelson sat alone and ate his breakfast struggling to drink coffee with his mouth still swollen.

He finished his meal and walked slowly out into the yard. He still couldn't talk very well and mumbled something as the welcome-back card was handed to him. He looked at it without emotion or a word, folded it up and stuck it in his back pocket. He then walked around the men and finally spoke. He did not mention the incident, but just went on about how he would be back to his 'old self' in time, but that clearly things would not be the same.

"If you thought I was mean before you ain't seen nothing yet." He told the men. He continued to walk around and then stopped and glancing out of his swollen left eye, fixated on the hand of one man standing a few feet away, the hand with a ring. He stood motionless and then slowly pulled his glance away and dismissed the men to return to work.

John approached Nelson and said, "You might want to take it easy on the men, they feel pretty badly about what happened."

Nelson stared away from John and simply mumbled, "Yeah, sure…I'll do that."

John noticed a peculiarity about Nelson that he couldn't quite pin down. The man seemed humbled by the experience but not angry, maybe more distant. John gave it some thought and dismissed it thinking that perhaps he was on some pain medication and his thinking was cloudy. John ended the awkward silence saying a little loudly, "Okay then, I'm going to catch up on some paperwork. I'll see you later." Nelson was silent.

John went to the canteen to get a pot of coffee to take back to his office. Hanna managed a broad smile for John. She respected John.

"I kept a bowl warm just for you." she said as she took a bowl from the warm oven where she had made biscuits earlier.

"Well, I've already eaten, but I know who makes the best oatmeal around here so I guess I'm going to have to eat breakfast again." John said with a smile.

Hanna laughed and this was actually the first time that John had seen her in such a good mood. She poured a generous handful of raisins on top as well as a big spoonful of brown sugar, a large dollop of melting butter and a handful of chopped walnuts. John looked out the window staring at Nelson only to see that after several minutes he still had not moved. John stood with his bowl, fixated on Nelson. Finally Nelson moved and John felt some relief. He sat down and Hanna came out from behind the counter and stood near John.

This seemed a little unusual to John and so he broke the ice, "Sit down, Hanna." She wiped her hands on her pants, pulled over a chair and sat down. "What's on your mind? Everyone treating you okay?" he asked.

"Oh, yes sir." she said.

"The accommodations aren't the greatest but…" John said.

"Oh, the room's fine, sir…much better than I had at Krueger's. I was wondering…with Nelson being back to work and all, they shouldn't need anymore help…but then maybe they could use someone to look in on them…well, you know… I was wondering if it'd be okay for me to stop in and check on his wife once in awhile." Hanna asked.

"Well, when your chores are done during the day the rest of the time is your own and so I have no problem with that. Since you don't have a car you'd have to use one of the company trucks, which you do anyhow when you run to town for supplies. No, I don't see any problem with that, Hanna. You do so as you please. A woman should have company with other women." John said.

"Oh, thank you sir. You can be sure I'm not one to take advantage." she said.

"No, I think I'm a pretty good judge of character, you can be trusted Hanna. As long as the men are fed and no one complains about the meals. And I sure don't expect that to happen." John said.

"I haven't gotten any complaints yet…least not to my face. If you don't mind John, there's a yellow car here with an automatic transmission, could I use that?"

"Well, you drive stick shift…you have since you got here." John said with some surprise in his voice, but then he saw the look on her face and stopped in the middle of his thought. "You go right ahead, Hanna. It is a much nicer vehicle to be seen in. There's a lot of room in the back seat and the trunk to haul supplies...you go right ahead and use the car." John said. Hanna gave a broad smile again and John, seeing that whatever it was about using the car instead of one of the trucks that made her happy, it was worth it.

The next day after breakfast at the camp Hanna drove the big yellow car to visit Agnes Nelson. Agnes heard the car pull up to their house and looked out the window. She saw Hanna get out of the car and Agnes's heart started pounding. She wasn't sure why she was doing this, but she found herself running upstairs to her bedroom dresser. She opened a drawer and dug to the bottom, feeling around for the tube of lipstick. She had put it there a long time ago and only took out when she wanted to make herself pretty. This was usually only when she was home alone in front of the dresser mirror. She took off the top and twisted it enough to bring the lipstick out, and then carefully slowed herself down enough to put a light covering on her lips. She heard a knock on the door and thought she'd better hurry, she didn't want her guest to think no one was home.

"Just a minute please...I'll be right there." she called out. She put the lipstick back in the drawer under her delicates, quickly brushed her hair and ran down the stairs. She stopped a few feet from the door to compose herself.

"Who is it?" she called.

"Agnes, it's me, Hanna...come to see how you're doing." Hanna called back.

Agnes opened the door and a smile came across both of their faces.

"My goodness, Hanna, how nice of you to drop by...would you like to come in?" Agnes asked. It felt so good to welcome a guest into their house. She couldn't remember the last time someone had come by to call on her socially other than Hanna's previous visit to bring them food.

Hanna noticed the lipstick. "Well Agnes, don't you look beautiful today." she said. Agnes smiled almost as if in shock and then she turned away into the house. She was afraid she would start crying. She couldn't remember anyone ever speaking to her like this and the feeling brought joy and at the same time sadness that she hadn't heard words like this more often. In one brief minute Hanna had flattered her more than her husband had in all their years of marriage.

"Thank you…Hanna." she said.

"It's a beautiful day, Agnes…thought you might like to take a drive." Hanna spoke and felt a little tongue-tied. She felt uncomfortable but for that moment there was no place else on earth she would rather have been.

"We could take a drive into Minocqua." Hanna suggested.

"Oh, my…that would be nice." Agnes answered.

"I packed some sandwiches…if you'd like, we could take a drive to Bonn Falls and have a little lunch by the water, just us ladies. It's a little warm for this time of year and the fresh air might be nice." Hanna offered.

"Oh, Hanna, how thoughtful of you. I'd love to do just that." Agnes responded.

Hanna would just as soon have taken Agnes with her to Phelps, but feared that someone would notice them, someone would say something that would get back to Nelson, and she didn't want to do anything that could remotely end up hurting Agnes.

The ladies drove to Minocqua, thirty miles away. Agnes enjoyed the drive. She turned her head and looked at every house, read every sign and became ecstatic when they saw a doe and her two fawns walk across the road in front of them. She had seen plenty of wildlife living in the country, but this event was extraordinary - she was creating a memory with a new friend. At Bonn Falls they parked the car near the rushing water, close enough to see the waterfall, but far enough away from the sounds of rushing water where they could talk as they sat in the car and had their sandwiches.

Agnes felt like a young girl again and the experience was perhaps appreciated more now as an adult. She was enjoying every minute of this day and Hanna was as well.

"Agnes...I have a surprise for you." Hanna said with a grin.

"Oh, Hanna, you've already surprised me...and I've done nothing to deserve it." Agnes said.

"That's where you're wrong, you've done everything to deserve it...dear." Hanna spoke, hardly believing she had the courage to call Agnes "dear".

"I'm going to teach you how to drive, Agnes." Hanna exclaimed.

"Oh, my goodness...no...no, I can't...I just can't." Agnes said with obvious distress in her voice.

"Oh, yes, you can, Agnes...you can! You know you want to and you deserve it. Why, what if there was an emergency... what if that husband of yours never came out of the hospital? What would you do?" Hanna's words made sense to Agnes... she was right.

"One lesson...just one." Agnes insisted.

"One lesson, dear...and then we'll see how you do. If you want a second lesson, that'll be entirely up to you." Hanna's words comforted Agnes.

Agnes got behind the wheel. She had never told her husband, but she had taken a couple of lessons from her father as a teenager in an old car with a clutch and gears to shift...it all seemed pretty complex to the young girl. Then her father got sick and died and Agnes never sat behind the wheel again. Hanna showed Agnes where all the controls were and explained to her that all she had to do was shift that lever on the column until the arrow pointed to "D". Agnes was delighted. As often as she had seen her husband shift the lever, it had never occurred to her what 'automatic transmission' meant. This was going to be a lot easier than she had imagined and with a new friend who made her feel comfortable and confident, she knew she could do this. Within the hour Agnes was driving forty miles an hour. The thrill of going even faster as the car sped downhill was exhilarating. She felt alive. And then she noticed the little clock on the dashboard. The day had gotten away from them. Neighbor children would be coming home from school, and she had to get home to fix supper for her husband. She became anxious and flustered. Her driving now seemed to be in a panic. She put her foot on the brake and shifted the car into park.

"My God, Hanna, I have to get home...your drive from here – okay?" Agnes was flustered.

"Okay, dear...just relax. You did real fine today...real fine. You make me proud." Hanna spoke with comfort in her voice and Agnes immediately felt more relaxed. Now her new friend was proud of her...another feeling that she was not familiar with. If only her husband knew how to speak these words and make her feel this way.

Hanna drove the rest of the way back toward Phelps and then pulled over to the side of the road a few miles from Agnes's home. Agnes's heart pounded as she felt a nervousness she had never experienced before. Hanna put her arm over the back of the seat and on to Agnes's shoulder. Agnes continued to look out the windshield, her eyes darting around as if to see if anyone could see them. Hanna pulled Agnes closer. Hanna put her left hand on Agnes's right cheek, directing her face to hers. Agnes now looked into Hanna's eyes. Hanna gave Agnes a gentle kiss on the lips. Agnes did not resist although some voice in her head said she should. Her heart continued to pound and she felt flushed. Hanna pulled back and looked at Agnes.

"Your friendship means a great deal to me, Agnes. You are so special...and I'm so glad to be your friend...your special friend." Hanna said.

Agnes began to cry a little and she pulled a handkerchief from her purse to dry her tears.

Hanna looked at her with a sad expression. "I didn't mean to hurt you, dear…far from it." Hanna said.

"You didn't hurt me…I thought I was confused…but I'm not. I'm happy…you make me happy…and I'm glad to be your special friend, as well." she said. Then after a long pause Agnes continued, "No one must know."

"I understand." Hanna replied. As much as she knew it had to be this way, it was still a little hard to accept, but it was also a condition that made their relationship special.

Hanna gave Agnes another hug and Agnes hugged her back intensely. Hanna then drove up to a spot about a block from Agnes's house.

"I'd better get out here." Agnes said.

"Nonsense…I'll drop you off at your door. We're just a couple of ladies out shopping." Hanna said with a laugh. Agnes laughed as well. Hanna pulled up to Agnes's door. Agnes got out quickly and gave the door a slam. Hanna rolled her window down half way.

"See you again soon, Agnes." Hanna called.

"See you soon, Hanna." Agnes answered.

33

The doorbell rang and Stephen came to the door, looking at his wristwatch. It was 9:00 AM.

"Good Morning, would you be the young man that Miss Baker is expecting?" Stephen asked.

"Yes, thank you, I'm Robert Edgerton."

"May I take your hat and coat?" Stephen asked.

"Yes, thank you." Robert handed his hat to Stephen and then removed his coat and gave it to him as well.

"Thank you, please come in." Stephen stood aside as Robert walked in and then moved ahead to lead him into the living room.

"If you'd care to have a seat, I'll let Miss Baker know that you're here. Could I get you something to drink?" Stephen asked.

"Oh, no thank you." Robert replied.

Stephen took a few seconds to look the young man over. Stephen thought of himself as more than a gentleman's gentleman, he thought of himself as someone who should look after the family as well. There had never been a woman living here before and he wanted to make absolutely sure that she was going to be in the company of someone who could be trusted. Robert felt Stephen's gaze and almost felt a need to speak out and ask if there was a problem, but before the words could form, Stephen gave a slight smile and left the room.

He knocked at Abby's door. "Miss Abby, Robert Edgerton is here to see you." Stephen waited for a reply.

"He's early, please tell him I'll be ready in five minutes." she called through the door.

"Very good, Miss Abby, take your time." Stephen said in a comforting voice. No young man was going to rush his employer. Stephen returned to the living room.

"Apparently you're a bit earlier than she expected, Mister Edgerton. So if you wouldn't mind having a seat, she'll be with you in a few minutes. Perhaps now I could get you something to drink." Stephen suggested.

"Coffee?" Robert asked.

"I'll make a fresh pot, it'll be a few minutes." Stephen said and then bowed slightly before turning to leave the room.

"Fine, thanks." Robert replied. Anything to get away from this man's scrutiny.

Robert looked around the apartment. He had never been to the home of his employer and he was impressed with the beautiful furnishings. He got up and looked at the books on the shelves separating the living room from the dining room. He pulled a book from the shelf "For Whom The Bell Tolls" by Hemingway and opened it. It was a book that Robert himself had recently read. Inside the cover was the inscription:

> *Mister Baker, I hope you enjoy this book. I insisted that father give you one of the first copies. I thought of you when I created the character of Robert Jordan. I hope to see you next time I'm home. I've always looked to you with the deepest regard.*
>
> > *Sincerely,*
> > *Ernest*

Robert slowly moved his hand over the inscription as if it were something sacred. Then he looked around - almost as if he were touching a forbidden treasure of some sort - and gently closed it and put it back on the shelf. Stephen entered the room with a cup of coffee and saucer. He set it on the mission-styled table next to an over-stuffed leather chair.

"Your coffee, Mister Edgerton. Do you take cream or sugar?" Stephen said graciously.

"Thank you, black is fine. Say…um, excuse me, but I was browsing through Mister Baker's books. I hope you don't mind. I noticed the inscription in the Hemingway novel." Robert said.

Stephen paused for a second and realized that there was a question in there somewhere. "Yes, Mister Baker and Mister Hemingway's father were classmates. They were also neighbors in Oak Park." Stephen said.

Robert's face expressed how impressed he was. "That's really something. I didn't know that about Mister Baker." Robert said.

"If you don't mind me asking, Mister Edgerton, how long have *you* been employed by Mister Baker?" Stephen asked.

"Almost three years, sir." Robert replied.

"And with all due respect, Mister Edgerton, have you ever noticed Mister Baker to boast, display a sense of pride, or behave in a way that was braggadocios?" Stephen asked, although he knew the answer.

Robert smiled. "No, of course not. You're right. He is a very humble man." Robert said.

"Men such as Mister Baker, have no need to brag. He has achieved a great many things in his life. Any wrong that the man has ever done, he has endeavored to correct. Any debt was repaid tenfold. Any mistake he might have made was never repeated. He is a man of valor, a man of integrity." Stephen spoke with pride.

"Yes, of course. I believe you're right." Robert said. There could be no other response.

"And he makes every effort to make sure that his son and daughter are safe, secure and never put into a state or situation that is compromising to their integrity as well. Any peril that would befall his children would transpire as much to himself." Stephen smiled, sure that he had used this example to make the point that Abby should be respected.

Robert seemed slightly nervous by Stephen's comment, but thought that any attempt to defend himself and assure Stephen of his honor and good intentions would only be construed as culpability. Just then, Abby entered the room and Robert breathed a sigh of relief.

"Hello, Robert. Have I kept you waiting long?" she asked.

"No, not at all. You look…" Robert choked on his words. He wanted to say that she looked wonderful, but didn't want to give Stephen the impression that he was here for anything other than work.

"I look what?" she asked. Stephen smiled broadly.

"I think what the young gentleman hoped to say was that you look very lovely, Miss Abby." Stephen gave Robert a wink and it went a long way to ease the tension he was feeling.

"Yes…yes, you look very lovely, Abby. That's a nice dress, it'll look good in the photos." Robert said.

"Now remember, Robert, above all, this is charity work we're doing today. And you're going to help. If we get a photo in the papers and a nice story about how the company has donated in some way, all the better, but that is not our principal objective." She spoke confidently and was noticing that she was beginning to speak differently from the way she had spoken before her move to Chicago.

"Of course, Abby. I didn't mean to…"

"Oh, that's alright, you're a businessman and you're thinking about your responsibility, that is why my father hired you. You do your job and put the company first." She spoke with a smile and then continued, "But not today."

Robert took a long drink of coffee and handed his cup to Stephen.

"I'll get your coat, Miss Abby." Stephen said to her as he bowed ever so slightly and then he left the room.

"Has he been your dad's butler a long time?" Robert asked.

"Stephen's been in my father's employment for many, many years. He's like the glue that keeps this household together." she said proudly.

"I enjoyed our outing the other day, did you as well?" Robert asked.

"Oh yes, I can't wait to spend more time at the museum. The city has so much to offer. Freddie drove me to the library yesterday and I got my very own library card." she smiled with delight.

"That's wonderful." Robert said, although to Abby, his words somehow didn't seem genuine.

Abby's thoughts turned to John for a second. John was always sincere with her. John loved books and he would have been genuinely happy to hear about Abby's library card. She thought about the values they shared in common. They were simple country people who worked hard, played hard and prayed often. They had an ability to connect that she had never known before. She wanted to like Robert and nothing more. She was hoping that her instincts about Robert were wrong although her intuitions had never had been wrong in the past.

"Shall we go, then?" Robert asked as Stephen held Abby's coat for her to put on.

As if shaken from a dream, Abby responded, "Yes...yes." Then she turned to Stephen.

"Thank you, Stephen." she said.

Robert grabbed his coat and hat from Stephen and gave him a smile. The couple left the apartment.

The couple went to Copley Hospital where they met with the administration who warmly greeted Abby and talked about the various areas in which her services could be used. This day she would be working with a new group of soldiers who had just arrived days earlier from the war. She was assigned to a nurse who would work with her throughout the day. Abby would help move patients from gurneys to beds and from beds to wheelchairs. She would read letters to some and newspaper articles to others, sports, entertainment, politics - whatever the patient wanted to know about to become reconnected with his country.

She helped men with missing arms, legs, eyes and other men whose ailments were less physical than emotional. Her heart went out to every one of them and her beauty and smile warmed many a heart.

Robert was sent to a the children's wing of the hospital where he read stories to children. He was hoping to spend the day with Abby, but the hospital administrator insisted that they really needed him to help in the children's ward. He did, however, have the opportunity during his lunch break to get a couple of photographs of Abby working with the soldiers, and from the standpoint of his career, that was good enough.

34

In the weeks that followed Nelson's return each of the men noticed that he had become stranger in his behavior, suspicious and preoccupied. Even to Agnes the man seemed more quiet and pensive. She catered to him from the moment he would get home in the evening until it was time to help him into bed at night. It was more comfortable for both of them when he fell asleep in his chair. But in those evenings she would usually end up hearing him struggle in the middle of the night and would end up helping him up the stairs to the bedroom, anyway.

Agnes reminded her husband that they needed to go to Three Lakes the following Sunday to take their nephews and niece back home. They had been visiting the past three days and helped with chores so that Agnes could look after Robert. He had seemed to be more active and she thought that breaking their routine of resting on Sunday would help to cheer him up.

"We could leave the house shortly after Mass on Sunday, if that would be all right with you." she suggested. Nelson was quiet.

"Say eleven-thirty? Helen can have dinner ready for us. You know how she likes to cook a big meal."

Nelson finally answered, "All right, all right."

The next few days Agnes ran the list through her mind a dozen times. Have the children's clothes washed and folded so that they could pack up their suitcases and be ready. She thought of things they could talk about so that there would be some pleasant conversation at the dinner table. She even thought of how she would re-direct the conversation should Helen's husband start talking too much about Bob's obvious breaks and bruises. She baked a pie with cherries from Door County given to her by a neighbor. She had frozen about ten pounds and put the rest up as jelly. She felt proud of her canning skills. She had learned how to preserve fruits and make jellies from her mother. Though there was seldom a word of approval from her husband, the children loved her pies and would make such a fuss. Bob only seemed to shovel it in, washing it down with coffee.

Sunday had finally come. Agnes made sure to let anyone who spoke with her at church of their plans to go visit her sister's family later that morning. She was happy to have her nephews and niece with them at church. It made her feel a little like a mother. She was so alone and it was so seldom that her husband would have the motivation to do anything but eat a big meal and fall asleep in his chair. Even though the day would seem short, a few hours to be with family and share a meal was something she really looked forward to. She was determined to make the most of this day. She would help her sister with dishes and this would give them the opportunity to have a nice conversation. This was the woman with whom she shared everything as a girl. And although there was so much she wanted to share again, she was sure that she couldn't bring up the subject of her new friend.

The Nelsons arrived at home from church and the kids ran for the house. Agnes reminded them not to get dirty and that they would be leaving again shortly. It was a particularly warm day for winter and Agnes anticipated the children would be playing in the wet snow. She took the paper bags with clothes out to the car and with a second trip brought out the cherry pie, now concealed in a paper bag, as aluminum foil was scarce these days. Every scrap of metal was put toward the war effort. It was eleven-twenty five and she was moving the children to the car. Nelson was still walking around the house. She yelled back to him, "Do you need help with anything, dear"? She didn't call him dear very often, but felt an obligation to do so today as it felt like he was doing them all a favor by taking them to her sister's. There was no response and so Agnes got into the car. The three children did their little fight for space in the back seat. Their thirteen year-old girl, Mary Helen wanted to sit in the middle as a way of keeping the boys, Johnny and Gary from fighting. They sat now waiting for their uncle to come and drive them home.

"What's taking Uncle Bob so long?" the older boy, Johnny, asked.

"Aunt Agnes, should I go see if Uncle Bob needs some help?" Mary Helen asked.

"I'm sure he'll be along any minute." Their aunt said in her usual comforting voice. "Here he comes now." she said as she watched his every move. Her smile faded as she saw him walk around to the side of the house. He grabbed a bucket and started filling it with water from the spigot. Her look turned to concern and she didn't know what to think. He went to the shed and came out with a sponge and rag. He approached the car and Agnes opened her window a few inches.

"Robert? Robert, what are you doing, dear?" She asked with trembling in her voice. "Robert?" She repeated. As he began washing the car she tried again, "Robert, what are you doing, Robert? We were going to leave at eleven-thirty, Robert."

He continued washing the car, now splashing soapy water onto the windshield as if to drown out her voice. "Bob...honey?" her voice trailed off. She rolled up her window to keep the water out as Nelson continued to wash the car. The children sat quietly in the back seat so in shock and fear that they dared not even glance at each other for fear that it would somehow confirm that they weren't just having a bad dream. Nelson continued to wash the car. Every once in awhile he would bear the sponge down on a spot and focus on it, as he rubbed hard to remove what was there. Finally Mary Helen began to cry. Then little Gary began sobbing as well.

Agnes turned around and consoled the children, "It's all right, my angels. Your uncle just wants to make sure we ride in a nice clean car, that's all".

She turned back and put a hand up to her eyes to stop the tears that were forming. Finally Agnes dared to look at her watch, the watch she had saved money to buy years ago, the watch she only wore on Sundays and special occasions. It was twelve fifteen and, as her husband was finally putting the bucket away, Agnes opened her window to get some fresh air in the car. She could hear the phone ringing and was sure it was her sister calling to see if they were all right. Nelson came from the shed, got into the car and they drove off in silence.

The children stared out the window and didn't speak a word until Gary finally said, "I'm hungry".

Mary Helen elbowed him softly in the side and put a finger to her lips to silence him.

He whispered back, "But I am."

When they arrived, Helen came out of the house to greet them and her children ran to her, hugging her tightly. She had been sitting by the window watching for them.

"Are you all right, Agnes? Is there something wrong?" she asked.

"Oh no, we just got a late start, that's all." Agnes replied, holding back the tears.

"Well it'll just take a minute to heat things up for dinner." Helen said. She knew that something was wrong and it was best to sweep it under the rug.

35

Abby saw her picture in the newspaper and read the article which was about volunteerism in the time of war. The article mentioned Miss Abigail Baker of Baker Medical Corporation, a company that has donated tens of thousands of dollars and much more in medical equipment to the war effort. She had never been in the newspaper before and in a way found it flattering, but the more she read the article, the more she felt that she had been somehow used to draw attention to her father's company. Her feelings were mixed. As long as her father's company was doing so much good for the war effort, was it wrong to call attention to it?

She went to her father's library to get a scissors from his desk. The solid oak, roll top desk looked massive to Abby and she imagined movers struggling to get the large piece of furniture into the apartment. She pulled back his chair with the padded burgundy-colored leather that shined. Abby carefully rolled the top of the desk to open it and immediately saw a framed picture of a woman who looked much like herself holding two babies. It was her mother. Abby ran her hand fondly over the glass and a sadness came over her that somehow rushed all the way through her, leaving a smile in its place. She placed the photo back carefully, but kept her eyes on it for a few brief moments.

She opened the center drawer of the desk, and found a scissors and used it to cut her picture and article from the newspaper. She thought that maybe she would send it to John, an excuse to initiate another communication in hopes that he would respond. She put the scissors back into the drawer and slid it shut. Then she noticed a stack of stamped letters in a shallow wooden bin atop his desk. She would normally have shown consideration and discretion except that the envelope on top was addressed to the Spot Lunch Café. She calmly took the envelope and held it up to the light. She could faintly make out the shape and color of currency. A smile came to her face and with composure, she placed the letter back on top of the stack. She rolled the top back down and ran her hands softly over the oak, trying to imagine all the things her father might have thought about or acted upon while sitting at this piece of furniture. Abby got up and slid the chair back into place and returned to her room.

She began to address an envelope to John, but suddenly found herself distracted, thinking about Robert. After they had finished their work at the hospital, he had taken her for a light dinner a café on Erie street. She had enjoyed seeing new places in the city and Robert seemed like the perfect gentleman. They had shared a bottle of wine. There was an upright piano along the wall of the café and while they were waiting for dessert, Robert had played a song for her. He made her laugh and she was beginning to realize that she felt some attraction to this man and it made her feel a bit ashamed.

After a moment she decided the newspaper clipping would be placed in a scrapbook she had brought with her from home. When she opened the scrapbook, she saw the photograph of her and John taken at the fair. A few small pressed flowers were tucked behind the picture. John had picked them as they lay in the grass watching people walking the fair.

Abby pulled the picture from the black paper corners that held the picture in the book. She looked at the picture for a moment, reflecting on that day and the feeling in her heart whenever he touched her. She placed the picture in her dresser drawer so that she could look at it more often. Abby placed the neatly-folded newspaper article in her scrapbook, carefully closed the cover and put it under her bed.

She looked out of her bedroom window as she had done so many times, and wished she was with John, lying in front of her fireplace up north. She was confused by her feelings. There was so much change in her life and she wanted to go back to what she knew and the place where she had spent her whole life. But now she had something that she didn't have in Wisconsin, something she had never had anywhere or at any time. She had a family. She was starting a New Year and another month without John.

36

John had spent time last fall making repairs to the outside of his house which included chinking some of the logs on the outside of the cabin. It was late in January and he now he spent his time making repairs to the inside of his house. This day he looked around and felt that he had done enough. Kassendahl was in pretty good shape and so he decided that with all of the stress he had endured the last few months, it was a good day to rest. He was feeling proud of his work and thought this would be a good time to reward himself with a beer. John went to the refrigerator only to discover that he had had the last beer the night before. John had spent all of his free time on Kassendahl and hadn't been to Jesters in months. He thought this would be a good opportunity to see how his old landlord was doing. John cleaned up at the bathroom sink and brushed his hair. He drove to town and parked in front of the bar. There was only one other car there. John walked in and glanced around. He saw Dido sleeping on a chair in the corner with Mr. Eggbert nestled under his arm joining him in his nap.

At the bar there sat a young man in an Army uniform with his head lying over his folded arms. There was a cigarette in the ashtray in front of him, an empty shot glass and a bottle of beer. John sat a few stools away trying to be quiet as to not wake Jesters clientele. Jester came out from the back room.

"John!" Jester shouted. The young man sitting at the bar raised his head and an eyebrow.

"Hi Jester...I don't mean to wake your customers. They tell me this is a pretty wild place but I've never seen it quite like this." John said.

"They can't drink if they're sleeping and if they're not drinking, I'm not getting any richer." Jester said. And with that he threw a wet dish rag across the room at Dido. Dido woke with a stir and Mr. Eggbert stood on his hind legs, looked around and then wiped his eyes.

"It's good to see you, John. How's the cabin?" Jester asked.

"It's great, could use a woman's touch, though." John said.

"Say, any word from that girlfriend of yours?" Jester asked.

"Oh, I'm not so sure she's my girlfriend...it's been months... almost a year." John said.

"Don't worry about it, John...plenty of fish in the sea." Jester said. "How's things in the lumber business, heard you've been running things for some time. Pretty cold out there this morning?" Jester asked.

"Colder than Cheyenne in January." John replied.

The young man at the bar lifted his head staring at John. "What'd you say?" the young man asked.

John looked back at Jester with a curious expression. "Why...I said it was colder than Cheyenne in January." John said.

"Sounds like something my old man would say." the young man said.

John noticed the young man's red hair and could now see a vague resemblance to Doc.

"How're you doing, Michael Fitzgerald? Pleased to meet you." John said.

Michael cocked his head with a puzzled look. "Well, I suppose that makes sense. So...tell me...how's old Thomas doing?" Michael asked.

"Haven't you been to see him." John asked.

"Manage I'll get around to it one of these days." Michael said.

"Your father would probably appreciate knowing that you're home and safe. He's been worried. Last I spoke with him he hadn't heard a word from you." John said.

"And what business would that be of yours?" Michael asked.

"He's more than an employee, he's a friend...and a darn good man." John said.

Michael got up casually and then spun around quickly taking a swing and hitting John square in the chin, knocking him back.

"Now stop that!" Jester yelled. Dido grabbed Mr. Eggbert and put him in his box.

John backed away a few feet. "I've got no quarrel with you." he said.

Michael lunged forward and John reacted the only way he knew, by striking back hitting Michael square in the face. Michael looked startled and blood began running from his nose.

"Sorry Jester!" John shouted to the bar-owner as Michael lunged forward again this time ramming his head into John's stomach. The two young men wrestled and punched each other until John finally had the upper hand, striking hard with his left until Michael was staggering. Just then out of nowhere Jester hit Michael across the back of the head with a wooden club he kept behind the bar. Michael dropped to his knees and then forward to the floor.

"What the hell was that about?" John asked Jester.

"Don't know, but he's not welcome here again...at least not until he learns some manners." Jester said as he placed the club on top of the bar. "Give me a hand, John." he said. The two men picked Michael up and dragged him out the front door and set him on the wooden porch.

"Now what? We can't just leave him here." John asked.

"Doesn't matter to me, John...but I can't afford to have guys like this busting up my bar." Jester said.

"Well, give me a hand. We'll load him into my truck. I'll take him back to my place and look after him...he's the son of a friend and if he dies I'll never be able to forgive myself." John said.

"I didn't hit him that hard...but suit yourself, John." Jester said as he started picking him up again to load him into John's truck.

"Gosh, all I wanted was to pick up a few beers." John said.

"Wait here, John, I'll get you a few cold ones." Jester said.

John looked Michael over. He was unconscious and badly bruised. There was a large lump on the back of his head.

"Would you bring some ice too?" John yelled to Jester.

Jester returned with a few bottles of beer in a paper bag and a bowl of ice. "Here you go, John".

"What do I owe you." John asked.

"We'll settle up some other time...you get a move on before this guy comes to and starts in on you again." Jester said.

John drove Michael back to his cabin. He opened the passenger side door and slung Michael's right arm over his shoulder. Michael was coming to and sluggishly walked as John led him into the cabin and to the couch. He got a towel from the kitchen and dumped some of the ice into it, wrapping it up and placing it on top of Michael's head. After a few minutes Michael was moaning.

"Oh my God...oh my head...what the hell happened?" he moaned.

"Stay put...sleep it off." John suggested and the young man passed out again.

John returned with a few blankets and threw them over Michael.

The next morning John woke up and noticed Michael sitting up on the couch rubbing the back of his head. John got a few aspirin from his medicine cabinet and a glass of water and brought them out to his guest.

"What's your name?" Michael asked.

"John Miller, I manage the lumber company for C. A. Anderson. Your father's been an employee for a long time. I told you at the bar that he is a friend and a good man and that's when you took a swing at me. Sorry to hit you so hard…I have developed a pretty good left." John said.

"I remember now…sorry. I haven't gotten along too well with the old man over the years…not since my mother…" Michael stopped himself.

"Your father mentioned something to me about it once." John said.

"She was always so quiet and withdrawn…then other times she'd get this mean look on her face, no explanation…just pissed at something and there was nothing that I could do to make her happy. My God, I can't stand to think of it even after all these years." Michael said.

"If it makes you feel better to get it off your chest…go right ahead." John said.

"She had always been quiet but in those last few weeks… depressed, secretive…like there was something she was hiding. The old man just worked all the time. I came home early from school one day and the sheriff was at our house…I figured it had something to do with my dad beating her…she had some bruises on her face and when I walked in I could tell she had been crying. The sheriff left in a hurry, I assumed to go and arrest my old man, but that never happened. He came home that night and barely looked at her. I guess she put enough make-up on to conceal the bruises. She went to her room and dad slept on the couch. The next day I came home from school and found her. I wish I could get the image out of my mind.

You'd think that with everything I saw in the war it'd cover up the past…but it doesn't work that way. Then the sheriff came, no one even called. I guess he was coming to check on her…to see if the old man was still beating her. We didn't speak about it. Something the old man did, some way that he treated her put her over the edge…and I can never forgive him for it."

Michael stopped talking and just stared off into the distance. John couldn't bring himself to believe this about Doc…it didn't make sense.

"Michael…you don't know me, but I do know your father and whatever he might have done in the past…even though I find it hard to believe, he's not that man anymore. Maybe in time you can find a way to leave the past behind and move ahead. He's your father and it sounds like he's the only family you have." John said.

"I don't know…we'll see. You got any food here?" Michael asked.

"Yeah, I'll fix you some eggs…just take it easy." John said.

Michael got up and walked around the cabin. He looked above the fireplace mantle to see a couple of cane fishing poles.

"You fish?" Michael asked.

"When I can…got a sailboat, but no fishing boat. I mostly just fish off the bridge at Long Lake." John said as he was frying up bacon and eggs.

"You ever do any ice-fishing? I got a room over at Alice's. Just need to change into my civvies." Michael asked.

"Under one condition." John responded.

"What's that?"

"We stop by to see your dad first." John said. There was a long pause. John knew that the next man to speak would be the one giving in and so he let the silence go on for what seemed like minutes.

"Yeah…okay." Michael spoke with an ambivalent tone.

John called in to the other room, "Food's on."

Michael sat down at the kitchen table as John slid a couple of eggs and bacon on to a plate. Michael ate and when finished, cleaned up after himself.

"They teach you this stuff in the army." Michael said.

'What's that?" John asked.

"Cleaning up…good hygiene…all that. Were you in?" he asked.

John looked at the floor, and then raised his right hand up for Michael to see more clearly.

"Oh, yeah, sorry…how'd that happen anyway?" he asked.

"Farming accident…smashed with a sledge hammer." John said.

"You didn't miss anything…the war that is. Just a bunch of guys killing a bunch of other guys – savage when you think about it." Michael said.

"Your father told me you were a hero…saved some German guy's life." John said.

"Hero? Not likely. They don't hand out medals for saving the bad guys. Now, if I would have stuck a bayonet in his face, left his family wondering what ever happened to Fritz…that would have been heroic in somebody's eyes. I would have gotten a damn ticker tape parade, but no…I drag the guy back across the lines so that he can try to kill some more Americans for God and the motherland another day." Michael said.

"And what about your friend from Eagle River? The one over there with you." John asked.

"Didn't make it…poor bastard tried to out-do my little show. Threw himself on a grenade. Wasn't a pretty site…it wasn't instant either like you might think. He didn't aim very well and he hung on for a couple hours with the lower half of his body blown to hell screaming until someone could finally get a shot of morphine in him. Then he just lay there looking at his guts. I suppose he was wondering if what he did was worth it. I tried to talk with him a bit…tried to comfort him…told him what a hero he was and all that but all the while I was thinking, 'stupid bastard…what'd you go and do that for?'" Michael wiped his hands on a dish cloth. "And that's how that's done." he concluded.

"I was hoping to go…even thought maybe I'd catch up with my brother, Bill." John said.

"Listen to me, Miller, if you think the war is all about honor and glory, you're crazy. You've got a job, a house, food in your kitchen…a truck. You don't know what a lucky bastard you are. I come back here with nothing – nothing. The war ain't about nothing but killing and keeping yourself alive one day at a time" Michael spoke with a tone of bitterness.

"Come on…we're going to see your father." John said.

"I changed my mind." Michael said.

"No such luck, buddy – get in the truck. By the way…if you're looking for a job we could use you." John said.

"Yeah, I could use a job…just to get back on my feet."

"Great. Just stop out and ask for me and I'll get you going. Hope you don't mind hard work."

Michael gave John a dirty look. "Miller, I was raised on hard work. There's not a job you can throw at me that I can't do."

"We could use someone to drive a skidder. It's like a tractor…"

"I know what the hell a skidder is, John…for loading logs on to trucks, sleds, wagons and whatever." Michael rolled his eyes and John laughed.

"Well great…just come on out when you're ready to start."

"I'll be there Monday." Michael said firmly.

37

The apartment was empty and quiet. Stephen and Marion had the day off and Elizabeth offered to prepare meals for the Baker family until they returned. She promised to make Anthony a spaghetti dinner from an old family recipe. He had mentioned to her at one time how much he enjoyed the cooking he had had while stationed in Italy. Abby was restless and looking for an excuse to get out of the apartment and so she offered to help Elizabeth with the shopping to pick up fresh ingredients for tonight's dinner. Freddie picked up the two ladies to take them to the markets in an Italian neighborhood that Elizabeth had suggested.

Anthony had assured Elizabeth that he would be fine, and was actually looking for some time alone. He knew she needed to get out of the apartment and so his words were only to ease her. He had not been alone since he had left the hospital, and now he was beginning to remember the nightmares he had during those first few nights back from the war.

Anthony sat in his wheel chair and stared at the telephone across the room. He thought about calling some of the men from his troop who he knew had come back from duty before him. One man was Skip Morrow, a young man who had been raised in Toronto and moved to the States with his parents just a year before he was drafted into the United States Army. Skip was an ambitious young man who had confided to Anthony and many others in their troop that he wanted to become an artist someday when the war was over. He had planned on moving back to Canada where he would enroll in college and take courses in art and design. Anthony smiled as he thought about how Skip's eyes lit up when he talked about his plans. The young man would often be seen sketching scenes of the small villages where they were stationed. Then Anthony remembered the evening their troop was on route to Venice. They had just left Florence a few hours earlier and were traveling north through the countryside near a vineyard when they were attacked by a small group of German soldiers who had been separated from their company. The attack came quickly and was over in less than ten minutes, but that was all the time it took for the shell of an MP-40 to rip through Skip's forearm. Anthony recalled how he wrapped the young man's arm with an extra shirt from his pack as he waited for the medic to finish attending to another injured. He applied pressure to keep the bleeding down and comforted Skip, telling him things would be alright to keep him from going into shock. That night was long, a night Anthony didn't want to experience again, even in his thoughts. The next day their troop arrived at a hospital in Venice, where the injured were looked after.

Anthony remembered the vacant look in Skip's eyes when the doctor told him that they would have to amputate his right arm at the elbow.

He decided not to make the call and he looked away from the telephone.

He thought now about his last battle. He led his troop to the north of Italy at the Austrian border. It was a quiet wooded area and there was no sign of the enemy. Two men were sent up ahead to scout the area. Two hours had passed since the scouts had left and the men were beginning to relax, thinking that the Germans had already left the area. Anthony lit a cigarette as he sat on the backrest of his jeep, surveying the area. A few of the men were resting, exhausted. Two men played cards while a few others looked on.

Suddenly there was a loud explosion as the jeep behind Anthony's vehicle exploded, hit by a German grenade. Anthony was jolted from his perch and could hear nothing but a loud ringing in his ears. The men came under fire from machine guns and he saw men ripped apart by bullets from a machine gun being fired from a position just beyond the trees. He couldn't move, couldn't get up even though every thought in his head commanded the effort. He noticed his submachine gun a few yards away and crawled on his elbows, dragging his body behind him as the ringing in his ears continued. He reached the machine gun just as the German soldiers emerged from the wooded area fifty yards away. The enemy charged as Anthony lay close to the ground, unnoticed. Anthony flipped the safety with his thumb and in one long, continuous spray of fire, killed more than a dozen Germans.

Anthony recalled how he continued to look around, ready to continue his kill if anything moved. Things started to go white as he was losing blood and then his eyes closed. He was discovered by another troop of Americans the following day. There were no other survivors. The next time he opened his eyes, he could make out the figures of people in white walking around him. The ringing in his ears had diminished and he could hear voices speaking French. Then the steady infusion of medication took him away again into an unconsciousness so deep, he was bereft of all dreams.

He awoke again in another hospital, this time his vision clearer. A doctor, an older man, looked directly into his eyes no more than a few inches from his face and then spoke in a heavy English accent. 'My God, man, I thought you'd never wake up, good show, good show.' The doctor stood up and called to some nurses. From there, his memory was foggy, but he did remember being loaded onto the airplane and the long, uncomfortable ride home. He remembered straining to see if he had legs, as he had no feeling below his waist. He remembered the embarrassment as an attendant had to clean him up after he had accidentally relieved himself.

Now Anthony thought about the men who didn't come home at all - too many! He thought about the men who would come back as hero's, but would keep quiet about their courage not wanting to relive the war through stories they would be asked to tell a thousand times. He thought about a few men he knew who would come back and mask their cowardice by telling lies of where they had been, what they had seen and things they had never done. As a leader, his duty was to lead, but also to comfort. Regardless of who the man was, what he did or didn't do, he always told them that they would be alright. Everything would be alright. He was always telling people that things would be alright when he always seemed to know in his heart that, somehow, they wouldn't be. At least he could be sure in his own mind that things would never be the same.

Anthony would not call anyone today. The war wasn't over, not physically, not mentally and certainly not emotionally. A tear formed in his eye, but went no further. It was time to face the fact that he would probably never walk again.

The windows of the apartment were tall and heavy. He would never be able to open them. If dragging himself to the window and out on to the ledge to throw himself to the street below was going to be a part of his plan, it would have to wait until a warm summer night when he could convince Stephen to leave an open window in his bedroom. Slitting his wrists would mean ending his life in his father's apartment where he couldn't be sure of who would find him. He surely didn't want his dear father to find his only son lying in a pool of blood. And he didn't like the idea of Abby finding out for the first time in her life that she had a brother, only to discover him dead from suicide. For a young man returning from the war, he now had only one responsibility and that was to survive at all cost, if for no one else, for the benefit of his sister.

Anthony wheeled his chair to a cabinet where the liquor was stored. He reached to the cabinet and opened it, finding several cut crystal bottles filled with a variety of alcohol. He froze, staring at the bottles. This could be his escape, just for today. This could be a way for him to forget his situation. Thinking about the war and his situation was becoming a bad habit and taking a drink would only trade one bad habit for another. He slammed the cabinet door shut and let out a loud frustrated moan.

He now wheeled over to the bookshelves that separated the rooms. He would loose himself in reading. He stared up at the books. The one he wanted, an adventure book, "*West With the Night* a memoir by Beryl Markham, was near the top shelf. He wheeled across the room to an umbrella stand near the front door. Anthony grabbed a long, carved walking stick that his father had picked up during one of his adventures. He examined it closely. It had the head of a lion carved at the top. The lion's carved beard had edges just sharp enough to hook over the spine of the hard-covered book. He wheeled back to the shelf and taking the walking stick, reached up to the shelf. He carefully maneuvered the edge of the walking stick over the book. He snagged it and gave a sudden tug which brought several books falling from the shelf and landing on his legs.

His first reaction was of anger and frustration until he noticed that he felt something in his leg. He picked the books from his lap and now set them on the open shelf in front of him. He took the sharp edge of the walking stick and tapped the spot where the books had landed. He closed his eyes thinking that perhaps his eyes were telling him that he was feeling the sensation. He tapped a little harder and a smile came across his face.

38

John and Michael drove to one of the neighborhoods of Phelps to a small house. Doc's house was a company house surrounded by several other small houses, very plain and simple. It was late in the day and John could smell potatoes frying from one of the houses nearby. John could see the name "Fitzgerald" on the mailbox.

"I suppose this brings back a lot of memories." John said.

"It would if it weren't for the fact that I parked across the street the other day when I got back and stared at this place for about an hour. Five minutes…that's all, and then we go – right?" Michael said.

"Yeah, five minutes."

Thomas Fitzgerald pulled back his curtain to see who drove up. He was wearing a sleeveless t-shirt. He grabbed his shirt and threw it on as he opened the door and stood there watching to see what would happen next. Michael looked over at John, shrugged his shoulders and then opened the door of the truck. Michael walked toward his father and now his father was walking toward him as well. Thomas extended his hand to shake and Michael swallowed hard.

John threw Michael's duffle bag off from the back of the truck and drove off. Michael turned to see that his ride was leaving.

"Hello, Michael."

"Hi."

It was awkward for both of them. "Mike…I wish I could give you a hug…"

"No…listen…I'm not even sure what I'm doing here. I try to remember you as being a good dad, but then I remember seeing the bruises on mom…"

"I never struck your mother. Mike…I never struck your mother."

Michael finally made eye contact with his father. "That almost sounds believable."

"That's because it's the truth. Mike, I've never lied to you, not once – never. And I'm sure not lying to you now. Your mother, rest her soul…your mother had some problems, Mike. I couldn't figure it out then and I can't figure it out to this day. I mean…we all have problems from time to time…but your mother…she'd never say a word about what was bothering her. I tried to find out what was going on, I swear I did. And when I couldn't get an answer I'd get pissed off and go out drinking…I know that didn't help. I didn't know what to do…I didn't know how I could help the situation. I was frustrated…I was sad for her and I was alone."

"Are you sure you didn't hit her? Maybe smack her around a bit when you'd come home from the bar?"

This comment angered Doc, but he held back his emotions and looked Michael straight in the eye. "I loved your mother, Mike, and I told you I never, never struck that woman."

Mike looked off to the side. "Alright. Let's give this a try."

Doc felt relief. "You thirsty? Sure you are. Come on in, let's have something to drink…I'll get you a cold one."

"I'll grab my duffle bag" Michael said as he headed over to where John had dropped it. Doc looked at his son, this young man, and smiled. The two men went inside. Mike looked around and took it all in, the wallpaper, the furniture, even the smell seemed so familiar and he knew that he had missed it.

39

Abby and Elizabeth returned from shopping in the late afternoon and found Anthony sleeping in his wheelchair near the window. He had a book on his lap and a blanket wrapped around his shoulders. Anthony woke to the sounds of people in the apartment. Freddie was placing bags of groceries on the kitchen table and Abby was already taking things out of the bag that she carried in. Elizabeth came over to him.

"I'm sorry we woke you, Anthony. Would you like me to take you to your bedroom where you can continue your nap while we prepare supper?" She asked.

"No, thanks…I just dozed off while reading." he replied.

"Anything new happen while we were gone?" Abby asked from across the room.

"Not a thing, Sis!" he shouted back to her.

"Maybe you and Anthony would like to play a game of chess while I prepare dinner." Elizabeth asked Abby.

"I thought that maybe I could help." Abby responded.

"With all due respect, no one comes into the kitchen while I'm preparing a meal! It's nothing but chaos! But…when you taste how good it all turns out, you don't really care." she said with a smile.

"Alright, Anthony? A game of chess?" Abby asked as she walked into the living room from the kitchen.

"Sure, that sounds great." he said with a smile.

Abby sat in a chair and slipped off her shoes. She noticed Anthony smiling. "You're in a good mood." she said, looking for a response.

"Just enjoying the book I've been reading, that's all." Anthony set up the chessboard, taking the pieces from an engraved walnut box that was kept on a shelf below the chess table. Anthony smiled at Abby and she began to help set up the chess pieces.

"Elizabeth and I went to a wonderful neighborhood where there were bakeries and meat markets and all sorts of places where we could buy nice, fresh ingredients for tonight's dinner. It was really terrific and I want to take you there someday." Abby said excitedly.

"That sounds great, Abby. Someday we'll go there, I promise."

"Father will be home for dinner and I think he'll be so pleased." Abby moved her pawn and waited for Anthony to move. Anthony studied the board.

"I propose a glass of wine before dinner!" Elizabeth called from the kitchen. She came into the room with a bottle in one hand and holding the stems of three glasses in the other. She handed the bottle to Anthony and produced a cork screw from the pocket of her apron.

"You're a mind-reader, Liz." Anthony said with a smile. He opened the bottle and glasses were filled.

The ladies looked to Anthony with anticipation of a toast, as if it was a sense of duty belonging to the man. Anthony raised his glass and had an apparent look of thought as he glanced toward the window. At last, Anthony turned his glance toward the women.

"I propose a toast to the two indispensable women in my life, a sister, a twin who has come to me after all these years to fill a void I never knew existed, but somehow always felt. We will never be separated again." Abby wiped a tear from her eye.

"And to Liz, a woman brought to me by way of kismet to aid me in this time of need and help me rebuild my life through her hard work and friendship. Here's to you."

The glasses chimed as they observed this moment. Abby felt warm inside and for a fleeting second was aware that she wasn't thinking of John, but taking pleasure in the moment that was meant for family. Elizabeth excused herself and returned to the kitchen.

The telephone rang. "I'll get it." Elizabeth called out. Anthony and Abby wondered if they would ever get to their game. Elizabeth came into the room wiping her hands on her white apron. She picked up the receiver.

"Yes, this is where Anthony Baker lives. Would you like to speak with him? May I tell Mister Baker who this is? May I ask what this is in regards to? Oh…I see…yes, just a moment please." Elizabeth brought the telephone over to Anthony. He looked up at Elizabeth.

"Who is it?" he asked as he turned his wheelchair from the table toward her. Elizabeth held her hand over the mouthpiece. "It's a woman, her name is Margaret Rice, she says her brother was in the war with you." A look of concern came over Anthony's face and he slowly reached for the receiver.

"Hello, this is Anthony Baker."

"Mister Baker, this is Margaret Rice. My brother, Steve… Skip was stationed with you in Italy."

Anthony froze, fearing what would come next.

"Mister Baker, are you there?" she asked.

"Yes."

"I didn't know who else to turn to."

"Is Skip alright?" Anthony asked.

"Yes, well, in a way. He's been staying with my husband and I since he returned, since our parents have been gone for some time now. My husband took a loaded handgun from him this morning. We think he was going to…well…" Her words drifted off.

"Yes, yes I know. I understand. So he's alright then?"

"For now, but it's getting to be too much for us to handle. We can't afford to get professional help for him. We had our priest come over to the house, but that didn't go very well." The purpose of her call was becoming obvious.

"Would you like me to talk with him?" Anthony asked.

"Oh, yes…yes, please. He tells everyone how you saved his life, kept him from bleeding to death. Now maybe you can save his life again."

"Give me your address and phone number." Anthony's words reflected his take-charge character, a temperament he hadn't expressed since his days as the young man's sergeant. Anthony nodded to Elizabeth who had been standing there listening. She quickly produced a tablet of paper and a pen. Anthony took down the information.

"Now listen, Margaret, you tell him that I called you, tracking an old war buddy. Tell him I'm coming to visit. Leave it at that, nothing more…understood?"

"Yes, yes, Mister Baker."

"Sergeant Baker." he said to her. Elizabeth and Abby glanced at each other and words weren't necessary. They were witnessing a transformation. An altering of a man's persona to fit an exact need at an exact time. An assignment was being taken on by this man with the significance, fervor and commitment necessary to accomplish a purpose they could only imagine, to save a man's life.

40

It was an overcast day and the weather seemed to change every hour from sleet to snow although the temperature was unseasonably warm for late February. The men couldn't work and a few of them sat around the canteen playing cards. Most of the men stayed in the bunkhouse. They kept a fire going to keep off the chill and for once the temperature seemed comfortable, a good day to stay in. Some of the men slept and some wrote letters home. John would take the rest of the day off, but made the rounds this morning to check on the men, occasionally helping those who were writing home with the spelling or selection of a word.

Nelson came through the bunkhouse and shouted to the men, "Tomorrow will be a good day to stock up on some venison." The men were surprised and looked up from what they were doing. No one had heard him speak so loudly since before the attack. "I'll take one volunteer hunting with me - only one. Who's it going to be?" No one replied.

Without much time for consideration of the offer, Nelson shouted to Steeg "Okay, Steeg, tomorrow morning, Five AM, you be here and don't be late." Steeg looked around and made eye contact with John. John shrugged his shoulders.

Steeg said, "I have some chores to do here…"

"Forget it, Steeg, I ain't dragging a deer out of the woods in my shape. Besides, looks like you could stand to drop a couple pounds. Five AM and I said don't be late." Steeg looked again at John and gave a grimace, but got up off of his bunk and proceeded to grab his boots and gear. John slapped Steeg on the back and wished him luck, then proceeded to walk through the bunkhouse to be of help where he could. Steeg spent the rest of the evening carefully writing a letter.

The next morning Steeg came out of the bunkhouse wearing his heavy red wool coat and tall rubber boots for his trek in the wet marsh. Nelson came out of the canteen with a paper bag containing food for their hunt. Nelson barked orders to Doc to toss a couple pair of snowshoes in the back of his pickup truck. Doc nodded and hurried back to his shop. The two men met at Nelson's truck. Steeg stood with one foot in the cab and the door open.

"Where are we going?" Steeg asked.

"I saw some big buck tracks just off of Military Road. Thought we'd give that a try." Nelson replied. Doc had come out of his shop with the snowshoes and tossed them into the bed of the truck. He gave a couple slams to the side of the truck to get Nelson's attention that he had fulfilled his task and he gave a nod to Steeg.

"Good luck, Steeg." Doc said.

Two shotguns were resting in the rack behind their heads, an over and under shotgun and a double barrel. Nelson drove recklessly as if he was intentionally hitting every pothole along the gravel road. After about twenty minutes of driving they came to a fire lane off of Military Road. The fire lanes provided access deep into the forest so that fires could be fought with some strategy. Nelson slowed down and they drove deep into the forest. It was early morning and still no sun to be seen through the thick, dense fog. The trees and branches provided so much cover overhead that it became even darker. Steeg couldn't figure out why Nelson had picked such a poor day to hunt for deer. It would be hard to see anything and the deer usually went for deep cover on days such as this.

"You go about a hundred yards up this trail and sit. I'll move around to the south in a big sweep and see if I can drive a big buck out of that thicket." Nelson directed. Nelson handed Steeg a .410 shotgun that he had behind the seat of the truck.

"Why this gun? It's a pretty small gun to take down a deer." Steeg asked.

"'Cause this one's got good luck, that's why. Besides, this other one is my own lucky gun and I don't let nobody use it." Nelson replied. The .410 was a smaller gauge of shotgun and it would be hard to drop a large deer with so small a weapon. Steeg thought that this seemed like a wasted trip so he might as well just go up the trail and rest while Nelson moved around wasting his time. Steeg found a fallen tree that provided some protection from the wind, but there was still a heavy mist in the air and it chilled him to the bone. Steeg sat and waited, then finally pulled out his pocket watch. About a half-hour had passed since they split up and there was no sign of Nelson.

Nelson sat back at the truck eating sandwiches and hard-boiled eggs from the bag he had brought. When he finally had his fill, he shoved what was left of his sandwich into his mouth and closed up the paper bag. He opened the truck door very quietly, stepped out and took his twelve-gauge over-under shotgun from the rack. He closed the door quietly, just enough to keep it closed, but not to make a sound. Nelson walked slowly up the fire road one step and then another until he could finally make out the figure of Steeg leaning over the fallen tree. Nelson got down on one knee and put his gun up to his shoulder. He took steady aim and paused. Many thoughts raced through his head, images of his father beating him as a child, kicking him as he yelled and told him that he was worthless. His mind raced to his years in school in his teens, how girls would giggle and laugh behind his back and the other boys would laugh to his face and call him names. He thought of the nights he lay in bed crying because he felt like a failure all of his life and he had no friends. His job gave him a sense of being, of security and authority. Now it was his turn to push people around and make them do as he saw fit. He was still the foreman, the wood boss and the man that all men feared until the night he was beaten down. He was now the judge and jury and would sentence this man who had beaten him so severely. Wiping a tear from his eye with the thumb of his right hand and re-gripping his gun, he finally squeezed the trigger firing his shot directly into Steeg's back. The shot rang out loud and echoed as Steeg slumped over the fallen tree. Nelson brought his gun down from his shoulder and placed the butt of the stock to the ground. He remained motionless on one knee watching for signs of life from the man he had just shot. There were none.

After a few long minutes to take in what he had just done, Nelson got up and walked back to his truck. He opened the door, put his gun in the rack, got inside and slammed the door. He looked around the truck and then spotting the paper bag, picked it open to pull another sandwich out to eat. He sat there for a long time, then started the truck, slung his right arm over the back of the seat and backed out of the fire lane until he came up to Military Road. Nelson headed back to the camp. Arriving back at his office, he called the sheriff.

"Belke...you know who this is."

Ronald Belke was an overweight middle-aged, balding man with a thin moustache and glasses. He bore two long, faint scar's on his left cheek.

"What is it, Nelson?" he said after a long pause.

"Seems there's been an accident." Nelson said without emotion.

"Someone hurt?" Belke asked.

"Just...get out here." Nelson snarled.

A half hour later Sheriff Belke arrived at the camp and came into the office. Taking off his cap, he started to hang it on a hook on the wall.

"Not here." Nelson said. "Let's take a walk."

The two men walked over to the canteen where Helmut was mopping the floor.

"What's with that guy?" Belke said.

"He's one of the krauts – don't worry they don't speak English. Sit down…take a load off." Nelson ordered.

"What's going on…you said something about an accident. What kind of accident?" Belke asked.

"The kind that needs to be cleaned up." Nelson said.

"I don't work that way…not anymore. What are you doing asking me to come here like this?" Belke asked, now becoming more nervous.

"Seems to me you owe me one…or did you forget that mess of yours I had to clean up a few years back?" Nelson said. "It's kind of a sad thing… that kid coming home to find mom hanging from the ceiling…that kid's all grown up and just come home from the war. I'd bet he'd be good and pissed to find out that the sheriff that came to his house and comforted him was the one who choked the life out of his mother 'cause she wouldn't have anything to do with him." Nelson said.

"We had a deal…that's all in the past…you was supposed to forget all that…that was part of the deal." Belke spoke nervously and ran his fingers along the scars on his cheek.

"Well maybe I'm getting my memory back. Yeah, that's it…I remember now…you flirting with that woman, another guy's wife – guy works here as a matter of fact. She don't want nothing to do with you…you rough her up a bit. She's too scared to say nothing to her old man and so you keep after her. Then one day…my dear friend, Sheriff Belke, puts his hands around that poor lady's neck until she's real quiet."

"Stop it…what do you want? I ain't paying you nothing…" Belke said.

"Oh, Bob…what have I done? What am I going to do? I remember it very well now. So your old friend comes to the rescue…hangs that poor sweet woman and makes it look like an accident. My…she was sweet. You know Belke…she was still a little warm when I got there…"

Belke broke down, "Stop…stop…what do you need me to do?"

"Well, that's more like it. There's a guy's been shot…let's say a hunting accident. He's on a fire lane off of Military Road" Nelson said.

"You want it to look like an accident?" Belke asked.

"No…I don't think so…bullet went through the back. Just get rid of the body somewhere." Nelson spoke in a quiet voice. He looked over at Helmut and nodded smiling. Helmut nodded back with a blank expression.

"Anybody know he was with you?" Belke asked.

"Everyone here…don't worry about that. You just take care of your end…and make damn sure you put him somewhere deep….got that? Oh yeah…one other thing, take a look for my shotgun…a single barrel .410."

Sheriff Belke said nothing further. He got up from the table and left.

Nelson sat for a minute to collect his thoughts and then gave Helmut another look and left. He entered the bunkhouse where most of the men were resting.

"Any of you guys seen Steeg?" Nelson asked.

The men who were awake said no. One man shouted back, "Thought he was hunting with you."

"Yeah, he was…but I dropped him off at the road coming in about two hours ago…said he wanted to hunt a little more. He's got my gun." Nelson said.

There was no response from the men.

"Well, when you see him…tell him to bring my .410 back." Nelson said as he turned to leave.

41

Anthony and Stephen set out on their excursion to De Moines, Iowa for Anthony's visit with Skip Morrow. Anthony knew that travel would be a challenge and that he would need someone with physical strength to assist his needs. He asked that Elizabeth stay behind and with some reluctance she agreed. He also considered that a few days apart might give her the rest he felt she likely needed. Anthony also spent some time with his father, filling him in on the purpose of the trip and seeking his wisdom on how best to handle the situation. Stephen suggested going by car as he felt trains lacked proper accommodations for people in wheelchairs, but Anthony insisted they travel by train as it would afford them a more comfortable and relaxing ride.

His father's company fitted Anthony with leg braces similar to the ones they had provided for FDR. Anthony struggled with his crutches as he lacked strength below his waist, but knew it had to be this way to maneuver through the aisles. The crutches and leg braces drew some attention, along with the fact that Anthony was dressed in his formal military attire. One man stared until Anthony made eye contact and then gave him the 'thumbs up' and a wink.

The stationmaster assisted Stephen as they guided Anthony up the steps and to his seat. The trip took them across the flat farmlands of northern Illinois, and the two men sat in silence, each reading with occasional glances at the scenery which never seemed to change. Anthony produced a pen from his pocket and used it to underline parts of his book for future reference. When Stephen wasn't watching, Anthony ran the pen deeply into the upper part of his right leg. He was beginning to feel something, if ever so slightly, it was a sensation that had not been there the week before. He discretely switched the pen to his left leg and repeated the deep massage of the pen into his muscles. He smiled.

They arrived in De Moines by late afternoon. Stephen had arranged for a taxi service to pick them up at the train station. The taxi service would provide local transportation during their stay and the driver would assist Anthony from the train and into the back seat of the taxi cab. The driver, a thin middle-aged man who went by the name of Bigsby, helped Stephen put the crutches in the trunk of the car. Bigsby typically wore casual attire, but for this task he took his uniform out of the back of his closet and even made the extra effort of polishing his shoes the night before.

"Where to, Mister Chase?" Bigsby asked. Anthony was taken back as it had been years since he had heard Stephen's last name. He had always just been 'Stephen'.

"The Savoy Hotel, please." Stephen replied.

"No, no." Anthony put his hand on Stephen's forearm. "I think we should go straight to Skip's – you can drop me off there and Bigsby can drive you to the hotel. You can get us checked in with the hotel and then come back for me." Anthony spoke with inflexibility in his voice.

"As you wish, Anthony." Stephen replied.

"Bigsby, please take us to Seven Seventeen Oakcrest Drive. Do you know where it is?" Stephen asked.

Bigsby turned around to face his passengers. "Lived here all my life, Mister Chase. I sure do." Bigsby turned back around, looked in all directions and drove off.

The neighborhood was middle-class and the homes were well taken care of. The driver pulled into the driveway and shut off the car. Anthony noticed a curtain being pulled back and someone peering from behind. Bigsby unloaded the crutches from the trunk as Stephen walked around the car and opened the door for Anthony. Anthony lifted his right leg and dragged it out of the car, then lifted his left leg and let it also drop to the pavement. He sat for a moment, waiting for his crutches.

The front door opened and Skip walked out to meet Anthony, smiling.

"Sergeant Baker!" Skip came to an abrupt halt, stood at attention and saluted with his left arm. Anthony grinned and extended his left hand to shake.

"At ease...good to see you, Skip. Give me a minute here to get out of the car and we can go inside and get caught up," Anthony said as Stephen positioned the crutches for Anthony to take.

"Gosh, Sarge, I had no idea. What happened?" Skip asked.

"Took some shrapnel in the spine. They got most of it out, but there's still some small pieces causing havoc. Other than that, I'm just fine."

Anthony walked to the house with Stephen walking closely behind him. Anthony nearly lost his balance a couple of times, but quickly recovered. They made it into the house and Skip led Anthony to a chair in the living room. Skip's sister, Margaret, walked into the room.

"Margie, this is Sergeant Baker. I'm sure you've heard me talk about him a hundred times." Skip smiled as his glance went back and forth between his sister and Anthony.

"Nice to meet you, Margaret, we spoke on the phone when I tracked Skip down the other day." Anthony gave her a wink.

"Of course, I'm so glad you decided to come to Iowa for a visit." she said as she shook Anthony's hand.

"And this is Stephen, he's a friend of the family." Anthony said. Both Skip and Margaret shook hands with Stephen.

"Nice to meet both of you. I have a few things to tend to and so I'll leave you now for a couple of hours if that's alright?" Stephen asked Margaret.

"Oh, absolutely, take your time. I was just getting ready to start supper. If you'd like to stop back, dinner is at five." she said to Stephen.

"Thank you all the same, Margaret, but I'll probably be a bit later than that." Stephen directed his response to their host and then turned to Anthony. "I should be back by eight or nine. Is that alright with you?" Stephen asked Anthony.

"If Skip can tolerate my stories that long. What do you say, Skip?"

"That's great, it'll give us time to get caught up." he said.

Margaret's husband came home from work and the four of them enjoyed dinner together. After dinner, Margaret and her husband excused themselves to run a few errands although their real reason was to give Skip and Anthony some time alone to talk in private.

Anthony and Skip settled in the living room with a couple of cold beers. Skip turned on a brass floor lamp as darkness still came early this time of year. The men sat in chairs near each other and Skip watched as Anthony struggled with his leg braces. After a few uncomfortable minutes, Anthony was settled in.

"So how are you adjusting to the left-handed world?" Anthony asked point blank.

Skip looked down and then off to the side. "I don't think I can take it, Sarge. This God damned world doesn't have a thing to offer to a man like me." The words seethed from his lips.

"A man like you? I don't get it, Skip. You have two working legs don't you?" Anthony looked directly at the young man.

"I wanted to be a designer. I had talent, you know that. You saw my sketches of the villages in Italy before…" Skip drifted off.

"The talent is in your eyes, in your mind, the way you see things and interpret them. Is there anything wrong with your left hand?" Anthony asked.

"I'm not left-handed. I'm trying, it's not easy. I have a God-damn hard time getting dressed in the morning. I have to wear pants with a button fly so I can take a piss without asking for help! I get stares from people everywhere I go. Kids think I'm some kind of monster." Skips emotions were a mix of frustration and disappointment.

"Have you been fitted for a prosthetic arm?"

"You mean a hook?"

"My father's company manufactures and distributes medical equipment. Just recently my father purchased the patents to a new line of prosthetic limbs, capable of much more flexibility and movement than the '*hook*' your thinking of. From a distance, it looks like a real hand!" Anthony looked for a reaction from Skip. There was a pause as Skip thought about what Anthony was telling him.

"Where does a guy get one of these?" Skip seemed calmer.

"There are only a few prototypes right now. My father had purchased them along with some tooling from the inventor, an old guy in northern Wisconsin whose father lost an arm in a lumber mill accident."

"So how does this help me? I mean…" Skip was unsure of what to say.

"My father wants to know if you'd be willing to come back with us to Chicago. His company would fit you with a prosthetic arm."

"And what would this cost me?" Skip asked.

"That's just it – nothing! My father needs to have his engineers study all of the details, parts, look for problems, ways to enhance its features…you know."

"So I'd be a guinea pig?" Skip asked.

"You could look at it that way. Or you could consider that you'd be helping every other unfortunate guy who came back from the war to lead a normal life – or as close to normal as a guy can get with a handicap." Anthony paused. His father had taught him long ago that silence plays an important part in negotiations. After a long minute, Skip responded.

"Do you think I'd be able to hold a pencil…a pen maybe?"

"Well, that leads me to my father's other thought. His company has to package and label everything they manufacture. They've always left the commercial art to the packaging manufacturer, but if it's something that you think you might be able to do, he'd be very interested in talking with you about creating a new position in the company. You'd be a graphic artist, designing the logotypes, artwork, instruction manuals and anything related to the medical equipment they manufacture."

"You're kidding me – right?" Skip seemed stunned. Anthony smiled.

"It would take some adjustment. Do you think you could do it?" Anthony asked.

Skip was overwhelmed with emotion. Until this moment he thought his chance at a normal life was over. Here was an opportunity being dropped at his doorstep.

"Where would I live?" Skip asked.

"My father's company could give you an advance to get you started. There are some nice apartments near my father's company. I'm sure we can help you find something near the bus lines. After awhile you could get yourself a car – who knows, maybe meet some nice girl and settle down."

"When do we leave?"

"Stephen and I are going back tomorrow – early afternoon. Would that give you enough time to discuss it with your sister?"

"I don't really need to discuss it with Sis, I'm sure she'd be glad to see me get back on my feet, so to speak."

Anthony clinked the neck of his beer bottle against Skip's.

"That's it then!" Anthony stated.

"That's it." Skip agreed.

42

The next morning the men were having breakfast in the canteen. John came in and Hanna handed him a plate with eggs, potatoes and beans.

"Thanks, Hanna." John said. Then he took a seat at an open table.

One of the men came over and sat next to John. "Nobody's seen Steeg," the man said.

"What do you mean?" John asked.

"Nelson came into the bunkhouse around 4:00 yesterday... says he dropped Steeg off two hours earlier...that Steeg wanted to hunt some more on his own. Kind of funny since Steeg didn't want to go hunting in the first place." the man said.

"Where'd they go hunting?" John asked.

"I think he was talking about Military road." the man said.

"I'll go take a look around. Where's the German crew?" John asked.

"Nelson sent them out a half hour ago...they're cutting the forty in section seventeen."

John finished up his breakfast and headed over to the maintenance shed.

"Good morning, Doc." John said.

"Right back at you, John. Say, I never did thank you for... well, bringing Michael over and..."

"Don't mention it, Doc. Say, I heard Nelson and Steeg went hunting yesterday, you know anything about that?" John asked.

"Yep...tossed a pair of snowshoes in the back of Nelson's pickup." Doc replied. "Nelson was talking about seeing some big buck tracks up at Military Road."

John rubbed his chin in thought looking down to the floor then raising his eyes to meet Doc's. "Steeg's missing...didn't come back to the bunkhouse yesterday."

"Think there's something fishy going on?" Doc asked.

"With Nelson...absolutely." John said.

"You got another pair of snowshoes here, don't you?" John asked.

"I'll put then in the cab of your truck John. I'll toss in a few flares too...just in case. You want me to go with you?" Doc asked.

"No...thanks, Doc. I think I'll just take a little look around. Military Road you say, huh?"

John now came up to Military Road and slowed down. John could see a set of tire tracks leading into one of the fire lanes. The tracks had a light dusting of fresh snow on them. John parked his truck about fifty feet into the fire lane so it would not be seen from the road. He strapped on the snowshoes and went down the trail. He could see several tire marks and footprints where a vehicle must have been parked. John looked closely at the tire marks and thought 'two different vehicles'. Now, there was one set of footprints from the left side of where the truck had been parked. John followed the footprints about another fifty yards up the trail where he spotted the fallen tree. There was not much sunlight this morning but still enough to see a bloody mess. He touched the blood that was now hard and rubbed his fingers around. He held his fingers up to the light and now could be sure that it was blood. John lit one of the flares. In the erratic light of the flame John could see a massive amount of blood, broken branches, and apparent signs that something tragic had happened here. John could barely hold back his feelings and walked a few steps away to let his emotions catch up with him when he tripped across something in the snow. John backed up a step and stooped down. He brushed his gloved hands around in the snow until he uncovered what it was that he tripped over, a shotgun. John held the gun up with both hands under the sunlight to examine it more closely. It was a .410 shotgun. John trembled with nervousness as he struggled to think clearly about what to do next. He decided that he would have to hide the gun until details could be sorted out about what had happened.

John drove back to the camp and put the gun in his office behind some boxes.

43

Anthony, Stephen and Skip arrived in Chicago. At Anthony's suggestion, Stephen was preparing to take Skip by cab to a motel near the Baker Medical Corporation. Anthony said that he was exhausted from the trip and told Skip that Stephen would take care of all the details and get him settled in. Then he told Stephen that he would call Freddie to get a lift home from the station, although he had another plan. Anthony watched the cab driver load their suitcases into the trunk of the cab.

"Are you sure you'll be alright, sir?" Stephen asked Anthony.

"Yes, yes, just look after Skip. Make sure he gets settled into a nice place. I'll call him tomorrow. I'm tired and just want to go home and relax a bit."

"There's a pay phone over there, would you like me to call Freddie?" Stephen asked.

"No! Thanks, Stephen, I might stick around awhile…maybe have a beer. I can give him a call when I'm ready. I just need to relax a bit before I head home."

"I understand. I'll see you this evening." Stephen said with a smile.

Anthony just gave a nod and an assuring smile. Skip leaned out of the window of the cab and waved to Anthony and then called out, "Thanks!"

Anthony stood on his crutches and watched as the cab drove off. Something was racing through his mind. He wanted to try walking as far as he could. If he fell, he didn't want Stephen there to pick him up. If he was going to make it on his own, it meant a chance of failing on his own as well. Anthony took a step and then another. He was aware of how awkward he might look to some people.

He looked far ahead. He saw benches a half a block away and planned this as his goal. If he made it to the benches, he could turn around and walk back to the benches outside of the train depot. More awkward steps and then a few firm and steady steps. After about ten feet, he felt a pain shoot down his leg. Feeling pain was better than feeling nothing at all and it lifted Anthony's spirit. In a few seconds the pain subsided and he continued to walk. He walked past the benches that were his goal and paused at the corner. The traffic was light this time of day and so he cautiously planted his crutches in front of himself past the curb. He made it out into the crosswalk and walked to the other side of the street. He now knew how to handle curbs and so he stepped up onto the next block and rested at the corner. He turned himself around and now planned his walk back to the depot.

Anthony took a deep breath and began walking back. He noticed two old men sitting on the bench watching him. It didn't matter. He was making progress and now beginning to actually feel the concrete through the metal braces as his feet connected with the pavement. His mind raced ahead, planning his steps, measuring the distance between himself and the next goal. Step by step he felt less reliance upon the braces, less and less of his weight on the crutches and more of his weight was now being transferred to his leg muscles. He continued this exercise for the next two hours, only stopping to rest for ten minutes.

Late in the afternoon, Anthony called Elizabeth from the payphone that was mounted to the side of the train depot.

"Liz?" he asked.

"Yes, Anthony…are you alright?

"Yes, yes, I'm fine."

"Stephen called here an hour ago to check on you. I told him you hadn't returned yet."

"Well, I'm alright…just getting used to the crutches that's all. You want to come pick me up? I'm at Union Station."

"Yes, I'll call Freddie. We can be there in twenty minutes. I…" She stopped before telling him that she had missed him.

"What?" Anthony asked.

"Nothing, we'll see you in a bit." She hung up the phone.

Freddie drove Elizabeth in the limo and parked on Monroe street near the station. There was a street vendor selling flowers and Elizabeth thought it would be nice to buy a bouquet of mixed flowers for the apartment. She looked for Anthony through the crowd, but didn't see him.

Suddenly the crowd parted and from thirty feet away she saw Anthony. She smiled and waved. Anthony made eye contact and then raised his hand to stop her from coming closer. She looked puzzled, but stopped. Anthony walked with the crutches for a few feet and then stopped. Elizabeth nudged forward as if she was going to run to him, but stopped. Anthony removed the crutch from under his left arm and moved it over to his right hand. A shocked expression came across Elizabeth's face. Anthony paused, took a step and another with his crutches now out from under his right arm and being used only as a walking stick. He took a few more steps and then dropped the crutches altogether.

The flowers dropped from Elizabeth's hands and she raised her palms to cover her open mouth. Tears began to stream down her cheeks as Anthony continued to stagger toward her. She ran to him and stopped inches from him. She cautiously reached her arms out and slowly wrapped them around him. He sighed deeply as he threw his arms around her. She cried openly and a tear rolled down his cheek. Her emotions ran deep with joy, admiration and a small bit of fear that he would no longer need her.

44

Sheriff Belke came out to the camp. He was nervous about what he had to discuss with Nelson. He had convinced himself to be calm and in control, but all of that faded quickly when Nelson came storming up to his car.

"What the hell you doing here? I didn't tell you to come here!" Nelson growled.

"I know…I know…but…" Belke stammered.

"'*But*' nothing…stay the hell away. You take care of that situation?' Nelson asked.

"That's what I come about…it's done…taken care of…as best as I could."

"What the *hell you mean* the '*best*' you could? You better not…"

Belke became excited and quickly interrupted, "It's taken care of…but the ground's too frozen. I found a spot near the dump and covered him with some boards from the old shacks that used to be there during the depression. We'll have to take care of him in the spring."

Now Nelson was getting angrier.

"And another thing…I didn't see any gun.'

"God damn it…damn! You stupid son of a bitch…get the hell out of here, I'll take care of it myself. And don't you ever come out here unless I tell you to." Nelson demanded. Belke left and Nelson went back to work. Later in the day he got into his truck and drove out to the fire lane.

Nelson came up to the fallen tree and kicked around in the snow. He saw more tire tracks and then noticed snowshoe tracks leading right up to the spot where he had taken Steeg's life. He seemed frozen and then slowly looked up and around as if sniffing the air for a scent or trace of something. He looked around and didn't find his gun. At first he thought that Belke had come back out to finish his work, but then saw tracks in the snow. Nelson didn't know what to make of it and so he headed back to camp.

John was at the camp and seeing Nelson drive up, he came out of his office marching up to Nelson's truck.

"Where's Steeg Onsgaard?" John asked.

"Don't ask me. How should I know? I dropped him off down the road from here Sunday afternoon...even gave him my .410 to use." Nelson said and then realizing that maybe he had said too much, he stopped. Then he began barking orders to some of the men in the yard.

John went back into the office and then noticed Nelson walking near John's truck. Nelson had his back to the pickup and then leaned awkwardly backwards to look into the bed of the pickup. He turned around and spat a long trail of tobacco juice and then walked away.

When Nelson was out of sight, John took the snowshoes from his truck and carried them over to the maintenance shed. John spent the next few minutes in Doc's shop thinking. Doc was sharpening saw blades and didn't even notice John. John was careful not to say anything to Doc for fear of compromising the situation even more. John came out of the machine shop and walked up to Nelson. "As General Manager and Records Keeper for the company I'm going to need a sheriff's report and something to tell his family." John spoke directly and confidently to Nelson.

Nelson hesitated for a minute. A scowl came over his face and he finally said, "I'll give the Sheriff a call, but I don't know what the fuss is. The guy's only been missing a day. Not like no one's ever quit and walked off before."

"I think if Steeg had quit he would have collected wages due." John said.

"Not necessarily. From the story I heard, when he worked on your old man's farm he didn't collect his wages after smashing your hand in that little accident. Word gets around don't it?" Nelson spoke with re-discovered confidence. "You have it your way...I call the sheriff and have him file a missing person report or whatever you want...*boss!*" Nelson had a sneer on his face. He spat tobacco on the ground and walked off.

Late in the afternoon the sheriff's car pulled into camp. Belke made his way up to the office and passed Helmut who was walking toward the office carrying a ladder and a bucket of tools. The two men exchanged nods. Belke walked in, followed by the German.

"What the hell took you so long? You find my gun?" Nelson barked at Belke. Belke nodded toward Helmut and Nelson let out a laugh. He grumbled, "I told you already he's one of them krauts, he don't speak a word of English. Do you kraut?" he shouted at Helmut. Helmut looked puzzled.

"I didn't go back out there to look for the gun, I thought you were going to take care of that." Belke replied. Nelson looked puzzled.

"Miller...the guy running the operation here...wants to file a missing person report." Nelson said.

"No harm in doing that." Belke said.

"You take his report...tell him you already questioned me, then you stop back here and see me." Nelson said.

"Not a problem." Belke said.

Nelson yelled out the door to the men, "You guys tell Miller that the sheriff is here."

A short while later John came into the office as Nelson was leaving. Now, except for Helmut, John was alone with the sheriff.

"I'd like to file a missing person report." John said.

"Nelson already gave me the information. Not much we can do in situations like this and besides it's only been…what…a day or two? We usually wait at least a week in case the guy just went off on his own…maybe on a drunk…maybe with some whore." Belke spoke as an expert.

"But there's more." John said.

Helmut dropped his pail of tools, making a loud noise that startled both of the men.

"Nein., ist er mit dem fetten Mann. Hören Sie, vertrauen Sie nicht diesem Mann. Wir müssen sprechen."

"No, he is with the fat man. Listen, do not trust this man. We must talk." Helmut said.

"Was Sie bedeuten."

"What do you mean?" John asked in response.

Belke looked at John. "You understand him? You speak German?" He asked.

"Täuschen Sie Sie verstehen nicht viel vor"

"Pretend you do not understand much." Helmut quickly interrupted.

"Uh…not much…just a couple of words here and there." John said.

Belke nodded.

"Senden Sie ihn weg und wir Sprechen."

"Send him away and we will talk." Helmut said.

John gave a look as if he didn't understand and shrugged his shoulders, then turned to Sheriff Belke. "I don't know what he wants, I think he's complaining about the tools or something… this might take awhile to figure out. Sheriff Belke, you're probably right about this Onsgaard fellow…I'd hate to put you through a lot of work and then have him turn up drunk and broke in a couple of days. So if you think we should just let it go for now, then let's just let it go." John spoke as he got up and walked toward the door.

Sheriff Belke followed him. "That's a good idea. That's how these things work." he said. He left and John watched as he walked toward his car.

"Herr Miller," Helmut spoke.

John put his finger to his mouth. "Shhhh." He continued to watch until the sheriff's car was moving down the road.

"You speak English?" John asked.

"Yes…quite well I think. I did work in German Intelligence after all." Helmut said.

"Well, doesn't that beat all. How come you never told me?" John asked.

"You spoke German from the first time I met you. I thought you preferred it." Helmut said.

"So what did you mean before…about him being with the fat man." John asked.

"The other evening…Sunday, I'm scrubbing floors in the canteen and the sheriff comes. Nelson asked him to *clean up* for him…gave him the location of the body…all of that." Helmut said.

"The body? You mean Steeg's dead?" John asked.

"Yes, I'm afraid so." Helmut said with concern.

"Why would a sheriff go pick up a body...I don't get it..." John said.

"The two of them go back several years. Nelson covered up for Belke...something about a woman that the sheriff killed... put a rope around her and made it look like an accident. Now Nelson has Belke where he wants him...re-paying an old debt." Helmut explained.

"My God...it sounds like it might have been Doc Fitzgerald's wife. What about Steeg?" John asked.

"I'm sorry...shot in the back from what I could tell." Helmut said.

John sat down and put his face into his hands. Then John took a deep breath. "We've got to get this bastard." John spoke into his hands and then looking up, said again, "We've got to get this bastard."

"Helmut, tell no one of this conversation." John said.

"Yes, I agree." Helmut replied.

John went back to his cabin and prepared a fire. He paced the floor, sat and then paced the floor again. He knew he couldn't take any chances, his plan to bring Nelson to justice had to be well-planned from the start.

The next morning John drove to the sheriff's office in Florence County. He walked into the brick building. The ceiling was tall and there was a fan slowly circulating the warm air around the office. A woman was sitting behind a wooden desk typing. A Golden Labrador jumped to its feet and came over to John sniffing at his legs. John crouched down and stroked the dog's neck and ears.

"You made a friend." the lady spoke.

"Suppose so. Um...is the sheriff around?" John asked.

"Be back any minute, just went across the street to the hardware store. Old man Jacobson thinks a couple of young boy's been shoplifting fishing lures. Last time though, it turned out that he had them in his apron pocket. Think he's getting kind of foggy." She pointed to her head and made a funny face. Then she gave a little laugh and John smiled.

"Well, would it be alright if I wait?"

"Sure, have a seat. Anything I can help you with?"

"Um…no miss, it's kind of complicated."

"Oh, I see. Well, suit yourself. Want some coffee? Oh… here he comes now." she said. John looked in the direction of the door he had just come through.

Sheriff Olson was in his mid-sixties with white hair, brown eyes and a pleasant disposition. His work primarily consisted of arresting an occasional poacher or busting up a still after confiscating a small sample bottle or two for evidence. He didn't take much pleasure in putting a man in jail for trying to feed his family or make a couple of dollars from selling a few gallons of moonshine, and so most moon-shiner's got off with a stiff warning and the poachers would have their shotgun confiscated for a month or two. It wasn't the system, but it worked, and with any luck it would continue to work a few more months until his retirement.

Sheriff Olson took off his cap and noticed John sitting on the wooden bench a few feet away with the dog's head planted firmly on his lap.

"Ginger's got a new friend." The sheriff said with a grin.

"That's just what I said, Al…didn't I?" She said as she turned her gaze toward John.

John reached his left hand over to shake, trying not to disturb the dog.

"Name's John Miller, sir. I'm with the Anderson Lumber Company over in Phelps."

Sheriff Olson shook John's hand with a puzzled look.

"Injured my right hand awhile back…"

The sheriff nodded in understanding.

"I see. I'm Sheriff Olson, what can I help you with, Mr. Miller?"

"Can we talk in private?"

"Well…I don't know as if there is such a thing. You're looking at the whole sheriff's department." After a brief pause, he continued, "Nancy, you must have some errands to run. I see pork chops are on sale over at Haberkorn's grocery store. I remember that boyfriend of your telling me how much he liked your pork chops."

Nancy took a cigarette out of her purse and put it in her mouth. She put on a headscarf and gave the sheriff a smile. She put on her coat and headed for the door. Sheriff Olson lit his Zippo lighter and she paused long enough to light up.

"I'll be back in fifteen minutes." she said.

"Oh, you take your time Nancy. It's a slow day. At least I hope so."

As the door closed, Sheriff Olson took off his coat and hung it on the coat tree in the corner behind the door.

"Take your coat off, Mr. Miller."

"Thanks."

The sheriff made his way over to his desk and sat in his chair. He straightened up a few things from his desk as John came over to sit down.

"I'm not sure where to start, Sheriff. There's a man from our camp…actually a friend. I believe he's been shot in cold blood."

The sheriff leaned forward. "John, right?"

"Yes sir."

"John, you have a sheriff right there in Phelps. Why did you come all the way to Florence? It's out of my jurisdiction."

"Please, sir, let me continue and you'll understand."

"John, I'm going to take some notes as you tell me everything about this, but let's start at the beginning."

"Yes sir."

"What's the victim's name?"

"Steeg Onsgaard. S-T-E-E-G." John waited for the sheriff to catch up.

"O-N-S-G-A-A-R-D." John continued, "Tall, blonde hair with a big moustache and…"

"Where's the victim now?"

"I don't know sir."

"You don't know?" The sheriff leaned back. "Did you see the victim?"

"No sir, but…"

"Well, John, forgive me for asking this, son…but how do you know he's dead?"

"We have a German worker at the camp. He overheard two men talking in plain view…talking about how the one man shot the other and how the other man should hide the body…"

The sheriff laughed. "John…sounds like just maybe these two guys were playing a joke on your German friend."

"No, sir…you see…they didn't know that the German worker could speak English. They thought he didn't understand a word the two of them were saying."

"And why would they think he didn't know a word of English?"

"Because he's a German Prisoner of War. We have about thirty of them on loan from one of the camps in Calumet County."

"And who are these two men?"

"The one's name is Robert Nelson. He's been a foreman at the company for many years. He's a big, heavy-set guy…mean sir…very, very mean. We don't have any proof, sir, but last winter we believe he left one of the men out in the woods to freeze because the man crossed him."

"You sure it wasn't an accident? There are a lot of accidents in the lumber business…you probably know that better than me." The Sheriff said.

"Well, yes, sir…I do. But then there was another accident when our cook went through the ice and was drowned. Nelson's the one who forced him to take the load across the lake."

"I heard about that accident…but, John, no one can force a man to do what might be considered his job no matter how dangerous it might be. The worker can always refuse to do the task…even if it means quitting…he doesn't…"

"Yes sir, I understand. But after that accident Nelson got beaten…badly…it put him in the hospital. When he came out, he went after the guy or guys responsible. I think one of them might have been Steeg and that's why Nelson killed him."

"Careful, John. Slow down. This is just the two of us talking right now and we should probably keep it that way. Don't go making accusations without some hard evidence."

"But we have the German worker who overheard the two men."

"A German prisoner of war. John, I'm sure you believe everything this prisoner has told you and you've probably weighed it all in your mind, but *he is a Prisoner of War*. I can't think of a jury in the state who would take the word of a German prisoner. Especially with the sentiment toward the Germans. And John…where's the body?"

John became crestfallen. "What can I do? I mean…what can be done? Where do I go from here?"

"Who's the other man? The one who this Nelson was talking to."

"That's why I came here. It was Sheriff Belke." John said.

Sheriff Olson leaned forward again.

"Sheriff Belke? John, do you know what you're saying here? Do you have any idea of the implication being made? Do you understand what would happen to me…all of us, for that matter if...I mean, dear Lord...no evidence other than an overheard conversation?"

"Well, I do have a gun that was left at the murder scene." John said.

"Murder scene? Gun?"

"Yes sir. When I heard that Steeg was missing I went to where the two of them were supposed to have been hunting. There was blood everywhere and I found a .410 shotgun...a gun that Nelson told the men at camp he gave to Steeg to use that day."

"The two men were hunting together?"

"Yes sir. Nelson said he was going to get some venison for the camp...told Steeg to come along...didn't really give him a choice."

"What's to keep Nelson from saying it was an accident?"

"Well sir...he came back to camp alone...asked the men if they had seen Steeg and claimed that he dropped Steeg off with the .410 shotgun that he'd given him. Said that Steeg wanted to hunt some more."

The sheriff rubbed his chin. "It does sound suspicious, John...very suspicious, but this is going to take a whole lot more to build a case. Frankly, without a body you don't have much to go on. Have you told me everything that you can think of?"

"Yes sir." John said. There was a long pause. "No...there is more. When Nelson and Belke were talking, Nelson reminded Belke that he was owed a favor...that Nelson covered up a murder that Belke committed years before. A woman he strangled. Nelson put a rope around her neck..."

"And hung her in her kitchen." Olson completed the sentence.

"Yes sir." John said.

"I heard stories around the time that that had happened. Rumors mind you...but sometimes where there's smoke... anyway, story had it that Belke was new on the job...a little power-hungry, throwing his weight around. Thought he could put his moves on a woman…a housewife…pretty young thing, but she'd have nothing to do with him and kept telling him that she was a married woman…faithful. Rumor over in Phelps was that she was roughed up a bit. She told a friend…lady friend. The friend came forward after the woman's death, but there again…no evidence. Just one person's word against another. Now John, you don't repeat a word of this – you hear?

"No sir."

"I'll do some checking around." Sheriff Olson said as he got up from his chair.

"Thank you."

"I'll give you a call in a few days…let you know what I find. In the meantime, you try to relax a bit. I know that doesn't sound easy, but if a crime's been committed, we'll get to the bottom of it."

With that, John got up and headed for the door. He stopped and gave the sheriff's dog a few more strokes and then stepped out into the fresh air, the sheriff right behind him.

Nancy was walking across the street with a white paper bundle under her arms. She smiled at John as she got closer.

"Goodbye now." she said.

"Goodbye…and thanks." John said as he walked toward his truck. He looked back at the sheriff.

Sheriff Olson gave a nod and a slight wave. Then he went back to his desk and began looking over the notes he had taken.

45

Robert Edgerton read the Chicago Tribune as he sat at the corner of Roosevelt and Canal Street having his shoes polished. He poured over the words below the photo of Abby reading to a young child: 'Miss Abigail Baker, daughter of prominent Chicago businessman, Edward Baker, volunteers time reading to young patients at Copley Hospital'. He studied the photo with a smile. The article mentioned Baker Medical Corporation and the generous donations being made to several regional hospitals to help veterans returning from the war.

Now it was time for a press release mentioning the acquisition of patents for new prosthetic devices that would lead to the expansion of the company and even provide jobs for some of the men returning from the war. It was time to leverage the opportunity into a marketing move that would bring attention to his career. It was time to ask Abby Baker for a date. The young man polishing shoes, gave a tap under the sole of Robert's shoe with the handle of his brush, indicating that he was done. Robert looked down at his shoes and moved them slightly to see the shine. He got up, reached into his pocket and drew out a handful of change. He gave the young man two quarters, folded his newspaper under his arm, turned and walked away.

When he reached the office, Robert set his briefcase on his secretary's desk, opened it and took out a fresh copy of the

Tribune. He tossed it in front of his secretary, ignoring the fact that she had work spread out on top of her desk.

"Lillian, page four, second section. Cut out the article on Abigail Baker and give it to Mister Baker's secretary. Ask her to place it on top of Mister Baker's morning mail."

"Perhaps you'd like to give it to him yourself…you know, maybe get a pat on the back?"

Robert gave his secretary a look of disgust. "Don't be absurd. Mister Baker doesn't look favorably on people blowing their own horn." A look of embarrassment came over her face. "That's why I always make sure someone else is blowing my horn for me." His secretary gave a look of subtle agreement. "Now, that's our little secret, Lillian. Oh, and get Miss Baker on the phone for me."

"Yes, Mister Edgerton."

"And my coffee." He gave her a condescending look, she simply nodded.

Robert snapped his briefcase shut, went into his office and shut the door. He set his leather case next to his desk, hung up his jacket and went to the large window that faced Lake Michigan. He pulled the cord that opened the wide blinds and let the morning sun stream into his office. He looked out at the lake, it seemed serene, peaceful, and he thought about owning a large sailboat someday. It would be tied up in the yachting marina and people would walk by, pointing to it. It would be longer, more sleek and clean than any of the surrounding boats. He would have parties on his yacht and he would be mentioned in the society page of every newspaper in town.

Lillian's voice came on over the intercom, "Mister Edgerton, Miss Baker on line two."

He would normally keep people waiting a few seconds, it was his discreet way of implying his control, but he didn't want to upset the person on this call. Just the fact that he had a secretary to make his telephone connections proved his command. He hurried to the phone.

"Abby?"

"Hello, Robert, how are you?"

"Fine. Thank you for taking my call. Another article, this time in the Trib, did you see it?"

"No, no I didn't…" she said.

"I'll have my secretary send you a clipping, better yet, how about having lunch with me today and I'll give you a copy myself." Abby wavered, she wasn't sure that she wanted to give Robert any wrong ideas. He sensed her hesitation, and he was prepared with split-second execution. "I'd like to discuss an opportunity for creating more exposure for Baker Medical… something that will really help our returning vets." This piqued her curiosity.

"What is it?" she asked.

"It's really a bit complicated, not that you wouldn't understand it – you are a very bright and perceptive young lady. It's just that I've prepared some charts…a strategy that I'd like to show you." She was silent, and instinctively, he continued. "You know how we marketing men work, we like to demonstrate our ideas with supporting materials." He held his breath.

"Sure, that would be fine. I can meet you somewhere."

"Morton's at say…eleven-thirty?"

"That sounds good." she said.

"And it'll give us a chance to catch up on what you've been doing…how you've been." He added.

"Yes…yes, see you then." She hung up.

Robert heard the click of the receiver as he said, 'goodbye'. She was going to be more of a challenge than he was used to, and he couldn't understand it. City women were easy prey for a successful, well-dressed and good-looking young man. A man with goals, a man with a clear idea of what he wanted and a plan to get it. A simple country girl should have been easier to approach, in his mind. He was perplexed, but yet challenged by the opportunity. And the reward would be well worth the work. He looked around his desk, he hadn't put any ideas for the new prosthetic line on paper. He had only learned of the prospect a few days earlier and the young man, Skip Morrow, who would participate in the company's testing. It would make a great story, but how could he involve Abby? Then it came to him, she would make the announcement of the company's new project in a press conference, a dinner celebrating the return of several of Chicago's veterans, among them, Skip Morrow with his new prosthetic arm. A beautiful woman posed with a veteran in full army attire, maybe even saluting the American Flag with his prosthetic arm, would make a great photo for the papers. A man who might otherwise think of himself as less of a man, although a hero, posed with a beautiful woman…yes, this would be the angle.

Robert pressed the button on his intercom. "Lillian, come in here." In a matter of seconds, the secretary was in his office with pencil and pad of paper in hand. "I need one of the boys to put together a few sketches for me. Here's what I have in mind." Edgerton gave specific orders to his secretary and dismissed her with instructions that everything needed to be on his desk by ten o'clock.

Abby arrived at Morton's a few minutes after noon. She wore a new pink dress under her fur coat. She was still a bit uncomfortable wearing such an expensive coat, but it was warm and the weather this day was still a bit cold.

Freddie parked outside and conversed with some of the other driver's who dutifully brought their employers and guests to Morton's for lunch. Robert had arrived ten minutes earlier and had notified the maître d', a short man in his forties, to be on the watch for a young woman of Abby's description. He gave the man a five-dollar bill. The restaurant was lit with sconces that lined the rich oak-paneled walls. Abby looked around for only a few seconds before she was spotted by the attendant who hurried to assist her. He bowed graciously as he reached with both hands for her empty hand, and taking it, he spoke softly.

"Miss Baker, it is so nice to have you in our restaurant. Welcome to Morton's. May I take your coat?" Before she could answer, the maître d' nodded to another man who came up behind Abby and took the fur from her shoulders. There were businessmen sitting at the bar, several of which, ignored their conversations long enough to get a good look at the beautiful woman who graced them with her presence.

"A young man, Mister Edgerton is expecting you, please... let me show you to your table." The maître d' bowed sharply from the waist.

Abby smiled and the words, "*Thank you*" whispered from her lips as she followed the man. As she walked by, she could feel eyes on her. She was beginning to feel more comfortable with her beauty. She held her head high, her manner complimenting her stately beauty.

Robert stood up from the table. He was wearing a blue pin-striped suit, white shirt and yellow tie. His bright blue cufflink showed as he reached to take Abby's hand.

"Abby, so nice to see you. Thank you for coming." he said with a bright smile.

He was handsome, this Abby could not deny. She smiled in return.

The maître d' slid a chair back and seated the young woman. He stood upright and snapped his fingers.

A young man carrying a tray with a glass of water hurried to the table. The young waiter could have seen the maître d' and guest walking to the table and timed his approach accordingly, but like Mister Edgerton, the maître d' also had his display of authority, and it was this subtle expression that added to the show and impressed their guests while offering their customers a sense of importance. The clean, clear glass of ice water made a chiming sound.

"You look wonderful, Abby. I hope you don't mind me saying that." Robert raised his eyebrows in a pleading sort of way. Abby gave a discomfiting smirk which Robert took in an entirely different way, and it put him on his guard.

"I heard about your brother's recovery, it's truly a miracle." he said.

"Oh yes, we're all so happy. He's still walking with two canes, but with such confidence and surety, I'm sure someday he won't need them at all." she said.

"Wouldn't that be wonderful. And is he still having physical therapy?"

"Yes, for now. I believe that Elizabeth will stay at least a few more weeks to help him with his exercises and such." She felt slightly ill at ease talking about Elizabeth, her feelings were mixed and, in some way, she regretted mentioning her name. Abby looked away to a painting on the wall nearby and then quickly back to Robert.

"And so then, what do we have to discuss?" Her manner was suddenly all business.

Robert cleared his throat, took a sip of water and began to sort through the sketches that his staff had put together for this meeting. "We can look at these later at greater length, but I'd like you to get the gist of what the new campaign will be about."

Abby took a sip of water and then leaned forward to see the sketches that were being set out in front of her. Robert could smell her perfume and for a second, lost his train of thought.

"Baker Medical will be launching a new line of prosthetics, artificial limbs if you will…"

"Yes, I'm aware of what a prosthesis is, Robert. My brother explained it all to me and I think it's wonderful. Many lives will be made more comfortable, not just physically, but emotionally as well." Abby spoke with confidence and poise.

Robert became enthused. "That's it exactly, Abby, you're a natural when it comes to marketing." To this comment, Abby smiled and Robert continued. "Now, this isn't something that gets marketed to the public...not directly, that is, but through exposure at the hospitals and clinics throughout the country. Press is very important in a strategy like this. I'd like to get you directly involved with this. We'll need to spend a lot of time and effort on it so that we can get the word out and help our war hero's who have returned home with the loss of a hand, arm or leg." Robert studied the expression on Abby's face.

"Can I...can the company count on your support in this effort?" He looked into her eyes.

Without a moment's consideration, she answered, "Yes."

Robert stacked the sketches and tapped them onto the table to square them up. He set them aside and handed Abby a menu. He gave her a wink. "The veal is excellent." He gave her one of those Clark Gable expressions that hit Abby directly in the heart.

The couple enjoyed an amazing lunch. Afterward, Abby couldn't resist the dessert cart that was wheeled to her side. She enjoyed a large slice of chocolate cake with coffee. Harvey never served cakes at the restaurant and his coffee never tasted this rich. At one point, Robert put his hand over hers as he was telling her how much he appreciated her contribution to her father's business. She felt a bit uneasy but didn't pull her hand away and then resolved to herself that it was just his way of displaying a friendship.

46

It was Friday morning and Sheriff Olson came into the kitchen where his wife of nearly forty years was preparing breakfast. Her name was Mary. She had put on some weight over the years, so gradually that he never noticed and if he did, it certainly didn't matter, especially when he took a look at his own waistline. She was in every way a devoted wife and mother of their four children.

"Two eggs this morning, Al?"

"As always, Mary." He gave her a smile though she didn't notice as she was already picking two brown eggs from a chipped porcelain bowl that sat on a table next to the old gas stove.

"You think you might be able to get at fixing that rain gutter? The wind picked up last night and it was rattling against the side of the house." Now, she picked up the coffee pot and poured a cup that she would let cool while the eggs fried so that he wouldn't burn his tongue. She looked up from the stove, turned and gave him a smile, but he had already turned away.

"I didn't hear it." he said and he sat down at the old oak table.

She turned back to the stove, took the spatula and moved the bacon that sizzled in the old cast iron pan. Of course not… it's closer to my side of the bed." she said with a good-natured smirk.

He got up from his chair and walked nearer to her. "I've got a little business to get to this morning my dear, but when I get back, you can absolutely be sure...without a doubt in the world...that I will nail down that rain gutter if it's the last thing I do." He came up quietly behind her and placed his hands on her waist, giving her a squeeze. She turned her head and gave him a little kiss on his whiskered cheek. His face mirrored years of hardship and years of happiness, and he always tried to show his best side to her even this morning with the thoughts of a murdered man racing through his mind.

"You're the best there is, Mr. Olson." She turned around, spatula in hand and the two gave each other a little kiss. She turned back to the stove to turn down the heat as the eggs were frying and the bacon grease was popping and spattering.

"What kind of business takes you from your loving wife on this morning?"

"Need to take a drive over to Phelps, ask a few questions around town...nothing big."

"Okay if I come with you? He didn't answer. She continued, "Remember that time a few years ago in the fall, we drove over to Phelps and had our little picnic at the roadside near Big Twin?"

"How could I forget that? But no, dear...not today...you'd get pretty bored and besides, it's a little too cold for picnics."

"Alright, Albert Olson, but you better not be chasing down any dangerous criminals." She turned from the stove with his breakfast and raised one eyebrow with a suspicious look and it made him laugh.

"Not in a million years...not too many Capone-types up here since the thirties. And besides, almost forty years in this business and never had to shoot a soul. I sure wouldn't want to break that record."

She set the plate down in front of him, then turned as the toast popped up. She brought his coffee and then buttered the toast. The two sat and ate together. He found himself looking at her, thinking about what a blessing this woman had been to him. She looked up and gave him a smile.

Sheriff Olson took his own car this morning instead of the police car. He dressed in overalls and a red plaid wool jacket. He didn't make it over to Vilas County enough that he would be a recognizable character but going today dressed in uniform would certainly cause people to talk. The Sheriff drove to the Anderson Lumber Company. He hadn't been out that way in years, but still vaguely remembered how to get there. He drove up to the office and shut off the engine. He looked things over before getting out. The office ladies both craned their necks to see who was here. Sheriff Olson entered the office.

"Good Morning, ladies." he said with a smile.

"Good Morning." Both ladies replied in cheerful unison.

"I'm Sheriff Olson from Florence County."

"You're not dressed like a sheriff." one of the ladies replied. The other lady shushed her, a little embarrassed by her comment.

Sheriff Olson gave a little laugh and produced his badge from his jacket pocket.

"Well, you're right about that…I guess I don't look like a sheriff today. I mostly have personal business today and, well…you know that crisp, starched uniform can get a little uncomfortable."

The ladies chuckled.

"What can we do for you, Sheriff Olson?"

"Heard you have a man missing, is that right?"

"Yes sir, Norwegian man…Onsgaard." one lady replied.

"Swedish isn't he?" The other one spoke trying to correct her, but the first lady shrugged her shoulders.

"When did this fellow go missing?" the sheriff asked.

"Isn't that all in the police report? I mean, with all due respect, sir, I believe that the local sheriff already took that information."

"Oh I know, Miss…just looking to refresh my memory, that's all. And I'm from Florence County, we need to put together our own report as we're looking for the man in our county."

"I believe it was last Sunday he was last seen, when Nelson dropped him off on the road."

"That's what *Nelson* says." the other lady chimed in quickly.

"Would you mind telling me where I might find this Nelson fellow?" the sheriff asked.

"Not at all, that's him right there." the one lady said as she pointed out the window toward the front of the canteen. Sheriff Olson turned his head and looked out the window.

"Thanks very much, ladies." he said with a wink. The two ladies smiled and had lots to talk about after the door closed behind the sheriff. They seldom spoke with a man that had such a manner and smile.

Sheriff Olson made his way across the yard as Nelson was standing on the porch of the canteen rubbing his belly.

"Mr. Nelson?" Nelson did not respond, but gave the sheriff a stare.

"You Nelson?" the sheriff asked.

"Who wants to know?" Nelson responded.

"My name's Al…Al Olson. I'm the Sheriff over in Florence County." Nelson looked away nervously. "I picked up a vagrant earlier in the week. A tall Swede…or Norwegian…I can't tell, but he kind of fits the description of the guy who went missing from your camp here last Sunday. Just wondering if it's the same guy."

Nelson looked back at the sheriff. "You got a badge?" he asked.

The sheriff gave a little laugh again and produced his badge, holding it low as Nelson looked it over.

"What's this guy of yours look like?" Nelson asked.

"Just kind of tall...rough looking...smells like he hadn't had a bath in some time. What about your guy? What's he look like?" the Sheriff asked.

"About the same...you know, brown hair...whiskers... moustache." Nelson replied.

"Well now...the guy I got locked up has blonde hair. The ladies in the office there tell me your guy has blonde hair too." Nelson wiped his face with his hand.

"No...brown hair. Very, very light brown hair...well, I guess you could call it blonde...kind of a skinny guy." Nelson said.

"Your guy got a gun?" the sheriff asked.

Nelson hesitated for a second and it didn't go unnoticed by the seasoned sheriff.

"Yeah...I loaned him my .410 shotgun. We was deer hunting and he asked me to drop him off down the road. That's that last I saw of him and my gun."

"Well now, that's where my guy's different. He had a handgun – Browning...45 caliber. You see that's why I'm asking around. I pick this guy up and it turns out he's got a handgun. He doesn't say a word...you know a guy like this is up to something. No...I don't think we're talking about the same guy. Besides, you said your guy's skinny...my guy's got a big round gut. Kind of like yours." Sheriff Olson pointed toward Nelson's stomach as he winked and gave a smile. Nelson's face turned sour. The sheriff turned and headed toward his car.

"Thanks for your time, Mr. Nelson." he said loudly enough to be heard. Nelson continued to stare at the sheriff.

Sheriff Olson drove out of the camp and into town. He saw the sign for Jester's Bar and thought this might be a good spot to hear what's going on in town. It was still early in the morning, but the bar was open. Dido sat at his usual table with Mister Eggbert. Dido allowed himself one shot of whiskey in the morning just to open his eyes, but after that it was Jester's strong black coffee. Dido sat quietly and watched as the gray car pulled up in front of the bar. Sheriff Olson walked in quietly looking around and noticed Dido at the table in the corner.

"Good Morning, anyone here besides you?" he asked. Dido pointed to the doorway that led to the back. Just then Jester came from the back with a dolly stacked with cases of bottled beer. He noticed the sheriff and gave a nod.

"Morning." the sheriff said.

"Morning…what can I get you?" Jester responded.

"Nothing at the moment. I'm Sheriff Olson from Florence County. You have a few minutes?" Jester stopped long enough to eye up the man.

"You don't look like a Sheriff." This time the comment was getting a bit old and the sheriff produced his badge. Dido's eyes lit up.

"What can I do for you?" Jester asked. Dido put Mister Eggbert back into his box and quickly brushed the remaining peanuts from the table into the pocket of his new coat. He scurried toward the front door and left.

"I seem to have that effect on people from time to time." the sheriff commented.

"Wondering about a man missing from around here, a man name of Onsgaard."

"I only know what I hear in the bar. He's an old friend of John Miller. John's a young guy…kind of new to the area, used to live upstairs. Real nice fellow, works out at the lumber company. Anyhow, I just heard that the foreman took him hunting and the guy never came back."

"That's it?" the sheriff asked.

"That's it, but if I hear of anything I'll let Sheriff Belke know if you want." Jester offered.

Sheriff Olson produced a dollar bill from his pocket and left it on the bar. "No…that's alright. Let's just leave this one be." the sheriff said with an understanding nod. Jester winked, picked up the bill and nodded in return.

The sheriff came out of the bar and saw someone sitting in his car. He went to the passenger side window and gave it a wrap with his hand. Dido looked through the window at the sheriff with his eyes wide open. The sheriff gave a smirk, figuring the old man wanted a ride and so he went around the front of his car and got in.

"Need a ride, pal?" the sheriff asked.

"The jobber's camp." Dido replied.

"Now I'm not all that familiar with all the lumber camps around here...which one is the jobber's camp?"

"Shacks on the south edge of town...near the dump."

Just then Sheriff Olson saw Officer Belke's police car coming toward him on the main street. He had only met Belke a few times over the years, but didn't want to take the chance of being seen and so he turned his visor down and put his forearm over his face as Belke drove past the two men. Just as Belke passed by, Sheriff Olson looked over to notice that his passenger was slumped down in the seat trying to conceal himself, as well. Dido looked over his shoulder at Belke's car passing and then sat upright again.

"You live there?" the Sheriff asked.

"Where?" Dido asked.

"The dump."

"Near the dump...Sometimes." Dido replied. "Sometimes I see things too." he said. There was enough mystery in the old man's voice to intrigue the sheriff. He started the car and headed out on to the county road.

"That's quite the friend you've got there." the sheriff spoke as he glanced down through the wire mesh of the wooden box at the porcupine inside.

"His name's Mister Eggbert."

"And what's your name?"

"Dido...Daniel...O'Day." He sounded as if he had trouble remembering his real name.

"What kinds of things do you see?" The sheriff was asking his questions slowly so as to not intimidate the old man.

"For example, a man poking around last week, a few days ago. Sunday…yep…Sunday."

"People poking around in the dump? That doesn't sound too harmful. Lot's of people poke around the dump looking for things…scrap metal…glass, but usually not in the winter." the sheriff said.

"I was looking for pinecones for Mr. Eggbert. No, not the dump. Saw a man poking around the old shacks – too close for my comfort, but he didn't see me. I stayed low – peeking out between the boards."

"This *man*…what did you see him do that you think I'd be interested?"

the sheriff asked.

Dido glanced at the sheriff and then at the dashboard of the car.

The sheriff pulled over to the side of the road and stopped. He reached into his back pocket and pulled out his wallet. He pulled out a five dollar bill and held it toward Dido. The old man reached for it expecting the sheriff to pull it away at the last minute, but the sheriff wasn't this kind of man and let the old man take the bill. Dido smiled.

"Body." he said.

"What?" the sheriff asked.

"Saw the man put a body down under the boards. Then he covered it with some more boards…kept looking around, but he didn't see me. I breathed through some snow to keep my breath cold…no mist."

"What did this man look like?" the sheriff asked.

"Looks like he always does."

"You know the man?" the sheriff asked.

"Belke." Dido said as he looked out his window. Then he turned toward Sheriff Olson and looked him straight in the eyes.

"Sheriff Belke." he repeated.

The sheriff put the car in gear, checked his mirror and pulled back out onto the snow-covered road. The two men rode in silence for the next two miles until they got to the old abandoned jobber's camp. Dido sat up and pointed. The sheriff parked the car right on the road as the lane as it was covered with too much snow and he didn't want to risk getting stuck. He looked around and saw no sign of any other vehicles. He held his hand up to signal to Dido to be still. He opened his window and all he could hear was the sound of wind blowing through the ash trees and a few crows perched overhead.

"Now show me." the sheriff said.

Dido got out of the car, and pulled his stocking cap out of his pocket and tugging it down snuggly over his ears, he looked around and quickly crossed the road. He pulled at a few boards as the sheriff looked around. There was nothing. Then he pulled at a few more boards that were frozen halfway into the icy ditch, but still nothing. Finally he looked up and around. The sheriff continued to watch the old man. He slowly moved his head and then his eyes opened wide. Without a word he quickly moved to a spot about ten feet away. He pulled at the boards and then one snapped apart sending the old man falling on to more boards and remains. The sheriff quickly came over to help the old man.

"Careful there…your coat's snagged on a nail. You don't want to rip it." he said as he carefully helped Dido free of the old wood. He managed to get the old man back to his feet and brushed him off. Dido stared down and pointed.

"There." is all he said.

Sheriff Olson looked in the direction and saw the booted leg of a man. He had seen dead men before, but it was different every time and not something he ever wanted to get used to. He pulled some boards away and now could make out the snow-covered face of the man, powdery snow covering a long moustache. The body was frozen partially into the ice and he knew he wouldn't be able to budge the man loose. He scooped some snow on to the corpse to cover it.

"Mr. O'Day...I need you to come with me." Dido thought that maybe he was in trouble and had a nervous look on his face.

"I'm going to take you over to Florence where you'll be safe. I've got a nice warm place with good home cooking. We've got to keep you out of the area so nothing happens to you or Mister Eggbert. This sounded like a good idea to Dido, and so he nodded in agreement.

"Now if you don't mind, I'd like you to go sit in the car while I dust over our tracks. I'll get back over here this afternoon with my deputy, the county coroner and some help. I want to get him out of there before any critters find him."

Just then Dido made a comment totally unconnected to the subject, "The enemies will be crushed."

"What's that?" the Sheriff asked.

"Nothing...nothing."

Sheriff Olsen raised an eyebrow and didn't respond.

As the gray car moved through the countryside, Dido looked at the scenery intently. He hadn't been out of Vilas County in years and this was beginning to feel like an adventure. He picked up the wooden cage so that Mister Eggbert could look out the window. An hour later, the two men arrived at the sheriff's office in Florence.

"Nancy, this is Mister O'Day. He'll be staying with us for awhile as a guest."

"Pleased to meet you, Mister O'Day." she said.

"You can call me, Daniel, Miss Nancy."

She showed Dido the jail cell. It was warm and there was a homemade quilt on the bed and what looked like a very soft pillow.

"Now remember, Mister O'Day, you're our guest. The door stays open, but for your own good I think it'd be best if you stay in the neighborhood. Anyone asks who you are or what you're doing here and you just tell them you're my cousin visiting for awhile." The sheriff instructed.

Dido went into the cell and sat on the bed smiling. He took Mister Eggbert from his cage and showed him his new accommodations.

Sheriff Olson walked past Nancy and she gave him a curious look. He whispered to her, "I'll explain later. Could you get the Vilas County District Attorney on the phone for me please?"

"Yes sir…right away."

Sheriff Olson poured himself a cup of coffee and went to his desk. Nancy brought the phone over to him.

"Thank you for holding, sir. I have Sheriff Olson right here. I'm handing the phone over to him right now…your welcome… here he is."

"Mr. Wambach…this is Sheriff Olson over here in Florence County. Thank you for taking my call. Yes, I'm fine, sir, and you? Good. Well sir, it seems I have a situation on my hands and I could use your help."

Sheriff Olson went on to explain the circumstances relative to his call and asked for assistance from the county coroner.

The following morning the sheriff met his deputy and the coroner. They removed Steeg's body from the frozen ditch. It was a gruesome job and the Sheriff knew he would have trouble sleeping this night. The body was taken to the morgue, located in the basement of the hospital at Florence.

The next day, Sheriff Olson called John to come to Florence and identify the body. John had never seen a dead person before and it shook him up. He wanted to cry, but held it back. The sheriff put his arm around John's back and offered that he would do everything he could to find the person or persons responsible and bring them to justice.

47

Elizabeth prepared breakfast for Anthony. Stephen and Marion were out shopping and running errands for their employer. She wanted to do more for Anthony, but didn't want to make it obvious for fear that he would think that she was trying to extend her employment beyond his needs. But the fact remained that Anthony was becoming self-reliant once again. In the past couple of days there had been some tension between Abby and Elizabeth. There had been a chemistry developing between Anthony and Elizabeth that was obvious to Abby, and even the staff. Innuendos and allusions, although slight, were all filed away in Abby's mind. She had gone without a sibling her whole life until just a few short months ago. She didn't want to lose her only brother, and twin at that, to any woman much less a woman she felt uncertain about. If it weren't for her father's fortune, it would be easy to call it love, but since there was money, Abby couldn't be sure about Elizabeth.

Elizabeth heard the sound of Anthony's canes dragging along the floor in the hallway. She lit a candle at the breakfast table, placed the morning paper beside his plate and hurried to pour a cup of hot coffee. Anthony looked surprised to see how elegantly the table was set for a breakfast.

"What's all of this?" he smiled broadly at Elizabeth.

"I thought I'd start you off with a good, healthy breakfast. How are you feeling this morning?" she asked.

"Still a little wobbly with the left leg. And that sharp pain in the right leg still catches me off-guard. Other than that, pretty damn good I'd say!"

Elizabeth looked concerned. "I suspect that you might still have some nerve damage. We'll make an appointment to see Doctor Maguire next week." she said.

"It'll have to be this week, Liz. I want to start work at my father's company next week."

The comment took her a bit off-guard. Starting a job was a pivotal step that would further prove his lessening need for her. Anthony sat at the table and Elizabeth set a plate of scrambled eggs, bacon and toast in front of him.

"Well, Anthony, that brings up something we need to discuss." she said without emotion.

Anthony suspected what was coming next. "What's that, Liz?" He took a sip of coffee and looked at her and she sat in the chair near to him.

"Well, apparently there isn't as much of a need for me as before. You're walking…and that's what matters. Your body is healing and you've proven the doctor's wrong. My work here is finished." She forced a slight smile. Anthony took a minute to collect his thoughts.

"I suppose you're right, Liz. I'd like it if you'd still come by and help me with my exercise's – it helps, it really does." Now it was Anthony's turn to force a smile.

"That might be possible, but I need fulltime work. I've already contacted the hospital about re-assigning me." There was a moment of silence as Anthony looked down at the table, not sure of what to say next. "I'll miss it here." she said.

"I'll miss *you*." Anthony replied without hesitation, but this wasn't the time or place for a romantic gesture. These words could be taken in different ways and he thought it would be best to let her draw her own conclusions. Perhaps if the situation had been different, had he not been her employer, had she not been his captive audience - there to laugh at his jokes, listen to his dreams and hopes - things could be different.

Anthony began eating his breakfast and Elizabeth got up from the table to serve herself. She was anxious to brush off his comment. To her it would have been a good time for Anthony to express his feelings. It didn't matter if it were at the breakfast table or standing on the veranda on a moonlit night. She wanted to hear more from him, if not 'I love you', at least the word, 'stay'.

Abby walked into the living room and could see the couple at the breakfast table. She could sense a discomfort and so she kept her distance. Anthony could sense her presence as twins often can, and so he called out to her, hoping to finish off an awkward moment.

"Abby, come on in and have some breakfast!" he called. Abby didn't have a choice but to join the couple in the dining room.

"Good morning, Elizabeth." Abby couldn't help but notice a gloomy expression, but Elizabeth forced a smile.

"There are scrambled eggs on the stove, a few pieces of bacon, too. If you want, I can cook some more." Elizabeth said, and she started to slide her chair away from the table. Abby touched her shoulder.

"No, sit…I can get it, your food will get cold." Abby offered. Elizabeth would have rather moved from the table, but Abby's presence lightened the mood.

"So, brother, you're getting around pretty well, I'm so happy." Abby smiled at Anthony as she scraped the remaining eggs and bacon onto a plate. "Father was off rather early this morning." Abby spoke as she poured a glass of orange juice. Neither Anthony or Elizabeth commented.

"I'm going to start work for the company next week." Anthony said, hoping to spark a conversation.

"That's wonderful, Anthony. What will you be doing?" Abby asked.

"I'm going to be working in research and development, helping to document the quality and advantage's of the new prosthetic devices that you'll be mentioning in your marketing efforts." He smiled proudly at his sister.

Abby pulled a chair from the table and sat down. Elizabeth pulled a cloth napkin from a holder nearby and handed it to Abby. Abby nodded a 'thanks' as she took a drink of orange juice.

"Oh, this really is exciting, Anthony." she said as she prepared to eat. It became evident that Elizabeth would have nothing to add to this conversation, and so they let the exchange drop. Anthony became somber, glancing at the expression on Elizabeth's face.

"Elizabeth will be leaving us soon." he said. Abby knew this was coming but paid the usual comment.

"I'm so sorry to hear that, Elizabeth. But you will still visit, won't you?"

Elizabeth smiled politely and responded, "Of course, Abby, of course."

The three continued with breakfast in polite fashion, avoiding any further mention of Elizabeth's leaving.

48

It was now late March in 1946, the crews were now being filled with veterans working alongside the German Prisoners of War. The mix sometimes caused tension, but arrangements still hadn't been finalized for the return of the prisoners. While their future hung in the balance, and some showed concern for returning to their homeland, none of them seemed to mind having work to occupy their days.

John went out to Camp Eight and found Michael operating the skidder, loading logs onto the bed of a large truck. Camp Eight had been logged off several months earlier and Michael was working alone except for the truck drivers. John waved at Michael and Michael waved in return. John motioned with his hand crossing his throat which meant that he should cut the engine. Michael dropped the log, shut off the engine and stepped off of the skidder.

"What's going on, John?"

"Hi Michael, how's it going out here?"

"Good, I should have everything loaded in about another week. I sure could use some hot coffee!"

"As a matter of fact I have a thermos in my truck. Come on, it's kind of brisk out here and a lot warmer in my truck. Let's talk there." The two men walked over to John's truck and climbed in.

John reached for his thermos and poured some hot coffee into a white porcelain cup. He handed it to Michael. Michael took in the aroma and smiled as he closed his eyes for a few seconds.

"Earlier this week one of the German prisoners told me something that I think you should know."

"Boy, John, you really speak German well. We could have used a guy like you in the war."

"That's just it, Mike. His name's Helmut and he speaks English just as good as you or me. He was doing some maintenance in the camp office when two guys came in. They figured he doesn't speak a word of English and so they had a discussion that they thought was confidential."

Michael's face appeared curious. "Go on."

"It was Nelson and another guy. Nelson asks this guy to repay an obligation. Seems that this guy killed someone years ago and Nelson helped to cover it up."

"What the hell..." Michael gasped.

"Michael, what I have to tell you will come as a shock. Are you prepared to hear this?"

Michael's brow furrowed. The war had prepared him to endure many dreadful things. "Go on, John."

"Michael...I think the guy murdered your mother."

Michael became upset. "What the hell are you saying? You're saying my mother was murdered? Miller you better know what the hell..."

"Mike, Mike...listen to me. This isn't easy for me to tell you, but I'm telling you what I know and I'm pretty sure it's the truth. The guy was after your mom, trying to seduce her, but she wouldn't have anything to do with him. He kept it up and she kept resisting. He ended up choking her and calls Nelson to make it look like an accident. Nelson put a rope around her neck..." John didn't know what to say next.

"Are you sure? Are you absolutely sure?" Michael was still in shock.

"I met with the sheriff in Florence County two days ago – told him just what I'm telling you. He said he remembered it from the papers and heard a few rumors that pretty much backed up what I just told you. No hard evidence, nothing that could be proven."

"If that's the case then how come nobody did anything... huh?

"The case was written up as a suicide...because the guy who did it, the guy who I believe did it...was Sheriff Belke."

"What the hell are you saying, John? What the hell are you saying? Bullshit, John, I don't believe it...bullshit."

"Mike, how could I make up anything like this? And why would I? Helmut wouldn't have anyway of knowing any of this...God, Mike, the guy's only been in this country a few months. And the sheriff from Florence Country pretty much corroborated his whole story.

"Jesus, John. When I was a kid I was in the boy scouts... Belke was a troop leader. I even went fishing with the guy. And all the while I treated my own father like dirt. My God, John – do you hear what I'm saying!"

"Yes, Mike...I understand."

"No I don't think you do. I was wrong all these years...all these years." Michael was stunned and visibly shaking from the distress.

"Mike, it's not too late to forget the past and make things right with your dad. The Doc's a good guy – a decent man. He'll understand...he'll forgive. Give him a chance."

"And what do I tell my old man, Guess what dad, the guy I looked up to as a kid killed your wife – my mother, and all I ever did to you was treat you like dirt. Is that what I should tell him?"

"Mike, no…listen, Mike, things are heating up. Sheriff Olson is looking into things and if we're lucky it'll all come out – all of it. We'll get the evidence we need and put this guy away."

"Lucky? Don't count on it. If everything you're telling me is true – then he's gotten away with murder and there's no way to prove otherwise."

"Mike – listen to me, trust me. You've got to keep quiet about this – we've got to keep quiet about this. If word gets around, who knows, he might make a run for it. And Mike, there's more…Nelson killed Steeg. That I'm sure of."

"What?"

"Nelson had Belke go out and bury Steeg's body. The two of them are in deep and if we're not careful they'll both get away with it."

Michael quieted down and sat back in the seat. "Christ, John…I still can't believe this."

"Mike – you take the rest of the day off. I'll take care of your time card. Think about things, but whatever you do, just settle down and take everything slowly. Think about everything you say or do and don't let anyone…not anyone know about this conversation."

"Yeah, John…yeah, you're right. God, I could use a stiff drink right about now."

"Well, Mike you're in luck because I do know a tavern in town that has a bottle with our names on it. What do you say?"

"You don't have to ask twice. Just drop by my dad's place so I can pick up a few bucks."

"No, Mike – today I'm buying."

The two men drove off into town.

49

Abby was meeting with Robert to discuss a 'features and benefits' summary that Robert wanted to include in the sell sheets he was preparing for the new products. A delivery boy brought chicken salad sandwiches and soda's to the office and Robert's secretary, Lillian, timidly brought a cart with lunch into the conference room.

"Lillian, lunchtime, great…I'm starved. How about you, Abby?" Robert's mood broke from his all-business character.

"I'm famished." she said simply.

Lillian placed a checkered cloth out on the table. "Is this alright?" she nervously asked Robert as she spread the cloth. But Robert seemed like a completely different person when Abby was around.

"That's great, Lillian, good job!" he said. His words threw her off. Her eyes darted back and forth between her task and her boss as she took the sandwiches from the waxed paper and laid them on china plates. Robert watched with a smile and Lillian's mood began to ease. If there had been any anxiety on Lillian's part, Abby didn't notice.

"That's fine, Lillian, we can take it from here. Just leave the bottle opener…it's okay." Robert said. Lillian looked up at Robert with a shy expression and then gave a half-smile as she nodded and then left the room.

Robert got up, took a plate and offered it to Abby. "Chicken salad, I hope you approve." he said.

"I love chicken salad. Harvey used to make it at the café at least once a week…usually on Monday's after the Sunday chicken special." she said, reminiscing.

Robert concealed his smile. "Do you miss Wisconsin?" he asked and then waited for the answer he hoped to hear.

"Sometimes I don't…but most of the time I do. Soon it'll be Spring and it's the most beautiful place I know. There's a special place I used to go with…" She stopped herself, not wanting to mention John's name.

"With?" Robert asked.

"Someone I used to know."

"Someone special? It's okay, you can tell me."

"Well, yes…in fact, I thought someday we'd be married."

"What happened?"

"I came here. I wrote to him but he never wrote back." She took a bite of her sandwich.

Robert saw his opportunity. He looked directly into her eyes. "I'm sorry to hear that. Sometimes these things happen for the best…you know? I thought I knew someone at one time in my life…but time proved me wrong." He spoke with compassion, and Abby sighed. Robert felt that he had made a tactical success for the day.

"Well! I hate to be a slave driver, but we have work to do, Abby." He spoke in a light-hearted way and it was enough to bring a small smile to Abby.

She took a sip from her orange soda and looked at Robert as he started going through his notes and sketches. She felt like she had just seen a vulnerable side to him and it made him seem like more of a person to her.

50

Robert and Abby left the movie theatre. The cold Chicago wind blew through the streets and it only seemed natural for Abby to wrap her arm in Robert's. He flagged a cab that was slowing up as it approached the theater. Robert opened the back door and Abby got in. Abby was thankful for the warmth of the taxi. Robert got in and closed the door.

"Keeler and Cicero." he said to the driver as he loosened the scarf from around his neck.

"Where's that?" Abby asked him.

"That's where my apartment is." he said. There was an awkward silence and so he felt compelled to continue. "It's still early and I thought you might like to see the place, that's all." Abby looked out the window of the cab. "It's alright, Abby, my roommate will be there. I don't think I've ever mentioned him to you. His name is Harry Sieger, he's an old classmate from college." Abby seemed a little more relaxed.

"I hope you don't think I'm old-fashioned, but it's really not appropriate for a girl to visit a man's apartment." Abby spoke with some hesitation. It had been a perfectly enjoyable evening to this point and she didn't want to ruin it. Robert was careful not to laugh as she might be offended by such a reaction.

"It's alright, Abby, we're co-workers. And besides, I like my well-paying job way too much to do anything foolish." He gave her a reassuring nod and she smiled.

The cab reached their destination and Robert handed the driver a few bills. He got out and held the door for Abby. She looked around, it seemed like a nice neighborhood. The streetlights were bright and it gave her a safe feeling. She stood for a moment and looked at the signs of the shops, a bookstore, bakery and a grocery store. Robert noticed her looking.

"Well, I'd show you around, but I guess you can see it all from here. There are mostly apartments along this block and so it's pretty quiet." he said.

"I suppose it's very handy having a few stores nearby." she said, trying to add to the dialogue. Robert simply smiled.

"This way." he said as he led her up to a door. He pressed the button, expecting his roommate to buzz open the lock. He shivered and bounced a little bit on his feet.

"Harry's pretty slow sometimes." He smiled and pressed the button again. "Come on, Harry." Robert blew into his hands to warm them. Abby held her wool collar up around her face. "He must be asleep." Robert produced a key from his pocket and unlocked the front door. "Come on." He held the door open and Abby walked in.

The foyer had pale yellow walls and rich, dark woodwork. The carpeting was very clean and there was a beautiful light fixture hanging from the ceiling, the lamp shade matched those from the light sconces along the hallway. Abby felt a little uneasy. She was a single girl with a single man going to his apartment. She felt that she wasn't in her environment. When she actively thought about what her environment was, it was her little cabin back in Phelps, Wisconsin. She followed Robert down the hallway. A door opened and a middle-aged couple came out into the hallway and passed them. Abby felt their eyes on her as they walked by. Perhaps it was her imagination.

"Here it is." Robert said as he put his key into the lock and turned it. He gave the door a little extra nudge. "Sticks sometimes in this weather." He looked over his shoulder and smiled at her. He walked into the apartment and turned on a light. He held the door open for Abby, and she walked in slowly and looked around. The apartment was warm and remarkably in order and very clean. Somehow she expected an apartment with two young men to be in need of a *woman's touch*.

"Very nice, I like the mohair chair and couch – beautiful colors." she said as she continued to slowly walk around looking at pictures hung on the walls.

"We try to keep it neat, I can't bear a messy apartment... although sometimes it does get away on us." Abby noticed a note on the dining room table.

> *"Staying at April's – see you later. Don't do anything I wouldn't do!"*
>
> *- Harry*

Robert saw the note at the same time that Abby did and quickly snatched it and crumbled it up.

"Well, I guess you won't have a chance to meet my sometimes intolerable roommate this evening. But I can assure you, he is quite the joker!" Robert said with a wry expression.

"Take your coat off, can I get you something to drink?" he asked as he stepped briskly toward the kitchen. Abby wanted to leave but thought it would be impolite. Perhaps what she was feeling was unfounded. Maybe he was simply being friendly, proud of his apartment and wanted to show it to her. After all, it was a beautifully furnished apartment and they had been spending a lot of time working together. She supposed that it was the sort of thing that people do in the city. She had only worked at the Spot Lunch Café and had never been asked by Harvey or any of the older, married waitresses to visit their homes. She unbuttoned her wool coat and slipped it off, laying it over the back of the couch. She took off her hat and glanced over at a mirror as she fixed her hair.

"Yes…yes, just a glass of water I guess." she said.

"Are you sure? I have soda, juice, beer, wine anything you want." He held the refrigerator door open.

She wasn't sure what caused her to change her mind, but she called to him, "I guess I could have a beer." From where she stood in the living room she had no way of seeing the smile come over his face as she spoke those words.

Robert came into the living room with two cold, open bottles of beer and two glasses.

"Please…sit." he said as he placed the glasses on the coffee table. She immediately sat on the couch in response. He picked up one glass and slowly poured the beer and she watched, as if spellbound by the process. She hadn't had a beer since an evening the last summer when she was with John. Robert handed her the glass and she held it as he poured the second glass. He sat just inches from her and held his glass near hers.

"Here's to a good movie and a very nice evening." he said.

Abby suddenly seemed more alert. "Oh, wasn't the movie good?" she asked brightly.

Robert did his best to feign interest. "Oh…I suppose so." he said.

"Well, perhaps you wanted to see a different movie, something with more fighting?" she asked as she took a drink of beer.

"No, that's not entirely true, but there are a lot of good movies playing now. We could go see one next week too. Maybe a scary movie!" he said.

"No, thank you, Mister Edgerton. I don't care for scary movies." she said. Robert laughed out loud and took a drink of his beer.

"We'll meet somewhere in between. What do you say? How about a mystery?" he asked.

Abby was beginning to feel warm inside and took another drink. "I like mystery's." she said.

"There you go, I'm sure they're going to be coming out with another Sherlock Holmes movie, and when they do, we'll go see it. We'll compare notes and see who can solve the mystery first." He winked as he took a drink. Abby let out a little laugh and then took a long drink. She leaned back on the couch.

Robert discretely looked at Abby's shape. Her white cashmere sweater fit snuggly over her chest. He noticed how her eyes sparkled as she laughed. He had had many women, but he wanted her more than any of them. She was beautiful and a relationship with her not only meant never having to worry about money again, but being able to live a life of comfort. He'd be able to have any car, any home and more important than anything, he'd have status. Velvet ropes would part and people would stare at the couple as they'd whisper. "Would you like another beer?" he asked Abby.

Suddenly, as if someone had snapped their fingers, she realized where she was and what she was doing. She was enjoying Robert's company and maybe there *wasn't* anything wrong with that. She hadn't heard from John, but there had to be a reason. Before she could respond to Robert's question, he leaned over and kissed her. Abby moaned as she felt the warmth of his kiss and then his hand on her shoulder as he drew her close. She kissed him back and then suddenly with both hands, pushed him back.

"No...no, Robert." she said.

"Is there something wrong? I thought we were hitting it off pretty well." he said, speaking as if he were totally shocked by her reaction.

"No...it's not you, Robert. This just doesn't feel right...not yet, anyway. I need more time. This is only our first date...give it time." she said.

Robert liked what he was hearing. He was getting the signal that told him it would just be a matter of time before he could take her sexually. He knew that once he did, she would feel an obligation to stay with him and then marriage wouldn't be far behind. His business sense took over. He put the situation in terms of a strategic maneuver. What would she need to hear next?

"I understand, Abby. I understand. I'm sorry if I seemed too forward. I guess I just got caught up in the moment. You're so beautiful and the moment seemed so right." he said. She was flattered by his understanding, she liked hearing her name and she liked being flattered for her beauty. Abby stood up and grabbed her coat. She spoke as she put it on.

"It's alright, Robert...really. We don't need to make a big deal about it. We're grown adults." she explained. Robert stood up.

"Here, let me help you with your coat." he offered.

"Thank you." she said as he held it for her.

"I'll call you a cab and ride along to your place to drop you off." He was trying hard to salvage some sense of honor.

"No, Robert, just call me a cab. I'll ride home alone. It's only a twenty minute ride and it's cold outside." Abby had made her decision.

"I don't mind, really." he said.

"No, I insist, Robert." Abby responded emphatically as she put on her gloves. He picked up the phone and called a taxi. Abby sat on the edge of the chair.

"Are you sorry you came?" he asked.

"No, not at all." She spoke but her words didn't seem to match her mood and she became aware of it. "We'll see each other at work." she said.

"And give it some time." he replied. Abby nodded. "Maybe in a couple of weeks."

"Sure…sure…we'll see." she said.

Abby felt a little awkward as she sat for the next ten minutes waiting for the cab to arrive. Robert brought over some of his family pictures that had been sitting on top of his bookcases. It made her feel a bit more at ease as he pointed out family members and gave descriptions of their personalities. Finally a horn beeped and a sigh of relief came over her.

Robert walked her down the hallway and to the front door which he opened.

Abby gave him a quick kiss on the cheek and then pulled her scarf over her face as she prepared to step out into the cold. Robert watched as she hurried to the cab. He waved as she looked back and she waved briefly in return.

He went back upstairs, picked up the phone and dialed it.

"Harry…you can come back to the apartment if you want… No, I wouldn't call it a 'failed mission'…just the opposite. We'll talk. I'll see you later."

He hung up the phone and placed it back on the table as he smiled to himself.

51

Anthony sat at his desk in the office that his father prepared for him at Baker Medical. He leaned back and spun his chair so that he could look out the window. He was deep in thought and struggled with what he should do about his situation. He took a piece of paper from his shirt pocket that he had been carrying with him for a few days. He unfolded it and set it in front of him where he could see it. He picked up the phone and dialed the number that was written on the paper. He heard the phone ringing.

"Hello?" It was Elizabeth's voice.

"Hi." he said simply. Elizabeth was surprised and thrilled to hear Anthony's voice but wanted to keep her attitude cool toward him.

"Anthony." she said.

"Yes, Elizabeth. I'm sorry I haven't called sooner. How are you?"

"I'm fine, Anthony. I'm working an evening shift at the hospital. And you, how is your walking coming along?" she asked.

"I'll probably always need the canes, but at least I can walk. I've gotten used to the stares, I guess. My legs feel like their getting stronger...I'm still doing the exercises you taught me." he said.

"And how are Abby and your father?"

"They're fine…listen, Liz, the reason I called is…I miss…" He wanted to tell her that he missed her, but suddenly the words wouldn't come.

"Yes?" She tried to prompt him to complete his thought.

"I miss our routine, I guess. I was wondering if you'd consider coming over a couple of times a week to help me." He immediately felt disappointment in himself for not being able to tell her how he felt and frustration that he had now fabricated such a request.

"I'm sorry, Anthony. I don't think that'll be possible. My new schedule is keeping me very busy. I know another nurse who might be able to work with you. She's…"

"No, no that's okay." He interrupted her and now felt compelled to give her a reason.

"I…I don't want to bother you. Listen, I have to go. I'm running late for a meeting, but it's been nice talking with you. I'm glad you're doing well." His words became softer, weaker.

Elizabeth felt resentment, why couldn't he be honest with her? "I have to run too, Anthony. Thanks for calling." She hung up the phone.

Anthony looked around his office as if he were ashamed of the conversation he had just had or the words he had spoke. He hung up the phone.

He had survived the war, he had led men into battle, he knew he wasn't a coward. Although he managed to muster up all of his will to overcome the wheelchair, he still felt embarrassment about his peculiar walk and the dependence he would always have on his canes. He didn't want Elizabeth to be with a man who drew stares from people. People would point and whisper. There were also other physical concerns that made him so uncomfortable, he didn't even discuss them with Doctor Maguire. Elizabeth deserved a whole man, a man who was physically complete.

Elizabeth stood by the window of her small apartment and looked out at the thawing icicles that hung from the eave outside. Why did he call? She told herself that her life would be so much easier if he wouldn't have called. But she was lying to herself. She had been thinking of Anthony every day since she left his father's employment. She had also lied to Anthony, she wasn't working an evening shift at the hospital. She hadn't been working at all. She was struggling with depression and the sadness she felt whenever she thought about the wealth of Anthony's family and how it would always come between them.

Elizabeth came from a middle-class family that knew nothing but struggle. She had worked her way through college to become a nurse and physical therapist. She was proud of her family and her accomplishments. As a young woman in high school it seemed as if every other family came from wealth. She knew what it was like to hear girls whisper about her because she wore the same skirt several times a week. Her shoes were worn and she had one brown sweater that was handed down to her by an older sister. At one time she became close friends with one of the girls from the 'other neighborhood' only to have the girl's parents suggest that their daughter find another friend of background and upbringing more similar to their own. Although it seemed unusual, Elizabeth had developed a bias toward the wealthy.

That evening as Elizabeth sat quietly, reading in her small simple apartment. There were sounds coming from the hallway, but there were always sounds in this apartment building and she sometimes kept the radio on softly in the evening hours. There was a knock on the door. She was not expecting anyone and the sudden sound startled her. She put down her book and went to the door.

"Who is it?" she called.

"Anthony." he answered. She felt her heart pound. Outside her door stood the man she could not stop thinking about for the last two weeks. She opened the door a few inches.

"Anthony, what are you doing here?"

"I went to the hospital to look for you." he said in a somewhat firm voice. She suddenly felt uncomfortable.

"I have the night off…" her lie trailed off.

"Don't – *don't*, Doctor Maguire told me that you never came back." Anthony said.

"I plan to go back, I just need some time to think." She opened the door enough for Anthony to come in. He struggled to walk as straight as he could with his canes as he entered her apartment. "Is there something wrong, Anthony?" she asked.

"No…yes, that phone call this afternoon. Nothing came out the way I wanted it to and I didn't tell you the real reason for my call." He stood near the living room wall and discretely placed a hand behind his back to brace himself. His physical motions were a bit clumsy, but Elizabeth wasn't watching his movements, only his face and his eyes. Those dark brown eyes of his could be so demanding, so forceful and now, finally he was speaking to her heart.

"I miss you, Elizabeth." he said as she let out a deep sigh. The truth is that I love you and I want to be with you."

She turned slightly away from him. She didn't want him to look into her expression and know that she felt the same way. She didn't want him to see the tears welling up in her eyes.

"Anthony, you come from money – I don't…I don't fit into the same society that you were raised in." She wiped her eyes with the palm of her hand. "You could know no other lifestyle. I don't hold it against you…maybe I do." Her words became softer as she turned around now to face him.

"Look at Abby, such a sweet and simple girl. She was raised much the same way I was…in a modest home with people that loved her even if they weren't her real parents. And now, she's been here a year and she's changing. The wealth is changing her and before you know it she won't think about her farmer, John. She'll continue to go to the fanciest parties, wear the nicest clothes and be courted by every young man in Chicago. At first they'll be attracted to her beauty and then it won't take long before they're attracted to her money and everything it can bring." Elizabeth looked straight into Anthony's eyes and to her joy he looked straight back at hers.

"I didn't come here to talk about my sister. I came here to talk about us." Anthony said confidently.

"Don't you see, Anthony. *It is about us.* Your wealth will destroy me the way it's eating away at Abby. I can't lie to you anymore and I'm sorry that I lied to keep you away. The truth is that I love you, too, and the truth is that I enjoyed living in your penthouse. My God, Anthony, it was like living every little girl's dream. I enjoyed the feeling of not having to worry about money even though I knew it was fleeting, I enjoyed it with all my heart. I loved you from the start...and my God, Anthony, the way you looked in your uniform..."

"You're prejudiced against people with wealth. Is that it? Is that it, Elizabeth? Because if it is, damn it all. I'll give it all away to charity. I don't need my father's money to make a living in this world!" Anthony refused to take his eyes from hers.

"It sounds so wonderful to hear you speak like this, Anthony, but making you struggle through life when you can simply have it all handed to you will only cause you to resent me in time." She felt good inside for the first time in weeks. She was addressing the real issues and her words made sense to her, they would certainly have the same effect on him. Anthony smiled and it was always his smile that seemed to melt her heart.

"You might be right, Elizabeth...but you might also be wrong. Look at my father – does he strike you as the typical man of wealth? He told me about the weeks he spent in the north looking for Abby. With a shabby coat and a few days of whiskers on his face, he fit right into the environment." he said.

"But he was faking it." Elizabeth refuted.

"No – no he wasn't. He did it so that he wouldn't draw attention to himself – so that people would talk with him and not feel uncomfortable. He did it so that he could find his daughter, my sister. Money and power mean very little to my father. Look at what he does with his wealth, he gives everything he can afford to the hospitals so that they can help people. Think about the families whose pain and suffering have been eased because of my father's generosity." Anthony stood up straight and removed the hand that had been bracing his back.

"Do you know how much my father gave to the various charities in this city, in this country last year?" Anthony asked.

"No." Elizabeth answered softly.

"No one does…except maybe his accountants. I don't even know." Anthony said.

Elizabeth took one step closer to Anthony.

"*I am my father's son.* I have never denied my birthright and I won't reject my heritage because most people think the rich are arrogant. I know differently and, because I am my father's son, I have learned how to manage and cope with wealth in a way that seems to confuse my father's peers. In the Bible it says that it is easier for a camel to pass through the eye of a needle than for a rich man to enter the gates of heaven." Elizabeth moved closer to Anthony.

"Yes, I know the verse." she said.

"But what is rich? My father is rich because he has turned his knowledge into wisdom and has recognized that he is no better than any other man on this earth. There are people without a dime to their names who are rich because they've learned the same." Elizabeth put her arms around Anthony.

"You're right…and I'm sorry, Anthony." she said.

"Please, Elizabeth, please try to learn to accept me for who I am and not where I came from. Can you do that?" He asked her softly as he put his face near her hair and breathed in her familiar scent.

"I can do that, Anthony. We can do this...I believe it." she said.

Anthony held her face in his hands and kissed her passionately.

52

Officer Belke called Nelson at his home.

"Hello?" The voice didn't belong to Robert Nelson as he expected, but instead it was Agnes.

"Hello...is...is uh...is Bob there?"

"Yes, he is. Who might I say is calling?"

"This is Ron Belke." He hoped that she didn't recognize the name, but knew as he said it that she would know.

"Sheriff Belke?" There was a pause. She repeated, "Sheriff Belke? Sheriff?"

"Yes, yes...could I speak to Bob please?"

"Well this is Agnes." She expected the caller to recognize her, but after she realized that he wasn't responding she continued. "I'll have to go get him. He's out back at the moment. Can I tell him what this is about?"

"No...it's...personal." Again he choked on his words realizing that his call was beginning to sound suspicious, at least to him. "It's nothing, really...just..." His words drifted off.

"Okay then...okay. You just hold on a minute Sheriff and I'll go get him."

He could hear her put down the phone and her footsteps echoing. He could make out the sound of her yelling to him in the distance."

"Bob…Bob, Honey…telephone. Yes, the telephone. It's the Sheriff…what do you mean - which sheriff? Why, Sheriff Belke, of course, Bob. Come on, Bob…he's on the phone…waiting."

Sheriff Belke could hear a door slam and heavy footsteps getting louder as Nelson approached the phone. Nelson took the phone from the kitchen and stretched the cable as far as he could into the hallway. Nelsons voice was angry but hushed to keep Agnes from hearing.

"What do you want?"

"I'm nervous, Bob…I went back to do a better job of covering the body and he's gone!"

There was silence.

"Did you hear me, Nelson? Steeg Onsgaard's body's gone!"

"First of all – you don't call me. We've been through this. You don't call me at work, you certainly don't call me at home – never. Do you understand? Never. Secondly, I gave you a job to do, and as far as I can tell you've done it half-assed from the start. You just don't remember where you put him. Think about it, we had some snow, you were working in near-dark. You just done fouled it up and I strongly suggest you go back and look until you find him. Now…you don't ask me for help – you finish the job. And another thing, that snoopy sheriff from Florence come around the other day. You tell him to back off…you got that? I said do you got that?"

Agnes was in the kitchen wiping the kitchen dishes, but curious. She quieted down just enough to overhear part of what he husband was saying.

There was a long pause and finally Nelson said, "Do you think you're going to sleep well tonight?" There was another long silence and Belke hung up the phone.

Nelson hung up the phone. Agnes tried to make her tone of voice appear to be curious and not prying.

"Something important?" She asked in a nervously pleasant voice.

"What do you mean something important?"

"Well it was the Sheriff and all…I just thought…"

"There you go thinking again. It was nothing – nothing." Nelson gave Agnes a mean look and she looked away with a sad face.

Sheriff Belke spent the next two hours driving around trying to think of a way out of his situation, but he knew it had all become too complicated. Suddenly a voice came over the police radio in his car, "Belke, this is Al Olson from Florence County?" Belke hesitated and picked up the microphone.

"Yes, Sheriff Olson, what can I do for you?"

"I understand you might have a man missing." There was no response. "Did you copy?"

"Yes…yes…a missing man. I don't remember making out any report on a missing man are you sure? Belke's voice was nervous and seemed almost panicked.

"Just heard some talk around town and wanted to see what I could do to help."

"Well come to think of it there was some talk last Sunday about a guy who got lost hunting…but no one wanted to fill out a report or anything."

Sheriff Olson was getting to the point where he knew something had to be said to get things *tipped over.*

"Oh, I don't think he got lost, Belke. I heard he was dropped off on the road not far from the lumber company. Maybe we should meet up and go over this." Again there was silence.

"Did you hear me, Belke? I'd like to sit down with you and go over some information on this missing person. "Did you copy?" Olson asked.

"Yes, sir…yes, sir. You bet we can do that. My schedule is pretty busy…I could give you a call in a couple of days." Belke said.

"Actually, I thought we could meet this afternoon."

'No. No, that's not possible. I'll call you. I'll call you…get back with you real soon."

Belke shut off the radio. He drove down Military Road and parked his car. He took out his revolver and opened the chamber to make sure it was fully loaded. He left the engine running and walked down the fire lane. He looked up at the dark and cloudy sky and began sobbing. He trembled as he put the barrel of the revolver under his chin. Belke looked around into the sky as if someone or something would give him the courage to pull the trigger, but the courage didn't come. He put the gun down and slumped down to the ground and leaned back against a tree. There were too many loose ends and the pressure weighed heavily on him. He knew his choices were limited. Either he would have to continue living his lie or he had to confess now and face the legal system. Surely Nelson would tell everything he knew about the past that Belke wanted to forget, but perhaps he could just continue to deny what had happened. Surely people would not take the word of a man such as Nelson over the word of a police officer, especially one with so many years of duty. After some time Belke looked up to see the sun was now shining through the trees. Belke put his revolver back in his holster, walked to the police car and drove out of the lane.

Belke went to his office and picked up the phone. "Father Chambers?"

"Yes this is Father Chambers and to whom am I speaking?"

"A sinner, Father…that's all, just a sinner." Belke began to choke up.

"It's alright, my son – we are all sinners. Take a deep breath, how can I help you?"

"I want to confess my sins, Father…I want to be forgiven… I've done so many wrong things."

"We shouldn't do this over the phone. Would you like to come to the church?"

"No. No, I don't want you to know who I am...I can't be seen going into the church."

"Well then my son, talk to me on the phone as you wish. You're confession will be kept confidential. It is the Lord who will forgive you, but you must share with me what you've done. It's alright...go ahead."

"Many years ago." He began to sob again and the pastor waited patiently. Many years ago...I killed someone. I covered it up and made it look like an accident. I've carried this weight all of these years. When I would think of the lives I've destroyed because of what I did...it would drive me crazy. I smothered those thoughts over the years and tried to forget it all...but recently something happened and now it's all coming back to haunt me and I can't take it." There was a long pause and then he continued. "I thought about killing myself."

"No, no, my son, that is not the answer...no. There is help, there is forgiveness."

"What should I do?"

"Are you willing and ready to change your life? Are you ready to deal with the past and press on to a brighter future with the Lord?"

"I...I think so."

"You must pray hard for the Lord's forgiveness. The Lord will forgive you, but you must be willing to change your life and repay the Lord for his forgiveness. Are you willing to do that my son?"

"Yes...Yes I am."

"What is it that recently happened that made this all come back to you?"

"Another...another person was killed – not by me...but by someone who knows about my past. The person who helped me to cover up my crime...he killed someone and asked me to bury the body. Oh my God, I can't believe what I'm telling you…I was so scared I didn't know what to do and so I hid the body."

"How is it that you began this association with this person… the one who holds this over you?"

"We were teenagers…got into a lot of trouble together. We robbed an old lady's house one summer. She was supposed to be gone, but she wasn't. She caught us and started yelling at us to get out. This guy…my friend…he pushed her…pushed her hard. She fell backwards. The door to the basement was open and she fell down the steps – hit her head – probably broke some bones. He told me that if she came to, she'd be able to identify both of us. We'd both go to prison. So he grabbed her head and beat it against the floor hard. There wasn't any doubt about it, she was dead."

"Dear God." the priest whispered.

"We put everything back the way it was and left. She lived all alone and so no one discovered her body for more than two weeks and it had been real hot that summer. We figured it was such a mess to clean up that no one ever suspected that she was pushed. Neither of us spoke a word of it ever again…not even to each other. I thought about it every night – sometimes waking up in a cold sweat. Finally I thought about it less and less. I'd tell myself that it was her fault for being in the wrong place at the wrong time, but I knew better. Years went by and that's when I killed someone. I didn't mean to. I thought she was going to scream. I reached to cover her mouth and she was swinging her fists at me. My hands ended up on her throat."

The priest was silent.

"I called him to help me. I didn't know what to do. I needed his help and it's as if it was starting all over again. He made it look like she committed suicide."

"My son, listen to me…are you listening? You're talking about the Fitzgerald woman aren't you?"

"Yes, yes." Then, in that moment, Belke knew that he had said much more than he had wanted. There was no turning back, but somehow it felt good to him to tell someone after all these years.

"You must cooperate with the authorities. You must go to the authorities and tell them what you know. You must deal with what you've done and not be afraid. If you will trust in the Lord he will be with you…to protect and guide you. Will you do that?"

"Yes, Father…yes I will."

"Alright my son, I will pray for you but I do want you to call me back and tell me how things turn out. I will help in any way that I can. Are you alright now? Is there anything else you want to share with me or talk about tonight?"

"No. Thank you Father. I will call the authorities in the morning…I promise you."

"It's not me you must promise – it's the Lord."

"I will. Thank you, Father…thank you. Good night." Belke hung up the phone.

It would be a long time before tomorrow. He would have time to reason with what he was doing. He would have time to think of another way out.

53

Abby and Robert continued to work together on the new marketing materials in the days that followed their first date. Abby was beginning to feel culpable for having pushed Robert away that evening. She didn't regret doing it and if she were in the same position again, she would do the same thing, but she felt that she might have hurt his feelings. She caught herself wondering if there would have been a better way for her to have handled the situation. At work there was no mention of the incident and for that, Abby felt thankful.

Abby walked into Robert's office one Monday afternoon and found him sitting at his desk with his face planted firmly in his hands. She noticed him and suddenly slowed her pace as she looked at him with great concern. He slowly lifted his face from his hands, saw her, smiled and then shook his head as if in disbelief.

"What's the matter?" she asked. Robert flopped back in his chair and spun from side to side.

"That brother of yours! That's what's the matter." he said. Abby looked concerned.

"What did he do?" she asked.

"I'm kidding you know, your brother's a great guy – great guy. He just called to tell me that there's going to be a re-design on several of the products. It seems this guy named Skip is coming up with ideas to make the prosthetic arm more comfortable, easier to put on…you know…improvements." Robert rolled his eyes.

"Well, that's good, isn't it?" Abby asked. Robert looked at Abby and lightened up.

"Of course it is, dear. It just means that everything we've worked on for the past few weeks will have to be put on hold until R&D comes up with the modifications, new prototypes and a list of features." he said.

"Then, what do we do in the meantime?" Abby asked.

"Well, we could do some more public relations. Free press is always a benefit to the business. But I think maybe we'll just take the rest of the week off." Robert was now facing the window as he spoke. "What do you say?" he asked.

"That's a great idea, Robert. Anthony is getting along well and doesn't need my help. Maybe I could take the train up to Eagle River. It's been a whole year and I'd love to see my friends at the café, one friend in particular." Abby's voice was light and her spirit was soaring. Robert winced as he thought about Abby going back to see John. He spun around in his chair with a broad smile.

"Well then, it's settled. We'll finish off today and then meet here in the morning to tie up loose ends and then take the rest of the week off." he said.

"Loose ends?" Abby asked.

"Yes, we need to list all of the projects and adjust the timelines. Timelines are very important to your father. When he asks to know the timeline on a particular project, I make sure I always have it at my fingertips. In addition to that, I'd like to review where we are on each of the new sell sheets." he said.

"But…we're on hold." Abby replied.

"Abby, Abby, Abby…yes, we're on hold…but, we need to make sure our data is current and distribution is ready once the sell sheets are updated. I'd hate to take a week off and then have these guys in R&D surprise us by getting everything back to us early. Then we sit here and have to play *catch up*. That's the kind of stuff that doesn't go over too well with the old man...I'm sorry, your father. We get this all wrapped up by mid-afternoon and we're out of here...Wednesday morning at the latest." He nodded his head in a positive way. Abby felt somewhat reassured. Even if she left by Wednesday afternoon, she would have three full days back in Phelps.

Her father had paid a full year of Abby's rent at the cabin after they arrived in Chicago, never knowing if she would want to return to stay or if he would have to send someone to get her belongings, what few she had. Now Abby was thinking about her cabin. She was even looking forward to seeing the mounted animal heads and fish that were displayed on the walls. More than anything she wanted to see John. By this time she was beginning to tell herself that if he was dating someone else, it wouldn't matter. She would fight for John and win his love back. Her strongest hope was that John never even looked at another woman and was missing her as much as she was missing him. She decided that she would try placing a telephone call to John to determine if she should make the trip or accept that the relationship they once had was now over.

That evening, Robert picked up the newspaper from his doorstep and entered his apartment to find Harry sleeping on one of the living room chairs with his right leg crossed over his left at the knee. Robert took his rolled-up newspaper and smacked the sole of Harry's shoe.

"Wake up! Wake up!" Robert called in a loud voice. Harry was startled and swallowed a few times as he blinked his eyes and finally kept them opened wide.

"What the hell, Robert! What the hell! What's the matter? Christ, man I was sleeping."

"I might have a problem…damn, I can't believe I didn't see it coming." Robert was pacing the room, twisting the newspaper in his hands.

"Slow down, Robert. I can't help you if you don't tell me what it is." Harry spoke as he rubbed his right leg that was numb and tingling from falling asleep.

"My department is caught up – waiting for the boys in R&D to get back to us on some things and so I suggest taking the rest of the week off." Robert spoke tersely.

"Time off, doesn't seem like a problem to me." Harry said.

"Don't you get it? Now she wants to take the train up north and see her *boyfriend*." Robert said as he stopped for a few seconds to make face to face contact with his roommate.

"Oh…you mean, Abby?"

"Yes, of course, Abby. Damn, I'm getting *so close* with her… so close. I can't have her seeing her boyfriend and falling in love with him all over again."

"It's been what… a year? Maybe he's not even interested in her anymore. For all you know, he's married with a kid on the way. Maybe she'll go up there and not even feel the least little thing for this guy." Harry sat upright, thinking he was making very good sense.

"This is a woman who's been carrying a torch for this guy for a whole year now. Maybe he has moved on – he hasn't written to her, hasn't called. Maybe he's dating some hairy-legged lumberjack woman with bad breath and fleas! I don't know, but I can't take any chances. I have to think of a way to cancel the free days and keep her here." Robert said.

He paced the floor in silence and Harry, in fear of having more of his ideas shot down, kept to himself.

54

Nancy poured Sheriff Olson a cup of coffee. The sheriff stood, looking out the window deep in thought. She brought the cup and saucer over to his desk, pushed some papers aside and set it down.

"Penny for your thoughts, Al." He turned, caught off-guard.

"Oh…thanks, Nancy. Just kind of stuck on this case."

"What case is that?"

"Well I wish I could tell you, but I can't."

"Would I be right in guessing it has something to do with our guest?" she asked as she looked in the direction of the jail cell that was now being occupied by the disheveled old man and his prickly friend. Sheriff Olson looked over at Dido and gave a smile.

Just then the phone rang and Nancy turned to answer it. "Sheriff's office. Sheriff Olson, you bet he is. May I give him your name? Just a minute…Al, it's Sheriff Belke from Vilas County for you." The sheriff was surprised, not expecting to hear back from the suspicious lawman.

"Sheriff Belke?" The voice of the caller sounded distressed.

"Sheriff Olson…I know what happened to the jack…he's dead."

"Yes, I know," replied Sheriff Olson.

"You know?...how?" And then Belke realized that Sheriff Olson must have somehow uncovered the body. "You found him, didn't you?" Belke spoke softly like a man beaten at a game he never wanted to play.

"Are you ready to tell me everything?"

"It was Nelson – Robert Nelson…"

"I know, Belke. I'll need to take a statement from you, but not on the phone. I can come to your office."

"Yes…yes, but I have to settle up some old business first out at the lumber camp." Belke hung up the phone.

"Belke? Belke? Damn it!" Sheriff Olson hung up the phone.

Nancy was standing nearby listening in on what she could make out. "Can you tell me now?" she asked.

"I'd love to, Nancy, but I've got to get over to the Anderson Lumber Company right away."

"Do you want me to call deputy Nolan?"

"No, I'll go this alone. But have Nolan stand by just in case."

"Yes sir, right away."

Belke drove out to the lumber company and up to the office. John was surprised to see Belke's police car and a little nervous as well. He watched out the window as the officer made his way toward the door. John sat down behind his desk. In a minute, Sheriff Belke came in. The ladies looked up at the man, but there was something about his expression that kept them quiet and waiting for the officer to speak first.

"Hello…I heard you have a man named Michael Fitzgerald working here."

John stood and spoke up before the women had a chance to respond. "Yes, that's right."

"I'd like to have a few words with him. Where can I find him?"

"Can I ask what this is about?" John asked.

"It's personal...and it'll only take a few minutes."

"Camp Eight, just a mile south...lane leads in on the east side of the road." John's mind was beginning to race. 'What could Belke want with Michael?' Belke turned and without further comment, headed out the door. John stood again and watched out the window as Belke drove out of the company yard. The office ladies whispered to each other as John watched the police car leave the yard.

Belke found the lane and drove in. Michael was loading logs and as the skidder turned around he immediately noticed the police car. Belke parked alongside a load of logs and got out of the car. He stood, watching Michael.

A range of emotions ran through Michael. He knew it was time to deal with the past so that he could move forward. Michael slammed the brake forward and the huge log he had been lifting went rolling loose. The log crashed up against the officer, pinning him against his car.

Michael's heart began pounding as he shut off the tractor. He hurried up to the officer now trapped between the log and his car. Belke was in intense pain and Michael was surprised at how quiet he seemed despite the situation. But now he found himself moving slower as he came closer to this man who he thought of as a monster, struggled in agony.

"Mike...Mike." The man called out. Mike came closer and stopped. He reached into his shirt pocket and pulled out a pack of cigarettes. He shook the pack to loosen one up, put it to his lips and put the pack back in his pocket.

"Mike?"

Mike took out his lighter and lit the cigarette, taking a long draw and exhaled into the air. "Yeah."

"Mike...I came here to tell you something."

"I'm listening."

"I was the one responsible for your mother's death." There was no response. "Did you hear me, Mike?" Belke continued to moan in excruciating pain.

"Yeah." Michael now became calm. He had seen many men die in war and had developed a way to distance himself from the here and now.

"I took your mother on a date…one time…a long time ago…long before she met your father. When she married your father…I couldn't accept it. I kept after her…I'm so sorry, Mike…I'm so sorry. I didn't mean to kill her. She raised her voice…I reached to put my hand over her mouth, but as she was swinging her arm it knocked my hand down over her throat. I didn't know what I was doing…"

Michael continued smoking his cigarette and sat on another log close by.

"Can you move this? Can you move this, Mike? Can you help me?"

"No."

Belke began sobbing and then shouted his words louder, "My God, Mike…my God, I'm so sorry…I'm so sorry. Will you help me? Please?" Finally the pain became too much and Belke's eyes closed just before he slumped forward. There was silence. Michael continued to smoke his cigarette and then looked up at the trees. Just then, John's truck pulled up to the edge of the lane and stopped. John hurried out of the truck and ran over to where Michael was sitting.

"My God, Mike – what've you done?"

Michael took his last drag from the cigarette, dropped it to the ground and stepped it out. John was shocked at Mike's detached behavior. John lowered his voice. "Can you move this, Mike? Mike…can you move this log?

"No, John…no I can't." And with that, Michael pointed to the gearbox of the skidder. A pulley had cracked in half causing the cable lifting the log to spin loose.

"It was an accident?" John asked.

"Don't get me wrong, John, I wanted to kill the guy. In a way I wish I had, but the damn skidder beat me to it."

John reached over the log and pushed Belke's body back enough to get a hand on his heart. There was no sign of a heartbeat. John looked up as he heard a siren and Michael continued to stare into the treetops.

Having seen John's truck, Sheriff Olson drove in the lane past the truck and up to where the two men were sitting. The sheriff got out of his car.

"What's happened here? Is he...?"

"Yeah...he's dead. It was an accident, Sheriff...an accident." John said as he pointed to the broken pulley hanging loose from the gearbox.

"My God...he was going to give a statement. He was going to come clean on the whole thing about Nelson." The sheriff said. "Who's this? The sheriff asked John.

"Michael Fitzgerald." John said.

"You the one operating the equipment when it failed?"

"Yes sir."

"I'll need a statement from you." The Sheriff said, and then realized that this man must feel some mixed emotions about what had just happened. "It can wait a day or two." the sheriff continued.

"No problem."

"You're taking this pretty well. Are you alright...inside?"

"Sheriff, you have no idea of how I'm feeling inside."

"John, Michael, no one knows what happened here today – including Nelson. Let's keep a tight lid on this. Maybe we can flush him out." the sheriff said.

John went back to the camp and later came back with a large truck and chains to move the log. The sheriff called for a tow truck and the driver was instructed to take the police car to Florence County by way of the back roads. An ambulance was called to take the body and the attendants were instructed not to use the siren. The sheriff knew he couldn't keep a lid on this for very long and would need to move quickly.

55

Something came over Abby, a feeling that compelled her to pick up the telephone and put the receiver to her ear. It was one year from the day that she left Phelps.

"Directory Assistance, please." she said. A voice came on the line.

"How may I help you?"

"I'd like to place a long-distance call to Phelps, Wisconsin, please." she said.

"What listing?" Abby took a deep breath.

"The C. A. Anderson Lumber Company."

"One moment please and I'll connect you."

Abby felt excitement. She hoped that the next voice she would hear would be that of John's. After a long minute, she could hear the ringing sound.

"Anderson Lumber Company, how may I help you?" the voice of an elderly lady came.

Abby felt her heart pound.

"Yes, yes, I'd like to speak with John Miller, please." She could barely contain her excitement and yet she felt a nervousness.

"I'm sorry, John isn't here at the moment." the lady said in a detached voice.

"I'm thinking about coming up to visit for a couple of days. Can you tell me where he is...or when he'll be back?" Abby asked.

"No, I'm sorry, I can't."

Abby couldn't understand why the woman wouldn't make more of an effort. "Well then, could I please leave my telephone number? I'm calling from Chicago and I would really like to speak with John."

"He's very busy these last few days, I'm not sure when he'll be able to call you back." the elderly lady said.

"Well, it's very important...could you please give him this number?" she asked, now almost pleading.

"Go ahead." the lady said.

Abby gave the lady her phone number and first name and then repeated it so that there would be no mistake.

"Abby who?" the lady asked.

"It's okay, he'll know who it is...thank you." Abby said, now feeling as if a load had been lifted from her.

The lady hung up, and Abby sat for a second holding the telephone. She hung up the phone and placed it on the table by her bed. She had told herself that this phone call would help her to determine if there was still hope. She wanted to hear John's voice, telling her that he missed her and wanted to see her. Now she would have to wait for John to return the call. Surely he would return the call to her as soon as he received her message. If not, she would give up. A tear ran down Abby's cheek as she looked out the window. Then she grabbed a pillow and held it to the side of her face and cried softly.

56

In the town of Phelps, Michael Fitzgerald was walking up to his father's front door. The door opened and Thomas Fitzgerald greeted his son with a beer in his hand.

"Hello, Michael, would you like a cold one?"

"That'll do for a start, but I could use something a little stronger to warm me up inside."

"Sure…sure." Doc was pleased to hear that his son would join him in a drink and he hurried into the kitchen to grab a couple of shot glasses from the shelf. He then took a bottle of brandy from the shelf on the other wall, grabbed a kitchen towel, wiped the dust from the bottle and brought the glasses, brandy and another beer into the parlor where his son was sitting. Thomas set the glasses and bottles down and poured them both above the line.

"Dad…before we drink I have something to tell you."

"Sure, Michael."

"I want to tell you now so that you know it's me talking and not the brandy."

"Sure, Michael…sure."

"My mother…" Thomas's face began to distort a bit, afraid of what he **was** about to hear.

"My mother…she loved you, dad."

Thomas swallowed hard as tears filled his eyes. Michael put his head down into his hand and pressed his fingers tightly to his eyes.

"She…"

"I know son – I know. She loved us both."

"She didn't…" Michael stopped.

"She didn't what…didn't what, Michael?"

"She didn't want anyone but you, Pop…no one but you." Michael quickly took the shot and gulped it back. Thomas fought hard to hold back his emotion.

"I know, son…I know." He took his shot glass and tipped it back.

"I miss her every day…still talk to her." Thomas said.

Michael took the cold beer, gave his father a nod and took a long drink.

57

Freddie arrived at the apartment to take Abby and her friend shopping. Abby felt guilty for wanting to shop to take her mind off of John, but didn't know how else to take her mind off of him. She thought it a bit shallow, but then convinced herself that she would only buy a few things for her brother and father, nothing for herself. Freddie knocked at Abby's bedroom door.

"I'm here, Miss Baker." Freddie called through the door. Abby sat at her dresser brushing her hair.

"Alright, Freddie, I'll be out in a minute." She opened the small drawer where she kept the picture of John. It wasn't a very clear picture as it had now become quite worn. She looked the picture, held it up to study it closely. Then she set it back in the drawer and softly slid the drawer closed. She took her coat and walked out. She smiled and greeted Freddie with a nod as she walked to the front door. Freddie held the front door as she walked out and pressed the button for the elevator.

"Miss Baker?" Freddie asked.

Abby turned. "Yes, Freddie?"

"I'm sorry, Miss, may I use the bathroom before we go?" he asked with some embarrassment.

"Why, of course, Freddie, but the elevator's already up. I'll meet you in the lobby." And with that, Abby stepped through the open elevator doors as Freddie rushed back inside the apartment.

Just then the phone rang. Freddie called out, "Stephen? Stephen? Where the heck is that guy?" The phone continued to ring and so Freddie sprinted across the room to answer it.

"Hello?" Freddie said.

"Hello, I'm looking for Abby Spence." came John's voice.

"No one here by that name…Oh…oh you mean Abby?"

"Yes, I'm calling for Abby."

"Well, she's not Abby Spence…at least not anymore. She's Abby Baker."

"Abby Baker?"

"Yes sir, I really have to go. I mean, I really have to go. Would you like me to see if Tony is here?"

"Who's Tony?" John asked.

"Tony Baker. Would you like to speak with Tony?"

There was a silence and Freddie was feeling anxious. He didn't want to keep Abby waiting and really needed to move things along and so he repeated, "Would you like to speak with Tony Baker?"

The phone went dead.

"Hello?" Freddie called out. "Well, same to you, Mister!" Freddie hung up the phone.

58

Sheriff Olson tossed and turned most of the night and was up just as the sun was rising above the meadow around his home on the edge of town. He looked out of the window across a field stubbled with corn to see a large buck and a doe walking. He looked at his wife lying in their bed sleeping. He thought about all of their years together, the good times and the times they knelt together to pray for spiritual support. He knew he would be lost without her and she would be lost if anything happened to him. He didn't fear death. Although he had made it all these years with few harrowing experiences, he knew that it could still come to him without a moment's notice. He accepted the possibility, but it was not something he liked bringing up to Mary. He knew that today it would be best if he got dressed without waking her. Their dog raised her head and stood up looking for attention and expecting her ride to the office.

The sheriff whispered, "Not this morning, Ginger." As he patted her on the head.

He could see his breath this morning as he walked out to the car. He scraped a thin film of frost from the windshield, got in and started the car. He let it idle awhile as he blew into his hands to warm them, then put the car in reverse and backed out of the driveway.

Sheriff Olson drove to the Cozy Corner Café for breakfast.

"Good Morning, Al." The waitress said as she poured him a cup of coffee.

"Morning, Millie...a little frosty this morning." he said.

"Supposed to warm up pretty good by noon...at least according to the weather report on the radio. What'll you have?"

"Oh, how about two eggs over easy, toast, hash brown's, juice and some oatmeal."

"My goodness, where're you going to put all that?" the waitress asked.

"Got a big day planned today, Millie."

"Well I'd guess so...you're eating as if it's your last meal."

"Let's hope not." He knew she meant it as a joke and he responded as if it were such, but in the back of his mind he prayed that he would live to lie down beside his Mary again this night.

The Sheriff was quietly planning his day. Although he had no intention of reading, he picked up the newspaper from the counter and glanced at it. He turned pages, but not a single word registered. People were coming into the café now and occasionally he'd respond to someone's greeting with a simple nod without looking up from the paper. He wanted to be left alone with his thoughts. He wanted to think very clearly about every move he would make this day.

He arrived at the office long before Nancy. He turned up the gas heater. Then he took a key from his desk drawer and unlocked the gun cabinet. "Going hunting?" A voice came from the cell behind him. It startled him and he quickly remembered their guest, Dido.

"Good Morning, Dido...did anyone ever tell you it's not polite to scare people?"

"Sorry." Dido said as he wiped his hands on his pants.

"Got any coffee?" Dido asked.

"You're on your own for that, Dido. You know where everything is…I've got some business to attend to."

"Don't worry." Dido said.

"About what?" The Sheriff responded in a cool tone so as not to arouse suspicion.

"He'll never set foot in a jail cell." Dido said.

Seeing that he couldn't hide much from the clairvoyant guest of his, the sheriff said, "I suppose that's why I'm taking a little extra ammunition with me this morning. But listen, not a word of this to Nancy. She worries."

Dido put his forefinger to his lips, "Not a word."

And then he whispered, "Muddy boots." Sheriff Olson heard him, but was too involved with what he was doing. Then he glanced down at his boots which were clean from the snow. The Sheriff raised an eyebrow and shook his head. Then he took his rifle, a box of ammunition and left.

The Sheriff stopped in at the town garage.

"Good Morning, Rod."

"Good Morning, Sheriff."

"That police car you towed in yesterday. Where'd you put it?"

"Took it out to the farm…threw a canvas over it just like you asked."

"Anyone see you?"

"Not a soul. Took back roads all the way. Never passed a single car."

"Tell anyone about what you saw yesterday?"

"You told me not to. I figure you'll tell me when you're good and ready."

"Thanks, Rod – you're a good man."

The sheriff's next stop was at the court house where he discretely picked up the warrant for Nelson's arrest. He left by the back door. The sun was warming up the air and he could see the frost melting away from the metal roof on the feed mill across the street. He took off his heavy coat and got into the car. Before starting the engine he looked at the medal of Saint Christopher on the dash and then he turned down the visor and looked at the picture of Jesus he had placed there years ago.

"I could use a little help today, Lord. I've made it this far in my life...I'd like to go to bed tonight the same way I do every night. And I'd appreciate it if you'd let me wake up in my own bed tomorrow with the beautiful woman you blessed me with. I'm thankful for all you've given me...given us. I hate to ask too many favors...but today, Lord...today I could use a little help."

Half way across the county the sheriff called Nancy on his two-way radio.

"Nancy...Sheriff here. Can you get a hold of Nolan, I've been trying to reach him for the last hour. I could use some backup to serve a warrant this morning."

"He's right here, Al – I'll put him on!" She handed the microphone over to the deputy.

"Sheriff, I'm glad you called."

"Nolan, where've you been?"

"Car won't start, boss. I must have left the radio on last night – drained the battery. I can maybe borrow a car from..."

"Never mind, Nolan. You stay there near the phone."

By mid-morning Sheriff Olson pulled into the C. A. Anderson Lumber Company. John was in his office with the door closed. John heard the sheriff's car pull into the yard, then got up from his desk and stood near the window, watching. John tapped lightly on the glass and the sheriff noticed John. John pointed to the office door and the sheriff nodded. The sheriff saw Nelson walking around through the large window of the office. He took a deep breath and went inside, tightly clutching the warrant he had come to serve.

"Robert Nelson?" Nelson got up quickly as a boxer coming out of his corner for the next bout.

"What."

"I have a warrant here for your arrest in connection with the death of Steeg Onsgaard." The two office ladies gasped.

"What the hell you talking about?" Nelson responded firmly, but Sheriff Olson didn't back down.

"It's over. Belke told me everything. We have his written statement and he'll be testifying in court so this isn't the time to pretend. That time's long over."

John stepped out from his office with Nelson's .410 shotgun in his hands. Nelson's stare went back and forth between the two men.

"Where'd you get my gun?" Nelson asked.

"From that fire lane off of Military Road where you shot my friend."

"Naw…Naw, naw, naw…I didn't shoot anybody. I'll answer any questions you might have, Olson, but I'll get me a lawyer first." Nelson's voice was pacifying. He calmly reached up to the hook and got his coat.

"Watch him, sheriff." John said. "Ladies, I think it'd be a good idea if you step into my office for awhile until this is over." John had no sooner finished making the suggestion and his office door was already slamming shut. Nelson stopped and gave John a surprised look, tilting his head to the side.

"We'll just sit down and talk about this…clear it all up." Nelson spoke with a tone of complacency. John stood, nervous but prepared. The sheriff's hand moved slowly over his hand gun. In an instant Nelson threw the coat at the sheriff and then ran forward pushing him down. John raised the shotgun but couldn't get a shot off safely. Nelson bolted out the door, ran to his truck and drove off. John ran over to the sheriff and helped him up.

"You alright?" John asked.

"Hit my head pretty hard but I'll be okay. John can I swear you in as my deputy?"

"Sure, sheriff…what do I need to do?"

"Go after that bastard!"

John ran to his office door and opened it quickly which startled the two ladies.

"Look after the Sheriff, his head's bleeding."

John took the shotgun and ran to his truck. He sped out of the driveway. He could make out Nelson's truck in the distance. He had quite a head start, but John stayed on his trail. Nelson's truck quickly turned into a lane that led to one of the abandoned camps just south of town.

John drove as fast as his truck would let him and he could see the brake lights from Nelson's truck as it turned. John arrived at the lane and proceeded cautiously. He could see Nelson's truck up ahead and thought it best to keep his distance. John shut off the truck and listened in silence. The sun was warm now and John stepped out of the truck into a puddle. He reached back in and grabbed the shotgun. Only one shell, John thought to himself. John stood still. John walked toward Nelson's truck with the gun raised slightly in front of him. He couldn't see anyone in the truck. The driver's side door was slightly ajar. John stepped closer and pointed the gun toward the door. He opened the door with the barrel of the shotgun. No one inside. John quickly looked around, but there was no movement except for the birds enjoying the bright sunshine and warmth. He could faintly hear the sound of twigs snapping, but the sound was distant.

John looked down and could spot footprints in the muddy snow and he followed them. Nelson was headed north into the woods, but why? John would follow the footprints cautiously and then stop and listen. Again he could faintly hear the sound of twigs snapping and branches breaking. The sounds were perhaps three hundred yards ahead.

John had no trouble following the trail as there was still a lot of snow in the woods. John could see a spot where it looked as if Nelson had tripped. John bent over to look more closely. Just then a shot was fired and John could hear it hit a birch tree only a few feet from him. John lay low expecting another shot, but after a few minutes he could hear the sounds of running again. John pursued. After another half-hour of the chase, John could hear the sound of cars on the county road that ran east and west. Nelson's tracks led right up to the road and from there John couldn't tell where they went.

The road still had snow and ice on it mixed with melting snow that was steaming from the heat of the sun. Nelson had walked on the road sufficiently shaking any remaining snow or mud from his shoes that would have been enough to tell which direction he was going in. John looked around. He was on the edge of town near some houses, but everything looked very normal and quiet.

John saw Sheriff Olson drive up and stop his car. His window was rolled down.

"Any luck?" He called to John.

"No…I had him up to here, but I can't tell which way he went."

"Get in, we'll catch up with him."

John and the sheriff sat in the car for a few minutes trying to figure out what to do next. The sheriff mentioned to John that he could somehow sense that Nelson was still nearby.

Nelson had made it to the safety of his own house only a few hundred feet from them. He stood inside at the front door and watched through a sliver of glass as he held the curtain back an inch.

59

Agnes sat in her chair watching the suspicious movements of her husband. Nelson turned around and he was startled to see her sitting there. Mud on the floor and mud up to his knees, he looked from her to his feet and realized he had not given a thought as to what he would say to her and how he would explain his being there. "Agnes, Honey…I'm in a little trouble. There are some men, some very bad men chasing me." he began. Agnes put down her knitting as she got to her feet.

"What kind of bad men. What is this all about?"

"That man that was killed while hunting, I mean missing. The man missing, there's men who think I killed him. I guess the guy's dead." Nelson said, the nervousness of his voice was obvious.

"What men?"

"Just men from the camp. Friends of the guy, I guess… maybe some of the same guys that jumped me. I don't know why they would think…" His voice trailed off as he could see the disbelief in her face.

"I didn't do it, Agnes. Don't look at me like that." Nelson pleaded loudly. Agnes continued to study his face without making a sound.

"It was an accident. He got into the way. I didn't mean to shoot him. What am I supposed to do?" Nelson asked as if it was her problem. "I have to get out of town for awhile. You help me, Honey, please? Get some food and I'll pack some clothes. In a couple months this whole thing will die down." Nelson continued. Agnes still said nothing. "Damn it, Woman…I got to get out of here!" Nelson yelled with panic in his voice.

"I'll fix some food." she said quietly.

"That's my girl." Nelson said with a nervous grin. "That's my girl." He repeated as he carefully tried to place a hand on her shoulder. Agnes pulled away as if the gesture had never happened and headed for the kitchen. Nelson ran up the stairs to their bedroom to grab some clothes. She thought about the prospect of this man leaving, perhaps for months for things to die down as he said, perhaps for good.

Minutes later Nelson came running down the stairs, slipping on the mud and almost falling. He hurried to the kitchen. "Got that food ready yet, woman?" Nelson barked with impatience. "Jesus, hurry, Agnes. They could get here anytime." he added. She didn't speak a word, but continued to move at her own speed as he paced the kitchen floor. Nelson began rambling incoherently as he paced around the room. "Just another damn immigrant. Stupid ass got in my way. Not my fault he was there." Nelson said. "Don't know how to get out of the way when I'm shooting. No one gets away with beating me." Nelson continued, but then suddenly realized what he had said. Agnes froze facing the kitchen cabinets.

"He's the one who beat you?" she finally spoke.

Nelson mumbled, "Yeah, but that had nothing to do with it." It was an accident and nobody can prove a thing - not a thing!" Suddenly he realized that his own words were getting out of control. "You understand me, Agnes. You're my wife. You stick with me, right? Right?" Nelson asked.

"I'll get the car started." Agnes finally answered.

"Good girl. Where's our pin money? There's got to be fifty dollars saved up, right?" Nelson asked. This was money that

Agnes had set aside from the extra work she did around the neighborhood. It was from washing dishes at the café whenever there was a wedding that had been catered or sometimes doing laundry for the vacationers, odd jobs that paid very little but better than nothing.

"It's in the mason jar by my bedside." she said without emotion.

"Good girl. You get that car going now, you hear?" Nelson barked orders again as he hurried up the stairs to get the money.

Agnes went into the garage through the side door. She placed the sandwiches on the workbench in front of the car. Then she got into the driver's side of the car and started the engine. She sat with both hands firmly on the steering wheel, her window open. When Nelson came into the garage Agnes pointed to the sack of sandwiches and simply said "Robert?" Nelson looked at her and then at the sack lunch.

"What? You gonna drive? You nuts? You can't drive woman!" He laughed out loud, walked briskly to the front of the car and then squeezed between the front of the car and the workbench. In a moment, without giving it any more thought, Agnes put the car in drive and stepped on the gas crushing him against the garage wall. He was in excruciating pain, but could only make choking, gurgling sounds and stare at her for several minutes before he slumped over the hood of the car, motionless.

She shut off the engine and sat quietly for minutes after, as if she expected him to still be alive, to still be barking orders to her, to still be mentally abusing her again and again. She put her forehead to the steering wheel and cried. It was relief, it was sadness, and it was freedom at last. But she feared the inevitable and started the engine again. The garage began filling with fumes.

A few minutes later, the sheriff's car pulled into the driveway. Sheriff Olson had not heard the crash, but the garage door was shut and he could hear an engine running. He opened the door and the fumes quickly escaped. The sheriff reached into the car and turned off the switch. He pulled Agnes from car and walked her out into the fresh air. John made his way to the front of the car, clearing broken lumber from his path. He could make out the face of Nelson – his eyes still open. There was no need to check for a heartbeat, the man was obviously dead.

Seeing the police car so shortly after the crashing sound, a neighbor lady ran over.

"What happened here?" The sheriff asked Agnes.

"It was my turn to run him down." she said faintly.

"Be careful now, lady, you've breathed in a lot of fumes. You might not be thinking clearly." the sheriff said.

"Oh, Agnes don't know how to drive, sheriff…Agnes never drove a car in her life." The neighbor lady stated. "Ask anyone in town…" the lady said.

Sheriff Olson looked around. "Looks like an accident to me." Then he directed his next comment to the neighbor lady. "Are you willing to give us a statement to that effect?" The woman nodded.

60

It was early April and most of the snow was gone. Steeg's casket sat on the ground beside a hole that had been dug by men from the camp. The simple wooden casket, painted white, was covered in droplets of rain than trickled down the side. The day was wet, cold and gray. There was a gathering of people that included men from the lumber camp, Matt and Katherine Miller, a few relatives and people from town. John and his parents stood in the front of the crowd. A car pulled up to the cemetery just as the service was about to begin. It was Charles Anderson and his son, Charlie. Charlie walked around to his father's side of the car and opened the door. John thought that he should probably offer to help the man, but then could see that his son was managing well. The priest looked around the crowd and then at John. John gave a nod and the priest knew it was alright to begin.

The service was brief and not held in the church since Steeg did not belong to the congregation. The priest, however, was the only man in the area who could officiate such a ceremony and since Steeg was a Christian in his own right, the parishioners did not object as long as someone else was paying the priest for his time. John, his father and a few of the men took turns saying a few words about the man they simply knew as Steeg.

Each person threw a handful of dirt over the casket that had now been lowered into the ground. The priest wrapped his scarf tightly around his neck and headed for his car. Mr. Anderson went over to John's parents and introduced himself. John announced to the crowd that they were invited to Jesters for some sandwiches and a few beers courtesy of C.A. Anderson. The crowd quickly dispersed since the cold rain had now begun to come down heavily.

One by one the cars parked on the street at Jesters. People ran to the door with collars pulled up to ward off the rain. Jester poured pitchers of beer and set them on the bar. His wife brought out plates of sandwiches, potato salad and baked beans. Everyone had something to eat and a few brief toasts were made to the man to whom they had come to pay their respects.

John walked over to Mr. Anderson. Charlie nodded to John and John nodded in return. "Good to see you back, sir. Did you just get in this morning from St. Paul?"

"No, Charlie and I came in last night." Then without hesitation continued. "The production reports all look good, John. And now with the weather letting up we should be doing well going forward." Anderson nodded as he spoke and only paused to take a sip of beer. "You had your hands full here, John, you handled it well. That Nelson, I never did feel too good about him. It's not right to speak of the dead..." Anderson looked around and leaned closer to John, his voice reduced to a whisper. "But I guess he got what was coming to him. So, we'll leave it at that."

"Yes sir." John said quietly as he looked over the crowd.

"Before you go, we need to talk about some changes here at the company." Anderson finished his beer and handed his glass to his son with a look that made his request unnecessary. Charlie grabbed the glass, gave his father a nod and headed through the crowd to the bar.

"John, I want you to keep this to yourself." Anderson spoke quietly.

"Yes sir." John said simply.

"I don't know if this is the time or place, but I'll come right out and say it. I'd like to sell you an interest in the company."

John was surprised by the comment. "Mr. Anderson, with all due respect sir, where would I get the money to purchase a share in the company? I don't have that kind of money. Don't get me wrong, sir, it's a generous offer, but..." John's words faded. He looked over the crowd to see his parents looking over at him curiously.

"You'll run the operation...completely. And in exchange for that, you'll receive a generous salary plus a bonus. But any bonus will be applied toward the price of ownership. The ownership will be forty-nine percent, you'll be a partner. Over a period of time, let's just say five years, you'll have the option to finance the balance of the company at which time you'll own the entire company...lock, stock and barrel as they say."

John leaned back against the nearest wall to keep from losing his balance. He was excited, he wanted to shout the news to everyone, but knew that he couldn't. He would need to be steadfast and mature in his thinking and demeanor. By this time, Charlie was returning from the bar with a full glass of beer for his father. Mr. Anderson did not take the glass, but instead pulled his leather gloves from his coat pocket and put them on. Charlie stood there wondering what the two men had said and why they were now silent. Seeing that his father no longer wanted the beer, Charlie awkwardly set it on the window sill nearby where someone from the crowd quickly snatched it up.

"Now think about what I said, John. We'll talk more in the morning." And with that, Charles Anderson pulled up the collar of his wool coat and started heading for the door. Charlie quickly walked behind.

"What was that about, dad?"

"Nothing that concerns you." John saw Charlie look back at him with a puzzled look on his face.

Matt and Katherine Miller came over to John, each with a mixed drink in their hand. "Your boss seems like a nice man." Katherine said to John. Both were hoping that this would generate a comment from John about what Mr. Anderson had said.

"Yes, yes...he's alright." was all John said.

"When will you be coming down for a visit next?" Mr. Miller asked.

"I've got a bit of paperwork to catch up on. Maybe in a few weeks." And then John's thoughts shifted and he set aside the conversation he had just had with his boss. He turned to his parents and put his arms out and hugged them both. Katherine smiled, but tears still managed to form in her eyes.

61

This Sunday morning at Saint Mary's Church, a clean-shaven man in a beautiful dark wool coat came in and sat in a pew at the back just shortly before the service started. It was Daniel D. O'Day. He looked somehow different on this morning and a few of the children turned to look at the man and whisper to each other. They wondered if this was the '*porcupine man*' as the children in town called him. Daniel kept his eyes on the altar as he folded his aged but steady hands in prayer.

Before the service began, Father Roots was putting on his vestments in the Sacristy. He was smoking a cigarette and had to set it in an ashtray to brush the ashes that had dropped on his black robe. He picked the cigarette back up and took a long draw from it. He blew the smoke out in a long, steady stream as if aiming it for a corner of the Sacristy.

There was a visiting priest on this day, Father Partington, a Jesuit Missionary prepared to speak to the congregation about an upcoming mission trip to Ecuador. Father Partington was a young priest who had only been ordained two years earlier. Father Roots didn't feel as if he had too many common interests with such a young priest. He had become somewhat world-weary in his old age. Since the young priest was a visitor, he thought he should make an effort to start a dialogue.

"So…how's the fundraising going for your mission?"

"We're a long way off from our goal. With the war and the way everyone has had to sacrifice, frankly, many parishioners don't understand the importance of a mission trip to Ecuador. They can't seem to relate." To this, the old priest chuckled and then snuffed out his cigarette in the glass ashtray.

His eyes darted up from the ashtray to the visiting priest. "Well, good luck getting this bunch to relate. Despite all I have preached about tithing, this congregation is stretched to the limit if you know what I mean." The disparagement in his words was obvious.

"I understand, Father. I've spoken to a dozen different parishes over a dozen weeks and we've only managed to raise a couple hundred dollars. That won't go very far toward building a church, even in the jungle." The young priest looked discouraged. Father Roots hesitated and then put a hand on the young man's shoulder and patted it firmly.

"Well, well, you do what you can...that's all you can do." Then he removed his hand.

"Now, I'll do the Homily and that'll be followed by our collection. Then you take five, ten minutes, whatever you need to tell your story and then we'll have a second collection for your mission. And of course, you help with communion." The priest glanced over at the clock. "Looks like it's about time. Let's go." Then the priest looked back at the altar boys who were gathered at the corner.

"And Tommy, when you pour the wine into the chalice – don't skimp!" The old priest gave a glaring look that struck fear in the young boy's heart. Then he looked back at Father Partington, smiled and winked. "Well, I don't want to choke on the communion host!"

The priests walked out into the Sanctuary followed by the two altar boys. The congregation stood as the choir began singing. Father Partington followed the old priest. They stood before the altar for a moment as the choir sang and then separated, Father Partington going to a separate celebrant's chair.

Mister O'Day winced as he heard one of the shrill voices singing much louder than the others. He knew who this lady was, an old classmate from his youth. A slight smile came across his face as he softly shook his head. He felt the eyes of one young boy staring at him. He glanced over and pulled open his coat discretely, just far enough to let the young boy see a baby porcupine nestled on his chest, sleeping. It had turned out that Mister Eggbert had been very busy in the preceding months and Mister O'Day came upon the results. The young boy smiled and turned away.

Mister O'Day listened to Father Roots' sermon and was not surprised that once again it was about eternal torture and the flames of hell licking at our evil flesh. He passed the time by enjoying the light streaming through the beautiful stained glass. For awhile he focused on the statues of the saints and Stations of the Cross that were mounted high on the walls depicting the crucifixion of Christ. When Father Root's was done, the ushers came through with the collection plates. The usher that came to Mister O'Day's pew reached the plate past him, not expecting the town's character to put a gift in. Mister O'Day didn't disappoint the man.

Then Father Partington spoke about the work of the Jesuits and the trip they were planning to Ecuador to build a small church so that they could spread the word of God and the story of his Son, Jesus Christ throughout the neighboring villages and jungles. At the conclusion of his discourse, he asked that if anyone were interested in contributing to the mission, their donations would be greatly appreciated. Again the ushers came through the congregation. This time as the collection plate was again being rushed past Mister O'Day, he grabbed it with his left hand which startled the usher. He reached into his top left coat pocket and produced a piece of paper that he placed on his lap.

Mister O'Day looked at the usher in a way that told him to *stay put*! He reached for an ink pen and bottle of ink that sat on a stained wooden shelf at the back of the seat in front of him. He opened the bottle and dipped the pen in. The usher took a deep sigh, rolled his eyes and then looked over at the other usher who was getting much further ahead on his side of the church. In a few quick strokes, Mister O'Day signed the back of the check he had brought with him and placed it in the collection plate.

Near the end of the service, Mister O'Day left before anyone else in the congregation. It drew a few looks from people, but this was a man who was used to receiving looks.

Long after the service, the priests dismissed the altar boys and then prepared to count the gifts and offerings of the day. Father Roots pulled a check from one of the plates, looked at it and then pushed his wire-rimmed glasses up over his eyes rubbing them frantically. The glasses dropped back down onto his nose and he read over the check again. It was a cashiers check in the amount of $25,000 dollars that had been signed over to Father Partington and the Jesuit Mission. The signature was from Mr. Daniel D. O'Day.

62

Charles Anderson drafted up the terms of his sales agreement. By this time he had no choice except to tell his son what was transpiring. Charlie threatened to bring a lawsuit against his father which only reinforced to the elder Anderson that he had made the right choice. In one of Charlie's many fits that ensued over the days since he was told the news, he shouted to his father that his only hope was that his father would die in the next five years and leave his fifty-one percent of the company to the *rightful heir*. After the words were said, they couldn't be taken back and Charlie regretted saying them. He apologized and his father forgave him with a few kind words, but it was enough to change Mr. Anderson's mind about the details of the transaction.

John trusted his boss, but at Anderson's advice, brought an attorney to the meeting which was held at Anderson's attorney's office in Eagle River. John had only been there on one other occasion, but was still impressed with the setting. The desks, tables, and cabinets were all a beautiful red oak. They looked as if someone polished them regularly. The chairs in the conference room were stout in appearance and upholstered with a plush reddish-brown leather. John sat down and when he attempted to slide his chair a little closer to the table, the chair didn't move and he had to make a second attempt with a little more effort to get the heavy chair to move. He looked around, but fortunately none of the other men noticed.

John looked around the conference room and was stricken by the large beams that spanned the ceiling. This was an attorney's conference room and although it belonged to the law firm, it would not be what it was without the sweat of the lumbermen who harvested the oak. It would be nothing without the factory workers who milled the logs and the carpenters who planed the boards. They would be in sparse surroundings without the skill of the men who cut, mitered and glued the furniture, the men who sanded, stained and oiled the rich red oak. John felt good in this room.

John's attorney was in his early thirties and John had only met with him briefly to discuss his need. The attorney's shook hands and greeted each other on a first name basis as it was a small town and they were members of the same club. Charles Anderson came into the room and patted John on the shoulder, taking his attention from the beams. Anderson sat in the chair next to John and the two attorney's finally sat across the table from the two men.

"Would you like to begin with the proceedings?" The young attorney asked his elder. The answer was obvious and there was no need for such a question. It was Mr. Anderson's attorney who drafted the agreement. The older attorney considered making a snide remark, but quickly considered that he would like to retain his position as attorney for the C.A. Anderson Lumber Company and didn't want the new partner to have reason to consider anyone else for the position that helped to pay for this office. And so as he changed his expression and took a breath, simply said, 'Thank you.'

"Gentlemen, first of all, thank you for retaining the services of this firm to represent you in this endeavor." The attorney smiled at Mr. Anderson and then at Mr. Miller. "I've made the changes that you requested, Charles, and trust you discussed the changes with Mr. Miller?" Mr. Anderson leaned forward in his chair.

"Well, actually not. This was pretty last minute stuff you might say…just get on with it and if John has any objection we can discuss it before signing." John became a little uneasy upon hearing these words and looked over at his boss. Anderson nodded at John to assure him that it was alright.

"Well then, the C.A. Anderson Lumber Company, herein referred to as the company under the ownership of Charles A. Anderson, wishes to offer for purchase to John D. Miller, a percentage of said company in shares equaling one hundred percent with monies for proposed purchase to be taken from a combination of salary, bonus and proceeds realized from profits accrued annually…"

John interrupted, "The entire company?"

"Yes, John, I realized the other day that if you bought anything less and if anything would have happened to me until such time that you could have been in the position to buy the remaining stock, you might have been bought out by any of my heirs. I want this to be your company, the whole thing. The assets of the company can be leveraged to help make it affordable. I'll continue to receive payments over the next few years. My children never did a hard days work in their lives and I suppose I'm as much to blame as anyone for letting their mother coddle them. They'll still inherit my money…unless I can manage to give most of it away before I pass on…which wouldn't be a bad idea!"

"Thank you, sir." was all John could say in response. Then Mister Anderson laughed.

"What did I miss, sir?" John asked.

"I was thinking about the day we met. Pretty good return on your thirty cents worth of gas, wouldn't you say?" He smiled broadly at John.

"Yes sir, I'd say so. You won't regret this." John looked Mr. Anderson straight in the eye.

"I'm sure I won't, John."

The men concluded their business and Mr. Anderson walked out with John. They stood on the sidewalk in front of the attorney's office and breathed in the early spring air. It was a bright and sunny day and a flock of geese were flying north over their heads and it caused the two men to look up.

"I'll be leaving for St. Paul in a couple of days. It's basically yours now and although you're going to be making all of the decisions, you can always call me for advice."

"I'll wire you my weekly report as always, sir." John said.

"You don't need to, but it would be nice to keep abreast of how things are going since I'll still own the mill that purchases your harvest. Just give me a call now and then. Let me know if you have any problems I can help with, and John...call me Charles."

Later in the day, John drove out to the camp. He lit a fire in the cast iron stove to take the chill off of the air, then made a pot of coffee and settled in at his desk. John became absorbed in his work, pouring over the logbooks and making plans. John was startled when suddenly there was a knock at the door. He got up and opened the door. It was one of the men from the bunkhouse.

"I thought we'd best clean out Steeg's locker. I put everything in this box and this gunny sack. There's a letter here with your name on it." John looked at the envelope with curiosity, and then thanked the man.

John treated the letter carefully and felt it rather unusual that he would be receiving a letter from an old friend who had just recently died. John sat at his desk, took out a letter opener and gently opened the envelope.

"John,

I don't trust Nelson and I think he suspects that I was the one who beat him. If anything should happen to me you need to know this. I did beat him and I don't regret it. But one thing I do regret is hitting your hand that day in the field.

My family struggled through the First World War. I was young when my father was killed and my brother was lost in combat. I didn't want to see this happen to you. You wanted to leave the farm and join your brother in the glory of war. But there is no glory in war. At that very moment when you reached your hand over the post, I knew I could change the course of your life. I didn't hesitate but after I realized what I had done I was hurt for hurting you and knew I could not stay. I could not stay with you and your family knowing what I had done, I had done with purpose and it would be a secret that would eat at me for the rest of my years.

If you read this then something has happened to me as I fear. But know this John, you are alive today and maybe would not have been had you enlisted. I am sorry for all of your pain and suffering but I am glad that you came to the north and that you have grown to be the man that you are. Goodbye my friend."

Steeg Onsgaard

John folded the letter neatly, put it into the envelope and then after a few seconds tossed it into the fireplace. He didn't know what to think of what he had just read. It was all in the past now and it was time to start working on the future.

In the weeks that followed there were some adjustments that needed to be made as John took his place as head of the company. Michael Fitzgerald was promoted to Wood Boss, replacing Nelson. It was a gesture that made Doc very proud and the two worked hard at rebuilding their relationship and making up for lost time. Almost all of the Germans had been sent back to their homeland. A few, including Helmut, stayed on and became more and more settled into the community.

Nelson's widow, Agnes, was hired as an assistant to Hanna in the kitchen. It was John's way of helping the widow find a job to make ends meet since Nelson was now gone. Hanna was overjoyed when she heard the news. Her reaction was such that it made John a little curious, but he shrugged it off. Agnes was grateful to have a new life and she and Hanna were inseparable. Hanna moved into Agnes's house in town and people commented at how Agnes seemed like an entirely new person.

Sheriff Olson brought Dido out to the lumber camp one day and asked if John could find work for the man. John wasn't sure that Dido really wanted to work, but gave him a job tending to the work horses. He had a room fixed up behind the barn. Dido, Mister Eggbert, the Misses and the little ones were all thrilled to have a new home.

John's working hours were still long and the responsibilities were greater than ever. He tried not to take too much work home with him, but since every night he was going home to a house that was empty except for Rusty, it didn't seem to matter. Days and weeks seemed to blur together. He enjoyed his growing success, but wanted to be able to share it with someone. Now that things had settled down somewhat, he had time to think about her. He wondered what had happened and how she could have ran off and married some man named Anthony Baker without so much as giving John a chance. His heart was heavy as he would sit on a wooden bench that he made and had placed on the spot behind the barn where they spent that long afternoon. Chicago seemed like such a different place for a country girl like Abby. Whatever it was that took her away, he just hoped it would make her happy. He still loved Abby with all his heart and he knew there would never be another woman like her.

63

John drove up the lane that led to a clearing where a new cutting operation had started only a few days earlier. He sat in his truck and watched as Michael stood off in the distance giving direction to Helmut and his crew of loggers. John got out of his truck and walked over to the crew just as they were breaking up and walking off toward the trees.

"Michael, how's it going?" John asked. Michael gave a smile, pushed back his broad-rimmed hat and placed a pencil over the top of his left ear.

"It's going well, boss. We're trying out a different method of staging the trucks and trying to get a handle on timing so that the skidder's aren't double-handling." John could tell that Michael was proud of the way the crew was responding.

"That used skidder working out alright?" John asked. Michael looked over at the new piece of equipment that John had recently purchased from the Krueger's operation.

"It burning a little oil, but nothing too serious. Dad said to keep an eye on it and if need be, he'd put in a new set of piston rings and bearings. I think he's got enough to do to keep up with things the way they are...I don't need to add more work to his list." Michael wiped his brow and then looked back at John. "We've got a handle on things. If you have work back at the office, don't let us hold you up." Michael gave John a nod and

John smiled. It felt good to have responsible men running the operation. It meant that John could focus his attention on sales and driving the front-end of the business.

"Well, as a matter of fact, I have some paperwork to catch up on. I'll check back later this afternoon." John looked around and felt a sense of relief.

John drove back to the office and parked in his usual spot. He stood for awhile watching Dido on the other side of the yard. Dido had just cleaned and oiled all of the leather harness's and had everything laying over the railing to dry and John noticed that he had nailed a board across the top of a post and had sprinkled it with table scraps of bread crusts and pancakes that the chipmunks were 'sneaking' away. Dido was now brushing the horses that were being used less and less these days. John smiled and thought how nice it was that the horses seemed to be enjoying their retirement.

John stepped into the office. The ladies were chatting away while they worked. One of the ladies was typing payroll checks while the other was sorting mail. Without even looking up, the lady held up an envelope for John. John took the envelope and watched the ladies as they didn't miss a beat with the demanding chores they were involved with. John looked at the handwriting on the envelope, there was no doubt that it was Abby's handwriting. John felt a wave of emotion rush through him. He glanced around and then walked to his office, went in and shut the door. He sat down at his desk and took the silver letter opener from the desk stand that Mister Anderson had left for him.

He opened it, set the opener down, pulled the letter from the envelope and unfolded it.

> *Dear John,*
> *I am sad that I haven't heard from you. I want to believe that it's because you are very*

busy at work and I know that makes you happy. Then I tell myself that if you're happy, I should be happy as well. However, I am concerned these days as I believe that Anthony is in love with Elizabeth. I can't bear the idea of losing him and I don't know what to do about it. There are days I wish I had the strength to leave this city and come back to Wisconsin. I tell myself that if this makes Anthony happy, that it should make me happy. But there I am again, putting those I love ahead of me and I feel so alone. I'm sorry to burden you with this and hope that as a friend you will see it in your heart to give me council.

Love, Abby

John read the letter a second time and then looked out the window at the sky. He read the letter a third time and still wasn't sure what she meant. "Putting those I love ahead of me." Did this mean that she loved him? And if she did, was it the love of a friend or something more? Why would she write to him to tell him that her husband was in love with another woman? And then there was the line about coming back to Wisconsin if she had the strength. Maybe there was something he could do to give her the strength. But was it right for him to want to take a woman from her husband – even if he was being unfaithful to her? John thought long and hard about the situation. The camp was running well, the madness that Nelson had created was behind them. John was now the owner and things were under control. John was quite sure it would be alright to leave for a few days and go to Chicago. He would confront this Anthony Baker and teach him a lesson about being faithful to a woman – especially a woman as special as Abby. Maybe he had lost Abby, but he could still do something to help her and hopefully restore the happiness she deserved.

64

Doc re-packed a wheel bearing on John's truck, changed the oil, greased all of the fittings and filled the gas tank. He topped off the water in the radiator, checked the fan and generator belts and gave John his blessing to take the old pickup truck on the trip of over three hundred miles to the city of Chicago.

John started out early on a Friday morning and by noon had made it to his parents farm for a visit. Mattie and Katherine were thrilled to have a surprise visit from their son and John did his best to hide what was going on in his heart. His parents were proud that their son was now the owner of a lumber company and they had spread the news all over the town. John told his parents that he was going to Chicago to take care of some business and they were impressed. Ma asked lots of questions about where he would stay and how long. And of course there were plenty of little comments about how exciting it must be to go to such a big city and eat in fancy restaurants. Finally, Pa could sense that John needed to be on his way and so he gave his nod to John as he said, "I suppose you've got to get going, Chicago's a long way." It was just what John needed to hear to make his exit.

John arrived in Chicago by early evening. He had picked up a map at a filling station north of the city. The street names meant nothing to him and he finally decided it would be best to check into a hotel and take a cab to his destination. John arrived at the Drake hotel, just a few blocks from Ontario Street. He drew a few looks as he walked up to the reception desk dressed in his blue jeans, white shirt and dusty boots. He hadn't shaved for a few weeks and his beard was dark to his blonde hair. He wore a red bandana around his neck. It kept the sweat from staining his shirt and it was the closest thing he had to a tie. John realized that he looked a little out of place, but for some time there was really no need for John to own a suit. He thought about going out to buy a suit before going to Abby's, but this is the way she knew him and the investment seemed a bit extreme for what might be a very short visit. John did his best not to be too obvious as he looked around the extravagant hotel lobby. He was impressed by the large gold chandeliers, velvet ropes and plush red carpet. The desk clerk was a young man who was caught a bit off-guard as John approached the desk. He looked a bit surprised by John's appearance, but quickly changed his expression as John pulled a large roll of twenty dollar bills from his pocket.

"Can I get a room?" John asked simply.

"Yes, of course, sir. How many nights will you be staying with us, sir?" the young man asked.

"I believe just the night, thanks." John said. The clerk produced a key and simply thanked John, advising him that if there was anything he needed, to simply call the switchboard.

John went to his room on the seventh floor. He set his simple brown suitcase on the bed and looked around. The room was ornate, something John wasn't used to. He looked closely at the framed Currier and Ives print of a fox hunt. The curtains were thick and helped to block out some of the noise of the city. John looked out of the window to the traffic below. There were so many cars and trucks. How could Abby possibly enjoy living in such a place. John sat on the ornate velvet chair and looked around the room. With all of the time he had spent traveling to get there, he still hadn't come up with a plan other than to go to Abby's home and confront the man who was breaking her heart.

He unbuttoned his shirt and went to the bathroom sink where he splashed warm water over his face and arms. John dried off with the lavish towel and spent a few seconds looking at himself in the mirror. He couldn't compare himself with the refined and well-groomed men he had seen in the hotel lobby. John felt like a man out of his element, but he didn't want this to be his element. His environment consisted of rolling fields and the trees of northern Wisconsin, not the streets of Chicago. John wiped his hands through his hair and looked down at the sink. Then he looked at his reflection in the mirror and took a deep breath. John brushed his teeth and splashed a little bit of cologne over his face. He buttoned up his shirt and then grabbed his denim jacket from his suitcase.

John climbed into a taxi and handed Abby's address to the driver. John would normally have been inclined to strike up a conversation, but he was a bit tired from his long drive. He had a lot on his mind and so he sat back in the seat and looked out the window. John arrived at the building and the doorman looked suspiciously at John.

"May I help you?" he asked John.

"Yes, I'm here to see Anthony Baker." John said simply.

"Do you have business with Mister Baker?" the doorman asked.

John was taken back a bit. He was tempted to tell the man that it was none of his business, but John didn't want to risk being sent away after he had gone to such lengths to finally arrive here, and so he took a breath and simply answered, "Yes."

"And your name?" the doorman asked.

"John Miller."

The doorman continued to look at John guardedly as he went behind the desk and picked up the phone. He dialed a number and in a minute, John could hear a voice coming from the phone.

"Yes, Stanley?" the voice answered.

"Mister Baker, there is a John Miller here to see you." There was a pause.

"Yes, yes…um…please send him up. Thank you, Stanley."

The doorman waved his left arm toward the elevator. "Penthouse suite." he simply said to John and forced the slightest smile.

John nodded and went into the elevator. The doorman followed John into the elevator and placed a key into a lock and turned it. The doors closed and the elevator began to move. The two men rode in silence, but John could feel the man's eyes on him. When the elevator stopped, the door opened and again, the doorman waved his arm for John to exit. John approached the door and knocked. He looked over his shoulder as the elevator doors closed.

The door opened and Stephen greeted John with a smile. "Mister Miller, please come in." John entered the penthouse and looked around, again feeling a bit out of place. "Please have a seat. Mister Baker will be out in a minute."

John sat in a plush leather chair. His heart was pounding as he selected the words he would use to make his case with this man whom he had never met, but who had taken the woman he loved. Deep down inside, he wanted to teach the man a lesson with his fists. A few minutes went by and then John heard sounds come from the hallway.

Anthony appeared from the hallway walking awkwardly with his canes. He seemed to be struggling from the expression on his face. John suddenly felt sorry for what he had been thinking earlier.

"John! Abby's told me so much about you!" Anthony said with a smile. Anthony continued to walk clumsily over to where

John was sitting. John sprang to his feet and Anthony suddenly stopped and extended his hand to shake. This wasn't the greeting that John had expected. John took his hand and shook it.

"Anthony...I wasn't expecting..."

"She didn't tell you that I came back from the war a cripple? It's okay, if you think this is unusual, you should have seen me a few months ago. All things considered, I'm really doing well." Anthony tried to make John feel at ease. "Please, sit down." He pointed to the chair where John had been sitting.

John sat back down and rubbed his hand over his beard. Anthony plopped down into the chair close to John's and set his canes on the floor next to him.

"Did you drive down or take the train?" Anthony asked, trying to break the ice.

"Look, Baker..." John summoned up his nerve.

"Please, call me Anthony."

"I received a letter from Abby the other day and frankly, it has me a bit distressed. She said in her letter that she thinks you're in love with some woman named Elizabeth."

Anthony looked a bit perplexed.

"Yes, yes, Elizabeth is a wonderful woman. I'd have to say that Abby's right on that one." Anthony was smiling and John was too stunned to know how to react.

"Don't say anything, John, but I'm hoping to marry Liz." Anthony confided. John couldn't hold back his reaction. He leaned forward in his chair. "But you're married to Abby! What the hell is the matter with you?"

Just then, Stephen, who had been cleaning up the kitchen, dropped a plate and the crashing sound added to the culmination.

"What?" Anthony gasped and then let out a burst of laughter.

"Well, that would explain why you never wrote to my sister." Anthony said.

"Sister?" John looked confused and then heard Stephen laughing in the kitchen.

"My God, John, did you think that Abby was married?" John didn't respond. "That certainly explains a great deal. Our father brought Abby here after I returned from the war. He wanted us all to be a family again. I wish you could meet him but he's out of town on business, although he should be back in the morning if you're around."

"But Abby is an orphan…isn't she?" John asked.

"No…well, she thought she was. Abby was raised by an aunt and uncle who…well, hell, it's a long story and I should probably let Abby tell you when she gets back." Anthony leaned forward in his chair.

"Good God, John. All she ever did was talk about you and mope around this place wondering why you never wrote. How on earth was it that you thought she was married?"

"I called here awhile back. I asked for Abby Spence and the fellow on the phone said she went by the name of Baker now…I just assumed…" John said, still reeling in disbelief.

Stephen looked at Anthony and simply said, "Freddie."

Anthony nodded and then explained, "We have a young driver, Freddie. He's not too…how shall I put it, polished with his words and demeanor at times. Well, hell man, this must be a bit of a jolt!" Then Anthony called out, "Stephen, I think Mister Miller could use a brandy!"

"Yes sir." Stephen replied.

John smiled and nodded.

"Abby will be so happy to see you, John. My God, it's been more than a year, hasn't it?"

"A long year." John added.

"Well, you'll be happy to know that she's still available. But I must warn you that she has been seeing someone…although I'm not at all sure if it's serious."

"I see." John said simply.

65

John and Anthony were having their brandy and getting acquainted. Two hours had passed since John had arrived and the men were enjoying their time together. It was now past ten o'clock and suddenly Anthony heard the front door open and the sound of two people laughing. The smile left Anthony's face as he realized that Abby was coming home with Robert Edgerton. Anthony looked at Stephen and Stephen could only raise his eyebrows and shrug.

"What is it? Is Abby here?" John asked. Anthony lowered his voice in a half-whisper to John.

"Now, John, please keep in mind that Abby hasn't heard from you in some time..."

Just then, Abby opened the door and she came into the room laughing with Robert right behind her. She saw John and suddenly froze, dropping her purse to the floor. She didn't know how to respond and neither did John. It was apparent that the couple had had a few drinks and Robert broke the silence in slightly slurred speech.

"Who's this?" he asked of no one in particular.

"John." Abby simply replied. John stood up and Abby took a deep breath. She felt a bit embarrassed and felt she had every right to be with someone, but her heart pounded as she looked at him and he looked at her.

"Abby...I'm sorry, I should have let you know that I was coming. I got your letter and I came to..." John's words drifted off as he looked deeply into her eyes.

"Sis...he came to teach me a lesson. It's a good story, really it is." Anthony added.

"Aren't you going to introduce us?" Robert said in a cocky way that was obviously meant to take control of the situation. Abby was slow to respond and she still hadn't taken her eyes from John's.

"Sis, maybe this isn't a good time for Mister Edgerton to be joining us. After all, I'm sure you and John have so much to talk about." Anthony was doing his best to diffuse the situation.

"With all due respect, Anthony, your sister and I are on a date. We simply stopped in for awhile before we head back out to the clubs." Edgerton said as he struggled a bit to stand straight.

"Is that right, Abby? Are you with him?" John asked. It took a few seconds for John's question to register with Abby. She was still in shock to see John here at this very moment.

"Who?" she asked. Edgerton let out a laugh, thinking that she was kidding around. Then the smile left his face as he could see that she really had forgotten him the very minute she laid eyes on John.

"Well, this just won't do. Abby is my date for this evening and you'll just have to come back at some other time!" Edgerton spoke to John in a very stern voice. Anthony tried to conceal a smile and then made a signal to Stephen who moved behind Edgerton and opened the door.

"John..." Abby was lost for words as all of her memories of him came flooding back.

Then Edgerton stepped in front of Abby. "I think it's a bit rude for you to be here...I mean, be a good sport and all that. I'm sure you'll understand if I ask you to leave. You can call Abby in the morning if she wants to hear from you." Edgerton's words were becoming a bit more agitated and there was the slightest undertone of fear. Stephen left the front door open and now stood in the hallway at the elevator. Anthony leaned forward in his chair and continued to watch eagerly, anticipating the next move.

Edgerton walked abruptly over to John and grabbed him by the right arm. In a flash, John swung his left fist into Robert Edgerton's face with a quick blow that sent the would-be suitor falling to the floor in an instant.

"Excuse me, Abby." John said and then he picked Edgerton up and lugged him into the hallway where Stephen held the elevator door open. Abby felt too relieved to feel sorry for Edgerton. She knew all along that he had been playing her and although she certainly couldn't have predicted this outcome, it had already happened.

John came back into the apartment and before he could apologize for his swift action, Abby threw her arms around him and began kissing his cheeks and lips vigorously. Then John kissed her in return, long and passionately. After a few minutes, both Anthony and Stephen excused themselves for the evening and left the couple alone.

The remainder of that night was spent in a long conversation. Abby was saddened to learn of Steeg's death and even more so at the news of John's brother Bill being killed in the war. She now understood how the events, misfortunes and miscommunications of the past year kept her and John apart. The important thing was that they were together now and neither of them ever wanted to be separated again.

66

John woke up on the couch with Abby still in his arms. The sun was streaming in through the window and his movements awakened her. John watched her every move. Her face was angelic and in his heart he thanked God for the privilege of being able to wake up next to her.

"Good Morning…my goodness, when did we fall asleep?" she said as she wiped her eyes.

"I don't know, but it feels so good to be with you that I don't want to waste any time sleeping." he said with a little grin.

Abby went to her room to change clothes as John freshened up in the bathroom that had been a part of Elizabeth's quarters. The couple walked down to the lakefront and watched seagulls from a bench near the marina. Abby clung to John's arm still finding it hard to believe that he was actually here with her.

John held her head and smelled her hair.

"Abby, I came here on a totally different undertaking, but I can't think of a better time to do this." His words were soft.

"Do what?" she asked. John moved from the bench and got down on one knee in front of her.

"Abby, will you be my wife…my partner, will you marry me?" John then stood, pulling her from the bench and into his arms.

Tears streamed down her cheeks as she simply said, "Of course." Then Abby added, "But with one condition." John pulled back from her and looked into her eyes. She smiled and continued, "That you take me back to Kassendahl to live."

And now it was John's turn to say, "Of course."

The couple walked downtown to an open café called the Bon Ton. Along the way they made wedding plans, each of them presenting their ideas to the other. Then Abby asked, "Will you be able to take time off of work for a honeymoon?" John realized he hadn't told Abby about his recent investment.

"The new guy running the operation is really a pretty decent man, I don't think there'll be a problem taking a week or two." He held back a laugh.

"Good, and I'm sure my father would be glad to pay for the wedding." Abby said.

"Well, we'll see. I don't think we need to be concerned with that right now."

After coffee, the couple went back to the apartment building. Stanley, the doorman seemed much friendlier toward John upon seeing him with Abby. The couple rode the elevator up to the penthouse and Abby put her key in the lock. John turned her around and gave her a kiss.

"We have to make up for a lot of lost time." He whispered in her ear.

"I'm all for that, John."

She opened the door and the two went in. Anthony was sitting at the dining room table, joined by Elizabeth. Stephen was preparing breakfast as the couple drank juice and read the morning paper.

"John, I'd like you to meet Elizabeth, the *other woman*." Anthony grinned. John reached to shake hands, but Elizabeth put out her arms for a hug.

"Oh, John, I've heard so much about you. I was beginning to think Abby made it all up!" She gave John a little kiss on the cheek. "Oh, those whiskers tickle." she said with a laugh.

"You should have seen the show last night, Liz. Old John here has quite a left hook." Anthony said. John looked a bit embarrassed and rolled his eyes.

"It seemed like a perfectly natural reflex at the time. You must think I'm some sort of barbarian!" John said.

"Quite the contrary, John. I'd take you on my team anytime. Old Edgerton never knew what hit him. Anyway, sit and have some breakfast with us." Anthony pulled out the chair that was next to him. John looked at Abby who was already pulling out a chair for herself. John sat at the table as Stephen brought out a large dish of omelets. Marion brought a plate of toast and Abby poured a glass of orange juice for John from a large pitcher.

As they were finishing breakfast, Abby looked at John and asked, "Should we tell them?"

"Of course, Abby." John said as he reached across the table and put his hand on hers. Elizabeth and Anthony looked on with anticipation.

"John and I are going to be married." she said with excitement. Elizabeth let out a little scream.

"Anthony, you and I only just met, but I'd be honored if you'd be my best man." John said.

"You got it." Anthony reached his arm around John's shoulder and gave him a little embrace.

"Elizabeth, you're the closest I've ever had to a sister, would you be my maid of honor?" Abby asked with a pleading expression.

"Oh, absolutely, Abby." Elizabeth wiped a tear from one eye and then the other. Then she got up from the table at the same time as Abby and the two women hugged. It was clear to John that any reservations Abby had about Elizabeth and her relationship with Anthony were gone.

A few minutes later the door opened and Freddie came into the apartment carrying Mister Baker's suitcases.

"Oh, this is wonderful - father's home." Abby declared. Edward Baker walked in to see his children and their loved ones and a broad smile came to his face. Abby ran to him and put her arms around him.

"Oh father, I'm so happy. I have someone I want you to meet." Abby pulled her father by the arm over to John. The two men looked at each other and both smiled.

"Father, I'd like you to meet your future son-in-law, John Miller." Abby said proudly. John rose from his place at the table and extended his hand.

Mister Baker put his arms around John and gave him a warm hug. He whispered to John in a low voice, "Did you have a chance to read Hebrews 13:1-2?"

John whispered, "This is how some without knowing it, had angels as their guests." Edward pulled back to look at John's face and smiled.

Then John whispered again, "And you play the violin impressively." Abby and Anthony both wore curious expressions.

"Have the two of you met somewhere?" Abby asked.

"You might say our paths have crossed." her father answered.

Epilogue

John and Abby were married on a Saturday afternoon in the meadow at Kassendahl as Spring flowers were at their peak of bloom. Most of the men from the lumber camp were in attendance, as were most of the townspeople. Harvey catered the event, prepared the food and even baked the wedding cake with the help of Hanna and Agnes.

Dido attended the affair in the company of one of the office ladies much to the surprise of most in attendance. In a fine suit and a neatly-trimmed beard, on this day he could have passed for a member of a monarchy, a diplomat or perhaps a prominent businessman as he once was. He was heard to whisper, "Many babies" throughout the day. A number of people who heard him, assumed he was talking about porcupines. However, most knew it was another prophecy.

Everyone danced to the music of the band who let John's father, Mattie, sit in on violin along with Doc Fitzgerald. The two men played "My Wild Irish Rose" as John and Abby danced.

Charles Anderson was in attendance and during the reception, Abby took him by the arm and thanked him for giving John some time off so that they could enjoy their honeymoon. It was at this point where he told Abby that the company had been sold some time earlier to her new husband.

Anthony took Elizabeth aside at one point in the evening and proposed that their union be next and just as simple and lovely as John and Abby's wedding. When wedding gifts were being opened, Edward Baker handed an envelope with a very large check to Abby and to John, he gave a set of car keys. John looked curiously at the keys and Edward pointed to the 1937 Auburn Boattail that was parked at the end of the driveway.

At the end of the evening, the couple were left alone to spend their wedding night together at Kassendahl. In the morning, the couple took Rusty and drove off in the Auburn to see the United States. They had no plan other than to be alone and together. They traveled through southern Minnesota and the Dakota's enjoying every minute together. At every little souvenir shop, Abby purchased a sticker of that particular state, park or point of interest and placed them on John's suitcase. It would be years before they would be able to take their first trip to Europe together, but for this couple, it didn't matter. Being together was the greatest adventure either of them could hope for or dream of.

THE END

LaVergne, TN USA
14 September 2009

157867LV00002B/16/P